dead ROMANCE

Lawrence Miles

mad norwegian press | new orleans

"Toy Story" originally published in *Perfect Timing 2* (Dec. 1999) edited by Helen Fayle
and Julian Eales; "Grass" originally published in *The Magazine of Fantasy and Science Fiction*
No. 599 (Sept. 2001), edited by Gordon Van Gelder, also appeared in *The Year's Best Fantasy
and Horror, 15th Annual Collection* (2002), edited by Ellen Datlow and Terri Windling.

Copyright © 2004 Mad Norwegian Press (www.madnorwegian.com).

Cover art by Steve Johnson.
Jacket & interior design by Metaphorce Designs (www.metaphorcedesigns.com).

ISBN: 0-9725959-5-3   Printed in Illinois. First Edition: October 2004.

TABLE OF CONTENTS

FOREWORD: DISINTERRED ROMANCE

'Maybe this isn't a story at all. Maybe this whole book's just a list of the states of mind I was in when I wrote it...'

This novel was never supposed to be re-printed. It was certainly never supposed to become part of the Faction Paradox universe (or, perhaps more accurately, a kind of historical document on the "formative years" of the Faction Paradox universe). *Dead Romance* was, as most of you reading this will know full well, originally written as part of Virgin Publishing's New Adventures range - "fine-quality pulp SF since 1991" - so a lot of the characters and events referred to in the story aren't even my own creations.

The trouble is that I can never leave anything alone. The bits of *Dead Romance* which were "mine" have somehow started turning up again in the years since, even though I was theoretically supposed to be forging a spectacular new future for myself outside the New Adventures line. Christine re-invented herself to become a character in *The Faction Paradox Protocols*; the universe-in-a-bottle keeps coming back to haunt me, even though in retrospect it wasn't a very good idea; and even Cwej's employers, who quite definitely *weren't* my invention, are presented here in a way which foreshadows the appearance of the Great Houses in the more recent Faction Paradox material.

I mean, make no mistake, I always wanted the New Adventures continuum and the *Faction Paradox* continuum to be "compatible". After all, I'm the type of person who thinks that *Quatermass* takes place in the same universe as *I, Claudius*. Even Cwej himself, created by Andy Lane at least two years before I started writing for Virgin, made a guest appearance in *Faction Paradox: The Book of the War*.

So, at the very least, this book now looks... a little confused. As one of the last New Adventures ever written, it almost comes across as a half-breed, partly dealing with the loose ends of the Virgin "canon" and partly hinting at events to come in the Faction Paradox series. This presumably means that the new edition will be read by (a) New Adventures fans who missed it the first time round, and (b) newcomers to Faction Paradox who want to delve into its pre-history. This is how I like to see the book, anyway, as source material rather than as a novel in itself.

From my point of view, *Dead Romance* was published five years ago and since then I've learned how to write properly. I don't mind admitting that there's a lot of material here which now makes me think "oh, for Christ's sake, get a grip", and this is probably why I'm trying to underplay the idea that it might be a *finished work* rather than an item of historical interest. But the fact is, *Dead Romance* has (on at least two occasions) been voted the best of all the New Adventures. This is blatantly wrong, yet Mad Norwegian Press doesn't seem particularly interested in a "historical interest" piece, and probably wouldn't have asked to re-print it if it didn't have some kind of reputation.

For those of you who've come to *Dead Romance* via the Faction Paradox series, then, some back-story might be required.

When *Dead Romance* was first published in 1999, the New Adventures range had been going for eight years, and - to be insultingly frank - had gotten itself into a bit of a rut. Whereas the earlier stories had (unsurprisingly) covered the whole span of the history of the universe, after 1997 the range had become mired in the 26th century, and had begun to rely on lightweight, semi-comic "outer space" stories instead of anything more grandiose. Virtually all the novels revolved around Professor Bernice Summerfield, a character created by Paul Cornell as early as 1992, an archaeologist of the future (Bernice, that is, not Paul) now rather disturbingly remembered as a cross between the two Joneses: Indiana and Bridget.

Bernice had worked quite well, at first. The problem was that beyond a certain point, most of the stories entailed Professor Summerfield going to unconvincing alien planets and uncovering mysterious alien artefacts, or at least it *felt* like that was what she was doing all the time. The readership was getting bored, and the sales figures were dropping.

In 1998, in an attempt to bring an "epic" feel back to the New Adventures, the editors came up with a masterplan. Since this was the tail-end of the *Babylon-5* era, when massively over-extended story-arcs were the "in" thing, they decided to introduce a vast, all-encompassing storyline that could run from book to book to book. The details aren't particularly important now - to be honest, they didn't seem *that* important even at the time - but the upshot was that a bunch of nebulously powerful hyper-entities known as "Gods" would overrun the university-planet which Bernice called home.

It's possible this was meant to have mythic, apocalyptic overtones, either Biblical or Wagnerian. What we *knew* was that one way or another, all the major supporting characters who'd turned up in the New Adventures over the years would somehow get involved in this mammoth God-struggle. This included Chris Cwej, who'd debuted in the series as a young, over-enthusiastic future-policeman, but who'd since grown up (a bit) and become the agent of a time-travelling super-culture which had supposedly been running the universe until the Gods had turned up.

Did the story arc work? Well... it's not remembered *terribly* fondly by the New Adventures fans, and it's not hard to see what went wrong. With the sales figures already sinking, the Higher Powers at Virgin Publishing were constantly threatening to pull the plug on the range, which meant - insanely - that the editors couldn't commission anything more than three or four months in advance in case the series came to an abrupt end. Which meant, in turn, that the writers hardly ever had time to finish the books properly. Just when the novels were at their most vulnerable, on top of all their other problems, they started to become works of desperation. *Dead Romance* was done in six weeks, and I still can't believe it worked. Some writers didn't even get *that* long.

Of course, even *Dead Romance* didn't go to plan. If you'd read the synopsis originally pitched to Virgin, you would have expected something a lot more... *sci-fi*.

Christine's reference to books about "little bubble-headed rocket men", on the very first page, gives you some idea of how the proposal must have looked to the editors. Instead, the novel became something much denser, much stickier and much more personal. It became a book about betrayal, gender politics and emotional numbness, in which the supposedly "exciting" SF elements often seem to be nothing more than externalised versions of Christine's own obsessions.

If you know Ian Fleming's original novel, and *not* the movie which just happens to have the same name, then you might want to think of *Dead Romance* as *The Spy Who Loved Me* of the New Adventures. And like *The Spy Who Loved Me*, it was one of the last of its kind, so with hindsight it almost seems as if the series were entering its "mourning" phase. There were only four more New Adventures before the range finally expired. *Dead Romance*, the only book in the series to have been unexpectedly re-printed, is merely number 79 in a set of 83. (Incidentally, at this point I'd just like to mention that Simon Winstone - the last of the New Adventures editors - really didn't like *Dead Romance* much, and didn't see the point of most of it. In this respect, the ludicrously tight Virgin schedule was a blessing. If there'd been even a single week for changes then Simon would have made me re-write huge chunks of the text, in an attempt to turn it into a "proper" SF novel. Even today, every time *Dead Romance* is cited as one of the series' high points I feel like sending him an e-mail. He's just lucky I don't have his address.)

But it's like I said. I can't leave anything alone. The truth is, this new edition isn't *exactly* the same as the old one. Though I've stopped short of adding extra scenes, or turning all the guns into walkie-talkies, there are some differences. For one thing, I've "corrected" the copy-editing. The copy-editors used by Virgin Pubishing - and, later, by BBC Books - were notoriously draconian, and insisted on Correct English even when there was a good reason not to use it. The original *Dead Romance* had commas in places where commas should never be, and anyone who knows me will know that I'd rather have an editor give the story a happy ending than let him fiddle with the punctuation.

Worse, in 1999 it was copy-editing policy to put certain words in standardised places. "I'm only mentioning this because..." wasn't acceptable; it had to be "I'm mentioning this only because...", even if the character who was speaking would *never* phrase it that way. (Still, I got off lightly compared to some. Another writer I could mention made the mistake of using the sentence "the ship escaped the planet's gravity well", *gravity well* being a standard scientific / sci-fi term for a planet's gravitational influence. The copy-editor changed it to: "the ship escaped well from the planet's gravity...")

There are a few changes which might be more noticeable. The original text contained various historical errors and omissions, simply because the research (like everything else) was done in such a hurry. These glitches have now been fixed. Lastly, and most controversially, I've changed some of the phraseology. Whereas the original version has Christine half-seriously referring to Cwej's employers as just "aliens" or "time-travellers", in this version she occasionally uses the word "Houses" as well. Since the new *Dead Romance* is presented here as a Neanderthal fore-runner to the Faction Paradox line, we might as well be consistent.

Is the book set in the "real" Faction Paradox universe, though? Do the two universes really gel together? This is something you can argue about among yourselves, but the DVD-style Extra Bonus Features at the end of this volume might give you some ideas. "Toy Story" is another piece of fiction that was originally written for a different universe, and first published in the anthology *Perfect Timing 2*, although - like *Dead Romance* itself - it introduces characters and concepts which later turn up in the Faction universe proper. Explaining the back-story to *this* particular piece would take pages, so if you don't know the history then just try to pretend it's enigmatic rather than bewildering.

"The Cosmology of the Spiral Politic" is an essay which tries to explain how the big scientific / pseudo-scientific concepts of the Faction continuum fit together, and was originally written for the benefit of the other writers in the series, but it suits this volume better than any other. "Grass" first appeared in *The Magazine of Fantasy and Science Fiction*, September 2001, and like the rest of the material on offer here, it's so closely tied to the continuity of the other Faction Paradox books that this seems the ideal venue for it. Besides, I still think it's one of the best things I've ever written and it needs a permanent home.

It's curious, though. This is the first time I've had the opportunity to write a proper foreword to a book; the first time something I've written has been published in a way that demands some kind of explanation. I was imagining that when I came to do it, I'd be witty, personal and vaguely acerbic. Instead, looking back at what I've said, I seem almost… disinterested. It's more like literary criticism than personal reflection, as if I'm writing a commentary on a novel whose author has already died. Possibly I should have expected that. It's only been half a decade since the book was first published, but already, very little of the person who wrote it seems to be left. It is, in a sense, like finding something you wrote when you were a kid.

So now I'm going to leave you in the hands of someone else entirely. Someone younger and thinner, who never wore a beard and who thinks he's a girl.

- Lawrence Miles,
March 2004.

Notes on a Prologue

1

All right. Let's start with the basics, and see where we can go from there.

This book is called *Dead Romance*. That's what I'm going to put on the cover, anyway, although it wasn't the first name I thought of. I was going to call it *Living Space*, but then it'd have "space" in the title, and you might expect it to be all about little bubble-headed rocket men, like you used to see on the covers of those old SF magazines before everybody started dropping acid and seeing Starchilds everywhere. I *did* think about calling it *Real Life*, but then you'd probably want me to tell you exactly what "real life" is sometime before the end and let's face it, it's not going to happen.

So. *Dead Romance* it is. Not the most exciting title in the world, but it means something to me. And I'm the important one, seeing as nobody else is ever going to read this. I think the word for what I'm doing is "therapy". It'd be nice to think that someday, the archaeologists are going to be digging up these notebooks and treating them like important historical documents, or even like holy scriptures from a lost civilisation. To be honest, though, I don't think the next people who come here are going to care much about English literature.

The first thing I'd better do is invent my audience. I'll pretend there are thousands of you out there, and I'll pretend you're all just like me: young, smart, pretty, and sarcastic (N.B. I'm probably being ironic here, although I'm not really sure any more). Just so we've got some common ground, I'll pretend you were born sometime in the late 1940s... no, sod that. I'll pretend you were born on the 15th of August, 1948. All of you.

Well, why not? If you're going to invent an audience, why not invent one in your own image?

2

I've never written a book before. Come to think of it, I've never met anyone who's written a book either, even though I've spent most of the last five years of my life hanging around with people who think they're artists. Or at least people who think they're the kind of people who'd be close friends of Oscar Wilde, if they'd been born nearly a hundred years earlier.

Thought they were the kind of people who'd be close friends of Oscar Wilde. Past tense. Must remember that.

In fact, the only person I ever knew who came close to the world of publishing was Dorian. Three years ago in summer '68, Dorian suddenly decided to tell everybody that he was one of the great modern poets of our time, on the grounds that he'd been to university and had an ode to some South American revolutionary or other published in the student magazine. So in the year when the rest of us were all pretending to hate pop music and claiming to be deeply, *deeply* into jazz, Dorian spent most of his time hanging around cafés in Covent Garden, standing on tables and reading out poetry to anyone who'd listen until the waitresses came and told him to stop. At which point he'd tell them that they were just pawns in an imperialist conspiracy to stifle freedom of expression. Then they'd tell him to piss off, and Dorian would forgive them, in an act of Christlike benevolence. So there.

3

At this point, I'd just like to say that I'm writing all this from memory. I'm not making any guarantees that these memories are accurate, all right?

4

The reason I'm mentioning Dorian is that he *did* get a book published, although it was just a collection of his stupid poems. He spent about six months telling us how a major ('and I mean, you know, *major*') publishing house had picked up on his work, and was going to unleash it on an unsuspecting world early in '69. When he finally showed up one day carrying two dozen "author's copies" in a Tesco bag, they were all held together with staples, and the ink came off on your fingers whenever you touched them. We decided that these "author's copies" were probably the only copies in existence, but we never said anything, not even when Dorian tried to sell them off. He managed to unload a couple on to tourists, but the rest ended up getting stuffed under his bed, where they stayed for almost two years until they were (presumably) destroyed along with the rest of London.

So, who's more pathetic? Me or Dorian? After all, at least two other people got to read his masterwork, even if neither of them could speak English properly. I'm telling myself this is therapy, but who's to say that what Dorian did wasn't? In the end, I'm writing this for the same reason he wrote his poems: because everyone likes to imagine they're the centre of attention, even when they're talking to themselves.

5

Anyway. Those "basics" I was talking about.

First, the world ended on the 12th of October, 1970. That wasn't the final end, of course, not the very last day. Most of the property damage was after that - the big cities, the Tokyos and the Berlins and the Riyadhs, they didn't get torn out of the ground until a few days later - but the 12th of October was when *it* all started. (Note how I put *it* in italics, just so you know how big and scary it was. Just you wait; I'll be underlining things next.)

I was in London when the end came, which makes me unique, I should think. I don't suppose anyone else from my neighbourhood is still alive by now. Nobody human, anyway.

London. Let me tell you about London.

.

6

London was the capital city of England, which was a country that liked to tell itself it was the cultural heart of the whole world, on the grounds that it had invented all the things that were great. Like Shakespeare, and the British Broadcasting Corporation, and even the Beatles (who came from Liverpool, which was a small suburb of London, according to all the tourist guides). In 1970 there were about seven-and-a-half million people in London, although I think most of them would've liked to be somewhere warmer.

What was it like? Well ... there were gutters stuffed full of last night's chip wrappers, and there were roads packed with taxis, driven around by men with bad complexions who stank of cheap cigarettes. *Everything* stank of cheap cigarettes, because the adults smoked and the children collected cigarette cards that turned their fingers the same colour as dead newspapers. There were streets full of people who complained when nobody was listening and who shut up again whenever anybody was, people who said the government should bring back national service, people who wanted something Ted Heath couldn't give them even though they couldn't remember what. There were pensioners wherever you looked, talking about the war and drooling onto the pavements (yes, I know it's cruel, but I was only twenty-two so I had the right to take the piss out of old people whenever I felt like it). It was a dull, wet, bleach-down-the-walls kind of city, that tasted like grease or closed-down cafeterias. And I hope that's given you a good feel for the place, because it's taken me hours to get this part right.

That wasn't the city where we lived, though. Me, and Cal, and Dorian, and all the others. We didn't live in London. We lived in LONDON!.

LONDON! was different. LONDON! was the place you heard about in all the Sunday papers, the place you saw every time you watched the news on the BBC and heard the posh presenters talking about the Latest Fashions of Today's Youth. The place that was famous, all over the world, for being the city that had invented everything new and shiny and exciting from Carnaby Street to the Beatles. (And if there are any Americans left alive, they probably still think Ringo Starr was a cockney... if any human beings ever crawl out of the wreckage to restart their civilisation, I hope to God they dig an idol of Ringo out of the ruins and worship him as their messiah, because it'd be kind of fitting.)

Oh yes. It was LONDON! for us, all right. We ignored the soggy people, we ignored the soggy food, we ignored the dog shit on the streets and the germs in the underground. In fact, I'm not really sure what we didn't ignore. I don't know what we thought LONDON! actually was. Half a dozen shops on Oxford Street and a jazz club in Soho, probably.

7

Another good reason for not calling this book *Real Life*. Six pages in, and it sounds like a bad joke already.

So, this was the way things were in the last few months before the end. It was, according to the hippies, the dawning of the Age of Something-or-Other (and we were never, ever hippies: we thought we were much too sophisticated and bohemi-an for that kind of thing). Which meant it was a good time for putting things into your body that weren't supposed to be there, basically.

Sex? There was plenty of sex, most of it in dingy little café back rooms, although we'd heard orgies were supposed to be fashionable in Rolling Stone high society (I'm trying to imagine getting into an orgy with the people I used to live with, but I don't think I can do it without making myself sick).

Drugs? Obviously, although all the boys used to lie about the number of trips they'd had, the same way they used to lie about the number of women they'd slept with. There was a kind of subspecies of girl in WC2 that had been specially bred by the boys in the LSD crowd, just so they'd have someone to offload all their post-beatnik bullshit on to. Girls who'd take as many tabs of acid as they were told to take and then lie down with their eyes and legs wide open, with big stupid I-can-see-through-time smiles on their faces. Girls like that must be extinct now, I sup-pose. I wonder what happened to them, when *it* came to the world. They must have just stood there, staring at *it* as *it* flooded into the city, smiling and giggling and -

No. Now I'm just fantasising.

8

I hope you've got the message by now. I am not, repeat not, the kind of woman who's likely to drop one tab of acid and end up staring at the carpet for six hours, looking for the hidden Jesus-faces in the pattern. Which is important, because of what I'm going to tell you next.

What I'm going to tell you is that at eleven o'clock p.m. on the 27th of September, 1970, I wouldn't have been able to tell you who I was, where I'd come from or why I even bothered getting up in the mornings. And the first thing I can remember about the night is being stuffed into the back of a police car.

I only remember *that* much because of the smell. Police cars used to smell like no other car on Earth, like everyone who'd ever been arrested had left sweat-marks on the upholstery. I was lying on my side on the back seat, with the weight of two police officers (neither of them women) pressing my face down into whatever it was police car seats had instead of leather.

The reason the policemen were sitting on me was that I was trying to throw myself out of the rear door of the car. This wasn't a good idea, seeing as the car must have been swerving along the Strand at the time, but what can you expect? Logic? I was screaming like a baby, kicking my skinny little legs, probably shouting 'get off get off, you fascist bastard scum' or something. Full-on paranoia. Full-on bad trip. Which was kind of surprising, seeing as I hadn't taken any acid, but we'll come to that later.

9

I was sane again by the time I got to the station. Sane and miserable. Just some skinny, badly dressed dropout girl with spit dribbling down her chin, staring at her plimsoles like a six-year-old.

The desk sergeant was a big square-faced man with whale meat for skin, and he looked like he'd been moulded that way. One of those people who get stuck in a dead-end job for so long that they end up changing shape to fit the office furniture better. You could tell, you could just *tell*, that he'd gone into the police force because he'd expected it to be exciting. He'd probably seen *Z-Cars* when he'd been a teenager, and thought, *that's the job for me*. Poor sod. Judging by the look on his face, I must've been the eight millionth burden-on-society who'd been pushed in front of him that week.

'Name?' he said.

'Christine,' I told him. I tried to sound sorry about it.

'Christine what?' he asked. He said it like it was a question on the official form, like everyone who came to the station got asked 'Christine what?'.

'Mmmuh-muh-muhh,' I said.

'What?'

'Summerfield,' I said. I felt stupid saying it out loud, for some reason. Like I'd only just decided to be Christine Summerfield, and still didn't really believe it yet.

Then the arresting (meaning: sitting-on) officers gave him all the facts. Apparently - and I *had* to believe this, seeing as I didn't remember any of it - I'd been found hanging around a building site near the Embankment, in the middle of a space that was going to grow up to be an office block one day. According to the official report, I'd been walking around in circles and making gurgling noises in the dark. One of the officers told the desk sergeant that my pupils had been dilated, so as far as he was concerned I had to be on drugs. (Fact: whenever the police arrested someone on a drugs charge, they always said the victim's pupils were dilated, even though most of the force didn't even know what "dilated" meant.)

I tried to tell them. I tried to tell them that I wasn't on drugs at all, that I was actually having a nervous breakdown, that I was suffering from stress and that my family had a long history of manic depression. But they weren't interested.

Besides, it was a lie anyway.

10

It's only just struck me. What I told you about London, earlier on: it doesn't make sense, does it? We used to say we were living in the pop culture capital of the world, where all the boys were in rock'n'roll bands and all the girls had Union Jack knickers. We used to say our city was the hippest place on Earth. But it's only now, now London / LONDON! doesn't exist any more, that I've spotted the big lie.

London wanted to be great by being just like New York. It's true, isn't it? We'd read all those stories about Greenwich Village in the *NME*, and we thought we could be exactly like that, like a little community of artists and dropouts protesting against the Establishment (that's the actual Establishment, not the club) by doing fuck all with our lives. Let's face it, even Dorian's useless poems were just bad Bob Dylan lyrics in a Hampstead accent.

We thought we were part of the best make-believe city on Earth, because we were English, and we were Londoners, and we were great. But we were trying to prove how great we were by being New Yorkers.

Why didn't I spot that before?

11

All right. Seeing as I've started talking about America, I might as well go all the way, and tell you exactly what was happening to LONDON! in 1970. Because this is where things get all twisted and sinister, and it's pretty much down to one man, plus a few of his friends. Because this was the year of Mr. Charles Milles Manson.

We did some of the most embarrassing things on Earth in the last couple of years before the end, just because we'd found out that we could. The stupid clothes, the stupid sex, the stupid drugs, the stupid everything. It was the dawning of the Age of Whatever-It-Was-I-Said-Before, and if we wanted to live in dirty stinking communes wearing no clothes and writing love letters to the Dalai Lama, then that's what we'd do. Even the TV programmes that were supposed to be in black and white had gone psychedelic on us.

The Californians were telling us that this was a whole new step in mankind's evolution, that we were turning into a new kind of super-species, a race so advanced it could stare at pink-and-green wallpaper for hours on end without freaking out. Everywhere we looked - the music papers, the record sleeves, the boutiques (because let's be honest, those were the only places we *did* ever look) - the message was the same. We weren't sure what the message was, but it had something to do with tomorrow being a better day, probably.

Manson changed all that. Like all the other important icons in our lives, he was an American. He looked like a guru, he had a big black Jesus-beard, and he lived on a ranch somewhere on the West Coast, where he built up a whole family of followers until he had what people liked to call a "cult". And, let's face it, on the surface he wasn't that different from the rest of us: if *we'd* had a ranch of our own, then we'd have hung around taking drugs and getting naked as well. Or at least that's what we liked to tell each other we'd do, but we were still pretending that a ground-floor flat off Endell Street could be the HQ of some kind of revolutionary social movement, so what did we know?

In August 1969, a bunch of five nearly-famous people in Hollywood all got killed off in one night, and at the time everyone said it was down to one of those American guerrilla groups we always used to get excited about, like the Weathermen or the Black Panthers. A few months later the papers told us all about Charles Manson, who was exactly like the kind of supercharged super-hip personality we all looked up to, but who'd ordered his "family" to hack people to bits for no good reason at all.

12

Everyone felt a bit down after that.

It wasn't just us, me and Cal and all the others. The whole of LONDON! (which, let's not forget, wanted to think it was a major - 'and I mean, you know, *major*' - American city) felt it. Suddenly, all the big acid-coloured shopfronts and the smiley-face badges started to look ... well, I can't think of a better word, so let's just say "sick".

Manson finally went on trial in 1970. By that time, we were still pretending to be the beautiful people, but none of us were talking about turning into higher beings any more. We weren't talking about LSD much, either. Cocaine, yes. LSD, no. In 1970, LONDON! wasn't Day-Glo: it was turning brown. Brown and orange. In a way, maybe it's a good thing that the world ended when it did. The 1970s would have been too ugly to live through. Or is it in bad taste, saying a thing like that?

In Covent Garden, there used to be a big piece of graffiti on the side of the Kean Street library, which had been there ever since late '68. It said, in huge psychedelic green letters:

GIVE PEACE A CHANCE

Then, sometime in early 1970, someone wrote a second message underneath it in no-nonsense black. The second message said:

NO

As far as the beautiful people were concerned, the writing was on the wall. If you see what I mean.

13

Incidentally, Charles Manson's trial never ended. Events got in the way, really. I should think he's dead now, or turned into something less human than he was to start with.

The trial started in July 1970, and we all followed it in the papers. The prosecution lawyer was a man called Vincent Bugliosi, which is something I remember without having to look it up, because at the time I thought it was exactly the kind of name a big American lawyer *should* have. Vincent Bugliosi told the whole world about the helter-skelter, about how Manson and his followers wanted to kick-start the revolution, and none of us back in London (it didn't feel like LONDON! that day) knew where to look.

We felt like we'd helped, I think. We didn't exactly feel guilty, but we were all on coke by then, so it didn't take long for the paranoia to kick in. We were paranoid about getting blamed, about the CIA sending agents to England to round us all up and have us all shot. I remember everyone (not just us in the flat) reading the parts about the apocalypse at the end of the Bible, just to see if there really were secret messages there, like Manson was supposed to have said. Especially in September. In September there were two or three big 'plane hi-jacks in some Arab country or other, so of course everyone was finding Bible prophecies about "winged things" causing death and destruction in the Holy Land. Then the papers started talking about the risk of the Manson-style "families" coming to England, and people started turning up dead even in London... but I'll get to that later.

Wouldn't it be funny if it turned out that Manson was innocent all along? If his defence had been planning on pulling out some breathtaking piece of evidence at the last minute, proving that everything had been a terrible mistake and saving him from the electric chair? Well, it might have happened. We'll never know, now.

14

I just pulled a scrapbook out of my rucksack, and something fell out from inside the back cover when I did it. It's a newspaper, a whole one, not just a clipping. The *Daily Mirror*, dated the 12th of October, 1970.

I'd forgotten all about that. There weren't many of them printed, and I picked one up on the morning after the end, just because I was one of the few human beings in London who had time to think about things like that. I should think most of Fleet Street stopped existing just after the first few issues came off the presses.

There's no story on the cover, but there's a great big photograph and a great big headline. The end of the world must have been a real hold-the-front-page kind of event, and the journalists couldn't have had much time to rewrite the issue, so all the pages inside are full of snippets they already had lined up; things so stupid and trivial that it's almost funny reading them now. Only page two says anything about the lead story, and it was obviously written by people who didn't know what was going on.

But I like the front page. There's a photo of the sky over London, taken just after it split open. The picture isn't great, probably because the cameraman was somewhere around Holborn, which was much too close to the centre of the action to get a good view of it all. But you can make out the basics. The shapes. The shadows. The hole in the world.

It's the headline I like, though. Well, what would you write, if you had to come up with a headline for the last day of your planet? The editors of the *Mirror* decided to try summoning up what they used to call the Old Dunkirk Spirit, which was named after a battle in World War Two that the British lost horribly, I think. The idea of the headline was to tell the people of the world that however bad things got there was always a chance of living through it.

The headline, which doesn't look like it's got anything at all to do with the photo underneath it, is this: NEVER GIVE UP.

15

Oh, the irony.

I've just realised why I like that headline so much. It's because it sums up this whole story. Or, rather, it sums up what this whole story isn't.

This is a story about giving up. Giving up your life, giving up your world, giving up on everything you've ever had. Am I being too pessimistic here? Well, I don't have anything to prove. There's nothing clever about coming up with a tragic ending, just because you want to look laid-back and cynical. But we already know what the ending is, don't we?

The Dunkirk Spirit. Never give up. Not even if you know your whole planet's finished.

Is that a moral, d'you think?

Maybe. We'll see. For now, let's get back to the police station.

Notes on the Station

16

Ending up in a police cell was a whole new experience for me. I wasn't naturally the kind of person to get into trouble, which is kind of ironic, bearing in mind what was happening to me in the last couple of months before the end. Or what I *remember* happening, anyway. I'd been on the LSD, and I was still on the hash (who wasn't?), but that didn't count. You didn't get arrested for that. Not usually.

If it gives you some idea of the kind of law-abiding citizen we're talking about here (for "law-abiding citizen", read "someone too scared to do anything much in a public place"), try this for size: after the graffiti on Kean Street got changed, I found another Day-Glo message, this time outside the queer toilets in Leicester Square. The graffiti was probably the work of the person who'd scrawled the GIVE PEACE A CHANCE slogan, and it said:

ALL YOU NEED IS LOVE

I came up with my own side-splitting reply to this. I even went as far as buying the spray-can, so I could add the words:

AND A FEW BASIC PROTEINS

But I didn't. I got as far as the entrance to the Square, then bottled out. Can you imagine that? One of the crowd who wanted to overthrow the fascist machine that controlled the freethinking people of the world, and I was too scared to even add a couple of words to some graffiti *that was already there*. That's so pathetic, even I'm impressed.

So how had I ended up in the middle of that building site, bawling my head off? What had pushed me over the edge and into screaming bloody delirium, to the point where I couldn't have cared less who was listening, or how many panda cars there might have been in the area?

Well, if you'd asked me that night, I'd have told you that the answer was simple. It was the cocaine.

17

I won't go into details. I won't bother. Back in the late 60s - oh yes, all those long, long months ago - the shops were full of books about drugs, about drug subcultures, about how drugs would turn people into supermen (but never superwomen, funnily enough), about how any number of happy little journalists had taken peyote on the side of a mountain and suddenly turned into American-Indian shamans. I'm only mentioning this because it might just turn out to be important to the story. Possibly.

Cocaine doesn't make you see things. It doesn't make you want to fly, either: I'm telling you this because, according to the newspapers, all drugs make you want to jump out of a hi-rise window. But if you're under stress, if you're in the right frame of mind, then maybe, just maybe, a couple of lines of coke are going to be enough to push you that one step further. Enough to make you decide that all the things you've been brought up with in your life are worth next to nothing, enough to make you drop all your defences and get you crying like a baby. Like something in you suddenly breaks open, and makes you realise how hard it's been, pretending to be a living, thinking, grown-up human being all these years. The same kind of shock you get when you realise that *nobody's really listening* when you talk to yourself, even if you think you're being really witty and clever. Nobody cares, and nobody's there to hear you.

Is that the reason I ended up in the cell?

Well, what do you think?

18

There was another woman in the cell with me. There were plenty of empty cells at Charing Cross police station, so I don't know why they made me share. Cal used to say it was some kind of policeman game, like when schoolchildren play with conkers. The police hang around outside the cells, putting bets on which of the prisoners is going to end up with the top bunk, and then moving the winner to another cell where there's an even harder hard-case to deal with... you get the idea.

I don't remember much about the way the woman looked. I remember her wearing a lot of black, and having a lot of pockets. She was probably overweight. All I remember for sure is that she'd been taken in for some kind of theft. She kept telling me, over and over again, how she'd been arrested. But the details changed every time, like the story was evolving inside her, until it was just the right shape to fit into my head properly.

'There's so much *stuff* in the world,' the woman said, more than once. 'You wouldn't think they'd care, y'know? You wouldn't think they'd care how much of it I've got in my pockets.'

She isn't important to the story. But I think about her a lot these days, like Cal, and Charles Manson, and all the others. I wonder what happened when *it* came, and turned her into just another piece of "stuff" in the world.

I think I'm over-emphasising the *it* here. Let's move on.

19/20

I'm sitting in the middle of some ruins as I write this, although I'm not sure what they're the ruins of. I'm a long way from London now, but I brought some things with me when I came here. To remind me of home? I don't think so. I don't think I care enough any more.

One of the things I brought is the scrapbook. It belonged to someone who used to be my boyfriend, and he let me have it when the end came, on the grounds that he was never going to find any use for it once he'd left Earth.

There's a cutting from the *London Evening Standard* on the first page. The headline reads THE MOST GROTESQUE TRIAL OF THE TWENTIETH CENTURY, and there's a big picture of Charles Manson in the middle of the text, staring up at the God in the ceiling and trying his best to look like Christ.

There are more clippings from the Manson trial after that, most of them taken from the London papers. Then, after a while, things change.

There's a piece from another copy of the *Standard*, dated the 1st of September: a front-page piece this time, with the headline "CULTS IN LONDON" WARN POLICE. Which isn't the most respectful headline ever, seeing as the story's about a murder. I won't bother copying out the text, although the details are pretty straightforward. Girl, aged about twenty, found dead near Constitution Hill. Face slashed. Hands slashed. No identifying features left. The police are calling the murder "ritualistic", an idea that obviously gets the reporters excited. Suddenly, the story "girl found dead" turns into "look out, Charles Manson's bunch have got to England". The *Standard* starts warning everybody that this could be the work of a cult, even though there's not one shred (oh, nice word to use, very tasteful) of evidence.

More front-page stories, after that. A second murder, two weeks after the first one. Same MO, like they used to say on *Dragnet*, and the same kind of weapon. As far as the papers are concerned, two deaths is a crime wave, so the conclusion's simple. There really is a cult at work on the streets of London. Forget the fact that the Manson family never bothered with "ritual" killing, whatever that's supposed to mean. Forget the fact that Charlie himself is up in court in LA, denying he's got any interest in black magic at all. This is obviously the work of some kind of Satan-worshipper, like in *Rosemary's Baby*. Maybe, say the papers, this is the real reason why nobody's reported the dead girls missing. Maybe they were both members of cults, who'd cut off all connections with their real families.

You're probably wondering whether I was scared, that September. Being a woman in her early twenties, with the same kind of build as the two victims (they were both size nine, one bigger than the size I told everybody I was), wasn't I paranoid about walking through London on my own?

Don't be stupid. There were three and a half million women in London, for God's sake. How was I to know I'd be the next in line?

21
Wait a minute. I'm getting ahead of myself.

22
Also, I've just remembered who made *Rosemary's Baby*. Is that in bad taste, d'you think?

23

I didn't spend more than an hour in the police cell before the big square-head desk sergeant came to let me out. (Square-head! D'you remember that old comic-book hero we used to have in England, who fought in World War Two and called the Germans "square-heads"? See how all authority-figures end up looking like Nazis, in my world.) To be honest, I don't think the police could be bothered charging me. They must have guessed I was on something, and I suppose they had blood and urine tests that could have told them what, but why bother messing around with a girl's urine if there isn't a major crime involved?

But there was another reason they let me go, and it's this: they had better things to think about. I found that out when the sergeant led me back to the main desk, down the big sweaty corridor that joined all the cells together. I kept my eyes fixed on my plimsoles while I shuffled along by his side, still feeling kind of embarrassed about ending up here.

We were halfway down the corridor when I heard the noise from the front desk. Men grunting. Furniture being shoved around. I'd been hanging out in South London pubs since I was too young to legally be there - too young to legally be in South London, I should think - and you didn't have to tell me what a fist-fight sounded like. The sound of men trying to out-tough each other by pushing chairs over.

The sergeant didn't speed up when he heard it. I got the feeling he was happy to let the other policemen deal with the problem, whatever it was.

'We've got the fucker,' he told me.

'Mnuh,' I said. (That was me trying to sound interested.)

It took me a while to figure out what he meant by that. Like I said, you could tell he'd had it with his job. You just knew he'd have given anything to go after real criminals for a change, instead of having to process scrawny little coke-heads going in and out of his station. So there was really only one person that "the fucker" could have been. After all, how often was there a celebrity killer on the loose in that part of London?

24

I've seen the police report on the suspect who was brought into the station that night, the man who was arrested 'in connection with' the two murders around Constitution Hill and Regent's Park. Obviously I didn't see the report at the time, but I was shown it later on, after ... well, we'll come to that.

The report says that at around a quarter to twelve on the 27th of September, a group (herd?) of three police officers spotted a man behaving suspiciously in the Embankment area, not far from the building site where they'd found me drooling in the rubble. The suspect looked like he was searching the streets for something, although when the police questioned him he wouldn't say what. When the officers pressed the point, the man got aggressive and had to be "restrained". When he was searched, he was found to be (and note the quote marks) "carrying several electronic components of uncertain manufacture". The officers took this as evidence that the man was mental.

There's a reason for this. In the early days of the trial, some of Manson's would-be disciples in California had started saying that their guru was transmitting instructions to them whenever he was on TV, using some kind of special hippie radio technology that only the Children of the Revolution could understand properly. Ever since then there'd been stories about deadheads walking around with radio parts strapped to their ears, so they could hear any messages that might have been sent by whatever icons they believed in. And when it came to technology, the suspect on the Embankment was loaded.

He was carrying what looked like a weapon, as well. The report didn't say exactly what it was, but - another quote - it "had a sharp edge, and could well have caused injuries consistent with the wounds from which the two victims died".

In other words, as far as the police were concerned, they had the fucker.

25

And there he was, in the police station, being mauled at the front desk by his three arresting officers. I stopped looking at my feet when I got there, because if there's one thing you can't look away from, it's a fight.

Yes. That was my first sight of him. I'm going to stop for a few moments' thought here, because this is important.

My first impression? He was powerful, for a start. Built. All three of the policemen were on top of him, pulling at his arms, trying to wrap themselves around his neck. Most of what I saw was blue, the colour of the uniforms, and the same colour as the suspect's suit. He was right in front of the desk, holding on to the edge of it, to stop the officers dragging him off to the cells. One of the policemen dropped to the ground at about the time I came in, clutching his stomach (although you couldn't tell exactly who'd hit him, not while there were so many arms flying about all over the place). The other men were grunting and swearing, telling their victim to calm down, telling him it was no use struggling, telling him that - *Christ, Jim, this is a sodding live one* - there was nowhere he could *go*.

The suspect wasn't listening. He was making a lot of noise as well, shouting over the grumbling sound the policemen were making. His teeth were clenched, you could tell.

26

'You've got to let me go,' he was saying. (Yes, whole sentences: so much more eloquent than the people who were attacking him, don't you think?) 'You don't understand. You've got to let me go.'

27/28

I remember reading a book about Jack the Ripper when I was fifteen, a crap old paperback in the school library back in Manchester (the book had ended up in the library by accident, and I only read it because all the other kids said the pictures were really sick, so I thought I'd better take a look before the teachers figured everything out and took it away from us). I can't remember what the book was called. I remember the point, though. The writer said he was sure that Jack the Ripper was the leader of some black magic cult or other. The murders were part of a ritual, meant to call forth devils and so on and so on. That's why Our Jack took the wombs out of some of his victims, because wombs were an important part of the ceremony, apparently. The writer talked about the ceremony a lot, although it sounded to me like he'd made the details up off the top of his head. More therapy writing, maybe.

The pictures were sick, like everyone said. There was a police photo, the one they took of the last murder scene back in the 1880s. There was a woman sprawled out on a bed, but she'd been pretty much turned into dog food. Parts of her body had been hacked off, and her head had been ripped up until all you could see of her face was a big grey smudge. And this was, according to the caption, something that had been a walking, talking human being just one day before the photo had been taken.

You had to laugh. I mean, not at the photo: you had to laugh at the idea that the person who'd done this was some kind of voodoo magician. The idea that he'd planned all this out, as part of a plot to call up whatever ghosts he was supposed to believe in. I keep thinking about the murderers who were around when I was younger, the ones whose faces kept turning up on the BBC for months after they were caught. Men like John Christie. Scrawny, wrinkly little men with ugly glasses and too many personal problems. Would anyone ever have written about *them* as being magicians?

But the rules were different, if you were talking about things that happened a hundred years ago. Why? Because there's something about that point in time, the way you see it in all the Hammer Horror movies, that makes you believe things might have been different then. That there really could have been bad magic in the middle of London.

1970 was the same. Probably only the second time in the city's history when people could seriously think there were devil-worshippers on the move. It was like the killer had been born out of all the dead skin left over from the 60s, like those two women had been killed by the culture instead of by a mad bastard with a knife.

(By the way, if you think I'm starting to sound cynical... let's not forget, you're talking to someone who must have been to a couple of dozen different planets by now, and not just in the marijuana-and-astral-projection way. You're talking to someone who spent her last days in London sharing a flat with a spaceman. Someone who's held a whole universe in her hands, a whole miniature universe, squeezed into a tiny magic bottle. Once you've seen all the little galaxies spinning around between your fingers, you start to get different ideas about what it means to be "realistic". That's all I'm saying.)

29/30

Where was I? Let me look. Oh yes. The man in the police station, with all the blue uniforms around him.

Just for a second, the policemen backed off, enough to let me see the suspect from head to foot. He was tall, although he was buckled up, so he'd obviously been kicked about by the policemen even before he'd arrived here. He was thin, but not sick-thin; there were big knots of muscle under that suit of his, you could see it. A suit! And since when did mass murderers wear suits, anyway? I could see his face, all pale and covered in bulging veins, with big scary teeth between his lips. I could see hair, short blond hair, sticking up in prickles all over his head. What else? Oh ... a little gold earring, just a stud. His face was so twisted up, there was no way of saying how old he was, but you could tell he was young just by the earring. Young, or a bit on the Leicester Square side.

The next thing I knew, someone was prodding me in the back. The desk sergeant. We were still standing at the end of the cell corridor, just spectating.

'Go on,' the sergeant told me. 'Sod off.'

I didn't argue. I headed for the doors, between all the chairs that had been scattered across the floor in the fight.

'You've got to let me go,' the suspect kept shouting. 'It's going to happen again. There's going to be another killing. You've got to let me *go*.'

You'll notice the emphasis I've put on that word: go. Why? Because on that word, the blond man decided to use up what must have been the last of his strength, and make a break for it. I didn't even know it was happening, seeing as I was only watching out of one eye, and trying not to trip over any of the chairs. (Coming down from the coke, yes, but still not exactly light on my feet.) There were yelps from the policemen. A grunt of something like 'get the bastard!'. That's when I turned to look at the desk full-on, and that's when I saw the face of the blond man, hurtling towards me. Just the face. At that exact moment, the rest of the body didn't matter much. Just the face, the teeth, the earring ...

Then the hand. There were fingers, reaching out for me. Not going for the throat, though. It was more like he was reaching out for help. I didn't even jump. I could feel the tips of his fingers brushing against my face.

'Please -' he said.

He didn't say anything else. He couldn't, not with the first of the policemen getting an arm around his throat, the second one pulling his elbows behind his back, the third getting up off the floor and swearing at him. And me? I just stood there, staring like an idiot, watching him being punched in the stomach and dragged to the ground.

Then the desk sergeant told me to sod off again. I did.

31

This is the kind of story that used to get you on chat shows, or at the very least got you column inches in the *News of the World*. How I was the first woman to stare into the face of the Butcher of Buckingham Palace and live. (The first killing hadn't actually been anywhere near Buckingham Palace, of course, but Constitution Hill was close enough for the papers.) You can just see my story, sitting there on page four underneath the topical cartoon. How the killer reached out and touched me, with hands that had been rummaging through God knows what kind of offal. So I'd like to be able to say that I was shocked, or stunned, or that the experience made me understand how brief and fragile life on Earth could be.

It didn't, though. In fact, the only thought that went through my head when his fingers brushed against me was this:

Wow!

Which probably isn't the right reaction, ethically speaking. So you might think it was some kind of cosmic karma that less than an hour after it happened, somebody tried to kill *me*.

32

I've been wondering, recently, what London must be like these days. It can't all have been destroyed, can it? The intelligence that runs the city now is ... well, intelligent. Cultured. I can't imagine the new ownership clearing away the ruins under the rubble, any more than I can imagine Lady Diamond clearing her shelves. (And yes, I'll explain that in a minute.) The ruins were still there on the day I walked out of the city, anyway.

So, this is how I see London now: I imagine a whole part of the city that's been walled off and left intact, or at least, as intact as it was the last time I saw it. I imagine the Houses of Parliament with their towers broken off, and St. Paul's Cathedral cracked open like an egg. I imagine all the cars that were in the capital, piled on top of one another in the wreckage of Leicester Square, set alight and turned into a bonfire that never goes out. I imagine a sky that's the colour of smoke, where the air's been burning for so long that it's been stained brown forever.

And then what happens is this. The spectators let humans loose in the ruins, inside the walled-off battlefield. They've chosen the humans carefully, these spectators: they've picked all the big icons, all the best madmen we ever came up with, but the icons have been pumped up with drugs and machines to make them pretty much indestructible. They come from all over the world, the way I imagine it. I can see Chairman Mao, and Ian Brady, and John Christie, and - yes, all right - Charles Manson, stalking the streets with knives in their hands and spit all over their clothes. The spectators start placing bets, trying to guess who'll be the last man standing.

Even the dead get the chance to play. Even Jack the Ripper might turn up as a special guest star. When only one of the humans is left, the spectators settle the bets and start the game again, bringing the bodies back to life and patching up the holes. Icon-soldiers in a fight that never ends. Let's be honest, it's not much different from the way we did things when we still ran the world. It's just more direct, that's all.

This is the way I imagine things. I've got no way of knowing if any of it might be true.

Anyway. Back to the 27th of September. Or rather, the early hours of the 28th.

Notes on Lady Diamond's Shop

33

By now, the question you're asking yourselves is: what was she doing, anyway? What was she doing coked out of her head in the middle of a building site, at that time of the night?

If you'd asked me that at the time, I probably would have answered by staring at you. Blankly. Well, why shouldn't I have been there? That was the way we were, before the end. Me, and Cal, and Dorian, and all the others. No job, no routine, just starting my fourth year at an art college I'd only actually been to once. (My family had only been middle-class for a couple of decades, in case you were wondering, and none of them had ever even seen London. They didn't have a clue how higher education worked, which is why I could get away with telling them that it could take me anything up to ten years to get my diploma, and why they kept sending the money for whatever it was that art students were supposed to need. Yes, it worked. Really.) The point is, I didn't have any reason to be anywhere. I was a goddess of the new bohemian age, remember?

No, the important thing wasn't where I'd been. It was where I was going to go next. Just think how I was feeling when I stepped out of that police station, and into the freeze-your-tits-off air of Charing Cross. Confused; coming down from a buzz; excited, seeing as I'd just come face to face with the man who'd probably end up being called "the English Charles Manson"; and, most of all, itchy. The way I saw it, the police had got in the way of what might have been a perfectly good cocaine experience. If you could ignore the screaming. What I needed was to find someone I knew, preferably someone with a good supply of their own, and tell them all about what had happened.

How civilised. 'Darling, you wouldn't believe what I've been through.' (Snort.) 'The police were positively everywhere. It was an absolute *nightmare*.' (Snort.) 'And, darling, guess what I saw while I was at the station.. .' (Snort, snuffle.)

34

Halfway along Henrietta Street in Covent Garden, there used to be a shop owned by a woman called Lady Diamond. Once upon a time it'd been a bookshop, but it had changed over the years until the windows were full of Laughing Buddhas and psychedelic zodiac charts, while the glass in the door was covered with little bits of card advertising palmistry and tarot-reading sessions. I can't remember what the shop was called in September 1970, because it changed every couple of weeks. It was probably Mysteries or Secrets of the Light or something. (Lady Diamond was her real name, by the way. Her family were the last great English Colonials in India, and they'd come up with the title "Diamond" a couple of generations earlier, to make it sound like they'd been in India as long as the rocks. I don't know why they'd called one of their daughters Lady, though. Maybe it was a social-climbing kind of thing.)

Lady Diamond was the most accurate fortune-teller in the city, according to the woman herself. Anybody could make guesses, but she claimed that when she saw into the future, she always - *always* - saw what was really there. She was even on television, once. A man from ITV came to her shop, asking about the 'new resurgence in spiritualism' or something. Lady went through her usual routine, and ended up doing the reporter's horoscope, for the entertainment of all the country.

She told him he was destined for great things in broadcasting. which is kind of funny, because a couple of months later he was in a head-on car collision, lost the use of his legs, and had to retire from TV (they didn't let cripples be celebrities back in England, they thought it'd look cheap). Lady Diamond wasn't put out by that at all.

'When I look into the future, I always see what's really there,' she said, when she heard about the crash. 'But that doesn't mean I have to tell the truth about it.'

Right up to the last time I remember seeing her, she was still claiming her visions were 100% accurate. After all, as she kept telling her customers, she'd predicted the death of Bobby Fuller two weeks before it had happened and had personally tried to warn the man about it. Which was a pretty safe claim to make, seeing as Bobby Fuller himself wasn't going to be arguing with her. But by 1970 hardly anyone could remember who Bobby Fuller was, until in the end all he was famous for in LONDON! was being the subject of Lady Diamond's most accurate prediction.

35

Bobby Fuller was an American rock'n'roll singer. He died in the mid-60s, when he tried flirting with a Mafia don's girlfriend in a nightclub, and ended up having his lungs pumped full of petrol by the don's bodyguards.

36/37

The reason Lady Diamond was so popular was that she kept adding new ideas to her repertoire. When Buddhism was fashionable, she started using Buddhist chants in her readings. When the Beatles went to India, she painted Indian letters (or things that looked like Indian letters, anyway) on her tarot cards. When LSD was popular - and when wasn't it? - her holy guardian spirits suddenly turned into psychic aliens, who were trying to speed up humankind's cosmic evolution. She kept throwing new bits and pieces into the window of the shop, until it turned into a kind of jungle, where natural selection could get on with its work as usual. The interesting-looking religions ate up the boring ones, until what was left was a kind of super-faith, ready to chew up and spit out any other beliefs it ran into. Laughing Buddha with pointy teeth and armour plating. Remember what I said about what London must be like now, with all the icons fighting it out in the ruins? Same principle.

And as for the inside ... The shop took up the bottom two levels of the building, but Lady had taken out the ceiling of the ground floor (something the council probably wouldn't have approved of, but there you go) to turn the place into a kind of well, with the bookcases set all around the walls and the roof a long, long way overhead. The wall space above the bookcases was taken up by Lady's "collection", leftovers from all the cultures she'd absorbed over the years, some of the items nailed to the brickwork and some of them resting on little shelves and balconies.

There were animal skulls from India and Africa, with blotchy red glyphs painted right between their eyes. There were candles that never got lit, carved into the shapes of Chinese women in "erotic" poses. There were Victorian anatomical charts, telling you the best places to drill holes to cure people's madnesses. There was a grubby white robe that had been singed around the edges, which Lady claimed had been worn by one of the men who'd burnt Joan of Arc (N.B. obviously a lie). There was even the foetus of a kitten preserved in a jar, which should have looked pathetic and embarrassing, like that rock star in LA who had a jacket made out of donkey embryos. But somehow it looked *right* there in Lady's shop. And everywhere, whichever way you turned your head, there was a smell like dust and old grandfather clocks. Like Lady had sprayed the place with something to make it feel older than it was.

The rule in the shop was this: when you went in, you didn't look up. If you looked up, your eyes tried to focus on the ceiling, but the ceiling was too far up for you to find. You just kept raising your head, and raising it and raising it, taking in all the bones and the charts and the dead things, until you started to feel dizzy. Like you were standing at the bottom of some kind of archaeological dig, looking at centuries of history all pressed together. Most people gave up before they could get as far as the roof. Then they had to sit down for a bit, usually on one of the big fat karma-friendly beanbags that'd been arranged in the middle of the floor.

Clever Lady. She knew how to get people in the mood for business. She knew how to make you feel vulnerable. But the shop was supposed to be her home as well as her workplace, so it's kind of impressive that she had a crypt for a living room and still stayed pretty sane.

38

The shop was the first place I went after I left the police station, for a couple of reasons. Firstly, it was close. Secondly, Lady was just the kind of person I wanted to tell about my run-in with the (alleged) almost-mass-murderer, seeing as I knew she'd have to pretend not to be impressed. She was getting on for twice my age, so there was always a lot of posing going on between us, what with her claiming to have once had tantric sex with Brian Wilson and everything. Thirdly, there was the cocaine.

Just as a matter of course, Lady kept stashes of all the fashionable drugs in the shop, in case a client wanted a full-on head-trip reading with all the *2001* special effects. She kept half a dozen Chinese puzzle-boxes on one of the lower bookshelves, each one full of a different illegal substance. She knew she didn't have to worry about the police. Even if the Met felt like raiding the place, there wasn't a policeman alive who'd bother messing with a Chinese puzzle-box to get hold of the evidence.

Cocaine again. Am I starting to sound like an addict? Maybe I'm just missing the comforts of home.

39

The shop was closed when I got there, and there weren't any lights on inside. That wasn't much of a setback. The front door might have been locked, but there was a rear door at basement level behind Henrietta Street. The lock had been broken for months, and Lady had dealt with this by shoving a pile of old D. H. Lawrence paperbacks (where did they come from?) up against the door. Anyone who was a friend of hers knew that all you had to do was give the door one big shove, and send the copies of *Sons and Lovers* flying.

I didn't have any problem with the idea of "breaking into" Lady's place. It's not like I was the only one doing it. Lady was famous (notorious?) for the number of skinny, hairy men she managed to end up in bed with, and most of her lovers and ex-lovers used the shop as a crash-house sooner or later. Lady had forgotten who a lot of them were. They just ended up hanging around the back rooms, spending their lives smoking dope and sleeping on old mattresses. She lost track of her partners the way most people lose track of spare change. Dig your hand down the back of a sofa in Lady's place, and you were bound to find a hippie toy boy or two.

I didn't see anyone in the back rooms when I "broke in", although the light was on in the back passage, and there was the smell of cannabis and dead skin everywhere. I didn't bother poking my nose into any of the spare rooms. By that time, the need to finish off the evening's coke experience was a damn sight more important than the need to find Lady and tell her about the police station, so I headed straight up the stairs and into the main part of the shop.

40/41

I'm thinking of starting a magazine, for people just like me. Seeing as I'm the only human survivor of London (I think), I'll be the only one who actually reads it, but that doesn't matter. The magazine's going to be called *It Might Never Happen: The Journal of Mindless Optimism,* and I'm going to fill it with all the things I tell myself to make me feel better about the world. I must have come up with millions, over the last few months. All the way down from 'at least I'm alive' to 'it wasn't a very big planet, anyway'.

What do you think I should make the cover story of the first issue, then? Should I go with 'there's always drugs', or should I just stick with the Dunkirk Spirit?

Anyway. It didn't take me long to crack the "coke" puzzle-box, because practice makes perfect, and on Henrietta Street you could always spot a user by the astonishing puzzle-solving skills he or she had picked up from hanging around Lady's shop. In the end, I was disappointed.

There was nothing there. A couple of empty paper wraps, and some white gunk in the corners of the box. Sure signs that someone had beaten me to it.

So I did what I had to do. I started scraping the stuff out of the corners, using my fingers, my nails, and - when all else failed - the amazing suction power of my nose. I ended up squatting on one of the beanbags, tilting my head back with the puzzle-box in front of my face, snuffling like a pig.

Which wasn't a good idea. I'd turned the lights on when I'd walked into the room, and the lights were right up there in the ceiling. Which meant that when I lay on my back and looked up, I could see all the dead things leering down at me, casting their big spiky shadows on the walls. I was staring straight at the animal skulls, things that had died in India and never been buried, covered in horns and hieroglyphs. There was the front part of some kind of lizard, mounted like the head of a moose. And - yes - there was that inevitable foetal kitten.

Don't look up. That was the first rule. The second rule was: especially not if you're on coke. Coke may not make you hallucinate, but it gets you paranoid enough to make you think that you're going to hallucinate, that the walls are going to start moving in on you any second. And there wasn't much in the box, but taking just one sniff was enough to remind me of all the times I'd taken more, and that was it: the trigger, the thing that made the paranoia kick in. All of a sudden I was staring into the eye sockets of a gazelle, waiting for it to move, or to blink, or to speak, or anything else that'd push me over the edge. Waiting for the lizard to crawl down from the wall with its hindquarters missing, waiting for the kitten to turn its head and look me in the eye.

The gazelle. The lizard. The kitten. The dead bodies on the Victorian charts, getting ready to bleed for me. Buddha smiling down from a print of some old Tibetan painting, grinning like death, psyching himself up to grab one of Lady Diamond's fake sacrificial daggers and say 'fuck karma, let's all kill something' -

And then something moved. I didn't see it, but I heard it, and that was enough. Feet shuffling. A noise that could have been anything - someone clearing his throat, someone scratching an itch, anything - but that sounded, just for a moment, like the scampering of little tiny feet.

That was all it took, really. That one sound. Suddenly I was seeing movement out of the corner of my eye, out of the corners of both eyes, the things crawling across the walls just out of my vision and then stopping dead whenever I turned to look at them. And I was pulling myself up off the floor, and yelling, and stamping my feet, and clawing at the dead kittens that I was sure were clawing and sucking at me, crawling around under my T-shirt, or nuzzling their way up my legs.

At some point, I must have realised I wasn't alone in the room. I must have figured out that I had company, even apart from the dead things. I'm not sure what that point was.

42

I just remembered something else about Lady Diamond. You know how I said earlier on that Dorian was the only person I ever knew who (kind of) got a book published? Well, Lady Diamond used to write as well, although she never had anything in print and she never tried to read any of her stuff to waitresses. In fact, nobody ever got to read the things she wrote, because she used to burn them as soon as they were finished.

It was what Lady called sympathetic magic. It's like in those old black magic movies, when the voodoo man makes a little doll of someone, then starts mutilating it. The idea is that if you kill someone's image, part of that person dies as well. Lady used to say that there was no way you could do any real damage to someone with just a doll, because a doll wasn't detailed enough. Even if you made it look exactly like your victim, it didn't say anything about the kind of person the victim was. How was the bad magic supposed to know who to target, out of all the billions of people in the world?

Lady Diamond had a solution to that. She used to write stories, but the lead characters in the stories were all based on real people. She'd make likenesses, just like the voodoo men in the old movies did, but she did it with words instead of Plasticine. She'd describe her victims in full, all the details of who they were and why she thought they had to suffer. At the end of each story she'd make sure that something bad happened to them, which was (she said) just as good as sticking pins in a doll.

Finally, Lady would burn the story in a little bowl, keeping the fire burning with herbs and lighter fluid. Filling the air with the smell of incense and cheap fiction.

'Sympathetic magic for *literate* people,' she'd say.

43

I wonder sometimes if proper writers do that. If, when publishers pay them to write books, they're actually being hired as assassins. Who can say?

But it's funny, really. Here I am writing my first "novel", and it turns out that the only other writers I've ever known also wrote things they knew nobody would ever read. Why do we artistic types do these things? Is it really therapy, or are we just doing voodoo? Am I trying to change the way things happened by writing about them, by some kind of magic that only Lady Diamond would have understood properly?

44

There was a man standing in the doorway. The doorway between the main part of the shop and the stairwell, that is, so you could see the cannabis smoke wafting up the steps behind him. The bulb-light was making the little puffy clouds sparkle around his head. Looking back on things, I suppose it must have been him I'd heard, moving up the stairs and into the room. This wasn't the way I saw it at the time, though. As far as I was concerned, he was probably in league with all the dead things.

You can just see me there, can't you? Eyes open wide, lungs ready to burst with all the heavy breathing I'd been doing, scummy bits of white powder dribbling down my lips. Clothes a mess. Hair a mess, all the big black strands tangled up around my ears. I think I remember putting my hands up in front of my face, like a boxer would have done. I must have looked ridiculous.

I didn't recognise the man. He was thin, and he was white, and he had too much hair sprouting out of his face, so I must have thought he was one of Lady Diamond's lost-property boyfriends. But he was too clean for a hippie. Not clean like you're clean after you've just washed, but clean like a piece of paper's clean before you write on it, before you've even left any of your dirty fingerprints behind. He looked too tall to be real, but then, everything looked bigger than it should have done at that point (even the kitten was puffing itself up in its jar; although it was doing this behind my back, I was sure). And as for his face...

There are two kinds of expression you see on people's faces when they're going out of their minds. There's the surprised, baby-faced look, when the acid kicks in and they realise that - Jesus Christ - the world really *is* a beautiful place underneath it all, if you ignore stupid little details like 'matter'. Then there's the other look. The dangerous one. The staring-dead-ahead one. The man's features were pretty grim anyway, with all those wrinkles and scars hidden behind the bushes of black hair on his face, but at that point in time it was much, much too easy to imagine him pulling out a Stanley knife and carving the words FEAR ME, FOR I AM THE BEAST on his forehead. In capitals, even.

Come to think of it ... doesn't it strike you, after what I've just said, that I'm describing a kind of second-hand Charles Manson? Even his clothes, the ripped (but *clean*) jeans and the cheap (but *clean*) vest, made him look like he'd been living out in the desert with the coyotes for a month. Not like he belonged in the middle of London at all. Or is that just how I'm remembering him, in the light of what happened afterwards?

45

The man didn't say anything, not straight away. He stared and he stared and he stared, so I started wondering whether he was really looking at me, or just watching the atoms dancing around my aura.

'You're not supposed to be here,' he said, in the end. His voice was so ordinary, I don't even remember what kind of accent he had. There was no feeling there, though. I didn't have an answer to that. After all, he was right, kind of. I remember wiping my nose. Hiding the evidence, maybe?

'I'm a friend of Lady's,' I said.

The man didn't say anything. He just kept staring.

'Are you staying here?' I asked. Which was a polite way of asking if he was Lady Diamond's current sleeping partner.

Still no answer. Instead the man stepped forward, heading right for me, and when he moved I saw little echoes of himself in the space behind him, as if parts of him were sticking to the air when he walked through it. That didn't surprise me. Like I said, coke doesn't make you hallucinate. But it pumps up your senses to the point where you sometimes end up seeing things that have stopped being in the space where you're looking.

This was kind of distracting, which is why I missed the fact that the man was still heading straight for me, and also why I didn't do anything to get out of his way even when it should have been obvious that he was getting ready to reach out and throttle me.

46

I've just read through the last couple of paragraphs and, no, it doesn't look right to me either. I'm sure there should be more to it than that. More suspense, while the two of us face each other across the shop. More of a confrontation. More drama.

But who am I kidding? I was a stupid, paranoid, coked-up cripple, who could hardly move without having a panic attack. And him? He just wanted to kill me.

Maybe I should rewrite it. So you genuinely think I'm being attacked by the dead things in the shop, and just when you think it's all a red herring, and I'm perfectly safe ... ta-daah! The real danger turns up. What do you think?

Also, you're probably thinking that this is a bit of an unlikely plot twist. I leave the police station, where they've just arrested a man for being the English Charles Manson (I'd patent that line, if there was any point now), only to stumble into a building where there's a real-life psychopath waiting for me. You're right. It doesn't look good. For now, though, you'll just have to believe me when I say that the same thing would have happened even if I'd gone somewhere completely different. I mean, I was the chosen victim. Not that I knew it then.

47

Judging by the cannabis smoke in the passage, there was at least one hippie hanging around in the back rooms, but I suppose he must have been too far away from Earth to hear the struggle when the man went for my throat. And Lady Diamond herself? I never did find out where she was, when her shop was wrecked and somebody tried to kill me. I only saw her once after that night, and by then I was already mixed up in the events that were leading up to the end of the world, so I never got round to asking her about it. I suppose it's all academic now. For all I know Lady looked into the future, saw the danger coming, and made sure she was out of the shop that night.

Notes on the Killer

48

This is the way violence works, in the real world. One minute you're getting on with your life - say, imagining there are dead kittens crawling up the leg of your jeans - and the next thing you know there's a flurry of arms and legs, and there's spit raining down on your face, and the only thing you can feel is the breath of some maniac who smells like he's been chewing on raw eggs.

There's that "real world" thing coming into the picture again. I'll have to watch out for that.

49

So. At half past one on the morning of the 28th of September, 1970, you would have found me hobbling down the side streets of Covent Garden, bleeding on to the pavements from the wound in my leg. The roads were pretty much empty by that time, so there weren't any crowds gathering around me, nobody listening to me grunting and blubbering while I dragged myself along the street. I must have seen a couple of passers-by on the way, people who were too slow to figure out that it was well past closing time, but so what if I did?

London was like any other city on Earth. Everything was contagious there. If you saw someone on a bad trip, you crossed the road to get away from them, in case the little pixie-demons jumped straight from their head to yours. If you saw someone with a bloody great hole in their leg, you stayed away from them as well, in case it turned out to be catching.

I remember the wound being huge. I remember looking down through the gap in my shredded-up jeans, and being able to see all the way to the bone, where the man in the shop had bitten a whole chunk of flesh out of me. But I'm sitting here now, looking down at my right thigh, and I'm tracing the scar tissue where the skin grew over the hole later on. And it looks tiny. Hardly a mouthful. Is that because of the way the wound healed? Or does blood just make everything look worse than it is?

50/51

So how did I get the wound in the first place?

Picture me splayed out in the middle of the shop again, with my back pressed against Lady Diamond's all-purpose therapeutic beanbags. Imagine a pair of hands around my windpipe. Not trying too hard to strangle me, not even trying to break my neck, but just keeping me pressed down, maybe hoping I'll get swallowed up by the beanbags if I stay down long enough.

Now see things from my point of view. I'm looking up, up towards the lights in the roof of the shop. (Don't look up, remember? That was the rule.) But I can't see the source of the light, because hovering over me is the head of the man who these days I remember as looking like a cross between Manson and Long John Silver. That's all I can focus on: the shape of his head, all black and hairy, until the pain doesn't matter any more and I start thinking about those stories you hear from people who've had near-death experiences, who say they saw Jesus Christ waiting for them in the light at the end of the tunnel. And that's what I can see now, just a big shaggy face wearing a halo that's been supplied by the London Electricity Board, and suddenly all I can think about is how confusing it'd be if he killed me, because how would I tell the difference between this and the afterlife?

Then he shifts his weight. He tries to get a better grip on my throat. He still isn't trying to kill me (much), just keeping me still, although that makes me wonder what he's keeping me still for. At this point, I'm thinking: it's not murder: it's rape. And the thought's annoying, more than anything, because it makes my whole lifestyle feel worthless. Here she is, modern cosmopolitan woman, always telling her friends that she knows how to look after herself, but when the big horror comes to get her it's the best she can do to hold up her fists like a five-year-old and squeal like a pig. The panic gets worse after that, because when he shifts his weight he moves his head, just a little to the side. So all of a sudden I can see right the way up to the ceiling, and see all the layers of dead things hanging over me. I'm not worried about the dead things moving any more: this time they're the spectators, waiting for the man to turn me into just another dead thing, or maybe even get me pregnant with a dead-thing baby.

Then everything changes again. It's not until after it's all over that I work out why. My arms have been flapping around by my sides, working on automatic. My hands have seen that bit in *Dial M for Murder* with Grace Kelly and the scissors, and they've got a hunch that they'll find a weapon if they flap hard enough. So far, they haven't. They've just been tearing at the beanbags, ripping them open, feeling those little polystyrene balls popping between their fingers. Now the man's shifted his balance, my body's starting to roll over, so the arms can reach out further. Finding something solid, but not that all-important pair of scissors, sadly.

My fingers grab it before I even know what's going on. I pull at it. Try to bring it towards me. It's round about now that my hands figure out what it is: it's a table, the one Lady Diamond keeps her teacups on in the middle of the room, so it's not exactly the weapon I've been hoping for.

I can't stab the man with it. Or even hit him over the head with it. They've got nothing better to do, so my hands just tug harder, and pull it over. Teacups are smashing against the floor. I can feel papery things falling on to my bare arm, and I guess that there were tarot cards on the table. All of a sudden it's raining wands and cups and discs and swords, and they're all made of cardboard.

Finally, the man lets go of my neck. There's something heavy on the side of my face, twisting my head to one side, pushing my cheek against Lady Diamond's best Persian rug.

This is when he bites me.

52

The cards, as it turned out, weren't tarot cards at all. They were Zener cards.

You might have seen Zener cards on TV at some time; at least, you might have done if you're the way I've imagined you. They're like a set of playing cards, but each one's marked with a different symbol in thick black ink. There's a star, there's a square, there's a circle, there's a bunch of wavy lines. Scientists (at least, the kind of scientists who thought they had better things to do with their lives than stare at bacteria) used to use Zener cards in special lab tests, to see whether or not people had telepathic powers. They didn't, usually.

But Lady Diamond's Zener cards were different. Let's not forget: she'd reached the point where she didn't see any difference between magic, psychic powers, Buddhism, spiritualism and drug abuse. As far as she was concerned, the only reason magic worked was because people were scared shitless of it, so when she decided to make Zener cards part of her routine she went out of her way to draw the scariest cards she could come up with.

When the man in the shop twisted my head to one side, the first thing I saw, lying on the floor in front of my eyes, was a black line drawing of a naked man being hanged. The second thing I saw was a picture of a syringe, with something nasty dripping from the end of the needle. The third thing I saw was a swastika. The fourth thing I saw ...

You get the idea. 'Try reading my mind, and you'll have the shock of your fucking life.' That's what Lady Diamond told the people she did her own telepathy "experiments" on.

53

A hanging man. A syringe. A swastika. A cartoon phallus. A Black Power symbol. A hammer-and-sickle emblem.

These were the things I saw, lying there on the floor of the shop with my neck being broken. Like a kind of breadcrumb trail of cards, leading across the rug. And there, right at the end of the trail, was the skull. A great big carved candle, the centrepiece of Lady Diamond's table, never meant to be lit. It was just sitting there with its jawbone missing, trapping the last of the cards under its teeth. All those symbols, all those little pictures of human culture, all ending up in that big bony mouth.

You can read what you like into that. You can say it's symbolic if you like. A couple of hours earlier I probably would've agreed with you, but at that point I'd just started screaming, seeing as I'd lost a good amount of flesh from my right thigh.

54

There are a lot of symbols in this book. Then again, I suppose that's what you'd expect. Everything was symbols, back in LONDON!. A couple of years earlier the only posters you could get in the shops had photos of pop stars on them, but now Lady Diamond was doing good business selling cheap four-colour prints of Buddha and Jim Hendrix (especially after his spectacularly crap death), not to mention a couple of cartoons showing Jesus as a pot-head in khakis. You could buy portraits of foreign revolutionary leaders in Woolworth's. Woolworth's, for God's sake!

Sometimes I think that was why the world ended when it did. Because the human race had reached its limit. We'd spent thousands of years making things, designing things, coming up with symbols to keep ourselves happy, and now the symbols were taking over. We were building a world where only the icons mattered, and the people were a kind of embarrassing side-effect. Humankind was bound to die out, because it wasn't needed any more, because it wasn't as important as all the bits and pieces it'd left behind. If everything hadn't come to a stop, we probably would've ended up living in a country run by smiley-face badges. The smiley faces are another thing the end of the world saved us from, like decimalisation and another four years of Tory government.

Why am I telling you all this? Oh yes. Because there's something I want to share with you. I want to tell you exactly what I was thinking, when I dragged myself out of the shop, after I'd finally got away from the maniac.

What I was thinking, at half past one on the morning of the 28th of September, was this ...

55/56

We're all dead things. We're all dead things, but the fact that we're still moving stops us seeing it.

My mother used to tell me something about the night I was born. She told me that in the maternity ward, in the bed right next to hers, there was a woman whose baby came out sick. She couldn't remember what kind of 'sick', but it was something bad, something the doctors couldn't spot before the actual birth. The woman somehow managed to keep quiet right the way through the delivery but, when the baby finally came out the way it did, something just snapped. That was when she started screaming. Screaming and screaming and screaming, until the doctors had to wheel her out of the ward. But she was still there when my mother started having the contractions, so I suppose the screaming could've been one of the first things I ever heard. I wonder if that's important?

The baby next door was definitely alive the day after the birth. Not that I remember this, but I know it slept in the cot next to mine in the hospital. I can't help thinking of all those babies, all lined up in their little boxes. All of them crying, all bald and slimy, but one of them different from the rest. Sick. Maybe dying.

Look, this is what I'm getting at. We're like the things in Lady Diamond's shop, like the skulls of all those animals from India. We're collections of bones, which have been given skin and fat for a little while, just so we can move around. And why do we move around? So the bones are spread about a bit after we die, sorted into pretty patterns, just like Lady's relics. The things we come up with while we're walking around, the symbols and the smiley-face badges, they're all part of the collection as well. We stop moving, the fat falls off our bodies, and the other dead things in the world lay us out in the ground, making sure we look nice for the archaeologists.

Think about it. How long do we move around for? Seventy years? Eighty? No time at all, in the big picture. But how long do the archaeologists need us for? How long do we stay useful, once we've been stripped down to the bone? Centuries. Thousands of years. Forever.

So which is more likely? That we were put here to live? Or that we were put here as part of the bone collection, and just don't know it yet?

That's why I keep thinking about the maternity ward. All the babies in their little boxes, just like that kitten, pickled in Lady's jar. Let's not kid ourselves, it's the baby in the cot next to mine who'll be the prize of the collection, not me. Little mutant. Little curiosity.

Which makes me wonder... who's the collection being assembled for? I can just imagine them, the curators and the collectors, stalking the world whenever they think we're not looking. Making sure we're all still breeding and dying, taking inventories of us on the quiet. Changing the world around behind our backs, to make room for the exhibits. Giving us more space to fill up with symbols and bones.

Is that how the world's going to end? When they decide there are enough exhibits, and take all the skin and fat away from us in one go?

57

That was what I thought while I was running, anyway. But I was confused, and I was upset, and I was coming down from a buzz. So don't think it's a lifetime philosophy or anything.

But I suppose some parts of it are close to the truth. Let's go back in time again, just a few minutes. Back to the shop.

Ready?

58/59

I'm looking into the face of the wax skull. I'm staring at the Zener cards under its teeth, because they're the only things I can focus on. I can feel the blood on my leg, and there's a kind of pain I've never felt before, stinging like somebody's injected floor-cleaner into my leg (in fact the flesh that's hurting isn't really there any more, but I don't know that yet). I'm keeping my eyes on the cards, wondering if the picture right under the edge of the skull really is a porno version of a drawing from *Alice in Wonderland*, which is what it looks like from here. With the pain shutting off most of the rest of the world, this is all I can think about.

I definitely don't have the presence of mind to ask the obvious questions. Who is this man? Why has he bitten me? If his mouth's all the way down there, then what part of his body is he using to crush my head against the floor?

I can't move my left arm. It's pressed against my body, against my ribcage, with all the man's weight on top of it. My right arm's twisted under me now, but the fingers are still moving, crawling across the rug, looking for the weapon that's never there when you need it. My legs are kicking, although my feet feel like they're a world away, and I can't say I care about them much anyway. No, I'm more interested in the noise I can hear, over the heavy breathing that could either be his or mine.

A slapping noise. Wet. To hell with the pain, to hell with the cards: this is the important thing now. That sound. Like a tongue, rolling around inside somebody's mouth.

Christ. He's tasting me. He didn't bite me to hurt me, or to get some kind of sex kick. He wants to know what I taste like. This man, who came out of nowhere and attacked me for no good reason (because it's starting to look unlikely that he's one of Lady Diamond's sleeping partners), is in fact a cannibal.

For the first time, I start to think about the other murders. I try to remember what I've seen in the papers. Whether the victims had any bite marks on their bodies. Would the police mention it if they did?

The pain isn't important. It's like when you're a kid, and the antiseptic goes into your cut and it feels like you're going to sting forever, but after a while you face up to the fact that you're going to be in agony for the rest of your life.

All of a sudden, there isn't so much weight on the side of my face. I turn my head, because I can. Not all the way, just enough to be able to see the killer out of the comer of one eye. His halo makes my eyes burn. There are tears, although I don't remember crying. I can't see properly. There's just a silhouette, as the man lifts up his head on the end of a long, long neck.

I realise that I can't see the dead things any more, because the man's big enough to blot them out, taking up too much light for a skinny thing like him. He pulls his head back even further, until I can see the outline of the lump in his throat.

There's a howling sound. No, "howling" makes it sound like a mammal noise, like a wolf noise. This is more primal, more basic. Give an amoeba a set of vocal cords, and this is the sound it'd make. It isn't him. It can't be him. It's not human. I decide it must be the dead things, complaining that they can't see me dying. My arms are still flapping, and my legs are still kicking, and I can feel the man's weight shift again, so the lower part of my body comes free underneath him. My body starts to realise that all it'd take is one good shove, and -

And suddenly my left arm's free, and before I can tell it what to do it's curling up into a fist, punching the air. I try to follow it with my eyes, but my eyes are full of water. I feel my knuckles press against him. He feels like leather. I don't remember him wearing anything made of leather, so I start to wonder if it's his skin I'm touching.

It takes me a while to notice that all the weight's gone. The man isn't on top of me any more, and I'm free, and I'm rolling on to my back, pushing all my limbs into the air, kicking and clawing like a baby (this is when I first start thinking of the maternity ward, natch). I feel my hands move against him. I feel my legs kick his stomach. Something in the back of my mind tells me that, if all four of my limbs have touched him, then he must be bigger than I thought.

The dead things are furious. The howling's getting worse. Also, I can hear something else, like rippling air. Like a great big pair of wings, flapping around inside the shop. I don't remember any of the dead things having wings, but I can imagine. Some kind of stuffed vulture, maybe, one of Lady Diamond's relics I've never spotted before. I think about it ripping itself off the wall, and circling overhead, waiting for the cannibal man to finish his job.

Except that there isn't a man at all. I can't feel him now, not even with my fingertips. I keep kicking, even though the howling's stopped, and even though nothing's touching me.

There's just the stinging in my leg, so I start to get angry with that part of my body, blaming my leg for trying to put me off.

60

The next sound I heard was cracking glass.

In and out. Over in a few seconds. One minute he was trying to kill me, the next he was gone. At the time, I didn't really care why he'd left me. I must have thought I'd been too much of a struggle. I must have thought I'd fought him off, with all that kicking and clawing. If I'd been thinking, I would have realised how ridiculous that was.

And if I'd been thinking, I would have guessed that he just hadn't liked the way I'd tasted. Which would have been a lot closer to the truth, really.

61

I once saw a documentary on BBC2, about a man who said he remembered fighting in the English Civil War, even though it had finished about three hundred years before he'd been born. He had all these memories about the places he'd been and the weapons he'd used, and he even remembered the name he'd had (I can't remember what it was, so we'll just say Davy Jones, like the boring English one out of the Monkees). Researchers from the BBC went through the old museum records, and found out that there really *had* been a Davy Jones (or whatever) fighting in the English Civil War. Also, he'd fought in all the battles the man had talked about.

The people who made the programme said this was good evidence of reincarnation. Which makes you think, doesn't it? Whoever you are, however unimportant your life is, just remember this: hundreds of years from now, your name could be all over TV, and your birth certificate could be dug out of the libraries by researchers whose names you'll never even get to hear. Because it's not just your bones you leave behind. All that rubbish, all those possessions, all those symbols and bits of paperwork. It doesn't matter how deep you bury them, somebody's bound to dig them up and rearrange them sooner or later.

62

The window of the shop was cracked right across, so it looked like the posters on the glass were the only things holding it together. The front door was open, and the panels there were smashed - not just cracked, but *smashed* - so I guessed that the man, whoever he'd been, had made straight for the exit after he'd let go of me. He'd thrown himself at the door, broken the lock and shattered the glass on his way out.

No, I didn't stop to think about that, either. About the logic of someone, even a madman, forcing open a locked door instead of taking the back way out. It can't have mattered to me much. The next thing I remember is moving along Henrietta Street, grunting and whimpering, with my hand pressed against the hole in my leg to stop the blood flow. I hadn't even bothered trying to find help in the back rooms of the shop. You can't trust a hippie in an emergency.

I was going back the way I'd come. I was heading for the police station. Because, in a crisis, even an anti-Establishment waste of space like me isn't too proud to go to the police.

63

By the way, I know not much of this will be making sense to you yet. There are too many questions. So, although I didn't know any of the answers at the time, I'll give you some clues now.

I wasn't the hairy man's main target, not really. Think back to what I said about the police station. Think back to the moment when the big blond man reached out for me, and I thought I'd been touched by the English Charles Manson (pat. pending). Suppose I told you that it was the big blond who'd been the real prey of the man in the shop. Suppose I told you that the man had ways of "sniffing out" his target, and that he'd just happened to pick up Blondie's scent on my skin. Suppose I said that he didn't realise his mistake until he'd taken a good bite out of me.

It probably wouldn't help you much. After all, it sets up as many questions as it answers. You'd just say that no human being could possibly have a sense of smell that good, and you'd be right. Besides, wasn't the blond man supposed to be the Butcher of Buckingham Palace, according to the police? So how come he's the victim all of a sudden?

Answers. More trouble than they're worth, that's what I say.

Notes on the Thing in the Cell

64

Really, it's a miracle I got as far as the police station. I fell over at least once on the way, ending up face down in a gutter somewhere off the Strand, bleeding onto the papers and Pepsi cans in the road.

Not that I want to keep reminding you of this, but I still had the coke in my system, and coke's got a way of boosting your senses. Just then, it was boosting my sense of drama more than anything else. Even while I was making my way up the station steps, I was imagining the big entrance. Throwing the double-doors open. Standing there in the doorway, obviously still in agony, all wounded and windswept. I was thinking about the faces of the policemen inside, looking shocked and startled, amazed that I'd made it there alive. I was thinking how surprised and sorry they'd be, when they figured out that the girl they'd arrested for being a useless junkie was, in fact, the victim in this story. *Yes, you fascist bully-boy pigs, that's right. Look embarrassed.* Then they'd rush towards me, catching me just as the last of my strength gave out...

But there wasn't anybody in the station. At least, not in the foyer.

The foyer was a kind of waiting room, painted in the same greys and greens you saw in waiting rooms everywhere. The front desk was on the other side of the floor, half a universe away from where I was standing, a great oblong piece of tack that was pretending to be old, expensive wood just to give offenders that up-before-the-beak feeling. There was the smell of disinfectant on the floor, and there were neon strip lights flickering in the ceiling, but there weren't any signs of life. The cartoon posters on the walls were telling me to fasten my seat belt and watch out for pickpockets, and that was all anybody was saying.

I must have stood there for a while, dripping blood on to the tiles. I was standing in the exact spot where I'd been planning on passing out. Frankly, I was pissed off that I wasn't going to get the chance.

In the end, I managed to stagger over to the other side of the room, still clutching the gash in my leg ("gash", she says; see how I make it sound smaller with every page?). The chairs were still scattered across the floor, more higgledy-piggledy than they had been before. I remember thinking that the big blond man must have kept struggling, which made me wonder if maybe he'd won the fight, if the reason there was nobody here was that all the staff had been torn limb from limb. I tried not to let it worry me.

65

Keep one thing in mind here: about an hour earlier, I'd met the alleged killer face to face, and he'd made a lunge for me (or at least that was how I was starting to remember it). My very first meeting with a possible mass murderer, and yet almost immediately afterwards, I'd been half-strangled by another one. You can imagine how paranoid I was about that. If you'd told me at the time that something had happened to the world while I'd been looking the other way, and that 50 per cent of the human race had suddenly turned psychotic in order to finish the species off once and for all, I would have believed you. The theory fitted all the facts, let's be honest.

66

And I'd just like to say sorry for saying "higgledy-piggledy" earlier on. I can't stand that.

67

There was somebody behind the front desk at the police station. I hadn't seen him from the door, because he was slumped down on the other side of the desk, with his back to the wood and his legs stretched out in front of him. I didn't spot him until I headed for the corridor where the cells were.

It was the desk sergeant, the one who'd told me to sod off earlier on. His skin was covered in sweat, so thick and gooey that it made him look like all the fluid inside his skull had started seeping out of the pores, and he was staring dead ahead at the blank wall in front of him. His face wasn't square any more. It had gone all blubbery. Also I remember that the phone on the desk was off its hook, and the receiver was dangling from the cord, swinging backward and forward next to the man's head. Like he'd started to make a call, but had given up.

It took him a while to notice me standing there. When he did, he turned his head towards me, very, very slowly.

'Name?' he said.

'Christine,' I told him. Automatic reaction, that.

'Christine what?' he asked.

'Mmuh-mnuh-mnuh,' I said.

The sergeant nodded, but carefully, making sure the movement didn't make his eyeballs drop out.

'Name?' he said.

68

I've heard people talk like that before, but usually only when they've been on amphetamines. They get caught up in a kind of cycle. They get fixed on one single part of their lives, and keep going through it again and again, building whole rituals out of it until it's the only thing that matters to them.

It'd be nice ("nice" as in "interesting") to say that the sergeant had gone mad. That he'd seen something so horrible he'd lost his mind right there and then. It'd be nice, but it wouldn't be true. In fact, he'd seen something so horrible that he'd run away from it the only way he could. He'd dug a little trench for himself, and covered himself over with his paperwork. In shock, yes. Mad, no.

I know this for two reasons. Firstly, it was only a couple of minutes later that I saw what he'd seen, so I know how he must have felt. Secondly I know for a fact that the sergeant recovered, retired from the police force, and tried to find a new career for himself in Hertfordshire, a career that was cut tragically short when the concept of "Hertfordshire" stopped meaning anything on the 12th of October. It was in one of the local papers, although the reporter was smart enough not to print the details of what had actually happened at the station. I've still got the cutting. It's in the scrapbook I brought with me from London. Am I the only person left who cares about these little historical details, d'you think?

And, by the way, his name was Elliot Bishop. If that helps give him any kind of personality.

69

'I need help,' I told the man who was actually called Elliot Bishop. I took my hand away from my leg when I said it, and help up my fingers, to show him all the blood that had dried over the wound. The sergeant nodded again.

'Christine what?' he said.

70

Now I'm writing all this down, I'm wondering about the telephone, dangling by his ear. Did he try to call somebody, when the bad thing came to the police station? If he did, then who? And why did he give up?

I think I can answer that last one, anyway. I could have dialled 999 from Lady Diamond's shop, but I never even thought about it. I mean, by then I'd convinced myself that the world was run by dead things, and that the only reason we were all still walking was so we could scatter our bones around for artistic effect. And I know I needed medical help, but phoning the emergency services would have felt pathetic, almost a joke. 'Hello, operator? The world's just stopped working, and all life on Earth is effectively meaningless. Is it police, ambulance or fire brigade I need?'

Sergeant Elliot Bishop must have felt the same way. How English can you get? Scared to make an emergency call, because of how stupid he thought he'd sound.

71

I headed down the cell corridor after that, and the sergeant didn't try to stop me, although I could hear him shouting after me while I walked away from him. Asking, 'Christine what? Christine what?' over and over again. I didn't listen. I was going to find the other policemen in the station, and make them help me whether they wanted to or not. (Yes, that's right: by this point, I was sure the desk sergeant had lost his mind just to make things harder for me.)

My leg was numb by now, the same kind of numb you used to hear arctic explorers talking about in radio interviews. That you'll-be-dead-soon-so-stop-worrying kind of numb. I knew I didn't have long before I fell over again, but even the cell-block corridor was against me, getting half a step longer every time I took a step forward. I tried counting off the cell doors as I walked past them, making sure the building wasn't stretching out the passage to slow me down, but I kept losing count and having to start back at one again. Then I tried counting footsteps, the number of times my plimsoles squeaked on the tiles. Then I tried counting the number of times I heard the words 'Christine what?' from behind me. Nothing made the corridor any shorter.

It could have been paranoia, of course. And it's a fact that the more tired you are, the longer things look; it's probably all part of the theory of relativity. But remember what I said before? There were things in the world, things that came out of the shadows only when our backs were turned, things that - and here's the important bit - moved space around when we weren't looking, making sure we had just enough room to bury our leftovers. And there, in that grey, squeaky cell-corridor, they were making sure I had too far to walk. Making sure my bones were going to drop to the ground in exactly the right place.

Again, I'm not claiming any of this was literally true.

72

Halfway along the corridor (can something that doesn't have an end have a halfway point, d'you think?), I stopped. All the cell doors had little hatches at eye level, sliding peepholes the policemen could use to stare at the prisoners, just to get them extra-tense. And one of the hatches was open. I think most of the cells must have been empty, but that one wasn't. You could tell. There was a pair of eyes behind the peephole.

It was the cell I'd been in, an hour or so earlier, and the eyes belonged to the woman I'd shared it with. The "stuff" woman.

'It won't work,' she said, when she saw me. The door made her voice go all muffled, so she sounded like she was talking through a gag.

'Uh,' I said. I was too tired to put proper sentences together.

'They're trying to freak me out,' the woman told me. 'That's why they're making all the noise. They're going to try to make me sign a confession.'

'Noise,' I repeated.

The woman nodded. Her eyes bobbed up and down on the other side of the hatch. 'The pigs. They've got someone next door. Screaming. Y'know?' Her eyes wobbled to the left, just in case I couldn't work out what "next door" meant. 'One of them. One of the pigs. Screaming. They reckon it'll mess our heads up.'

'Screaming,' I said.

'Screaming,' she said. 'But it's not going to work.'

73

I never found those other policemen. The desk sergeant was the only uniform in the building, as far as I could tell. The local papers never said anything about any police officers going missing, or any of them apart from Sergeant Elliot Bishop retiring for health reasons. And I'm sure somebody would have said something, if they'd all been killed right there in the station.

Perhaps they just ran for their lives when the bad thing came, and let Sergeant Bishop deal with things on his own. But that's not what I like to think. I like to think I was right, about the corridor being stretched. I like to imagine that the bad thing just made the corridor so long that nobody could ever reach the end of it. I like the idea of all those policemen, running past an infinite number of cells, trying to get back to the front desk but never quite making it.

Still, I suppose that would have got a mention in the papers as well, wouldn't it? Never mind. We've got to dream.

74

The cell next door wasn't locked. I didn't realise that straight away, not until the "stuff" woman rolled her eyes at it.

The door was only open a crack. The corridor was lit by the kind of strip lighting that had brightened up the foyer, by tubes of neon that were the same colour as varicose veins, but there was no light coming through the gap from behind the door. The lock was broken, though. Bits of metal latch all over the floor.

'Have a look,' said the woman. 'There's one of the pigs in there. Bet you any money.'

Screaming, the woman had said. Screaming from the cell. I mean, I didn't seriously believe the police were torturing suspects in there. This was WC2, for God's sake. They might have beaten the shit out of the occasional drunk outside Tottenham Court tube station, but since when had English policemen used professional torture? And I didn't believe it was one of the officers making the noise, either, just to wind up the prisoners. No, I was remembering what had happened back at Lady Diamond's shop.

There'd been that sound. The sound the Jesus / Manson lookalike had made, after he'd got fed up of throttling me. I'd told myself it'd been the dead things making the noise, on the grounds that it couldn't have come from a human being, but all of a sudden the theory was starting to look a bit on the shaky side. I was remembering the man rearing up over me, just before the window had cracked. I was remembering his head, being lifted up on a neck that looked much, much too long for his body. Like his skin had been stretching in front of my eyes.

Had that actually happened, though? Or was I starting to imagine things now it was all over?

'Name?' said the desk sergeant, from the end of the corridor. He'd obviously given up asking 'Christine what?', and gone back to the start of the loop.

And there was something else. Another sound. Not the sergeant, not the woman, but a voice from inside the open cell. Someone talking, or muttering, on the other side of the door.

75

It wasn't much of a shock for me, finding out that there really were dark, slippery, scary things in the world. Everybody knows it, and everybody pretends they don't, in case they get put on medication. If you pretend hard enough, you even get to be a psychiatrist.

I remember believing in fairies when I was younger. I remember believing that the world was full of beautiful shiny little winged people, who worked magic while the rest of us weren't looking, and who lived in all the places where nobody else could go. Then I grew up, and went through puberty, and got cynical.

After that, I believed that fairies were totally malevolent, and utterly inimical to all human life. I wasn't far wrong, either.

76

What I heard from the other side of the door was the voice of a man, reading what turned out to be poetry. I couldn't make out most of the words at the time, but since then I've heard the poem again - actually, I've learnt most of it off by heart - so I know that what the voice was saying was this:

Dank roofs, dark-entried, closely clustered walls,
Murder-inviting rooks, death-reeking gutters;
A boding voice from your foul chaos calls,
When will men heed the warning that it utters?

'See?' the woman in the other cell was saying, through the hole in the door. 'He's praying, y'know? They reckon it's going to put the shits up us.'
'Name?' shouted the desk sergeant.
I remember lifting up my hand. Holding back for a second.
Then putting my fingers on the door of the cell, ready to open up the crack. I could hear somebody moving inside, shuffling across the floor. And the voice was still speaking, carrying on with the poem:

There floats a phantom on the slum's foul air,
Shaping, to eyes which have the gift of seeing,
Into the Spectre of that loathly lair,
Face it; for vain is fleeing!

I pushed the door open. By that time, I couldn't remember what I was supposed to be doing, or even why I'd gone to the police station in the first place.

77

And if I'd known? If I'd known I was about to come face to face with the worst thing in the world, and see the real shape of the "cannibal" who'd attacked me in Lady Diamond's shop? If I'd known that, by walking into the cell, I'd be walking into the middle of a war that didn't even belong on my planet?

If I'd known, would I still have done it?

Well, let's not pretend I had a choice.

78

There was a man in the comer of the cell, crouching on a bed that had been stripped of just about everything except the springs. The blond man. The suspect. His legs were curled up under him, with his feet on the edge of the bed, so it looked like he was getting ready to leap off and into the air. But his eyes were shut, and he wasn't moving. The blue suit looked wrong here, like it was too neat for the cell, like it didn't match either the moonlight from the tiny little window or the neon from the corridor. The man looked smaller than he'd looked before. Less powerful. Less aggressive.

Of course, it's not hard to figure out why. It was because of the other thing in the cell, so much bigger and so much worse than a (supposed) maniac-cult-killer that it'd probably make Charles Atlas look small. If Charles Atlas was still alive.

To begin with, it was just a heap. A lump. Something the colour of rotting meat, so my first guess was that it was a pile of bodies. And that made me jump, thinking that maybe I was looking at the corpses of all the policemen, that the blond man had dragged them into his cell and torn them apart with his bare hands. But it was one thing, not lots. All the bodies were joined together.

Then it turned its head. Swung its big brontosaurus-neck towards me. Letting me see the muscles rippling under its skin, with every move it made setting off a kind of fleshy chain reaction, sending out ripples all over its body. Something huge, black and flat swung towards me, and I remember ducking, even though the shape - the wing? - stopped before it reached my head.

It had been in the shop. It had stretched its wings there, for the first time on Earth. It had forced its way out through the shop door, breaking the glass as it went, probably deciding that I wasn't worth finishing off. Then it had come straight here to find the blond man, the person it had been after all along. It had moved through the streets of London, keeping out of sight the way these things always kept out of sight, finally pushing its way into the station and forcing open the cell door with its sheer weight.

How it had squeezed through the door, I didn't ask. Its body could have been made of putty for all I knew. I'd heard it shuffling around the cell from the corridor, moving in what little floor-space there was, with its wing tips scraping the walls. Purely by accident, it had pushed the door half-shut behind it. I don't think it cared much about privacy.

79

There's another memory I've got that I'm not too sure about. I didn't mention it earlier, because the more I think about it the more it feels like something I imagined afterwards, or maybe even dreamt about. But it's like this ...

I remember looking up from the floor of Lady Diamond's shop, and seeing the Manson clone just before he flew off. I remember his skin splitting open, and his clothes splitting open as well, like they were just another part of his body. I remember wings tearing out of the hole in his back, even though I know I couldn't have seen his back from where I was lying. Of course, I didn't have this memory in my head when I arrived at the police station, so if it's real and not just a dream then I must have blotted it out of my head after it happened. And can you blame me?

80

The blond man opened his eyes when I peeked in through the door of the cell. That's one of those little details I probably didn't pick up on at the time, what with everything else that was happening. Another "little detail" is that some of the electronic parts he'd been carrying (remember those?) were scattered around him on the bed. The police must have let him keep them when they'd put him in the cell. They'd probably thought it couldn't do any harm.

If I'd been thinking things through, those electronic bits and pieces would have reminded me of something. The way they were arranged around him, like some kind of chalk circle, Dennis Wheatley style. Like a barrier against the thing that had come to get him in his cell. And the poem? All part of the ritual. The thing must have got to the police station a long while before I did, but the blond man had been keeping it at bay all that time.

Now I'd interrupted him. Broken the spell? Probably. The thing finished swinging its neck around, until its head was just a couple of inches away from mine, and I could see its face in full. The features were kind of vague, but at least they were human. Dark eyes. Haven't-slept-in-days eyes. Bad skin, a wide open gawping mouth, skinny cheeks that were much too narrow for its big head. Dark hair on its scalp, stuck together in ugly, sweaty clumps.

'Can you see them?' shouted the woman next door.

'Name?' asked Sergeant Elliot Bishop.

The second-to-last thing I remember was realising that I was staring at a reflection. It was my face I was looking at, because where the thing in the cell should have had its eyes and mouth there was just glass. A great big lens that had grown in the middle of its head like ... I don't know. Like a pearl inside an oyster? A shiny oval, as smooth and blank as a TV screen with the power off. And the last thing I remember was the sound of the thing screaming at me.

Which, along with the shock, the terror, the exhaustion, and the fact that I was only a couple of minutes away from dying of blood loss, was more than enough to make me pass out.

Notes on the Flat

81

This is what I dreamt about, after I passed out.

Space. Space looks full, when you see it on *The Sky at Night*. The stars are all clustered together, so you can imagine taking taxi rides from one planet to another. It's not until you're right in the middle of it, swimming through a vacuum with your lungs tearing themselves into little pieces, that you realise the truth. However hard you swim, and whichever way you turn, none of the stars are going to get much closer.

Except that it's not a vacuum, not really. Space is made up of black winged things, all locking together like the salamanders in that M. C. Esher picture Cal used to have on his bedroom door, so you can't see any gaps between their bodies. They *are* space. Living space. You're trying to claw your way through them, looking for oxygen and choking on the black putty-flesh. The planets and stars? They're not solid at all: they're just the spaces the winged things haven't filled yet. The spaces where they keep their odds and ends.

From here, in the dream space, you can see all the planets the way *they* see them. All those cultures, all those races, leaving behind their bones and icons in interesting patterns. Each of the planets makes its own kind of relics. Some planets build big spiky ships to nuzzle their way through space; some planets build great big cities or great big grave-yards. If there's any difference, from this point of view. You can't see Earth, for some reason, although you can bet that its contributions to space culture are its murderers and T-shirts. And there, close to the centre of the galaxy - 'galaxy' being the collective noun for the winged things - you can see a world that's way ahead of all the others, where the people have invented machines for taking time apart. The people probably hope the machines are going to be enough to hold off the winged things, to stop the darkness swarming over their Homeworld. They've got to live in hope, I suppose.

The surface of that world is dusty and dry, and all the cities are empty. The locals have gone underground, where they're breeding special soldiers for the fight ahead, stitching the time-travel machines right into the soldiers' skins. The only living thing on the surface is the blond man, the one from the police station. He's standing in a circle of computer parts, looking up at the sky, with a frozen look on his face and something that might or might not be a knife in his hand.

You can tell what he's thinking. He's thinking: you're not getting past me, you bastards.

82

What's the point of dreams, anyway? I mean, the human race is supposed to have evolved over millions of years, and ditched all the parts it doesn't need. So why's evolution left the dreams behind? They don't do anything, except make you feel itchy and give you clues about who you're supposed to want to sleep with. (And don't tell me they're a way of clearing out your short-term memory. Why would all the pictures be held together with stories, just to do that?)

Maybe evolution's getting us ready for some kind of future technology, not that my planet's ever going to develop it now. Maybe it thinks that if we keep dreaming, we'll be kept on our toes, and be ready when people really do start turning into talking dogs. Or whatever.

83

I woke up in a strange man's bed in a strange man's flat. This wasn't a new experience for me, so to begin with I didn't panic.

The bedroom wasn't big, and there wasn't much in the way of furniture. The bed against one wall, a bookcase against another, orange curtains pulled across the window. Daylight on the other side, making *everything* orange. You could still smell the splinters on the bare floorboards, as if whoever owned the place hadn't lived here for more than a month or so, hadn't finished unpacking his things and unloading all his old scents into the building. There was a duvet pulled over me, but even the duvet didn't have a cover. I could hear dogs and cars from outside the window.

The way I saw things was this: I'd taken coke, and the coke had sparked off something in my head, maybe some old acid that had got stuck in the middle of my brain (N.B. I have no idea whether this is actually possible), setting off a complete paranoid breakdown. So, I'd been arrested. So, I'd met some-one while I wasn't thinking straight, and ended up in bed with him, not that he was here to welcome me back to the world with a cup of coffee or anything. Everything in between...

Everything in between made sense, as long as you looked at it in a kind of psychiatric way. That thing in the police station. The great long neck, the shiny bulb of a "face" on the end... if that wasn't Freudian, then what was? It was so obvious, it didn't even count as a hallucination.

84/85

There were a lot of people seeing Freudian monsters in 1970. In the scrapbook, which I can't be bothered getting out of my rucksack again right now, there's a clipping from a magazine called *Fate* which used to be the journal of choice for the kind of people who wanted to believe that there were giant owl-monsters living out in the wilds of Canada. According to the article, asylum inmates "all over the world" had been having weird visions in the early months of 1970. If that's true, then it must have been something to do with the things I'm describing in this book, although I'm sure *Fate* always used to say that asylum in-mates had been having weird visions. But this particular crisis reached its peak in a mental hospital in India, sometime in June.

A "dangerous psychopath" there started developing strange symptoms - changes in the texture of his skin, changes in body temperature, that kind of thing - which the staff at the hospital thought must have been psychosomatic. The electric-shock treatment didn't work, though, and what happened next is harder to swallow. According to the one surviving doctor at the hospital, the patient went through a complete physiological (did I spell that right?) mutation. The skin on his face stretched out of shape. His hip bones shifted around, so he almost looked like he was supposed to walk on four legs instead of two. Finally, the skin on his back split open -sound familiar, this? - and wings grew out of his body, making some of the doctors give up their medical training and turn back to religion.

All of this was bad enough, but it turned out to be contagious. It happened that way in mental institutions, apparently. If one of the lunatics came up with a new symptom, it got spread around the place. Once the inmates in India heard about the man with wings, they all started showing signs of change as well, until the staff couldn't tell which ones were faking it and which ones were really growing scales. Just picture it: all those little cells, all those madmen and madwomen, twisting out of shape one after another. Why does that make me think of the maternity ward again?

Eventually even the staff gave in to it, until one night the whole institution exploded into a fleshy, bony mess. One of the doctors, the one who ended up being the only survivor, reacted in the only way he could. He took out a gun (*Fate* doesn't tell us where he got the gun from, so maybe we're supposed to believe that Indian asylum staff are armed around the clock) and started to put the creatures out of their misery. He said he had to shoot some of them through the head three or four times before they stopped screaming.

Of course, as the things magically changed back to their normal human selves once they were dead, the authorities only had the doctor's word that any of this had happened. Just like we've only got *Fate's* word that the hospital ever really existed.

86

Somehow I managed to get out of the bed, and headed straight for the window. Pulled back the curtains. Looked out. I was a couple of floors up, but I didn't recognise the neighbourhood. Backstreets, parked cars and council dustbins, stretching out as far as the eye could see. The kind of daylight that hurts you. Hangover daylight. Could have been any part of London.

The next stop was the bookcase. You could tell a lot about someone by the books they kept. I mean, I had my pride to think about. Suppose I'd ended up in bed with someone who still read Allen Ginsberg, *and* took him seriously. How could I have lived with that?

Some of the titles on the bookshelf were: *Life Under Glass*, by Marion Reardon; *Ozma of Oz*, by L Frank Baum, or Frank L Baum, or whatever it is; *Dawson's Concise English Dictionary*; *The Final Programme*, by Michael Moorcock (!!!); *Confessions of an English Opium Eater*, by Thomas de Quincey (yum); and the script of *Pygmalion*, by George Bernard Shaw. (Of course, these are just the books that stick in my mind, so the list probably says more about me than about the person who owned them.)

It looked like someone had bought the bookcase, then realised he didn't have anything to put on it. Like he'd gone around all the second-hand bookshops in the city, buying up any cheap paperbacks he could find and stuffing them on to his shelves in no real order. Like he thought that'd be the best way to find out about modem culture. (Funnily enough, that was exactly what he had done, but it took me a while to find this out.)

There was also a scrapbook on one of the shelves, although I didn't notice it then. Which is a good job, because it was full of press cuttings about famous murderers, and I might have got the wrong idea.

87/88

The other thing I noticed about the bookcase was the cardboard box on top of it, full of bits of grey plastic. A model kit, made by Airfix. According to the label on the side of the box it was a (quote) GENUINE SHIP IN A BOTTLE, modelled on some Tudor warship or other that had made history by sinking without trace in record time.

It wasn't a proper ship in a bottle, of course. Real ships in bottles are more complicated than the kits you used to get in Hamley's. With the Airfix sets, they gave you a see-through plastic bottle in two halves, which you were supposed to glue together around the finished ship. That was cheating, in my book. And I guessed the owner of the kit must have felt the same way, because the ship was only half-finished. A few parts had been glued together, but you could tell he'd given up out of boredom, like he couldn't see the point in anything so simple.

I stood there for a while, looking at the cracked spines of the old paperbacks, trying to get a grip on the person who'd put them there. My leg was itching, so I started scratching it, not taking my eyes off the books until one of my nails slipped into the hole in my leg.

The *hole* in my *leg*. Eventually, it clicked.

I looked down. There was a wound in my leg all right, where the Freudian thing had bitten a chunk out of me. The wound had been cleaned, so there was no blood, although I could see lots of red under the skin where it'd been broken open. The hole must have been about an inch and a half across (again, I could be mis-remembering this), so the thing that had been planted there was about the same shape and size as a small boiled potato.

Let's go over that again. Someone had planted what looked like a small. Boiled. Potato. In the hole. In my leg. I could even see tiny shoots coming out of it, working their way into the flesh. The little bastard was taking root. In. My. *Body*. The thing was turning pink around the edges, like it was trying to hide in the middle of all the other cells, hoping I wouldn't notice that it wasn't part of me. It was itching, the way wounds always itch once you notice how bad they are, and I wanted to scratch the lump right out, but I could see the shoots either pumping something into me or sucking something out. I wondered how much blood I'd lose if I took it away.

My jeans were folded up at the end of the bed. Folded badly, the way only a man could have done it. Next to them were my shoes, my socks, my belt.

I didn't bother taking any of them. A T-shirt and a pair of pants were all I needed to face the world. I just headed straight for the door.

89

The hallway of the flat was a lot like the bedroom. Bare boards, no carpet, although an old rug had been stretched across the floor near what looked like the front door. There was a phone nailed to one wall, and plenty of doors leading away from the hall, most of them closed. All of them unmarked. No cutesy little plates saying things like JOHN'S ROOM, nothing to give me any clues.

Not that I had to do much exploring. I heard the voice as soon as I walked into the hall.

It was coming from the far end of the passage, from behind a door that had been left half-open, so bright daffodil-colour daylight could pour into the hall from the other side. The last time I'd heard that voice, it'd been reciting poetry. The voice was in the middle of a conversation, maybe even an argument, although I couldn't make out who the owner was arguing with. I guessed he was on the telephone. The fact that the telephone was right next to me in the hall didn't put me off. The voice sounded young, but a bit croaky, like an eight-year-old who's been smoking fags on the quiet. He even went up and down at the end of words, so however serious he was trying to sound, you could imagine him asking you to buy him an ice cream at any second.

I'll tell you what the voice was saying, or at least, as much of it as I can remember. I'll fill in the blanks myself. Call it creative writing.

90

'No, of course not. Of course we won't. We don't want a war. We've got enough enemies already, we don't want to ...

'No. No, that's not what I'm saying. We don't want to end the treaty completely. Really. We just want to change a couple of the clauses, that's all. Listen, it's in your favour. All I'm saying ... No, listen ... all I'm saying is that we're ready to change the bits about ... about you not being allowed to have time-technology. That's all.

'Yeah, I know. I know, but ... look, we always sound like we're up to something. It's not like that. We're scared, you know? We need all the friends we can get, and ... the way we see it, if your people get time-active, that makes you stronger. That's what we're talking about here. Making your people stronger ...

'No, I'm not saying that. We don't want you to get involved in any, um, in any military action or anything. All we're saying is, we'll let you have time-tech, but if we get into some kind of face-off then you won't side against us. I mean, you don't have to side *with* us. Just as long as you don't make any deals with ... with anyone we might be at war with.

'Trust me. We're going to make the offer in a couple of days. I mean, officially. I'm just telling you now because ... I thought you should know how things are going, that's all. Right?'

91

None of this will mean anything to you yet. It all comes together in the end, though. Wait and see.

92-4

It was the living room of the flat, and it was big. You could tell it must have cost a fortune to rent the place. The ceiling was higher than any ceiling in London had a right to be, and the whole of the far wall was made up of windows, so you could see several miles' worth of tower blocks and back-streets whichever way you looked. Soho. Definitely Soho. There was sunlight, plenty of it, shining through the rain clouds (any minute now, the sky was saying, any minute now it'll piss down) and lighting up the old wooden floorboards.

Just about everything in the room was made of wood. There weren't any chairs, just a handful of wooden bunk-beds pushed against some of the walls, as if the person who'd decorated the place was still enough of a kid to think that bunk-beds were a really smart idea and had furnished the whole of his living space with them even though he knew hardly any of them would ever get used. There was a colour TV opposite the door, against the big bright windows, stuck inside a fake wooden cabinet. The furnishings were pretty new, you could tell. You could still smell the packaging material on them.

And then there were the ships. Ships in bottles. Not like the Airfix kits, but proper ones, some of them anything up to two foot long, things you knew must have come from antique shops. They were arranged around the walls, or nesting on the mattresses of the bunks, or even hanging from the ceiling on skinny wires. A couple of the ships weren't bottled, like they'd escaped, or maybe they were just too complicated to get squeezed into the glass. Some of them even had oars, like Viking ships, and some of them...

Some of them had engines. But even the spaceships in bottles were carved out of wood. That was it, wasn't it? That was why there was wood everywhere, because whoever had decorated the place had wanted to feel like he was inside one of the bottles himself. From here, looking out across the city, you could almost believe that London was the world outside the bottle, the world you'd see if you could stare out past the cork. Or maybe London was the world *inside* the bottle, depending on where you were standing.

The first moving thing I saw was Bill Grundy, reporting live from the Labour Party conference on ITV. The sound was turned right down, so for a second I thought he was the one talking about treaties and time-travel. It took me a while to take in the rest of the room, and to see the blond man, lying sprawled out on one of the bunks in the corner. He was the only other person in the room, but somehow he still managed to look really pleased that he'd ended up with the top bunk.

He stopped talking when he saw me. There was a shocked kind of expression on his face. He was holding something dark and plasticky next to his ear, which I must have thought was a telephone, even though it didn't have a cord and wasn't connected to anything.

'I'll call you back,' the man said. With that, he stuffed the might-have-been-a-phone under the mattress of the bunk, then turned back to look at me. He smiled. You could tell he was forcing it.

'Hi,' he said.

I looked around the room. Nobody was there to give me any cues. Even Bill Grundy didn't look like he wanted to help.

'Hullo,' I said. 'Where am I?'

The blond man opened his mouth to say something, then changed his mind, and closed it again. He sat upright on the bunk, so I could see all the sinews flowing under that blue suit of his. Yes, he was still wearing it; dark-blue jacket, dark-blue trousers, white shirt. It didn't look like he'd slept in it, though. Eventually, he hopped down off the bunk, and there was a heavy thump when his huge bare feet hit the floorboards.

I jumped. He must have seen this, because he decided against coming any closer. 'Um,' he said. 'Um. This is where I live. I mean, I've only just moved in and everything. Just been here a few weeks.' He shrugged. 'Sorry, look. This is really difficult. I know how you must be feeling, and ... maybe we'd better start from the beginning, yeah?'

'You're not the killer, are you?' I asked. God knows why I thought I'd get an honest answer to that.

He looked embarrassed when I said it. He glanced down at his feet, but his toes just wiggled up at him, so he looked up again. 'Er. I think you're getting confused.'

'Okay,' I said. 'You're right. Let's start from the beginning.'

He smiled again then, a great big baby kind of smile. That's when I noticed how old his face looked. In the police station, I'd thought he was young, maybe my age. Why? Because of his hair, all short and spiky, like he wanted to look exciting and dynamic. Because of that earring. But he was older than I was, at least a decade older. Even so, he still looked uncomfortable in that suit, like his body wanted to prove how young it really was by squirming out of his "proper" clothes and running around half naked.

Half naked. Was I thinking about what he'd look like half naked, even then? (No. I don't think I was.)

He took a step towards me, but just the one. 'My name's Chris,' he said. 'Chris Cwej. And I'm, um, friendly.'

'What a coincidence,' I said, trying to pretend I was at some dinner party or other. 'My name's, uh -'

'Christine Summerfield,' the man who called himself Chris Cwej said. I must have looked surprised, because he shrugged and grinned, the way (as I'd later find out) he always did when he thought he'd said the wrong thing. 'It was in the records,' he told me. 'At the police station.'

The police station. Oh yes. I decided it was probably time to face the ugly truth, and ask the big question.

'What the fuck is *happening* to me?' I asked.

Chris Cwej sighed. His lungs were huge, so it took him a while to fill them up and empty them again.

'That's really complicated,' he said. 'Look, are you hungry? Only I haven't had any breakfast yet.'

95

There was a lot of embarrassment in Cwej, that first day I spent with him. Even before I'd got to know him, I'd figured out why. He was embarrassed that I'd ended up involved in things. And he used to apologise a lot, for getting me into this. For messing up my life. That was what I thought, anyway.

As he told me later on, it was him who'd planted the potato thing in my leg.

'Copycat tissue,' he said. 'Best way of healing that kind of damage.' I'm sure he could have given me a proper scientific explanation, but to be honest I couldn't have cared less about the details.

One question's got to be asked, though. Cwej said he took me back to his flat because I was injured, because he didn't think he could leave me in the hands of the local authorities without them finding out too much about the winged things (we'll come to that in a minute). But the policeman, Sergeant Elliot Bishop, was hurt just as badly as I was even though most of the damage was psychological. Why didn't Cwej take *him* home? Why wasn't the sergeant given some "copycat tissue" that could heal over the cracks in his head?

Cwej never gave me an answer to that, but I came up with one pretty quickly. It was because Cwej didn't fancy Sergeant Elliot Bishop. Somewhere in every human male (and Cwej *was* human, at least to start with), there must be something that makes them do whatever they can to look after the skinny women, but leave the wounded men for somebody else to deal with.

96

I remember this girl who used to beg for spare change outside Tottenham Court Road tube station. Cal always used to give her money, even though he never had anything for the other sixty-million beggars in London. I asked him about that once. Why he gave money to only that one girl.

"Cause she's cute,' he told me.

That made me angry, at the time. I asked him if he thought this was a fair way of deciding who should have money and who should be left to starve in the gutters. So Cal shrugged at me.

'You give money to fucking Save the Whales,' he said.

'So?' I said.

'You don't bother giving any money to cancer research, do you?'

'So?' I said,

'You do the same as me,' he said. 'You just give money to the causes you like the look of.'

And, all in all, that's what I felt like while I was around Cwej. Just a cause he liked the look of. But you'll want to hear his explanation, about why my life had suddenly turned to shit and everybody wanted to kill me. I think it's about time I got round to that.

Notes on Cwej

97

We were both sitting on the floor of the living room with our legs crossed, poking at identical bowls of cornflakes. Cwej had picked the cereal that came with the free plastic toy. Very into toys, Cwej. You could tell, just by looking at the living room, with all its bottled ships and model starfighters or whatever they were called.

The TV was still switched on, but Cwej had turned the sound up a little. I think he wanted to give me some kind of normal background noise, to make me feel more at home. I had my eyes fixed on the cornflakes, while the room filled up with the theme tune of *Pogle's Wood*.

'I know this is going to be kind of hard to deal with,' Cwej was saying. 'It was hard for me as well, you know?'

It was almost funny, hearing him trying to be all caring and sensitive. He sounded like a five-year-old, saying sorry for bursting someone else's balloon. His face still looked too old for his body. For the way he acted. Was that why the aliens used him as their agent, maybe? Because they knew all they had to do was show him a piece of their super-technology, and he'd go 'wow, cool!' and not ask any more questions?

'How old are you?' I asked. I didn't have anything better to say.

Cwej shrugged. He kept tapping his soggy cornflakes with his spoon, like he was trying to wake them up and make them do something more interesting. 'I've kind of lost track. I've been living outside linear time for the last couple of years.'

'Mmm,' I said.

98

Cwej was the kind of person who'd never throw away his old washing-up-liquid bottles, just in case he saw a piece on *Blue Peter* about how to turn them into rocket ships. (I'm exaggerating, but not much. Even people with their own time-machines get the urge to make things out of squeezy bottles sometimes.)

I'd tell you in full what Cwej told me about his "employers", but there wouldn't be much point. I told you about my dream, didn't I? Well, most of it was right. That happened a lot around Cwej. I'd wake up in the mornings and know stuff about his world that he'd never actually told me. I'd say he was the kind of man to make my dreams come true, but that'd be missing the point, I think.

Just like in the dream, there really were planets all over space where people had crawled up out of the dirt and built things to keep themselves happy. I'm talking about people here, with arms and legs and proper faces. Cwej's bosses had been around longer than anyone else, so they'd got the jump on the rest of us. They'd been the first ones to come up with time-travel, which made them the most powerful people in space, or at least that was what they liked to tell everybody.

Yes, I know: there's a point in every acid-head's life when he or she starts to think that maybe the real world isn't real, that maybe the hallucinations are the real thing, that by stuffing more tabs down his or her neck he or she can go all the way and see what's really there, behind the dirt and matter that clogs our lives up most of the time. The point when you can either call it a day and move on to something else (like, say, cocaine) or do what your instincts tell you and run away to live with the hippie machine-elves in hyperspace. There in the flat, I knew I must have reached the point of no return, and not even noticed it. Which is why I believed, without asking too many difficult questions, that the man called Chris Cwej really was working for a bunch of old alien wizards who thought they ran the universe. If I'd been thinking straight, I would have just told myself it was the world's biggest and stupidest practical joke. Ever.

There's a lot to be said for not thinking straight.

99/100

On the TV screen, the puppet people were still going through the motions of life in *Pogle's Wood*, scratching their heads and looking surprised while the narrator explained what was supposed to be happening to them. In the "real" world, I was going through pretty much the same thing.

'But you're human,' I said.

Cwej nodded. 'I was born on Earth, yeah. I just work for them, that's all.'

Them. He said *them*. In all the time I knew him, I never once heard Cwej call his employers by name. He talked about "Houses" sometimes, as if the people who gave him his orders had cliques and families and feuds of their own, but names? He never used names. I think he was scared to. Like some kind of magic was going to kick in if he did, like all he had to do was say the word and they'd appear right there in the room with him, all blood and fire and thunder.

'Why?' I asked.

'Why do I work for them?' Cwej looked surprised. I don't think he thought it was a decent question to ask. 'You mean, how did I end up getting together with them?'

'Yes,' I said. It wasn't really what I'd asked, but it was close enough.

Cwej put on his "serious" face, which was never very easy to take seriously. 'I didn't have a choice. I got kidnapped. Abducted.'

'So these employers of yours ... they're not nice people.'

'No, you don't get it.' He shook his head, and waved his spoon around, getting wholesome flakes of wheat and corn all over the floorboards. 'They've got rules, where they come from. Laws. You've got to have really strict laws, if you've got time-travel. They're not allowed to get involved in other people's cultures. They can watch, and they can make notes, and maybe if there's a crisis they can step in to stop the whole galaxy blowing up or something, but they can't mess around with humans. Normally. It's the rules.'

This wasn't making a lot of sense, and I said so.

'There are renegades,' Cwej told me. He tried to make his voice sound all dark and sinister when he said it. 'They're like criminals. They steal the time-travel capsules, and they go on the run.' He leant forward then, poking his big face over the top of the cereal packet I'd put between us. It was the last line of defence I had. 'They're mad, you know?'

'Right,' I said. 'So you were abducted by ... ?'

'He was one of the renegades. One of the worst. We'd been chasing him for years. I mean, his people had been chasing him. He was kind of a mad scientist, yeah?'

'With a stolen time machine,' I said.

Cwej nodded. 'You know what he called himself?'

'No,' I said.

'He called himself the Evil Renegade. With a capital E and everything. Like he wanted everyone to know he was this...'

'Mad scientist,' I suggested.

'Yeah. He used to go around the universe kidnapping people. He'd take them on board his timeship, and he'd... do things with them. Play with their heads. Make them think they were having exciting adventures. He had all these laboratories on board the ship.'

'So, this time machine,' I said. 'Was it ... big?'

'Oh, yeah.'

'And that's what he did to you? Experiments and things?'

Cwej shuddered. No, I'm serious. He really shuddered. 'I think so. He must have done. I don't remember much of it. There were a couple of others on the ship while I was there. One of them came from the same place as me. She died. I had to watch her die. The Renegade ... he sent her out into the middle of a war, just to watch what she'd do.' He was getting upset now, you could tell. 'She was lucky, though, next to some. When he got fed up with us, he just left us wherever he felt like. Anywhere in space-time. Just for a laugh.'

'Sounds like a big road trip,' I said. 'Very sixties.'

'He was mad,' snapped Cwej.

It was scary, the way he said that. It's like when you're combing a cat or a dog, and for a while it's fine, it's enjoying the attention, but then you get the comb snagged on its testicles and suddenly, bang, you're in trouble. (Have I really just compared Cwej to an animal with snagged testicles?)

101

I looked down at my bowl. Cwej looked down at his.

'Sorry,' he said.

'Uh-huh,' I said.

'It just gets to me, you know? What he did to my life, it's just. . .' He started shrugging again. 'I don't want to think that's what I'm doing to you. That's what I'm saying.'

'Uh-huh,' I said.

'The thing is, I got lucky, in the end. My people ... I mean, his people ... they caught up with him. Brought him back to the homeworld. They were good to me, you know? They gave me a choice and everything. Either they could put me back in my own time, and blank out all the memories of what he'd done, or I could stay with them. I think I did the right thing.'

I risked looking back up at him. 'But you didn't think ... after what had happened. . .' (I wasn't sure how close to his testicles I could get here.) 'You didn't think it'd be better to forget it all?'

'It would've been a cop-out,' said Cwej.

102

I wonder, now. I wonder how much of Cwej's memory was real. But, then, I spend most of my life wondering how much of *my* memory's real, so what can you expect?

His employers knew how to play around with people's memories. Cwej said they left his mind in one piece, but I can't help thinking of the way he'd snap, when I came anywhere near saying good things about the Evil Renegade. Why was that? Because Cwej had really suffered, or because the aliens wanted him to *think* he'd really suffered, so they could be sure he was on their side?

Also, I don't believe anyone would choose a name like the Evil Renegade. It sounds silly. If that isn't a faked memory, I don't know what is.

103

Two weeks later, I was lying under a night sky that was a totally different colour from any of the night skies you used to see on Earth, looking at constellations I knew I'd never remember the names of. Blue grass under my head. Cwej's face next to mine, close enough for me to be able to feel the warm air every time he breathed out.

'Tell me something,' I said, trying to sound wacky just so Cwej knew I was joking with him (he was never very good with irony). 'Why do aliens have funny names, *Cwej*?'

I felt him frown, rather than seeing it.

'They don't,' he said. Then a pause. 'Do they?'

'Cal used to have all these old sci-fi novels,' I told him. 'And the alien characters always had stupid names. It's like, on Earth, we get proper names. We've got Christian names and surnames and middle names. But aliens get these one word, four-letter names, like "Darf" or "Vrij" or "Gorp" or something. Any idea why that is, Cwej?'

He finally got the point. 'Cwej is a good name,' he said. 'It's Polish.'

'So what about Khiste?'

I felt the frown get deeper. 'I don't know where Khiste comes from. I don't think he's from Earth.'

'He's not ... one of your employers.'

'No. Just an agent.' He turned his head, so his lips were nearly touching my cheek. 'Christine?'

'Mm?'

'Why do you call me "Cwej" all the time?'

'Because you're an alien,' I said. 'I told you. Aliens don't have first names.'

104

In fact, Cwej was a bit sensitive about how human he was. I knew he'd been born on Earth, but his employers had given him 'biological advantages' when he'd signed up with them. The aliens were so advanced, they'd even made machines they could sew into the cells of their bodies. Things that let them time-travel more easily. Things that helped them heal if they got hurt. Things that sharpened up their senses. Cwej always started mumbling whenever I asked him about it, so I never found out exactly how un-human they'd made him, although towards the end I started to get some idea of what they'd done to his body.

I didn't think his genes were very important, really. I mean, I didn't know him for long enough to think about having kids. Besides, what was the difference between shoving machines into your body so you could see in the dark, and shoving chemicals into your body so you could see pretty colours? Maybe that's what really defines a culture: the way its people mess around with their own bodies. Ask anyone who's ever had a tattoo done. Or anyone who's ever had an ear pierced.

God. Have I really written over a hundred pages already?

105

Anyway. All this was in the future. On the 28th of September, when we sat there in the living room with a big fat yellow sun crawling over Soho, Cwej was still trying to explain who his people were and why they'd sent him to London. I told him I'd heard him on the 'phone, which confused him, until he figured out that I was talking about the thing he'd shoved under the bunk bed mattress. I told him I'd heard him talking about some kind of face-off. He tried to look serious again.

'It's a busy kind of universe out there,' he said. 'Look ... my people are the oldest civilisation, yeah? They're the most powerful race there is, because they worked out time-travel first. Right?'

('My people', that's what he said. See what I mean, about me not being sure how human he was?)

'There are things that are even older, though,' Cwej went on, once he saw me nodding dumbly. 'Not people. Not civilisations. Just ... things.'

'Yeah,' I said. Which meant: you mean, like the thing in the cell?

Cwej waved his arms around, to make sure I knew he was talking about things that were big and scary. 'They're like gods. I mean, I'm not saying they are gods, but they're *like* gods. For all we know, they're, um . . . they're fundamental parts of the universe. Like they're parts of the universe's framework. They might have been there since the beginning of time, we don't know. But we've always kind of assumed they'd never wake up. That they'd never show themselves.

All the civilisations in the universe - like my people, like the humans, like whatever - they've kind of been growing up in the shadow of these god things. Is this making sense?'

Obviously it was making sense. I was remembering the dream, where I'd seen space, made up of all the winged things. Where I'd seen the people, building their homes in the gaps between the spaces. The way I saw it, the Gods were the ones who shifted our bones around, the ones who were making collections out of our leftover bits and pieces.

106

Later on, I found out that things weren't as simple as Cwej had made them sound. It wasn't a two-way fight between the Gods and the people, for a start. The people were split up into factions, and so were the Gods, and you could never be sure who was working for who, like a big James Bond story stretched over the whole of space. And there were a hundred and one theories about where the Gods had come from as well, although most of the popular stories said the Gods were just figments of someone's imagination. The rumours said the Gods had been made millions and billions of years earlier, by a bunch of super-aliens so powerful that even their ideas were dangerous. Still, nobody seemed to know where these super-aliens had gone, or why they hadn't left behind any records of why they'd done what they'd done.

The Gods were there. Whatever the reason, it was one of those things you just had to deal with. Why were there gods? Well, why was there anything? Why was there gravity? Why was there a universe?

107

Come to think of it ... why *is* there a universe?

108

Another thing I've got in my rucksack is a newspaper, dated the 30th of March, 2596. I've already told you that Cwej's people weren't stuck in one time like the rest of us, so this shouldn't surprise you much. I say "newspaper", although to be honest I don't think there's any paper involved. I don't know what the thing's made of. All I know is that when you poke the little photos of the columnists with your finger, they start talking, in case you can't be bothered reading the words.

(Interesting fact: at least twice, I saw Cwej poking photographs in the newspapers of 1970, and scowling when they didn't talk to him. But that's beside the point.)

The front-page story in the 2596 "paper" is about a planet called Dellah, which, like the story says, is a colony planet on the gloomy side of the Earth empire. That's right: the human race leaves Earth one day, and scatters its bones across space for all the universe to see. Not bad, for a race that died out in 1970, but we'll deal with these paradoxes later. The point is that in March 2596 something happened to Dellah, something the Earth authorities didn't know how to deal with. The reporters didn't know how to deal with it, either. The story's a bit vague about what the catastrophe might have been, but one columnist calls it an "infection", and the feeling is that Dellah's going to have to be off-limits to human beings for a while.

What actually happened to Dellah was this: the Gods took over. It was the second planet they sank their teeth into, the first being a planet nearby called Tyler's Folly, another Earth colony nobody ever really cared about until things started going wrong. The takeover on Dellah upset just about everybody. It upset the Earth authorities, who wondered whether they should try launching missiles at the planet, but never got round to it. It upset Cwej, who just happened to have friends there (I asked him whether time-travellers were like sailors, with a girl in every year, but he didn't know what I was talking about). Above all, it upset Cwej's employers, who hadn't been expecting the Gods to show themselves like that. It made them feel a bit helpless, I think.

I'll get back to the story in a moment. Right now, I feel like poking the faces of the columnists. Poking all of them at once. Hearing them arguing and talking over each other, until the ruins are full of their stupid whining voices. It'll feel like being in London again. Like being in a pub in Tottenham Court Road.

109/110

'They've found something out,' Cwej told me, over the cornflakes.

'Who have?' I said.

'My people. They've been kind of ignoring the Gods for years. We always thought they weren't important. I mean, a couple of them have shown their faces every now and then, but there are just so many other hostile powers in the universe, you know? *People* powers.'

I tried to look all serious and thoughtful. Cwej folded his big fingers in front of his face. 'We've been putting all our research people on this. Finding out what the Gods are, where they really come from, that kind of thing. Just in case they spread. In case they're a major threat.'

'And are they?' I asked.

'Um . . .' said Cwej.

The truth is, he didn't know. I didn't figure that out until later. Cwej's employers had found something out from their research, something crucial about the Gods, but they'd never bothered telling Cwej what it was.

Actually, we never *did* find out what it was, although I can make a few guesses. I know it must have been something bad, something about the Gods' powers that got the time-travellers on edge. Cwej's employers always thought they had a chance of fighting the Gods, if it ever came to that. I think they must have worked out that they couldn't.

They were scared. That's what I'm saying. And, at the end of the day, that was the reason they'd sent Cwej to Earth.

'All right,' I said. 'I'm going to see if I've got my head round this. First off, your employers are worried about the Gods.'

Cwej opened his mouth to say something. I didn't let him.

'Let me finish,' I said. 'Please. Your employers are worried about the Gods. Because the Gods are trying to take over the universe or something, five or six hundred years in the future. So. They've sent you back in time to 1970. They want you to change time, or something like that. They want you to get rid of the Gods now, so they won't be a problem in the future. That thing in the police cell was one of the Gods. It followed you back here to stop you, but you killed it off somehow, after I blacked out. Which is lucky, because it's been going around London killing people. Right?'

Cwej looked worried. 'Are you sure you're feeling okay?'

'Fine. Am I right?'

He cleared his throat, and started counting off points on his fingers. 'Well, to start with, I haven't been sent back in time. It's not that simple.'

'Simple,' I muttered.

'Also, you can't change time. It doesn't work. The whole universe falls apart if you try it, I think. That's not why I'm here. Three, the thing in the cell wasn't a God. It was just a sphinx. Gods are bigger. Four, I didn't kill it. I just shut it down.'

'Okay,' I said. 'But apart from that, how did I do?'

'I don't know,' said Cwej. 'I've lost track.'

111

I don't remember all the details about the conversation, obviously. Writing it all out now, I'm probably filling in more details than were really there. Cwej didn't give me all the answers, not at once.

The truth was, there were things he didn't like to talk about. For example, stuck in that scrapbook I keep mentioning there's a letter, dated September 1970 and written (in an ugly, scrawly kind of handwriting) on notepaper headed with the name of a prison in Los Angeles. It's an answer to a question, which Cwej had asked the writer a couple of weeks earlier.

The writer tells Cwej that, yes, he does think the fall of civilisation is imminent. Except that he doesn't use the word "imminent", and he's spelt "civilisation" with a "Z". There'll be a time of reckoning, when all the "pigs" and "niggers" will wipe each other out in a war of blood and fire. While all this is going on, the lucky few are going to be in hiding somewhere underground, ready to build a new, white, police-free utopia once the bloodshed's over.

I don't know how Cwej managed to get in touch with the letter-writer, although I suppose anything's possible if you're working for aliens. But I do know why Cwej asked the question in the first place. It was because he wanted to understand. He wanted to know all about Earth, and about all the things we thought were going to happen to it. Cwej must have decided that the writer was the right kind of person to ask, even if he was a complete paranoid maniac. (The writer, that is. Not Cwej.)

The letter isn't signed, although it's pretty obvious who wrote it. And it's easy to see why Cwej didn't like to talk about it, why he didn't want me to know exactly who his friends were. Scared to talk too much, that was Cwej.

Notes on the Bottle

112

Ancient Egypt was always popular with Lady Diamond's customers. Let's face it, it was the perfect civilisation. Old enough for Lady to pretend that the Egyptians had passed down all kinds of "lost secrets" to fortune-tellers, but big enough to have left a bunch of bloody great pyramids behind. As far as Lady was concerned, the reason they'd built the pyramids was so people like her could use them as props, thousands of years later.

'There's a whole city in Egypt that used to belong to the priests,' Lady Diamond once told me, in the days before she'd figured out that I wasn't going to be impressed. 'A whole walled-off city. And nobody else ever found out what they did in there. Orgies, they said. Sex magic. Can't you just imagine?'

'Have you been there?' I asked.

'Darling, of course I've been there,' said Lady Diamond, the woman who'd also claimed to have been in the bedrooms of every male rock'n'roll star who'd had a top ten hit between 1963 and 1968. 'There are dirty pictures all over the walls. *There's* something they don't show you in the Natural History Museum. The Egyptians invented mathematics, you know.'

I didn't see what that had to do with orgies or dirty pictures. Besides, it sounded like she'd made it up. I nodded anyway.

'It was all about geometry,' Lady went on. 'The priests knew they could get in touch with their gods through the power of mathematics. That's why they made so many great buildings. All those straight lines and angles. That's where the Masons get their ideas from.' She tapped the side of her nose, like she wanted me to think she'd been having sex with Masons for most of her adult life.

'Oh,' I said.

'They used to sacrifice slaves to their buildings. They used to use their crushed-up bodies as mortar. Did you know that?'

I didn't know that, mainly because Lady had got the idea from watching *The Ten Commandments*.

'I mean, you can just imagine, darling,' Lady told me. 'The things they must have found out, locked away in that city of theirs. The things they must have built. What kind of devices must there have been, hmm? What kind of diabolical engines, fed by the blood of their followers?'

'They didn't have engines, did they?' I asked. Although if she'd said that the first steam train had been invented by Tutankhamen, I probably would have just shrugged.

113/114

By two o'clock on the 28th of September, 1970, I was standing in the kitchen of Chris Cwej's flat, scraping my leftover cornflakes into a plastic pedal-bin. I felt like I hadn't eaten properly since the day I'd been born, but somehow my mouth didn't feel up to chewing.

'It was a sphinx,' Cwej said. At long last, he'd decided to tell me all about the thing I'd seen in the police cell. 'They're like the Gods' servants. We think.'

The kitchen was tiny, hardly big enough for two people. There was no fake wood panelling here, just smooth shiny white surfaces, tiles that had been splashed with the juice of old tea bags. You could tell it was a man who owned the flat. Nobody had even tried to decorate the room. The forks and spoons were lying in a messy heap by the sink, and under the bare lightbulb (there weren't any windows) you could see every blob of grease on every piece of metal.

Cwej stood in the doorway, with his big lanky body leaning against the frame. He'd scooped up a jar of peanut butter from a sideboard, and now he was busy running his finger around the rim.

'Sphinx, as in Egypt?' I asked.

'Er, not really. People call them sphinxes because ... it kind of fits them. We've known about them for years.'

'I thought you said the Gods had only just woken up.'

'Um. The thing is,' said Cwej. Then he stopped, and sucked the peanut butter off his hands.

'The thing is, the Gods aren't all the same,' he went on. 'They fight with each other, just like we do. We think - we *think* - they've all got different agendas. Most of the Gods have been, er, asleep for the past few million years. But there've been sightings. We think a few of them have been slumming it around the universe. Exploring. Finding stuff out about the other races.'

'Like your Evil Renegade did,' I said. Cwej immediately stopped slapping his tongue around his gums.

'I suppose so,' he said. 'Dellah - that's the planet I was talking about, the one the Gods took over - it wasn't the first place the Gods have popped up on. There's another planet, on the edge of the galaxy. The other edge from Earth, I mean. It's kind of been a colony for the Gods for as long as anyone can remember. We think it belongs to one of the ren... to one of the *rogue* Gods. I mean, most of this is guess-work, seeing as nobody's ever been there and come back again. We're not even sure it's a planet.'

'You can't tell whether something's a planet or not?' I asked. Cwej looked doubt-ful.

'Space goes funny around the Gods,' he said. 'The usual laws don't work proper-ly. Listen, you said something about Egypt, right? Do you know anything about the old Egyptian priests?'

'Ah,' I said.

115

Bear with me here. We're getting close to the part of the story where I tell you the secret of the universe.

116

I could write a whole thesis now, about the biology of the sphinxes. Most of it would probably be wrong, mind you, but it'd still be a thesis.

The one thing you've got to remember is this. Sphinxes aren't "natural". They didn't evolve. I mean, just look at the things: big sharp wings, bones that move around under their skins so you can't tell whether they're supposed to walk on two legs or four legs, and bloody great TV screens popping out of their faces. They *look* like TV screens, anyway, although I suppose they're just lenses. Maybe to help them focus on what they're doing.

The Gods made the sphinxes for a reason. They're not like slaves, they're like tools. Because sphinxes can make space.

I've read the books, all the theories written down by Cwej's employers. Sphinxes feed on stuff from outside normal space-time, although apparently you'd have to have eyes that see in five dimensions to guess what this stuff might actually look like. The important thing is, sphinxes eat material from outside the ordinary uni-verse, then excrete it again as raw space-time. I'll never, as long as I live, forget the way Chris Cwej described this process to me.

'They poo reality, basically,' he said.

That was why Cwej's employers couldn't even be sure whether the part of space owned by the renegade Gods was a planet. Because the Gods had been adding to it for thousands of years, getting their sphinxes to make more space in the area, almost like they were building their own little microcosm universe on the edge of the real one. The sphinxes had been there for thousands of years, beavering away like nobody's business, stopping only to kill off any travellers stupid enough to get too close to their territory.

117

"Microcosm". I've decided to make that the word of the day, mainly because I just flipped through my dictionary to check the spelling, and by pure chance I ended up opening the book at the exact page that starts with (ta-daah!) "microcosm".

Just luck, really, but it happens a lot. Cwej once said that it's because all dictionaries are a bit telepathic, although he could have been joking. He was the one who bought me this dictionary, by the way. It's a twenty-sixth-century edition, packed with all the latest words from the far-off corners of the Earth empire, and it's about the same size as a Mars bar, with letters so small you need a special mini-computer to read them.

On the day Cwej bought it for me, the first word I saw - after a random flip through the pages - was "fake". Just bear that in mind when you read these next few pages, that's all.

118

'Listen, you said something about Egypt, right? Do you know anything about the old Egyptian priests?'

'Ah,' I said. I didn't know whether to mention what Lady Diamond had told me, seeing as I knew she'd made most of it up.

'They were more than just priests,' Cwej said. 'They were like masons. Mechanics. They built -'

'Engines,' I said. 'Fed by the blood of their followers.'

Cwej blinked at me. 'Really?' he said. He sounded impressed.

'Never mind,' I said. 'Carry on.'

Cwej put the peanut butter back on the sideboard, although he didn't bother screwing the top back on. I did it for him, without thinking. 'What I'm saying is, that's what the Gods' followers are like. That's what we've heard from Dellah, anyway. We think it's probably the same in the part of space where the renegade Gods live. We think they've got human worshippers there. We think the humans are the ones who look after the sphinxes. They use the sphinxes to build things for the Gods. Like I said. Masons.'

That made sense to me. The worshippers were doing what the rest of us do all the time, building things to keep the Gods happy and telling themselves they were doing something important and noble.

'Can you imagine,' I said, trying to remember what Lady Diamond had asked me, 'the things they must have built?'

'Yeah,' said Cwej. 'That's it. That's the problem.'

119/120

And now, a story. Are you sitting comfortably, children? Then I'll begin.

Once upon a time, there was an alien called the Evil Renegade, who used to kidnap people and carry them off through time just to see what would happen. The Evil Renegade was proud of his reputation, as a reckless, dangerous adventurer who'd run away from his people and was quite happy to spend his whole life running. To prove to everyone how fearless he was, he challenged just about every other race in the universe, and he never lost, because he was as much a criminal mastermind as he was a mad scientist.

But there was one kind of monster the Evil Renegade hadn't ever taken on, and that annoyed him. He'd never gone head to head with the Gods. So, one day, the Evil Renegade decided to do something about it.

Along with his human slaves, the Evil Renegade took his time machine to the place where the sphinxes lived, the world that the runaway Gods had been building for themselves on the edge of the galaxy. Nobody else has ever come back from sphinx-space alive, so it's hard to say what happened to the Evil Renegade in the Gods' world. There are stories, although nobody's sure where the stories come from. All the rumours say there was a big fight, with the Evil Renegade waging a one-man war against the Gods, just for the hell of it. The cities where the Gods' worshippers lived were wrecked. The Gods themselves were injured, and their blood rained down over whole countries. Astronomers, watching the home of the Gods from a billion trillion miles away, sat and stared while the whole of sphinx-space lit up with fire.

(By the way, you should hear Cwej tell this story. He somehow manages to squeeze in a couple of dozen spaceship battles along the way. Believe me, this is the edited version you're getting.)

In the end, the Evil Renegade was beaten. The Gods were too strong even for him, so he made his escape while he could, leaving his doomed human slaves behind and getting away in his time machine. But he didn't go away empty-handed. He stole something from the rogue Gods, one of the 'devices' their worshippers had built in their honour. The Evil Renegade spirited it away and hoarded it in his trophy room, along with all the other things he'd taken from the worlds he'd visited, all the stolen relics and severed heads of his enemies.

The thing he stole was a bottle. A very special kind of bottle that had been built by the sphinxes, working to the plans of the Gods' followers. And the bottle stayed on the Evil Renegade's time machine for years, until finally the Renegade's own people caught up with him, and the relic ended up in the hands of Chris Cwej.

121

I've seen that bottle, of course. I saw it not long after the conversation in the kitchen. It was sitting on a velvet cushion, being treated like the king of the world by Cwej's people. I remember seeing it for the first time, looking through the glass and gawping at what was inside.

There's no way of saying how it feels, to see something like that in front of you.

To see whole stars, whole star-systems, spinning around inside a bottle not much bigger than a foot long. To see all those galaxies, squeezed into a space about the same size as your own head.

'It's true,' I remember saying. 'It's fucking true.'

'Sorry,' Cwej mumbled.

'A whole universe,' I said. Behind me, I heard Khiste - who I haven't told you about yet, but we'll get there, don't worry - snorting to himself under his breath, like he thought I was too stupid and primitive to understand anything that important.

'A whole universe,' Cwej agreed. 'In a bottle.'

122

'A whole universe,' said Cwej, some time before that. 'In a bottle.'

We were still in the kitchen of his flat, and I was putting the milk back in the fridge, on the grounds that Cwej probably wasn't going to bother. I was starting to feel itchy, like my body didn't think it could take in any more of this without chemical help.

'You're kidding,' I said. 'The sphinxes can do that? They can build something that big, and just...?

'Yeah,' said Cwej. 'Cosmic, isn't it?'

I got the feeling he only said 'cosmic' because he'd heard the hippies saying it. 'But it's not a real universe,' I said. 'Not like this one. I mean, it's only like a model universe, yeah?'

Cwej frowned. Then he looked down at his feet. They were still bare, and they still weren't giving him any answers.

'Hard to say,' he said.

'Are there people in it? Living inside the bottle?'

'Um, yes.'

'Do they know, though? Do they know they're not real?'

Cwej was still toe-staring. 'I didn't say they weren't real. They were just made by the sphinxes. That's all.'

I didn't argue. 'Don't the Gods want it back?'

'I should think so,' said Cwej, looking up at last. 'I think that's why the sphinxes are following me.'

'You mean, you've got it here?' I said. 'You've brought this universe-in-a-bottle thing with you? To London? In 1970?'

'Not exactly,' said Cwej. 'Look, I haven't made a report to the Homeworld yet. I'm not sure I should be telling you everything this soon ...'

123

A few more memories, which may be real, or may just be things I've imagined after the fact:

1. It was something I'd thought of while I'd been running away from Lady's shop with the wound in my leg, when I'd first worked out (or just imagined?) that there

were things moving around in the shadows, shifting our bones into patterns even the priests of Egypt would have been proud of. I'd imagined that these monsters, whatever they were, had been changing space so we all had enough room to die in. Was that a premonition, or what?

2. The corridor of the police station had gone on for ever. Earlier on, I'd put it down to the pain and the coke. Looking back on it, it's easy to imagine that the sphinx had shat out raw space when it had gone through the station, stretching out the corridor behind it. Does that make sense?

3. A definite dubious memory, this. Think about the man who'd attacked me in Lady Diamond's shop, the man who by now I knew had been a sphinx, somehow disguised as a human being (by changing its own private body space, maybe?). Sometimes, I remember turning around and seeing him already standing there in the doorway, staring at me. Sometimes, I remember it another way. I remember him stepping out of the shadows. Literally, I mean: stepping out of the shadows. Moving out of spaces in the building that shouldn't have been there. Did I really see him / it doing that, or am I fantasising again?

124
Not long now until the secret of the universe. Hold your breath.

125/126
Cwej led me out into the hallway of the flat. I thought we were going back into the living room, but instead he just stood there with his back against the wall, sticking his hands into the pockets of his suit as if he didn't know what else to do with them. There were still three or four doors in the hallway I hadn't been through, although I guessed that most of them led to spare rooms. One of the doors had a big padlock fixed to the handle, which I thought was odd.

Mysterious locked rooms. How gothic. What horrors could have been waiting for me on the other side? Well, that's not important right now.

'My people are scared,' Cwej said. He practically whispered it, so I started thinking about conversations in spy movies, wondering if we were standing in the hall only because the rest of the flat was bugged.

'Scared,' I repeated. 'You mean, of the Gods?'

Cwej nodded, keeping his eyes fixed on the grubby floorboards.

'So there's going to be a war?' I asked. I couldn't even imagine what a war on that kind of scale might be like, although I guessed there'd be a lot more to it than just spaceships shooting at each other.

'No,' said Cwej. 'My employers… they know they're outgunned. They know they can't beat the Gods. I don't know how they know it, but they know.'

Then he sighed, and lifted up his head, letting it thunk back against the wall. 'It's stupid. Really, really stupid. We always thought we were the best. Tougher than anybody else. Smarter. I never thought I'd ever see them scared.'

Note the way Cwej swung between saying "us" and "them" when he was talking about his employers, like he wasn't sure whether he qualified as one of them or just as one of their servants. Personally, I didn't know what to say, so I just shuffled my feet.

'The Gods don't just take over planets,' said Cwej. 'They take over whole cultures. You know what that's like for my people? Their culture's the oldest there is. I think so, anyway. They don't want to lose that. *We* don't want to lose that. We have to make sure the Gods don't take it away from us. We've got to make sure there's something left, even if the Gods take over. Something left of the Homeworld.'

'You mean, your new Homeworld,' I said. 'Where your employers come from. Yeah?'

Cwej looked at me, at last. His eyes were like shiny little blue buttons.

'We're going to send some of our people inside the bottle,' said Cwej. 'That's what all this is about. We're going to put together a survival team. Just a few of my people. They're going to take all our secrets, all our technology, and they're going to set up new lives for themselves inside the bottle-world. That way, our culture's going to be able to live. Even if most of us get taken over by the Gods. There'll be a ... a kind of colony. Like a time capsule. Inside the model universe.'

'I don't get it,' I said. 'Your people can go anywhere in space, can't they? Anywhere. So why not just find a new planet for yourselves?'

Cwej shook his head. 'You don't understand. The Gods aren't just threatening us. They're threatening *everything*. All of space. All of time. It doesn't matter where we go.'

The obvious question finally struck me. 'Wait a minute. Does that mean ... they're going to take over Earth as well?'

Cwej didn't give me a yes-or-no answer, which annoyed me. 'Nowhere's safe, that's what I'm saying. Nowhere real, anyway. But the bottle's different. The model universe isn't a perfect copy of the real one. It's a lot simpler. There aren't any Gods there. There aren't any really hi-tech cultures. There's a version of Earth, but there isn't a version of the Homeworld. No time-travellers. It's supposed to be safe. That's the theory, anyway. We hide our team inside the bottle, then hope the Gods never think of looking there, even if they manage to find the bottle again.'

There was something I didn't like about the way he'd said that. Something about there being a version of Earth inside the bottle. So I started wondering: is there a little model version of me there, or isn't the detail that good?

'Getting into the bottle's not easy,' Cwej went on. He was droning now, like he didn't want to have to tell me this. 'Our people spent years trying to work out how to get in and out without the two universes leaking. In the end, we had to copy the sphinxes. We had to copy their rituals. And even then, we could only get one person inside the bottle.'

'Who volunteered?' I said.

'I did,' said Cwej.

I've got to admit, I was impressed. 'You've been inside the bottle?'

'That was the plan,' Cwej told me. 'For me to get into the bottle world. To find a decent planet. To find a decent time period. Somewhere our people could... blend in. Then I was supposed to open up the bottle from the inside, so the rest of the survival team could make it through.'

'And did you do it?' I asked.

'Not yet,' said Cwej.

127

And that was it. The exact moment when everything clicked together; what Cwej was really doing in London, and what he'd meant when he'd said that he 'hadn't exactly' travelled through time to get here, even though he came from the twenty-sixth century. The secret of the universe. The secret of *my* universe, anyway.

'Oh, Christ,' I said.

Cwej just stood there, wiggling his toes.

'Oh, Christ, no,' I said.

128

And I've just reached the end of this notebook. Anyone would think I'd planned it that way.

Notes on the Sphinx

1

First page of a new notebook. I feel like scrawling something in big letters on the paper. THIS BOOK BELONGS TO CHRISTINE SUMMERFIELD, or maybe a dedication. Who should I dedicate it to, d'you think? I'll have to think about that.

2

Where were we?

Well. At about four o'clock in the morning on the 29th of September, 1970, I was on my hands and knees in the bathroom of Chris Cwej's flat, head down over the toilet bowl with my hands sliding around in a puddle of spilt disinfectant. I'd been trying to stick two fingers down my throat, but I'd bottled out (ha, ha) before they'd got all the way down. People aren't built to make themselves sick. Me, I never had the nerve to argue with nature like that.

I'd been trying to sleep, in the room where Cwej kept the spare bed, but it hadn't worked. I'd just lain there, with the cramp getting worse and worse in my stomach, feeling the sweat building up on the duvet. There on the bathroom floor, with the magic healing potato in my leg and a desperate need for drugs, for Valium, for *any-thing* to make all of this go away and leave me alone, I'd told myself that the only way to make life better was to throw up. Like I thought that shedding my stomach lining would make the whole world easier to swallow.

3

Later on, when we were walking through one of the cities his employers had built, Cwej told me that he didn't understand how I could ever have believed my world was the "real" one. He sounded almost embarrassed, telling me that. In his universe, in the "real" universe, things were different. The pyramids had been built by spacemen. There was life on Mars. There were "lost planets" inside Earth's solar system, covered with the ruins of old Inca-style civilisations. Humans were meant to start taking over other planets by the end of the twentieth century.

There was none of that in my world. Things were a lot simpler there, inside the model universe the sphinxes had made. 'I mean, where you come from, the pyramids were actually built by *humans*,' Cwej said, shaking his head in a disbelieving kind of way. 'That's just ... stupid.'

4

But all that was in the future. Let's go back to the afternoon when Cwej, for whatever reason, decided to tell me the truth. Or some of it, anyway.

I was sitting in the living room of the flat again, huddled up on the floor in the corner, next to the window wall. The TV had been switched off, so everything was quiet, apart from the sound of tiny little hailstones splattering against the glass. I was looking out at London, at Soho, trying not to notice that from here it looked exactly like the world in a bottle Cwej had told me about. Cwej had bought himself a few packs of cigarettes, more to blend in with 1970 than for any other reason, so I'd helped myself to a couple.

Cwej sat opposite me, on the other side of the smoke-cloud, folding his big limbs into the smallest space he could. He was pretending he wasn't staring at me.

We sat like that for a long, long time.

'Um . . .' he said, in the end.

It took him about five minutes to follow that up.

'Are you going to be okay?' he asked.

I shrugged.

Another long pause.

'Am I human?' I asked, in the end.

I could see Cwej squirming, out of the corner of my eye. 'Er, I'm not sure what you mean,' he said.

'Am I human? Do I count as a person?' I nodded at the window, at all the tiny make-believe people, shuffling along the streets of that little bottled world. 'Do *any* of them count? Or are they just ... ?'

I didn't bother finishing the question. I guessed Cwej would know what I meant.

'I'm sure you're human,' he said. 'You look human.'

That was his idea of a compliment. Maybe even a chat-up line.

'You didn't *have* to tell me, did you?' I said.

'You got involved,' Cwej said. He was almost whining now.

'Why? Because I know too much? Because I saw that bloody sphinx thing, is that it?'

'No, no.' Cwej shook his head, and waved some of the smoke out of his face. I wondered if they had cigarettes where he came from. He didn't look used to the air pollution. 'It's the ritual. You kind of got caught up in the ritual. That's all.'

5

Cwej taught me a lot about ritual, in the two weeks before the end. He even taught me the poem, the one he was chanting in the prison cell. I can still remember most of it. 'There is no light among those winding ways,' etc., etc.

The practice would go something like this: I'd sit in the middle of a circle, scratched into the floor of one of the spare rooms in the flat. The electricity would be turned off, so there'd be no light apart from the candles (Lady Diamond would've done the same thing, I'm sure). Then the computer parts would be laid down in patterns around me. The parts were junk, bits and pieces of old hardware from Cwej's beloved Homeworld, just there to help me focus.

The sphinxes were controlled by rituals. Well, of course. They were owned by people who were just like 'the priest-architects of ancient Egypt', remember? When the sphinx had broken into Cwej's cell at the police station, all those billions of years ago, Cwej must have had just enough time to scatter the computer parts around him. Props to help him fix his mind on the "spell", the chanting of the poem. Cwej had chosen the poem himself; it was nineteenth century, he told me, all about night-time and cities and ghosts and murder. A prayer to Jack the Ripper, or Charles Manson, or John Christie, or any other famous maniac you might want to think of.

The words of the poem weren't important. The point was, the sphinx knew what it meant. Cwej called this "programming" the sphinx, which was supposed to be something to do with computers. They had thousands of computers where Cwej came from, not just a handful like we had on Earth. In the cell, Cwej had managed to "program" the sphinx to stay where it was instead of ripping him to pieces.

Sitting in that circle, staring at those pieces of junk, I started to work out what he meant when he said that I'd been caught up in the ritual. I'd distracted the sphinx, while it had been trying to break out of its "programming" and attack Cwej. I'd become part of that "program". It was only after it'd been distracted that Cwej had managed to get deeper into its internal workings, and shut it down completely.

Could I have done that to a sphinx myself, after what Cwej taught me? I'd like to think so, although I never got the chance to try. I'd like to think I could squeeze one into any shape I liked, the same way the sphinx that had attacked me had squeezed itself into the shape of a modern mass-murderer, before it had decided that there just wasn't any point in pretending. But I don't suppose I'll ever know now.

6

'That's how you got rid of the sphinx?' I asked. I dropped the cigarette butt on to the floor, and Cwej winced, but he didn't say anything.

'With the ritual,' he said. 'Yeah.'

'So what did you do? Make it go back to ... wherever it came from?'

Cwej looked uncomfortable again. I was getting used to that.

'Not exactly,' he said.

'What do you mean, "not exactly"?' I asked.

'Are you sure you want to know?'

'No. What do you mean, "not exactly"?'

'It's in one of the spare rooms,' Cwej admitted. 'It's been there since last night. I didn't tell you before. I mean, I thought it'd freak you out.'

7

It wasn't in the room with the padlock on the door, which surprised me. I remember thinking at the time, *you mean, whatever's in the locked room, it's worse than the sphinx? Jesus Christ.*

Yes, I wanted to see the sphinx again. Why? Because the sphinx was, at the end of the day, the best proof I had that Cwej was telling the truth; that this wasn't all part of a desperate chat-up technique, or a way of getting me into some weirdo hippie-cult or other. ("The Children of the Bottle". It's got a kind of ring to it, I'd say.)

Cwej stopped at the door of one of the spare rooms, with his hand on the knob.

He looked over his shoulder at me.

'Are you sure you want to see this?' he said.

'Huh,' I told him.

So he opened the door.

8

It took me a while to fix my eyes on anything inside the room. There weren't any windows, and Cwej didn't turn on the lights. I could make out candles near the doorway - this was the room where I'd learn the rituals myself, later on - but the candles weren't lit. It didn't look like there were any furnishings around, either. There was one solid wedge of light from the hallway outside, but Cwej's body blotted most of it out, so I could just see...

Well, I could see something moving. I remember jumping. And all of a sudden there was the smell of something wet and leathery in the air, a deliberate kind of smell, like it had been chosen instead of being a natural animal scent.

'It's all right,' Cwej told me. 'It's under control.'

The thing was turning to look at me, swinging its big fat head on the end of its skinny neck. The light hit the lens at the front of its skull. I saw Cwej's face reflected in the glass, all cold and blurry and yellow.

Then it stretched its wings. I got the feeling I was standing in front of something huge, like a great big tidal wave rising up in front of me. Suddenly, I felt very, very dizzy. I took a few steps back, and ended up stumbling against the wall.

'Christ,' I said.

'D'you want me to turn on the lights?' Cwej asked.

'God, no.'

The sphinx moved its neck again. I could see the whole length of it in the shaft of light, long and grey-brown, with big solid muscles stretching under the skin. It was looking down at the floor, and in the big glass eye I could see the reflections of chalk lines, scratched into the boards.

It was inside a circle. The circle must have been a good twelve feet across, so every part of the sphinx's body was stuck inside the chalk line. I got the feeling it was trying to remind Cwej about that, waiting for him to let it go.

'Does it do what you say?' I asked.

'I'm not sure,' said Cwej. 'Do you?'

'ANSWER: THIS UNIT RESPONDS TO APPROPRIATE STIMULI,' said the sphinx.

9

No. I don't like the way that looks. It didn't talk in capitals; it wasn't that loud. It didn't sound like it was speaking through a mouth, though. How can I put this? It was more like the thing was rebuilding the space around it, so the air in that space just happened to have sound waves in it, sound waves that were the same shape as words. If that makes any sense.

Capitals just look silly. If I was better at this handwriting business, and wasn't just scribbling these notes in ballpoint pen, then I'd invent a special kind of ... what's the word? Typeface, that's it. God knows the sphinxes deserved one.

10/11

Actually, I've just thought of a comparison for what the sphinx's voice sounded like. But it's not a comparison that'll mean much to you, not yet.

If you were still wondering, I'll tell you now: yes, I did go to other planets with Cwej. Planets in his universe, that is, planets in the "real" universe, because nothing much was going on inside the bottle (where there were no Gods, remember, and no time-travellers). One of the worlds that really sticks in my mind - and God knows, I remember less than you might think - is the one we went to four or five days after we first met. I don't remember what the planet was called, so we'll just call it the Inside-Out World.

The visit was a big occasion, all arranged by Cwej's employers. I won't bother describing the planet in detail, except that it was inside-out only because the people who lived there wanted it that way. It had a great big yellow sun in the middle, and all the people lived on the inside of the shell, where it was warm. This was a miracle of engineering, Cwej told me, and that was kind of the problem. For years, Cwej's employers had been jealous of the people in the Inside-Out World, who were smarter than just about everyone in the universe apart from the time-travellers. So Cwej's employers had a treaty with these people, which said that the people weren't allowed to invent time-travel, because Cwej's kind wanted some secrets of their own.

Cwej was there to end that treaty. Or at least, to change it a bit. The ceremony was held out in the open air, if anything in the Inside-Out World could happen in the open air. I remember these two huge lines of soldiers, the honour guard Cwej's employers had sent, dozens and dozens of men in armour. Except that the armour looked like it had been stitched to their bodies. Cwej walked between the two lines with his head held high, dressed in a big red robe which was supposed to be traditional on "his" homeworld, but which his long gangly legs kept tripping up on.

He let me walk by his side. I don't know why. It's not like I had anything to do with things.

So we both marched across the grass, until we reached the podium in the middle of the field. There were aliens waiting for us there, two of the locals. Their skins were all shiny and sweet-shop coloured, like aliens from the covers of crap old SF magazines, and their eyes were huge. You could tell they only looked that way because they'd decided to. There were two scrolls on the podium in front of them, new copies of the treaty, covered in letters too small for anyone to read. Cwej picked up the quill pen they'd left there, and put his signature on both copies, as an official agent of the Houses.

Then a second signature appeared on the treaties. The planet signed on the dotted lines, like the ink had just coalesced (new word of the day) out of thin air. The aliens must have been there as witnesses. Even though they tried to keep staring dead ahead, you could tell the men in the honour guard were getting itchy. And who could blame them? Their employers had just signed away their monopoly on time-travel.

'Okay,' said Cwej, with a sigh. 'That's it. How long d'you think it'll be before you build your first timeship?'

'We've only got a population of about two trillion,' said a voice. 'I shouldn't think we'll have a working model in operation until, oh, about tomorrow lunchtime.'

I didn't know where the voice had come from, and neither did the men in the honour guard, although Cwej didn't look surprised. It felt like the whole planet was talking to us. And maybe it was, who knows? Maybe the Inside-Out World knew so much about its people that it even spoke for them.

That was the way the sphinx sounded, as well. Like it was the air speaking, not the sphinx itself. But the Inside-Out World sounded like the kind of person you wouldn't mind talking to, if you met it in a pub. On the other hand, the sphinxes were just machines, and they talked like machines. (Cwej once said they sounded like 'Grel on morphine', although I don't know what he meant by that.)

12

'I've been letting it squirm for a bit,' said Cwej, while the sphinx shuffled around inside its circle. 'It was getting kind of aggressive. I thought it needed time to calm down.'

The sphinx didn't have anything to say to that. In the shadows, you could see its head bobbing up and down, like it was sniffing at the architecture. Looking for weak points it could slip through.

'Can't you kill it?' I asked.

The sphinx turned its lens towards me. I pressed my back against the wall, for no good reason. 'I don't want to,' Cwej said. 'If I can figure out how to program it, I can use it to open up the bottle.'

He took a step forward then, probably because he didn't want to look like he was scared. 'Sphinx,' he said, and he sounded for all the world like Aladdin giving orders to his genie. 'How did you get here? Did you follow me into the bottle?'

The sphinx rested its front paws on the ground, and turned into a four-legged thing again. 'Reply: this unit has always been in operation within this environment. Summarization: no.'

You could tell Cwej was confused, even without seeing his face. 'You mean ... you've always been inside this bottle?'

This was my whole world Cwej was talking about, of course. I thought about reminding him of that, but I couldn't figure out how to say it. Sometimes English just isn't enough.

'Clarification: yes,' said the sphinx.

Cwej clicked his fingers. 'Got it. You're here as a kind of monitor. You're part of the operating system of the bottle. Part of the software. Right?'

'Reply: yes. Observation: your terminology is inadequate.'

'Good. Great.' Cwej was nodding to himself now, so his neck looked almost as long as the sphinx's. 'Are there any more like you inside the bottle?'

'Reply: no.'

'And you wanted to kill me because ... ?'

The sphinx didn't answer. It didn't even flap.

'That was a question,' Cwej pointed out.

'Reply: it's the procedure of this unit to remove all alien matter from this environment,' said the sphinx.

13

Or words to that effect, anyway. You're not expecting me to be word-perfect, are you? Just be thankful I've got a memory this good. I must have been made that way.

Also, you'll notice that I'm still describing the sphinx as being slippery and phallic-looking. That happens, apparently, when people have to come face to face with alien things for the first time. The only way your brain can deal with it is by seeing everything the way Sigmund Freud would have seen it, like it's all been dredged up from your own subconscious. I suppose that's why UFOs always used to look either tit-shaped or cigar-shaped.

14

'You're like an antibody,' Cwej was rambling. 'If anything comes in from the real universe' (he gave me a funny look when he said that, so I suppose he was embarrassed he'd reminded me that I wasn't 'real') 'you try to kill it off.'

'Affirmation: yes.'

'What about the other killings?' I asked. It was the only question I could ask that was on my level.

Cwej opened his mouth to say something, but the sphinx cut him off. 'Requirement: specify "other killings".'

I was starting to get the hang of this now, although I got the feeling Cwej would have preferred me to stay quiet. 'Have there been other, erm, "alien matter" things around here recently?'

'Reply: yes.'

'Like what?' asked Cwej.

'Record of relevance: this unit has recorded disturbances to the structure of this environment. Elements from the environment outside the bottle are emergent.' (I remember this line exactly, because I'd never heard anyone seriously use the word "emergent" before.)

'You mean, apart from me?' said Cwej.

'Affirmation: yes.'

'Wait a minute,' I said. 'Forget that. Why did you kill those two other women?'

'Statement of fact: this unit has killed no "women".'

'Look, I don't think -' Cwej began.

I ignored him. 'You mean, you haven't killed anybody in London? Apart from trying to kill Cwej?'

'Affirmation: this unit has not yet killed anybody. Affirmation: this unit attempted to kill "Cwej". Exposition: this unit has been recording other disturbances in this environment. These disturbances are subtle, and beyond the scope of this unit's senses. The attempt to kill the unit "Christine" and the attempt to kill the unit "Cwej" were this unit's first direct actions.'

I looked at Cwej. Cwej looked at me.

'So who killed those women?' I asked.

The sphinx reared up on its hind legs inside its circle, like it was getting restless, even if it was just supposed to be a machine with skin. 'Reiteration: other disturbances to this environment have been recorded.'

'Something's followed me here,' said Cwej. 'Something else has gotten into the bottle. Something the sphinx can't get a fix on.'

15

These days, I know what Cwej was worried about. Now I've met some of the other things in the universe, and learnt about the history of intergalactic civilisation. If you can call a bunch of big bangs and invasions a "civilisation".

Cwej's employers had a lot of enemies. Even apart from the Gods, there were plenty of people who had grudges against the time-travellers. As far as Cwej was concerned, any of them could have followed him into the bottle, to beat his people to their safe haven. Over the next couple of weeks Cwej visited a lot of those old enemies, to try to smooth things over now his people had a bigger threat to deal with.

I usually stayed in bed while he went on these missions. Once, I remember him coming home (if you could call the flat inside the bottle "home") with a horrible shocked expression on his face. His features had gone all pale and hard.

He told me he'd been to the home planet of one of his employers' oldest enemies, a race of machine people who, when they died, left their world littered with scraps of tin instead of bits of bone. These machine things were supposed to be the worst killers in the "real" universe, and you could tell it had shaken Cwej up, having to meet with them face to face. It was the thought, I suppose, that now the Gods had turned up these things were meant to be his allies.

'They said my people had dealt with them before,' he was muttering, when he climbed back into bed with me. 'We made a deal with them. Years ago. We even let them build time-machines. I mean ... I mean, it's just...'

'Mmm,' I said, without opening my eyes.

'We didn't even keep to the deal,' he said. 'We tried to wipe them out. Genocide. Can you believe that?'

But I wasn't really paying attention.

16

Yes. That's who I'll dedicate this book to. The machine people. Whatever they're doing now, this story's for them, even if they're nothing but a bunch of mass-murdering robot-things. Because the time-travellers double-crossed them, and they survived anyway. Good for them.

I just wish them luck, when the Gods try to take *their* planet apart.

Notes on Khiste

17/18

I remember having this dream, back when I still dreamt about things apart from collapsing cities, dead children, big fleshy winged things, etc., etc. I used to dream about an old house. Not a real house, not one I'd ever actually been to. A house made out of bits and pieces of all the other buildings I'd ever seen, so there were all kinds of chunks and points and spikes sticking out of the walls.

The house had more floors than you could ever count, all joined together by balconies and sloping passages and spiral stairways. There were no windows, and no lights; the lit parts were just the parts the shadows hadn't closed in on yet. Whole floors of the place were walled off by those shadows. The dungeons, the libraries, and especially the rooms that belonged to the older members of the family.

Oh yes. The family. This dream-house was occupied. Owned by one family, who'd been intermarrying and interbreeding there for so long that now they were just the house's caretakers, a whole race specially bred to see to whatever needs the house had. They'd shuffle through the corridors, great dusty skeletons in rags and monocles, redecorating the house the way it wanted to be redecorated. The caretakers were different every time I had the dream, so if I'd bothered to write anything down then I probably could have put together a whole family tree of the bone people. There was always a family resemblance, though. Sharp pointy smiles, like the skin around their mouths had been cut away with a Stanley knife.

In the beginning of the dream I'd be trying to escape, trying to find my way through the shadows to some kind of exit, but all the time I just ended up getting higher and higher, even though I knew the chances of finding a door to the outside got smaller every time I went up a level. By the end of the dream, everything would have changed. I'd forgotten where I was trying to get to. Because - and here was the surprise *Tales from the Crypt* punchline - by that time I was part of the house, and I was one of the family too. I'd wake up with my fingers in my mouth, just testing to see whether my lips had been taken away.

Chris Cwej never talked about his home, in the fortnight or so that I knew him. So I never found out what kind of house he had on the Homeworld, or who he might have lived with. But every time we got anywhere near the subject, every time he said the word "home", I'd start thinking about the dream. About how Cwej might have looked as one of the family.

Cwej told me about the changes his employers had made to his body, those 'biological advantages' of his, although he never went into the details. I suppose that means he was tied to his new Homeworld by blood. His people were supposed to be able to bring themselves back from the dead, and rebuild their bodies from scratch if they had any kind of nasty accident, so if that had ever happened to Cwej and he'd ended up with a new body built by his employers... well, that'd make him family, wouldn't it?

19

I was in the kitchen again, on my own this time. Cwej had sent me ... no, Cwej had *made a suggestion* that I should go and make some toast. When I'd left him, in the room with the captured sphinx, he'd been starting a new ritual to control the thing. He'd said the sphinx would help him do what he'd come here to do, to open up the bottle to his own universe, and let his employers' survival team in.

'Won't they be noticed?' I'd asked. 'I mean, it didn't take you long to get arrested.'

Cwej had almost looked hurt. 'Everything'll be okay. They're not stupid. They can learn to fit in. We'll work something out.'

I guessed he'd sent me... no, *suggested* that I make toast just to get me out of the way, while he did whatever bad magic he had to do to reprogram the sphinx. I didn't argue, although I had a weird feeling it might all turn out to be part of a great big wind-up. I had this image of Cwej and the sphinx waiting for me to shut the door behind me, and then both bursting out laughing.

'You're going to open the bottle?' I'd asked him, just before I'd left. 'Now?'

Cwej had nodded. 'I've got to talk to the others. If some kind of third party's got into the bottle, we could have problems. If they turn out to be hostile -'

'Hostile,' I'd repeated. I hadn't bothered pointing out that "they" had already killed two women on the streets of London, for whatever reason. That would have made me face the question of whether those people, being parts of a world that wasn't even real, actually mattered at all.

'If they turn out to be hostile,' Cwej had persisted, 'we could have a full-on war to deal with.'

'But if the worst comes to the worst ... ?' I'd asked.

'Then it'll be the end of the world, probably,' Cwej had told me. Trying to sound casual again.

20/21

The end of the world. Of course, back then it was just an expression.

Making toast wasn't as easy as I'd hoped. For a start, Cwej had a very definite place for keeping the bread, and that place was "wherever I put it down last". Also, there was a muffin jammed inside the toaster, one that had got stuck there and never been taken out. Leaving me to scrape away the mould with whatever tools I could get my hands on.

I was just putting the first piece of bread into the toaster when everything changed.

There are some things you can sense, even though you can't say exactly how. Like the way you can tell if a TV set's switched on or switched off, even if the volume's down and you've got your back to it. All of a sudden, I was standing in the kitchen with my ears popping and my skin prickling, and a kind of buzzing feeling in my skull.

Was that it? Was that the bottle opening?

Or was it just the end of the world?

I left the toaster to get on with its job, then headed back along the hall to the room with the sphinx. Whatever it was that had changed, this was where it had happened. All the pressure I could feel was coming from behind that door.

So I opened it. Really, I should have known better than to do something like that.

The spare room was the same as it had been, only ... different. All the walls were in the same places, but one of them, the one on the other side of the room, looked further off than it had done. The perspective had changed, even though the architecture hadn't. The wall was suddenly at the end of a tunnel, miles in the distance, but it was still attached to the two walls on either side of it and neither of them had grown any bigger.

I'm told this is what happens when universes get locked together. The sphinx obviously wasn't bothered by it. Even Cwej looked like he was used to this kind of thing.

And there was a third shape in the room, on the other side of the chalk circle. I got the feeling the man had just finished walking down the tunnel, like the wall had been shifted so far into the distance that whole worlds had been squeezed into the space between here and there, and the new arrival had walked straight out of one of those worlds.

That's how long it takes, I suppose, for your universe to fall to pieces and show you what's underneath. Less time than it takes to make breakfast. Faster than the speed of toast.

As I found out later, the man's name was Khiste. He was a friend, or at least a colleague, of Cwej's.

22/23

A word about Khiste here, seeing as this is the point when he starts to matter.

Like Cwej, he'd been born human (or something like it) and adopted by the time-travellers, who were using him as one of their off-world agents. He'd been working for them longer than Cwej had, though, and he'd had a lot more accidents. His body had rebuilt itself several times over, from the inside out. And every time it had been rebuilt, it had evolved a little, with his cells working out the weak points in his genes and coming up with new twists on his normal shape. It was like his body was building up whole layers of scar tissue around his skin. High-technology scar tissue. It happened like that, apparently, when Cwej's people gave their "advantages" to less advanced races like us. Cwej's employers could regenerate their cells in safety, sure that they'd always end up more or less the same shape as before, but "lesser beings" had less control. The things the aliens put in their agents' blood tended to get over-excited.

By the time I met Khiste, he was hardly a human being at all. He looked more like a knight in armour. There were plates of hard skin across most of his body, and even though he sometimes wore great big suits over it (out of decency?), he really didn't need to. His flesh was like armour now, blue-grey and smooth as a baby's backside, although little wrinkles would pop up whenever you touched it. His arms and legs were as heavy and as powerful as the rest of his body, more like tank parts than limbs. I still don't know, to this day, whether his hands really were as strong as they looked or whether he was just wearing gauntlets. I know he could crush rocks between his pincer-fingers, but so what? That was the kind of thing you'd expect aliens to do.

His head was the worst thing. The first time I saw it, I didn't know whether to jump or laugh. It looked tiny, compared with the rest of his armour-plated body. Like a little insect's head, welded to the top of a war machine. It was a normal-sized human head, of course, but the rest of him was much too big for it. His face wasn't armoured, although it was thin and grey, as if the rebuilding potions inside him had sucked out all the blood and flesh he didn't need. There were studs in his neck, smaller than Frankenstein-bolts but just as noticeable, which I eventually found out acted like extra eyes, seeing kinds of light that normal eyes couldn't see. Oh, and he had hair, scraped back across his head and down the neck of his suit. But the hair looked like wire, like strands of iron, or maybe silver. If you could ignore the pale skin and the machine parts, he didn't look much older than me. He smelt like warm leather instead of machine-oil.

Resculpted man. I must have wondered, even on that first day, whether Cwej would look like that in the end. As it turned out, Khiste had rebuilt himself only three times; God knows what he's going to look like in another century or so, if he's still alive by then. If he really makes himself more efficient with every rebuilding, he'll probably end up as a big armoured ball, covered in weapons hatches. I think he'd like that.

24

I never got on with Khiste. To him, I was a "lesser being". He obviously thought he was better than me, just because he'd leave all kinds of tin toys behind when he finally died, instead of plain old ordinary bones.

Once, while we were in the fortress on Simia KK98 (more about that later), I went ahead and told him exactly what I thought of him. I was having a bad day, that was all. I asked him why he thought he was so fucking great, when he'd been born just the same as me.

Khiste snorted, like he always did when I asked any kind of question (or am I just remembering him as more obnoxious than he really was?).

'How do you *know* how you were born?' he asked.

I didn't tell him the story about the screaming woman in the maternity ward. I just lied, and said I could remember it all. He snorted again.

'The sphinxes made your planet,' he said, hissing through those stainless-steel vocal cords. 'That means they made your whole species. Don't you know that?'

'So?' I said. 'How do you know you're any different? How do you know your universe isn't inside some other kind of bottle? It might be like Russian dolls or something. One universe inside the next one. And that'd make you the same as me.'

'You don't know anything,' he said, practically spitting in my face. I got worried, at the time, because it was easy to imagine him spitting acid instead of plain old flob. Then he stomped off, lumbering away like an animal that wished it'd been bom faster and lighter. Which he had, I suppose. With Khiste, you always got the feeling he'd built up scar tissue on his personality as well as on his skin, to help him cope with his new life.

(Incidentally, I don't know if I mentioned this before, but the name of Dorian's stupid poetry book was *Only Ants and Humans: An Evolutionary Thriller*. No, really. This was all supposed to be some useless metaphor about the race struggle in modern society - American society, natch - on the grounds that ants and humans were the only animals on Earth that attacked each other because of skin colour. In Dorian's world, anyway. But when I think about Khiste in his armour-plated skin, specially grown to help him fight all the other people and things in the universe... no, I'll stop right there. The next thing you know, I'll be saying that Dorian might actually have been right about something. Stupid idea.)

25

It made me think, what Khiste said. I'll own up to that. After all, Cwej had never told me *when* the sphinxes had built my universe. What I mean is, the world as I knew it might only have been made on the 27th of September, and all my memories could have been part of the blueprint.

Back at school, there was this Christian girl who used to cross her arms in history lessons, and sit at the back of the room looking upset while the teachers talked about the way cavemen used to live. As far as she was concerned, the world was only six-thousand years old. One day I asked her how she explained the dinosaurs. She must have been asked that a lot, because she had the answer straight away.

'God made the dinosaur bones,' she said. 'He did it so he could test our faith.'

I'm starting to sympathise with her now. If she ever existed, anyway, and she's not just a made-up memory. I'm sure the Christian girl wouldn't have believed what Cwej and Khiste told me about my universe, if she'd been in my shoes. She probably would have said they were just there to test her faith. And who's to say she'd have been wrong?

26

But the first thing I ever heard Khiste say, standing there in that half-lit room in the flat, was: 'Is that the girl?'

He nodded at me when he said it, with that little grey head of his. Apparently, Cwej had been telling him all about me while I'd been out of the room. Paranoia, paranoia, paranoia.

'Um, yes,' said Cwej, looking from Khiste to me and back again. 'But that's not the important thing right now.'

Thank you, Cwej.

'You're right,' said Khiste. His voice was like metal fillings biting down on tinfoil and no, I'm not sure what I mean by that. 'It's not. You'd better come and see what's happening on the colony. It doesn't look like we're going to have the bottle much longer.'

'Look, this is important,' said Cwej, waving his arms like a mad thing. 'There's a third party here. We could be talking about the end of the whole. . .'

Then he tailed off. I saw his skinny blond eyebrows crinkling up on his face.

'Not going to have the bottle?' he asked.

Khiste sighed, or growled, by rattling the metal-flesh in his throat. He took a great big breath, so his suit stretched to bursting point. 'We're wasting time,' he said.

Cwej bit his lip. Then he looked at me again.

'D'you want to come?' he asked.

'Cwej,' said Khiste. It was obviously meant to be a warning.

'She needs to know,' said Cwej, not facing him. 'She's involved. Christine ... look, I know this is hard. But I really think ... I really think it'd help, you know? If you saw what's out there. It'd help you understand.'

All of a sudden, everybody and everything was looking at me. The sphinx included.

'How do we get out of this ... universe?' I asked. Trying to sound like I was part of this whole operation. Khiste snorted, the first time I'd actually heard him do that, I think.

Cwej reached out for me. It took me a while to figure out that he wanted me to take his hand.

'We walk down the tunnel,' he said. 'Out of the neck of the bottle. You'll probably need a coat, though.'

27

There's this old movie called *A Matter of Life and Death*, which my parents took me to see at a cinema in Hulme when I was fourteen (at least, that's the way I remember things, but why believe any of my memories?). The hero's killed in an aeroplane crash at the start of the film, but there's some kind of mix-up in Heaven, so he gets sent straight back to Earth again. He spends a lot of the film moving between Heaven and Earth, trying to convince the people in both worlds that whatever the rules say, he's got a right to be alive. Which in itself strikes a kind of chord with me.

But what I remember most about the film is this: Earth was in colour, because everybody knows Earth's in colour, and Heaven was in black-and-white to give it that all-important otherworldly feel. Which drove me up the wall, when I was fourteen. The way I saw it - and this is real adolescent reasoning here - Heaven should be more real than Earth, not less. How you could get more colourful than colour I didn't know, but it bothered me for years afterwards. (These are adolescent years, which are about as short as dog years, so you can claim to be old enough to go into pubs even though the rest of the world thinks you're twelve.)

And moving between my universe and Cwej's? How did that feel? You'll just have to take it from me that the walk down the tunnel was a walk between worlds as different as black-and-white and colour, or as different as colour and more-than-colour. And all the time the cramps in my stomach were getting worse, and there was a headache coming together in my skull, like the universe (the "real" one) wanted me to know that not only was colour more colourful where I was going but pain was more painlike as well.

I still don't know what I must look like to the people of the "real" universe, as someone who was born inside the bottle. Do I look like a black-and-white character in a colour film? Or a cartoon character in the middle of a live-action scene, like that bit with the pavement pictures in *Mary Poppins*, only backwards?

28

You might have thought Khiste was unlucky, ending up in that stupid pin-head-ed tank-body. He got a good deal, though, compared with some. Cwej's employers were happy to regenerate themselves pretty much as they liked, but they had other plans for their followers. There were special drugs, which "advantaged" people could take to change the way their bodies would rebuild themselves in the future. I don't know this for a fact, but it wouldn't have surprised me if Khiste had been tak-ing drugs from a little bottle marked "heavy artillery". I know there were drugs like that in Cwej's bathroom, only without labels, so ... make your own guesses.

Cwej's employers had war machines, too. Big floating spheres, like great brass orreries (have I spelt that right? Oh, look it up), all held together with machine-parts too small to believe in. You could see the insides whirring and turning whenever they bobbed across the sky, and every now and then you'd get a glimpse of the pilots through the gaps in the machinery. The pilots would be sealed inside the things for life, wired into the life-support systems there and pumped full of the time travellers' drugs. When the pilots rebuilt themselves, their new bodies would fill up the cracks in the clockwork, until the spheres were perfect cross-breeds of skin and metal.

I thought that sounded cruel, although Cwej said it wasn't hard finding people who *wanted* to be machines, in a universe this size. Well, so much for his employers' policy of non-intervention. Khiste was lucky to keep his face at all, I suppose.

I'd be seeing a lot of machines like that, where I was going. At the end of the tun-nel.

29/30

The planet was called Simia KK98, and apparently it was one of the few colonies Cwej's employers had bothered setting up. Ten minutes after I'd arrived in the "real" universe, once I'd finished gawping at the bottle and Khiste had finished snorting at me, I was standing in the open air and taking in a landscape that looked like the front cover of one of those acid-head "adult" fantasy magazines they used to sell on the top shelf in W. H. Smith's.

The air was freezing, and the sky was psychedelic. There were orange, turquoise and black stripes as far as the eye could see, a kind of aurora you never got on Earth, and it was supposed to make you hallucinate if you stared at it for long enough (that was what Cwej said, anyway, but he was always a lightweight when it came to hal-lucinations). Under the sky, there was just snow, turned blue and gold by the auro-ra. The Technicolor Day-Glo clouds were making thick ripples of shadow on the ground, so it looked like the ice was going up and down all the time, like there were huge fat animals under the surface trying to force their way up into the air.

I felt sick. Later on, I found out that Simia KK98 made people sick even if they were used to the way the "real" universe looked.

And behind me was the one solid feature on the landscape, the building that me and Cwej and Khiste had stepped out of, to join the other armoured men standing on watch outside. The building was a fortress. It looked like a big broken tooth, pushing its way up through the ice and casting a great spiky shadow in front of us. The stuff the building was made of looked like rock, so I thought maybe it had been camouflaged to make people think it was a natural feature, although this was kind of spoilt by the fact that there was no real rock here on the planet.

My breath was making little clouds in front of my face, turned funny colours by the stripes in the sky. Cwej had made me put on a duffel coat and some thick trousers before we'd left his flat, although I don't know where the coat had come from. It smelt of cigarettes and second-hand shops, definitely not his kind of style. I pulled the coat tighter across my neck. My cheeks were starting to sting.

Cwej looked straight up into the sky when we walked out of the building, which is where all his colleagues were looking. Personally, I didn't have the nerve.

'Oh no,' he said.

I almost laughed at that. The understatement. Like it was such a small thing to say, in a place as bright and dangerous as this. If I'd known what he'd been looking at, I would have laughed even more. Probably.

'See what I mean?' Khiste grunted. 'What happens in the bottle isn't an issue any more. They've come to take it back.'

The word "they" worried me, the way Khiste had said it. So, against my better judgment, I looked straight up. Again, I don't know why I do things like that.

Notes on the Siege

31

I've just had another root around in my rucksack, and I can't help noticing that it's a lot emptier than I thought. It was supposed to be what Cwej called a "time capsule", a little cultural survival pod from London, but most of the collection's made up of souvenirs from other planets. Oh well.

I've found another twenty-sixth century newspaper, *The Times* (not the same one as on Earth?), following up the Gods' takeover on Dellah. There's a whole pull-out guide to the crisis, complete with a timeline, charting all the major events from the 22nd of January, 2591 (Professor Begarius of Loughborough University warns of the 'unseen consequences' of Earth's recent imperial policy), through the 18th of November, 2593 (sea serpents spotted on Tyler's Folly: there are monster sightings wherever the Gods go, although I don't know whether sphinxes can swim), all the way up to the 30th of March, 2596 (Earth finally admits that Dellah's a no-go area).

It's almost funny, reading that. Hearing the Earth politicians talking about the Gods as just another bunch of spacemen, maybe hoping to come up with some kind of political answer. The same kind of culture shock "my" version of Earth felt, when the first alien presence went public there on the 7th of October, 1970. Think about

Ted Heath, Prime Minister of Great Britain, going on television in September and talking about the state of the economy. Now think about me, standing on Simia KK98, looking up at the sky and seeing the end of the world coming. Makes Mr. Heath look a bit pathetic, doesn't it?

Another thing I've just pulled out of my bag is a stone paperweight, carved in the shape of a sphinx. Cwej bought it for me on a "planetette" called Cygni 8.6, and there's still a little sticker on the bottom of it that says GUARANTEED HAND-CARVED (which means, I've been told, that it was carved by a machine with hands ... I feel honoured). The sphinx is supposed to look like one of the Gods' servants, the fashionable alien species in 2596, but you can tell the sculptor's never seen the real thing. It looks too solid, like the stone Sphinx in Egypt.

I'm looking at the paperweight, and I'm thinking about the sphinxes in the sky over Simia KK98. I can't see the link between the two, just like I can't see the link between Ted Heath and Cwej's world.

32

It took me a while to work out what Khiste was looking up at, because I'd never seen KK98 before, and I didn't spot the obvious problem. The obvious problem was this:

The Day-Glo stripes in the sky were supposed to be only two colours, turquoise and orange. What I finally noticed was that the single thick black stripe I'd seen was moving faster than the others. All the stripes moved, the same way clouds move, but this one moved with *wings*.

It wasn't the air at all. The black stripe was made up of bodies, thousands and thousands of them, flapping across the sky in such a tight flight-path that you could hardly see the gaps. The stripe went all the way to the horizon, in both directions, and the tip of the fortress very nearly scraped the bottom of it. From ground level you could imagine that the black band went all around the planet, that there were billions of shapes locked together in one big solid ring.

None of the sphinxes looked like they were paying us any attention, but they weren't there by accident, either. They were there so we could see them. So we could see how many of them there were.

'Siege conditions,' Khiste said. He was getting ready for combat, just like the war machine he was.

33

Me and Cwej were the only people on Simia KK98 who still looked human. You couldn't tell what the other armoured men were, or what they'd been. Some of them were like Khiste, with their heads out-flanked by their bodies, but most of them had gone one step further. They'd been working for the time-travellers for so long that they didn't even have proper features. The armour had crept over their heads and smothered their faces. I wondered, in the days after the siege, whether they could still breed in the normal way. With humans, or with each other. In the end, Cwej told me that the reproductive system was supposed to be one of the first things to go, after your body rebuilt itself. (Note the words *supposed to* be'... we'll come back to this later.)

There weren't any of Cwej's employers at the fortress. They didn't like to leave their Homeworld, and it'd be another two weeks before I'd see any of them face to face. When Khiste looked up at the sphinxes and said those two magic words - 'siege conditions' - all the men outside the fortress listened, and turned to go back inside, to man the battle stations or whatever it was they did. Not because Khiste had given them an order, but because he'd been the first one to say what they'd all been thinking. Maybe he was the only one of the soldiers who was still human enough to bother saying it in words.

34

Cwej took my hand, and led me back indoors. All of a sudden, the fortress had come alive. The armoured men were taking up positions around the building, all of them knowing exactly where to go without being told. The tunnels were all the same, as far as I could tell, made of rock that looked like it had opened itself up to make way for the people instead of being burrowed out in the normal way. It was like being inside Ayers Rock, only less ... purple. The rock was mud-coloured, and ridged, so you got the feeling the walls were trying to do an impression of corrugated iron. There were streaks of black wherever you looked, seams of minerals running through all the ceilings and floors. The smell of rock dust everywhere. Dirty, heavy air.

Cwej was leading me along one of the passages that ran around the outer wall, where the floor was a rough slope, so we were spiralling up towards one of the higher levels as we walked. Yes; just like in the dream about the house. There were windows in the walls, one every eight yards or so, like the windows in one of those old Robin Hood castles. Not wide enough to let much light in, but wide enough to shoot out of. There wasn't any glass in the windows, although the building managed to keep the heat in anyway. You could feel warm air all around you in the corridors, like the building was breathing in and out, sucking the atmosphere back into its lungs before anything could get out through the cracks.

There were armoured men in front of most of the windows by now, all of them kneeling in exactly the same position. None of them were carrying guns, but who's to say what kind of weapons they might have had built into their bare hands? The passage was curved, so I kept getting the feeling we were walking round in circles, passing the same frozen statue-people again and again and again.

After a while, I tripped, and my hand slipped out of Cwej's. There was a stitch in my side now, as well as cramps in my stomach, so it felt like somebody was sticking needles through the part of my body where the two pains crossed over. Cwej must have stopped, because I remember staring at his feet, at the rubbery running shoes he'd slipped on just before we'd left his flat.

'Are you okay?' he asked. Sounding helpless for once.

'I want to die or something,' I said.

I didn't look up, but he was quiet for a while, so I guessed he was looking around the corridor. Wondering if he should ask any of the soldiers for help.

'Just a bit further,' he said, in the end.

35/36

Eventually, we came to a stop in front of a window that wasn't already taken. I leant against the wall, safe in the knowledge that if I felt the need to be sick, I could always do it through the opening. Unless the building wanted to breathe that back in as well, of course.

We had a better view of the sphinxes from here. You could just about see the spaces between their bodies now, and make out the shapes of claws and tails and wing tips in the gaps. The sphinxes didn't make a sound, not that you would have heard much anyway, over the metal-feet-on-rock noise that was ringing through the fortress.

'If you just hand over the bottle. . .' I said.

There was a look of pity on Cwej's face, as if he was sorry I didn't understand more about politics in the "real" universe. 'Not really an option,' he said.

'Okay.' My head was starting to click into "science-fiction" mode, which I guessed was probably the best way of dealing with all this. I remembered the evenings I'd spent arguing with Cal, telling him exactly why I thought *The Outer Limits* was crap, and pointing out all the stupid loopholes in his precious Brian Aldiss novels (which I hadn't read, but I was a good guesser). 'You said your people have got time machines,' I said. 'So there's no problem. You can go back in time and ... stop this happening. Somehow. You could get ready for them before they turn up -'

Cwej didn't actually cut me off, but the look he gave me was so sad and pitying that he might as well have done.

'There are rules,' he said, once I'd stopped talking.

'But you've got a way out of here, haven't you? A time machine or something?'

Cwej bit his lip, and turned back to the window. I realised he had his arm around me. Until now, my shoulders had been too cold to notice the body contact. 'We've got a way out, yeah,' he said. 'Look, this is kind of hard to explain. Our ... travel machines ... they work by taking you out of normal space-time, then putting you back somewhere else. Right? We ... um, how can I put this? We have to kind of cut through the different layers of space to get anywhere.'

'So?'

'The sphinxes can mess up space. That means they can shift around the layers. Tie us in knots. Basically, what I'm saying is that if we try to get out of here then they could just lock our machines into a loop.' (As with everything, I'm quoting this from memory, so excuse me if I get the technical details wrong.)

'It's worth a try, isn't it?' I said. 'If you don't have any other way out.'

'No,' said Cwej, not taking his eyes off the sky.

37

Note the way I said that. If *you* don't have any other way out. Like Cwej really didn't have anything to do with me. What was I expecting? For the sphinxes to zoom down on the fortress, kill off all the armoured men, but leave me standing? Call me cynical, but I don't think they'd have been likely to let me off the hook just because I've got skinny legs and a cute arse.

38

The "rules" of time-travel were complicated, and you couldn't get them in a handy little paperback, not like the *Highway Code*. Most of it was in the blood, apparently. It wasn't what you knew, exactly: it was what was in you.

I once tried asking Cwej about this, while we were out shopping one day. It was four days after the sphinx siege, by my reckoning. Back in LONDON!, my peer group used to go on shopping expeditions to Camden every couple of months, which we used to think was a long way away. I did the same kind of thing with Cwej, although the place we went to was Cygni 8.6, which was just on the edge of Earth's empire in the twenty-sixth century.

Cygni 8.6 was almost completely made up of markets. It was like a little bit of Camden had been planted in the dirt there, and it had spread its seeds all over the world, so wherever you looked there were racks of clothing and second-hand-music stalls. All under a sky that for some reason didn't have a proper sun, so you had to do your shopping by starlight. According to Cwej, it was only because the planet was so badly-lit that the first traders had set up shop here, hoping to sell off second-rate merchandise that didn't look so great in the light of day.

There was a reason Cwej had chosen Cygni 8.6 for the shopping trip. The reason was, it wouldn't be there for much longer. It was against his people's rules to warn the locals, but this was going to be the next planet to get taken over by the Gods. Cygni 8.6 was in the same part of space as Dellah, just a few short hops away, on the cosmic scale.

This didn't make sense to me, so I asked Cwej about it. At the time, we were standing in front of a stall that was selling novelty pets, bred on one of the nearby human-run planets. There were dozens and dozens of plastic bags on the stall in front of me, full of what looked like water. I'd been expecting to see goldfish in the bags, like at funfairs.

'Liquid cats,' the woman on the stall had told me.

In the twenty-sixth century "real" universe, people had apparently tried to build machines out of liquid, computers that could store their ideas on drops of water. It had worked, more or less, but the scientists couldn't make the machines smart enough to be really useful. On the other hand, it was pretty easy to give the computers the same kind of brain-power as a house pet. Some of the liquid cats had been let out of their bags as a demonstration, and now they were lying in puddles around the stalls, sloshing around and squishing into each other, so Cwej -

39

Wait a minute. I'm getting mixed up. Let me finish telling you about me and Cwej watching the siege, all right? We'll come back to Cygni 8.6 in a minute, I promise.

'All right,' I said. 'What about the bottle? We could go back inside the bottle.'

'No good,' said Cwej. 'Once the sphinxes get hold of it again, they'll come in after us. Besides, if we could get that many people inside, I wouldn't have had to . . .'

He tailed off. At first, I thought it was because he'd seen something outside, something even worse than the sphinxes. But he was just thinking things through.

'*You* could go back into the bottle,' Cwej said.

I blinked at him. 'Me?'

'You're not ... I mean, you fit in there,' he said, doing his best not to hurt my feelings. 'We could easily get one person back inside.'

He still wasn't looking at me. If I'd been thinking, I would have been grateful that he'd thought about saving me, even though things were looking rough for him and his own kind. At the time, I just shrugged.

Go back in the bottle? Go back home, having spent just a couple of minutes outside? I couldn't imagine living like that, spending the rest of my life knowing I wasn't real, that none of my friends were real, that nothing the human race ever did really mattered. Nixon could put as many men on the moon as he liked. Charles Manson could kill off the whole of showbiz, from Bill Grundy to Elizabeth Taylor. I could spend my whole life snorting spilt coke off the floor of every public toilet in Britain. What difference would it make?

'It's okay,' I told Cwej. 'I'll stick with you.'

40/41

Right. Back to the markets on Cygni 8.6, four days later. Cwej was getting distracted by the liquid cats, so I thought it'd be a good time to ask some tricky questions. I slid one arm inside his jacket, and wrapped myself around his waist.

'So, these rules of time travel,' I said. 'Can I learn them?'

'Um, no,' said Cwej. He picked up one of the bags, and weighed it in his hand, feeling the cat sploshing around inside. 'D'you want one of these?'

'You can mix dye with 'em,' the saleswoman told us. 'Have 'em any colour you like.'

'Why can't I learn?' I asked Cwej.

'You'd need to have stuff done to you,' he said.

'You mean, like those drugs you keep in the bathroom?'

There was a pained kind of look on his face when I said that. He carefully put the bag back down on the stall. 'Have you been messing about with my drugs?' he asked.

'Answer the question.'

'It's not that easy. Look ... the reason my employers are so tough is because of all the things they've pumped into themselves over the years, okay? Their grip on ... time. It's pretty much genetic.' (He whispered the word "time", so the woman at the stall wouldn't hear.) 'I mean, humans are only built to work in three dimensions, you know? Your eyes, your ears, they're made for three-D information. If you can rebuild yourself in the right way, you can rewire your nervous system, so...'

'So you can see in four dimensions?'

'So you can *think* in four dimensions,' said Cwej, eyeing up the saleswoman to make sure she wasn't a spy. She wasn't. She was busy stroking one of her pets with what looked like a cocktail wand. 'That's the only way you can understand the rules.'

'But you can time-travel. You can even take me with you.'

'Well, yeah.'

'So you must know some of the rules.'

He didn't answer. Natch. If he'd said 'well, yeah' again, he'd be admitting that he wasn't as human as he wanted everyone to think. Of course, the old reproductive system still worked, which made me ask myself: was I meant to be one last fling for him, before he lost his breeding power for good?

'So what about this place?' I asked, trying another tack. 'You said we should come here because it won't be around for long.' The woman at the stall glanced up at me when I said that, but she didn't say anything, so she must have just thought I was on narcotics. She was wrong, by that stage. 'Why bother?' I went on. 'You can come here whenever you like, can't you? By going back in time.'

'Yeah,' said Cwej, under his breath. 'So I must still be thinking in three dimensions.'

'Mmm,' I said.

I turned away from the stall. Then I froze.

'Cwej?' I said.

'Yeah?' he said.

'I think I just stepped in a kitten,' I told him. 'Help.'

42

I've seen some of the things Cwej's employers make, by the way. And their statues look weird, compared with the ones on Earth. Like there are patterns in them we poor sod humans can't see properly. It's only when you remember what Cwej said, about thinking in four dimensions, that you start to figure out why.

The statues are made so that when they get old and fall apart, they still look artistic. Decay's all part of the design. Even the time-travellers' ruins are well planned.

I bet their skeletons look fantastic.

43/44

Four days earlier, in the sky over Simia KK98, the sphinxes had stopped moving. They were just hanging there, hovering, with their wings still flapping away. If I'd been ten years younger, I probably would have tried counting them. I probably would have given up somewhere after the first two thousand.

From the window, you could see some of the ledges that had grown out of the side of the fortress. Great flat spikes of rock, like those cliffs the coyote's always falling off in Road Runner cartoons. There were men on the ledges, armoured men, sitting on horseback. That's how I remember them now, anyway. Like knights, perching on horses that had been covered in the same blue-grey armour plating. I can't really imagine the people in the fortress keeping horses, though, so I might be mis-remembering things. The shapes on the ledges definitely had four legs, but whether they were things being ridden or just agents of the Houses who'd grown themselves much bigger and heavier bodies, I can't say for sure. It'd make sense, I suppose, to turn yourself into a centaur. If all your weapons are built into your body, then a bigger body can pack more firepower. There could have been whole nuclear generators in the guts of those horse-people.

Even now, none of the men had opened fire. The planet was quiet, apart from the sound of the wind. The sphinxes were staring down at the fortress, and the fortress was staring up at the sphinxes.

'What are they waiting for?' I asked Khiste.

Cwej had left me, just after our conversation about going back into the bottle. He'd spotted Khiste in the tunnel, and told the pin-head to look after me. Then he'd bounded away up the slope of the passage.

Khiste snorted, more at the sphinxes than at me this time. 'They don't have to rush things. We don't even know if our defensive systems are going to scratch them.'

'So they're trying to psych us out?'

'Maybe. Doesn't really matter.'

I gave Khiste a withering look. He didn't wither. Six-and-a-half-foot-tall people with metal skins usually don't. 'So you don't care about their tactics? I thought you were supposed to be a soldier.'

'Not a soldier,' Khiste snapped. And when I say snapped, I mean, teeth-like-a-mantrap snapped. 'This isn't an army. We're just here to keep watch on the bottle.'

'But you still don't care about the sphinxes' tactics?' I asked, sticking to the only good point I thought I had.

Khiste shrugged. Chunks of armour the size of dinner plates ground together around his shoulders. 'It doesn't make a difference what they do. We can't fight them.'

'So we just sit here and die, is that it?'

'Don't be stupid,' said Khiste. 'We've sent for reinforcements. There's warships on the way from the Homeworld. We just have to hope the sphinxes aren't smart enough to figure that out. We might get lucky. They're not built to think for themselves much.'

'Oh,' I said. 'Is that where Cwej went, then? To send for help?'

'I sent for help,' Khiste grunted. 'While you and Cwej were busy screwing around in your world.'

I didn't know what to say to that, seeing as it wasn't true. Not at that point, anyway.

'He's got a thing about two-dimensional women,' Khiste added.

45

I'd like to be able to say I kept my dignity after that, and gave Khiste a piece of my mind. I didn't, obviously. As if to prove his point, I did what any two-dimensional character would have done. I stomped off, and went to find Cwej, who'd become the one thing in this world - no, in this *universe* - I felt I could safely cling on to. Whether I was screwing him or not.

If I'd known where Cwej had actually gone, after he'd left me... well, I suppose I night have thought twice. I don't know. But he didn't give me any clues about what he was up to. He didn't say, for example, 'excuse me a moment, I'm just going outside to talk to the sphinxes face to face'.

46

It's only just struck me, how much of this story sounds like a bad LSD trip. Those of you who still think I'm on a long-term high will be wondering whether the whole thing's a hallucination. I mean, is it really a coincidence that I somehow ended up on the only psychedelic planet in the galaxy?

Well, maybe that's a point. Maybe this isn't a story at all. Maybe this whole book's just a list of the states of mind I was in when I wrote it, like a catalogue of all the things I've been putting into my system. Paranoia for cocaine. Multicoloured planets for acid. I'll be relaxed again soon, so you'll think I'm writing it on dope.

Notes on the Face-Off

47

Imagine this:

There's a spire. and it's made out of solid gold, because the people who made it don't know about money and can get whatever materials they want from any time zone they can I think of. The spire's built for travelling through space, and it looks aerodynamic, even though it doesn't need to be. There aren't any fins and there aren't any booster rockets, although the gold's been twisted into a kind of corkscrew at the nose-end, like the ship has to burrow its way to wherever it's going.

Now imagine you're getting closer to the spire. So close that you can see the bodywork in detail, and you can see that it's not solid at all. It's like a cat's cradle of beams and arcs, all solid gold, woven together so tightly that there's no way you could untie the knots even if you had pincer-hands like Khiste's. You get even closer, so you can see right into the black spaces between the slats. And they are black, completely black, no way of seeing through the spire to the other side. You're looking at the big black heart of the ship, that's why.

It's about now that you start to work out how big the ship is. You're further away than you thought, and each of the gold beams is as wide as a house, so you can see blurry little figures moving about inside the framework. Figures in robes that make them look like monks, moving up and down and in and out and left and right across the ship. So how big's that big black heart? Bigger than you can get a grip on. And it's throbbing against the gold bars, trying to get out. Getting ready to bleed. You can tell, you can just tell, that one pump's going to be enough to push the ship halfway across the galaxy.

And if the heart breaks? Then all its power's going to be let out at once. Black lightning's going to burst over the metal. The ship's going to be the eye of a storm, and the storm's going to be big enough to tear up whole worlds.

Now imagine there isn't just one of these things in front of you. There are a dozen. A hundred. A thousand. Maybe more.

That was the kind of help Khiste had sent for, from his employers' Homeworld. That was what was on its way to Simia KK98.

Apparently.

48/49

I didn't know where I was going. I just kept walking, up the helter-skelter passage that ran around the fortress, past all the identical windows and identical soldiers, none of whom even noticed I was there. (By the way, did I mention that there weren't any female agents on the planet? Not as far as I could tell, anyway. It's funny, but I never thought about it while I was there.) Eventually, I found Cwej, mainly because I couldn't really have missed him.

There was a space in the outer wall, an archway, where the rock had opened itself up to let the light in. There was a bust set into the wall above the arch, a carving of a man's head and shoulders, glaring down like one of those gargoyles I remember throwing stones at on the school French trip to Notre Dame. The man was wearing a crown on his head, and there was a huge collar behind his neck, with shoulder pads so big they looked like armour. It was my first sight of one of Cwej's employers, I suppose, although the face had been made out of the same rough rock as the passage so that you couldn't make out the details of the face. At the time I wondered whether Cwej's employers actually looked like that, or whether they just wanted people to think they were faceless, the same way they wanted people to think they were nameless.

The ledge was a kind of pier, stretching out from the hole in the wall, ending in a point like another one of those Road Runner clifftops. There was no railing, nothing to stop anyone going over the edge. The archway was filled with sky, with those glowing orange-and-turquoise stripes. From here you couldn't see the ground. The only solid things in sight were the sphinxes.

At this height, the sphinxes weren't just a black mass. You could see the fingers clawing at the air, and the big glassy heads lolling backward and forward. Cwej was standing close to the end of the pier, staring up at them with his back turned to the arch. He had his hands stuffed into the pockets of his jacket. I got the feeling he was trying to look casual. The wind was blowing his little blond hairs in all directions, and his jacket was flapping around his waist, but somehow it never managed to blow any frost through the archway. Cwej looked wrong, standing there against the shiny sky. Like he was the only normal thing there, like his picture had been cut out of a newspaper and pasted on to the cover of one of Cal's cheap SF novels.

He hadn't seen me. When he finally said something, it wasn't me he was talking to.

'I suppose you can hear me,' he said, and his voice got buffeted around by the wind.

I didn't know what he thought he was doing. He'd got the sphinx to talk to him back in his flat, but only because he'd trapped it inside the circle. Here, he didn't even have any little pieces of hardware to use as crucifixes.

'Face to face,' Cwej added. 'If, you know, that's okay with you.'

The next thing I knew, there were new shapes blotting out the light from the archway. I counted about six of them. Six sphinxes, dropping out of their column, leaving holes in the middle of the black band. Slowly, and quietly, they got into position around the ledge.

The pier was surrounded. Cwej was surrounded. Half a dozen blank faces were staring at him, some of them floating just a few feet from his body, some of them hovering yards away. They were all focusing on him, so you could see his face reflected six times over in the lenses. The sphinxes kept flapping their wings, not making a sound, but other than that they didn't move.

I took a step back. So did Cwej.

For a few seconds more, nothing happened. Cwej looked down at his feet, then back up at the sky, then into the big glass eye of the nearest sphinx. He cleared his throat, and the wind carried the little grunting noise straight to me.

'I expect you're wondering why I've called you here,' he said.

I seem to remember the sphinxes turning to look at each other. But that would've been silly, wouldn't it?

'I want to talk to your leader,' Cwej said. 'Can I do that?'

50

There are all kinds of rumours about the place the sphinxes come from. We might as well call it "sphinx-space", which is what Cwej always called it. Who started the rumours, nobody knows, seeing as nobody's ever come back from sphinx space alive. Except for Cwej's Evil Renegade, of course.

(Don't you love that expression? 'Nobody's ever come back alive.' Like the Gods keep sending back dead bodies, with little notes attached. Well, maybe they do. I never asked.)

Even though sphinx-space has been twisted out of shape by the Gods, the stories say there's still a planet in the middle of it all. And on each side (hemisphere???) of the planet there sits, or stands, or floats, a great big sphinx. These two huge sphinxes are supposed to be the mother and father of all sphinxkind, although the rumours are in two minds about whether they're actually the Gods themselves, or just the Gods' own personal lapdogs. But all the stories say that one of these ultra-sphinxes is black ('as dark as a black hole', according to Professor Begarius of Loughborough Univer-sity) and one of them is white ('as bright as a supernova'. . . ibid., whatever ibid.'s supposed to mean).

It makes me think of that story about the white and red dragons they used to tell us at nursery school. I suppose that's the way it is with stories. You need these big contrasts.

The important thing is that these sphinxes are so huge, they can make whole worlds in the blink of an eye. So huge that their worshippers have started building cities under the glass of their face-screens.

Professor Begarius' theory says that sphinx "society" is based on a stupidly complex set of rules, and that these two great big sphinxes - the Kings of Space - are the ones who make judgments about sphinx law. But after what Cwej told me about the rituals, about "programming" the sphinxes, I've got my own ideas. If I've understood this properly, then the sphinxes are like computers, or maybe like solid versions of the "programs" computers run on. In which case, I think the Kings of Space (if they really exist) are just the bodies used by the computer's central databank, or whatever the most crucial part of a computer's programming is supposed to be called. That's what I think, anyway, and I'm the important one.

51

Cwej was always the diplomatic one among his people. That was his purpose, as far as they were concerned. I told you, didn't I, about the morning he came back from the planet of the machine people? I can't forget the way he looked then, the shock on his face, the horror of knowing who he'd been talking to. Dealing with the sphinxes was nothing compared with that.

I remember how he felt that morning. The tension in him, when he climbed back into bed and pressed himself up against me. When we had sex, it felt like he was doing it because he had to, not because it made him happy. Because he felt like he'd been touched by the machine people, and needed to get that machine-ness out of him. "Mechanical" is pretty much the only word for what we did.

Afterwards, he lay next to me and talked non-stop for about an hour, about the deal he'd had to make with the machines. I was half asleep, so all I can remember is a dream that didn't make sense, spiced up with snatches of Cwej-speak. In the voice-over of the dream, Cwej told me about the *other* deal his people had made with the machines, thousands of years earlier. About how his employers had let the machines invent time-travel, but only a simple kind. About how they'd promised not to scoop any of the machines out of time for their own entertainment, like they did with so many other races in the days before they knew better.

And in return ... no, I don't remember what the machines promised in return. All I remember is that after Cwej's visit, there was a brand-new treaty signed between the two planets. All allies together against the Gods.

I remember Cwej telling me where he thought everything had started to go wrong. The point when his people had really compromised their principles, for the first time in thousands of years. He said: 'It was that day on the ledge. When I went out to talk to the sphinxes. Fuck, what was I *doing*?'

52/53

'Question: leaders?' said the sphinxes. All six of them said it at the same time, changing the whole shape of the air around them, bending the wind into one big chorus of words. Even Cwej looked surprised at the force of it.

'The ones who give you your orders,' he explained. 'The ones who speak for ... um, the Kings of Space.'

It took the sphinxes a while to answer. Perhaps they were all trying not to laugh.

'Programming detail: all units speak for each other,' they said. I don't think they were speaking in time because they were telepathic, or anything like that. I got the feeling they were doing it because they were all sharing the same program. Mind you, I got the same feeling from the men in the fortress.

Cwej folded his hands behind his back. 'So if I talk to you now, your leaders are going to know about it?'

'Proposition: no discussion is necessary. Statement of fact: property has been stolen. Statement of intent: property will be reclaimed.'

'It wasn't us who stole it, though,' Cwej told them.

'Statement of fact: property has been stolen.'

'But we don't need to do it like this,' said Cwej, in a pleading kind of voice that made him sound very, very little. 'We don't want a fight or anything. Look ... your employers. The Gods out of, er, sphinx-space. They're renegades, right? They aren't allied with the other Gods. I mean, they don't care what's happening on Dellah.'

It took the sphinxes a while to unscramble his English. 'Statement: there are no renegades among God units. Second-ary statement: there is only self-interest. Clarification: the God units designated "Kings of Space" have no interest in the activities of those God units in the region of the planet designated "Dellah". Secondary clarification: the Kings of Space have no interest in the universe outside the area designated "sphinx-space".'

Cwej went 'hah', and clapped his hands. The sphinxes got a bit flustered by that, like they didn't understand the body language. 'So you *don't* care about the other Gods. That's what I thought. Listen, my people aren't worried about you. It's the rest of the Gods we've got a problem with. That's why we wanted to keep the bottle, after ... um, we rescued it. We want to get out of the way of the other Gods. We want to be left in peace. That's all.'

The sphinxes all bobbed their heads. Like they'd decided to end the conversation.

'Wait, wait,' said Cwej. 'Listen to me. All we want is the bottle. We want to put ... some of our people, some of our culture, on Earth. I mean, the Earth inside the bottle. That's all. Can't we come to some kind of arrangement here?'

The sphinxes considered this. Perhaps it just took them a while to remember what "Earth" was.

'Reply: there is nothing your units have which is of interest to our units. Suggestive secondary reply: nothing your units would offer.'

There was a long, long pause. I got the feeling the sphinxes were testing the water, seeing what Cwej would do. As it happened, Cwej just nodded a bit.

'Go on,' he said.

'Statement of fact: the Kings of Space have an interest in certain fields of knowledge in which your units specialize. Specification: time.'

'Ah,' said Cwej.

He left it at that, for a while. He paced across the width of the ledge, occasionally kicking at loose chips of rock at his feet, just to watch them tumble over the edge and down to the ground. (Cwej on the edge of the ledge. Now, there's a mantra for you.)

Finally, he looked up.

'All right,' he said. 'Let's talk.'

54

This was wrong. How did I know this was wrong?

Cwej's people never, ever, *ever* swapped their secrets with other races. It was a fact of life. Something so basic, it felt like I'd known it even before I'd been told. Like the Houses' control over space and time went so deep that one bad decision could make everyone in the universe feel ill.

How much of history gets decided like that, I wonder? In my world, or the "real" one? One of the time-travellers sneezes half a universe away, and whole wars start down on Earth. I'd like to think that this explains all the things I lived through in London. I'd like to think that the reason I've spent so much of my (remembered) life blowing and snorting my brains out is that I was trying to get over the shame of Cwej's employers, trying to shake the guilt they've always felt about the things they did in their past, when they were a lot younger and a lot more careless with their time-travelling. It's like original sin, I suppose. The oldest civilisation suffers, so we have to suffer along with them. We have to live out their nightmares, and deal with all their paranoia.

But I don't suppose any of this is true. I'm just trying to find excuses for everything I've ever done, all those mornings waking up sick with the taste of vomit in my mouth, all that time spent mixing Space Dust with the cocaine (for that extra adolescent buzz and no, it doesn't work, but I had to try). I don't think I can blame Cwej's employers for everything. Or the Gods, even.

55

Another conversation between me and Cwej, while we were lying on our backs looking up at the stars:

'How can the sphinxes do that, though?' I said. 'How can they just mess up the whole shape of the universe?'

'You mean, by making sphinx-space? Er. . .' Cwej mulled it over for a while. 'I don't know. Maybe it was always meant to happen that way. You know? Maybe there's something in nature that says things like the Gods have got to be there.'

'Like an appendix,' I said.

Another long pause from Cwej. 'Um ... ?'

'An appendix,' I said. 'Part of your body that doesn't really do anything except go wrong and give you gut-ache. Maybe that's what sphinx-space is. Maybe it's like the universe's appendix.'

'Right,' said Cwej. He sounded like he thought I'd gone a bit strange.

(We had a lot of conversations like that. If I've got space later on, I'll tell you Cwej's story about visiting a planet run by intelligent numbers. 'They were all between seventeen and eighteen,' he said. 'All the really complicated bits came after the decimal point.' You'll laugh, believe me.)

56/57

Now imagine this:

The warships, those twisty golden spire things I was talking about earlier, are burrowing their way through space towards Simia KK98. They used to have this story on Earth, which I never really believed, about the Great Wall of China being the only man-made thing you could see from space (why you should be able to see that, I don't know, seeing as it wasn't any wider than my old flat). Stick with that image for a moment. Stick with it while the warships get closer, because it's the best way of imagining what the pilots can see from up there on the other side of the atmosphere.

There's a line all the way around the planet, like an equator that's been drawn out in marker pen, all black and shiny. Then, when you get closer, the equator looks up at you. You can see billions and billions of dots of light, where the sunshine's glinting off the face-screens. Finally, some of the dots break away from the line. They're coming. Some of the sphinxes are coming, to eat their way into the warships.

Down in the clouds, the battle's already started. Those brass-coloured spheres I told you about, remember them? Spheres with pilots who've grown into the machinery. The spheres are rolling across the sky, trying to pick off the sphinxes that are breaking out of the formation. The sphinxes do their best to strike back, but it's not easy. The spheres, and the spheres' pilots, have got the blood of the time-travellers in them. A pilot stretches an arm, and his sphere stretches too, right into the middle of next week. One of the sphinxes twists space, tries to get a grip on the sphere, but the machine's already dragging itself into another time-zone.

This is a bad thing. The sphere pilot is halfway between one time and another, so right now only half of him is in the real world. But the sphinx is being tugged through time with him, so the two of them are getting scrambled together, and the sphinx's flesh is leaking into the cogs and gears of the machine. There's one object where there used to be two. A big black smear gets stretched along the timeline.

It must take months to unscramble a mess like that.

Meanwhile, the warships are closing in, meeting up with the breakaway sphinxes that the spheres haven't managed to deal with. One of the sphinxes sinks its teeth into the first of the ships, not that it's actually got teeth as such (no, don't ask about my leg, please). Space stretches. A gap opens up in the side of the ship. While the men in robes get sucked out into the dark, little bubbles of flesh pop out of the hatchways of the other ships, and start clustering around the damaged parts. The bubbles were probably human once, but since then they've been forced to rebuild themselves in the vacuum, so they're not held back by things like lungs any more. These are Swiss-army-knife people, who can spew out fluid that seals up holes as quickly as the sphinxes can spew out raw space.

You might be wondering how I know all this, seeing as I was on the ground when it happened. The truth is, Cwej told me. I know he wasn't there either, but if there was one thing Cwej was good at, it was describing space battles. Besides, there are so many faulty details in this story already that I didn't think you'd mind a few more distractions.

58/59

So there was Cwej, talking to the sphinxes about the secrets of his people. And there was me, standing in the passageway, watching history being made in front of my eyes.

I felt I had to say something. I wasn't sure what.

'Cwej?' I tried.

Cwej whipped round on his heels, almost falling off the ledge when he did it. The sphinxes stretched out their necks, until my own pale, skinny, empty-looking face was staring back at me six times over.

'Christine,' Cwej said. 'Listen, you shouldn't -'

He didn't bother finishing the sentence. A second later, his face had gone from "surprised" back to "serious". He turned to look at the sphinxes again, without saying another word to me.

'She isn't important to you,' Cwej said. 'I'm the one you want to talk to. You want to know about time-travel, is that it?'

'Reply: these units are interested in the concept,' chanted the sphinxes.

'All right,' said Cwej. 'Here's the deal. We get to use the bottle. We don't want all of it, we just want to be able to get to Earth and back. But the bottle still belongs to you. You can guard it, if you like. As long as you never let the other Gods get their hands on it. Okay?'

The sphinxes didn't answer. They were waiting to hear the other half of the deal.

'I can't speak for all my people,' said Cwej. 'My, er, employers can tell you what they've got to offer. I don't know the details, I'm not an expert, but ... you can have what you're after, basically.'

'Rejection: this deal is too vague.' Was it just me, or did the sphinxes sound angry? No, it was just me.

'But this isn't the deal,' said Cwej. He looked so frustrated, he was practically stamping his feet. 'All I'm saying is, we promise we'll *make* a deal. We can sort things out later. We have to stop this fighting, that's all. You can have what you want. I promise.'

The sphinxes thought about this for a moment. I absolutely didn't hear them muttering among themselves, whatever I might remember now.

'Question: your units give their word that negotiations will take place with regard to supplying time-technology to the Kings of Space?'

'Yes,' said Cwej. He was almost screaming by now. 'Just say you'll deal with us. Please. Before the warships get here.'

Even while he was saying it, things were happening. The sky was getting dark. The psychedelic stripes were fading away. Something black and heavy was forcing its way through the clouds from the other side of the atmosphere.

From where I was standing, I could see the side of Cwej's face. I could see him looking up at the sky with his mouth dropping open. Like he wanted to tell the sphinxes to hurry up and make a decision, but thought he'd sound stupid saying it.

'Decision: the conditions are acceptable,' the sphinxes said. Then, and only then, they swivelled their necks to watch what was happening up above them.

Notes on Afterwards

60

I don't know what it was that filled up the sky over Simia KK98. At the time I thought it was the sphinxes, coming down to the fortress in their billions, like the locusts in that part right at the end of the Bible where God freaks out and everybody dies. But the sphinxes weren't expecting it, I don't think. So it must have been Cwej's employers.

That worries me, and I'll tell you why. It's because I've seen the time-travellers' warships, and they're gold and spiky, not fat and black. Which means one of two things. Either the warships were just an escort, bringing something even worse to Simia KK98 to face down the sphinxes, which is bad enough in itself. Or ... or ... the warships had already fired up their weapons by the time they got to the planet. That's how the ships work, I've heard. Everything goes black, and then the world ends.

Which means that Cwej's employers, who were supposed to be the good guys in this face-off, were ready to let their warships wipe out everything on the planet. Us included. They've apparently done that before, sterilized (or do I mean cauterized?) whole satellites if they think there's some kind of threat to the grand order of things.

Would they have done that? Killed all of their agents, and even sacrificed the bottle? It makes sense, in a kind of if-we-can't-have-it-nobody-can way. Or am I getting paranoid again?

61

It was only the next day, when the world I knew about had come back again and I was sitting drinking chocolate in the flat, that I asked Cwej about the deal he'd done.

'If the sphinxes get time machines, won't they mess everything up?' I asked him. 'You know. Do damage to the space-time continuum, or whatever.' (I always used to say 'or whatever' at the end of sentences like that, just so I didn't sound like I was taking the whole time-travel thing seriously. Even if it was supposed to be real now.)

He sipped at his chocolate, although he must have known it was too hot for him. 'Doesn't make much difference,' he said, once he'd finished making slurping noises. His voice was quiet, maybe even a bit on the broody side. 'I think the universe is finished. I mean, my universe. I think that's the bottom line here. Pretty soon, nowhere's going to be safe. If the sphinx-gods get their hands on time travel, it's not going to change much. They're not interested in the rest of the universe anyway. Just their patch.'

'And your people go along with this, do they?'

Another shrug. 'They okayed the deal. I'll be putting my name on the treaty, pretty soon.'

'Cynical,' I said. I was stirring my own drink with a teaspoon, watching the chocolate flakes dissolve on the sur-face and wondering if it was supposed to be a metaphor for something.

'Maybe I'm just starting to think in four dimensions,' Cwej told me. Back then, of course, I didn't know what he meant.

62

Two hours before that, as I think I mentioned before, I was crawling around on the floor of Cwej's bathroom and wishing I had the nerve to make myself throw up.

We'd got back to the bottle at about ten o'clock in the evening, the 28th of September, 1970. Before we'd left Simia KK98, Khiste had started taking the piss out of Cwej for wanting to stick with me and wanting to go back to the flat inside the bottle. I think Khiste saw me as being like one of those rubber woman-shaped dolls you can get in Soho. Something for Cwej to take his frustration out on, without getting involved in a "real" relationship.

That hadn't made Cwej happy. It hadn't made much of an impression on me, though, because by then I was so sick and tired that I probably wouldn't have felt much if I'd been hit by a bus. Name-calling wasn't going to have much of an impact.

As soon as we'd got back to the flat, Cwej had headed straight for the kitchen, and forced me to eat something. He'd pretty much ignored the sphinx in the spare room, just telling it to close the passage out of the bottle. He'd shut the door to that room behind us, and tried to pretend that it was perfectly normal for someone to have a sphinx in the house, like it was a television or a washing machine or any other mod con.

I hadn't felt like eating, even though my stomach lining had practically been chewing itself up by then. Cwej had talked me into swallowing whatever he could get his hands on, more cereal, more toast, pieces of celery stuffed with peanut butter (most of Cwej's recipes involved peanut butter). He'd watched me like a hawk while I'd sat in the spare bedroom and chewed, just in case I tried stuffing any of the food down the back of the headboard.

He'd put me to bed after that. I hadn't slept. The cramps in my stomach had got worse, and the food hadn't helped. I'd ended up convincing myself that the peanut butter had poisoned me, that Cwej had spiked it with some kind of drug, to turn me into one of the armour-plated beetle-people from the fortress. Or worse. I'd imagined wings bursting out of my back, and that was before I'd even read the cutting from *Fate* magazine.

63/64

I never did manage to make myself sick, which is probably a good thing. Once I'd finished leaning over the toilet bowl, I turned on the strip lighting and leant against the sink, feeling dizzy at having to stand upright again. I remember looking at my reflection in the bathroom mirror, all pale and blurry, just the way it had looked in the face of the sphinx. Like the wind had changed direction and I was stuck that way for good.

Cwej was waiting for me in the hallway when I left the bathroom. He was leaning against the wall opposite the bathroom door, with his eyebrows raised. The same look policemen are meant to give you when you've been the victim of an accident, and they want you to think they're sympathetic.

'You're not going to be okay, are you?' he asked.

I shrugged. Cwej looked ... pained. I suppose that's the word.

'I could make you forget,' he said. 'I mean, my people could. We've got ways of doing that. Chemicals. To break down the memory acids.'

"Memory acids" sounded like the kind of medical slang Cwej would just make up on the spot, but I got the idea. 'I thought you said I was involved,' I said.

'You've had a shock,' Cwej told me. (What, just the one?) 'We could make you forget. It's just... the technique's not totally reliable. Bits of memories get stuck in the back of your head. You wouldn't know about any of this, most of the time. But. . .'

He paused. I could tell he wanted me to say 'but what?', so I'd feel like I was part of the conversation instead of just being lectured to. I did what he wanted. As ever.

'You might have dreams.' Cwej went on. 'About the sphinxes. About seeing your world from the outside. And you'd start getting paranoid. You might not be able to look at anything without having ... that feeling, you know? You'd suffer. Psychologically.'

'You mean, I've got less of a chance of going mad if I know what's happening,' I said. Or at least I said *something* like that, although I probably wasn't so lucid. My stomach was still killing me.

Cwej stepped forward. He tried to make the action look casual, but I could tell, even while he was reaching out for me, that this was all part of the "reassurance" programme he'd been taught by whatever people had taught him to be a soldier. I didn't care. He held out his hands, palms up, and I held on to them. I felt myself stumble forward, like my body wasn't sure whether this was a good time for a hug or not.

'I want to help you,' he said. 'I mean that. I really, really mean that.'

65

They say that kidnap victims, female kidnap victims, sometimes end up falling in love with the people who are holding them prisoner. It's not surprising, is it? The kidnappers are the only things those women have got to hold on to. The only things they can touch.

It's the same with cults. If you took all the cult leaders who were around in 1970, all the gurus and hippies and terrorists, I don't think any of them would have been as convincing as Chris Cwej. He'd been trained by people who weren't human, who could see people from the outside and spot all the stupid little flaws in the way they acted. And the irony is, he really *did* want to help me. He just wanted to help me in a way that involved my clinging on to him all the time, him and nobody else.

He tried to keep me away from my friends, and he tried to keep me away from my own home. Back then, I thought it was just because he didn't want the "knowledge" to spread. Oh yes, make no mistake, on my home planet the secret of the universe was contagious.

66

I said I didn't sleep, that first night after I'd come back from the universe outside. That's not strictly true, now I come to think about it. I slipped away a couple of times, but never for more than a minute or two, so I spent most of the early hours of the morning in that state when your brain doesn't need any help to start seeing things. Not hallucinating, but being so scared of hallucinating that you end up seeing little spider-people anyway.

That morning I saw the world the way the Gods would have seen it, the same way I'd seen it in the dream, the one I'd had the night before. The planets were great big collections of leftovers, with the sphinxes perched on top of all the gravestones, or wrapping their tails around the spires of the churches. But this time the perspective was different. I was looking at the universe from the outside, so I could see that even the planets, even the stars, were just more pieces of "stuff" the Gods had shifted around.

This time, of course, I knew it was true. The universe really *had* been made for the Gods' benefit, and all the things my race had left behind were just parts of the collection inside the bottle. But in all the time I spent with Cwej, I never got over the feeling that it went further than that. That even his world, his "real" universe, had been put there to keep someone or something happy. And who's to say I was wrong (apart from Cwej, who quite often did say I was wrong)? Cwej never could tell me exactly what was on the outside of *his* universe.

67

That afternoon - after a morning spent dozing in Cwej's living room, drifting in and out of sleep while the Labour Party conference went on in the background and Bert Foord read out the weather forecast - Cwej and I went out for a walk together. He said he thought it'd be a good idea for me to get some fresh Earth air back into my system. Something about the way the blood works.

We ended up in Leicester Square, drifting across the road from the underground station and along Cranbourne Street, past the boutiques and the "special interest" bookshops, up towards the cinemas. The roads were clogged up with black cabs, the way they usually were, and at least half of the passers-by were tourists. It was warm, for that time of year. There was prickly orange sunlight beating down on my right side, cold wind coming in from the left, so I just slung "my" duffel coat over one shoulder and kept walking. Running hot and cold at the same time, the same feeling I used to get from a buzz, before I ended up not feeling anything.

There was a street performer who'd made a space for himself on the pavement outside Leicester Square Gardens, in the big gap between the cinemas. The tourists were gathering around him in a semicircle, taking photos while he waved his arms and shouted. I think he was a street performer, anyway, although most of what he did was just shouting. I suppose he might have been a preacher, like one of the end-of-the-world-is-nigh people you used to see in Hyde Park before the world ended and surprised the lot of them.

If I'd thought about it, I might have pushed the man out of the way and told all the tourists the truth, two weeks before they found out the important bits for them-selves. Not that it would have changed anything. On the 29th of September, while the sunlight was making the railings sparkle and lighting up the posters for *Women in Love*, from my point of view everything was suddenly part of one big doll's house. Cwej bought me a cardboard cup full of Coca--Cola from a street vendor, and I remember being surprised by the logo on the side, like it'd make more sense for it to say ACME and for the man who sold it to me to have a little "Made in England" sticker on his back.

68

We stopped by a bench in the gardens. We were opposite the statue of Shakespeare, who used to stand on top of a fountain with a marble scroll in his hands, carved with the words THERE IS NO DARKNESS BUT IGNORANCE. And that made me laugh, because there was at least one other kind of darkness I knew about - made up of the bodies of sphinxes - and I'm pretty sure that even Shakespeare would have picked ignorance if he'd known about it. Cwej had bought a copy of the *Standard* from the newsstand outside the tube station, so now he start-ed to flip through it, frowning at most of the pages.

'What're you looking for?' I asked him.

'Um,' said Cwej, which was his usual answer when he didn't want to talk about something.

'More specific,' I said.

Cwej fixed his eyes on something in the paper, doing his best to look interested. 'Anything that doesn't look normal. Any clues. There's something else here on Earth, remember. That third party the sphinx told us about. We're going to have to help the sphinxes figure out what it is.'

"Help" the sphinxes. What a concept. I looked around the gardens, watching the students from St. Martin's rolling around on the grass and flirting with each other.

'I was going to ask you,' I said. 'The third party's the thing that's been doing the killings, yeah?'

'Mmm,' said Cwej.

'But the papers are saying that whoever's doing it is like Charles Manson or someone.'

'Mmm,' Cwej added.

'So,' I said. 'So I thought, is it maybe possible that...'

69

I can't believe I said it. I can't believe I actually asked whether Charles Manson, whose followers had hacked up nine innocent Hollywood lounge lizards (one preg-nant movie actress among them), might have been some kind of alien. Luckily, I don't remember how Cwej reacted. I must be blotting the embarrassment out of my memory.

Romance. If "romance" is the word. Hammer Horror romance, the kind that makes people think Jack the Ripper was a vampire or a magician or a science experiment gone wrong. I'd say things don't happen that way in the real world, but the truth is that the "real" world is exactly where they *do* happen. They just didn't happen in my world, that's all. Where Cwej comes from, Jack the Ripper was probably a renegade time-traveller from a parallel universe, and John Christie was probably in charge of an alien invasion force that was trying to take over the world by drugging, raping and murdering as many women as possible. For some reason.

I keep thinking about all those Barbara Cartland novels Lady Diamond used to read (although she hid them inside copies of the *Spiritualist Journal*, natch). Full of shy, good-hearted, blushing young Victorian gentlemen, making nervous passes at noble and free-minded heroines. Never mind the fact that young Victorian gentlemen were nothing but misogyny and VD, never mind the fact that they spent most of their time beating up their wives and hanging around male brothels. You get the same shit told to you over and over, the same old stabs at rewriting history, whether the stories are set in the French Revolution or ancient Babylon. You never get told about the lies, or the brutality, or that desperate paranoid fight to stay in control when someone else gets his claws into you. And my great romantic hero? I think about Cwej on the morning he came back from the world of the machine people, grinding himself into me in a last-ditch attempt to get his humanity back, and I don't know whether to laugh or scream.

70

The first time I went to Simia KK98, Cwej made sure we left before the warships landed, before any of his employers arrived to work out the deal with the sphinxes. On the day the treaty with the Kings of Space was signed, the time-travellers didn't show up at all. They let their agents handle the diplomacy.

The signing was done on the top level of the fortress, a room with no ceiling, so the snow and the cold had to be kept out by an invisible roof and the floor was covered in ripples of orange and turquoise light. There was a kind of podium in the middle of the floor, a little stepped pyramid made of the same rock as the rest of the building. The beetle-skinned men (Khiste included) lined up in two rows on either side of the podium, standing dead still, like clockwork toys that needed rewinding. I stood at the back, trying not to be noticed, while Cwej stepped up to meet the sphinx that was hovering over the podium. Floating in a bubble of its own personal space-time. It couldn't have squeezed into the room otherwise.

I saw a lot of ceremonies like that - I've already told you about the Inside-Out World, haven't I? - but this was the first of them. This signing was different from all the others I'd see, because there was only one copy of the treaty on the podium. The sphinxes had their own way of sealing a deal.

While the other men watched, one of the armoured people stepped out of line, and knelt down in front of the pyramid. His joints made little squealing noises whenever he moved. Cwej stepped back, just in time to get out of the way, as the sphinx reached out with its front paws and twisted the man's head off.

There wasn't any blood. It wasn't even violent, as such. The sphinx had re-folded space, that was all, so the place where the man's head had been suddenly wasn't next to the place where his neck had been. The sphinx kept working, picking at the air with its claws, until it had unfolded a space it could squeeze itself into. The victim's body had been expanded, and then hollowed out. Once it had climbed inside the man's armour, the sphinx stretched itself, flexing its muscles and slipping its fingers into all the body's little cavities. As soon as the sphinx had control of the victim's arms, Cwej offered it the pen, to add its own mark to the treaty.

And was I shocked by all of this? Good question.

71

It's funny, isn't it? Ever since I started writing this book, I've been telling you about the end of the world, about all the millions of people who must have been swept away when it came on the 12th of October. But somehow the bit about the soldier having his head ripped off seems much nastier.

You can't care about genocide. That's what I think, anyway, now I've seen a fair amount of life and death in the outside universe. Is that how the Gods get away with so much, do you think? By doing things so big, by wiping out so many whole populations, that nobody can really care about all the victims? It was the same on Earth, I suppose. Nixon must have sent thousands to die in Vietnam, but if he'd gone on TV and tortured some kittens in front of a live studio audience then the revolution would have started in a second.

72

'So the sphinx is going to kill him?' I'd asked, when Cwej had told me about the ceremony an hour or so earlier.

'Not really,' Cwej had said, like he'd thought it was possible to "not really" kill someone. 'It's just going to fill up the extra space inside his body. Er, once it's finished making the extra space.'

I'd blinked, because that had been the only thing I'd been able to do. 'And this man ... did he volunteer for this?'

'Sort of. He's not real.'

That had annoyed me. 'You mean, like I'm not real?'

Cwej had looked shocked. Then confused. Then upset. 'No, I don't... look, what I mean is... he's been engineered.'

I'd already locked my head into "SF" mode, so this information wasn't too surprising. 'You mean he's a clone?'

'Er. It's not as easy as that. But he's been put together by my people, yeah. Specially for this ceremony. They do stuff like that all the time.'

'Bred for slaughter,' I'd said, suddenly wishing I was a vegetarian, just so I could sound even more holier-than-thou.

'Kind of,' Cwej had admitted. 'Look, you don't have to come to the ceremony, all right? I mean, I just thought you should know what's going on.'

73

I felt sorry for that soldier, being sacrificed to the treaty just because that was the way the Gods wanted it. ("Felt sorry". Does that sound like ironic understatement? It wasn't supposed to be.) I felt a kind of sympathy with him, for pretty obvious reasons. Still, it didn't shock me, not as much as you would've thought. And it didn't make me think any less of Cwej, either, although by that time I was starting to wonder exactly how happy he was working for the time-travellers. He tried to hide it, but I saw him wince when the head came away from the shoulders, just like anyone else would have done. Well, apart from Khiste.

That evening, we went back to the flat inside the bottle, just like we always did. By then I was so used to moving between worlds that I hardly noticed the difference, the same way you stop noticing that an old film's in black and white after the first twenty minutes. That was the first week in October, the one week when I could honestly say I was starting to feel comfortable with this new kind of life. Apart from the decapitations, anyway.

When the night came, we drew the curtains in the living room and snuggled up together on one of the bunk beds, the one that gave us the best view of the colour TV. We lay curled up next to each other, Cwej's arm draped over my side, the back of my head tucked under his chin. I think I remember us being under a duvet, although I don't remember there actually being a duvet on any of the bunks. Maybe I just think about duvets whenever I think about being warm and cosy.

So there we were, shaking our heads at *Tomorrow's World* ('discoveries ... inventions ... ideas that will affect you in the future!'), talking over the sketches on *Not Only... But Also,* and giggling at the period costumes on *Thirty Minute Theatre.* Outside, the world kept turning, and all the little model people got on with their Pogle's Wood lives, but neither of us cared much any more. I let myself drift off to sleep, feeling Cwej's fingers stroking the hairs at the back of my neck, knowing that all I had to do to live through things was stick close to him.

He had to protect me. Cwej was dead set on his duty, like a little kid playing soldier, and I knew that meant he had to look after me. It was his way of making up for everything, for dragging me into his world to begin with. His way of dealing with the guilt, and that was fine by me.

At least, that's how I saw things. But then, what did I know? I wasn't even real.

Notes on Trafalgar

74/75

I don't know where Cwej got the ship from. And it was a ship, not in the way that one of his employers' space-corkscrews was a ship, but in the way that the things pirates and Vikings used to use were ships. It wasn't big, although it was shaped just like a longboat, right down to the dragon figurehead at the back (if it was supposed to be a dragon... for all I know, it was a portrait of the person who built it). It was made of gold, like a lot of the aliens' things were. Even the sails were gold, sheets of metal cut so fine that they rippled whenever the wind blew. The sails were huge, kept up by great big webs of wire, so I got the feeling that they'd been made to catch more than just wind. That the ship could run on sun or rain or snow or anything else Cwej's people felt like running it on.

The deck was like a mesh, with gold beams tied together at the prow and the stem (whichever one was which), and if you looked through the gaps you could see the internal workings. The machinery that made the ship fly. The pilot sat somewhere down there under the deck, of course, although I didn't know it at the time because by then Cwej hadn't told me about the way his people would rebuild themselves to fit their machines. This was just a couple of days after I'd met him, before we'd even started sleeping together. All I knew was that sometimes, if you looked down through the deck, you could see something soft and fleshy moving through the clockwork.

But I didn't spend much time looking down. I spent most of it standing at the front of the ship, leaning over the edge of the railing, letting the wind slam into my face. The ground of Simia KK98 would roll past, and there wouldn't be much to see, except for the stripes and clouds that Cwej had told me not to look too hard at. Every now and then he'd come up behind me, put his mouth close to my ear and mumble things over the sound of the wind, telling me about the landmarks down below. All the landmarks were the same, bad teeth sticking out of the ice-fields, fortresses just like the one where the bottle was being kept. There were shiny little people crawling over the ledges and walkways, all looking up at the same time when we flew overhead.

After a while, I started laughing. I told Cwej that it reminded me of an old Errol Flynn movie I'd seen on ITV, and that it was like we were the pirates, swashbuckling from city to city so the people never even knew what hit them. We started playing with make-believe swords after that, leaping backward and forward across the deck and shouting 'avast!' whenever one of us fell over. Cwej finally won the game by scaring me into submission. He hopped up on to the railing of the deck, and teetered. Deliberately teetered. Flapping his arms around and everything.

He wasn't in any danger. The ship was trapped inside one of the aliens' magic airbubbles, which knew what to keep in and what to keep out. The bubble let us feel the wind whipping around us, but it stopped us getting cold. It let the snow fall on the deck, but Cwej knew it wouldn't let him go. On the other hand, I didn't know. I kept gasping at him until he agreed to come back down.

I went back to the front of the ship after that, to watch another fortress rolling past. Cwej stood behind me, with his arms around my waist, while I leant forward to pull faces at the soldiers. He wasn't worried about me falling, of course.

76/77

Three days later, the two of us were lying together in the room at the top of the fortress, where the treaty had been signed and the engineered soldier had been ritually decapitated (something that, I admit, I'd completely forgotten about by then). Even though the room didn't have a roof, the heat was kept in by another magic bubble. The bubble had decided to let some spores in from the outside, and they'd settled all over the room, covering the floor with patches of fungus that were tinted funny colours by the light from the sky. There were clumps of blue grass all over the place, and it felt like stubble when you ran your fingers through it.

We lay next to each other, staring up at the night sky with our faces almost touching and our heads resting on the grass. Night was the only time you could look at the sky without feeling ill, because the stripes faded away when the sun (suns?) went down, leaving behind deep-blue clouds that never quite managed to cover up the stars. Cwej was mumbling me to sleep.

'That bright one is where we come from,' said Cwej, using the word "we" in a not-human kind of way. 'That's our sun. It's a supernova.'

'Supernova,' I muttered.

There was a pause. 'Aren't you going to ask me how we can live on a planet near a supernova?' Cwej asked.

'Supernova,' I repeated.

'You don't really care about the universe much, do you?' Cwej asked. He sounded puzzled, more than disappointed. Like it ought to be perfectly normal for someone to know the difference between a supernova and a black hole and a white dwarf and a jolly green giant.

'Jolly green giant,' I mumbled.

'What?' said Cwej.

And that was when Cwej's 'phone rang. I say "phone", but like I've already said, I don't think it was connected to any of the telephone exchanges on Earth. Unless it wanted to be, I suppose. I heard Cwej pulling it out of his jacket, and tapping one of the buttons.

'Cwej,' he said. I sniggered. I still couldn't take his name seriously, not when he said it himself. *Kwedge.*

I could hear a scratchy little voice at the other end of the line, and Cwej interrupted it with lots of 'um' and 'yeah' noises. Finally, he said 'okay' and hung up.

A few moments later he started nudging me, testing to see whether I was really asleep.

'They want me on Earth,' he said. He meant my Earth, of course, but he was too polite to say it.

'Mmm,' I said. 'Back to the flat?'

'No,' said Cwej. 'Trafalgar Square.'

78

I remember one other thing about that evening, lying under the invisible roof and looking up at the stars. It was the first time Cwej started opening up to me, about his family and his friends, about the people he'd left behind when he'd started working for his employers.

I'll be honest, I don't remember all of what he told me. All I remember clearly (and there's a very good reason for this) is that he said he had friends on the planet Dellah, there in the twenty-sixth century. He *had* had friends on Dellah, anyway, before the Gods had come.

One of them was called Bernice. Bernice Summerfield. When I asked Cwej if she could have been a descendant of mine, he didn't answer.

It took me a whole minute to figure it out. We couldn't have been related, because she was a "real" person and I wasn't. So I ummed and ahhd, and asked if maybe when the sphinxes had made everybody inside the bottle, I'd been inspired by this Bernice person. Cwej said he didn't think it was likely, because I was nothing like her, and it was probably all just a coincidence. I could tell he didn't really want to talk about it.

79

I've only just realized that I use quotes whenever I write the word "real". Why is that, do you think? Am I just trying to convince myself that Cwej's world wasn't any more "real" than mine, or is there more to it than that?

I sometimes wonder whether those artificial people the time-travellers made came with instruction manuals, or with one-year guarantees, like you get with TV sets. It'd make things easier, wouldn't it? Giving everyone who came off the production line a little leaflet called "How to Have a Happy and Successful Life (At Least Until We Twist Your Head Off)". But then, I suppose I should have had an instruction manual too, seeing as I'm just as fake as that soldier who got taken over by the sphinx. Or maybe I should have a little label on my arse, telling people not to machine-wash me.

80

It was close to midnight by the time we got back inside the bottle, and made our way over to Trafalgar Square from Soho. The square was empty at that time of night. You could still see Nelson's Column by the streetlights, but the only people in the area were passers-by, coming home from the pubs and clubs around Charing Cross. Most of the human beings we saw were huddling together in little drunken crowds, moving through the streets around the square rather than heading straight through it, which was lucky for us. Maybe it was an English thing, not wanting Nelson to look down from his perch and see his countrymen as a bunch of alcoholics.

For those of you who haven't been there, and who now never will: Trafalgar Square was a bit like an old amphitheatre, a big square pit in the middle of London, cut off from the rest of the city by whole walls of benches and railings. There was a huge phallic column in the dead centre of the square, and a statue of Admiral Nelson used to stand on top of it, although the statue was so high up that you couldn't see it and it could have been Adolf Hitler for all anybody really knew. And around the bottom of the column there were lions. I don't remember exactly what they were made of, but I know they were huge, I know they were black, and I know that children and art students used to spend hours sitting on their backs. Swinging their arms around like they were Boadicea riding into ... whatever battle Boadicea had ridden into.

That was in the daytime, anyway. At night, things were quieter. We hopped across one of the roads that ran around the square, dodging the late-night taxis that rolled past, then came to a stop on the edge of the amphitheatre. Looking for the person who'd called us there.

Actually, it was impossible to miss him. Khiste was pacing up and down between the lions, the only human(ish) shape in the whole square. In the light from the streetlamps, his little grey face had gone all yellow.

'Is he stupid or something?' I said. 'Everyone's going to see him.'

Cwej chewed on his lip. 'I don't think he cares,' he said.

No, of course Khiste didn't care. There wasn't anybody important on Earth, was there? He could have zoomed over Oxford Street in a warship, and not thought twice about it.

81

There was a statue in the fortress on Simia KK98 as well, and if you'd picked a random alien from one of the other planets in the "real" universe then he, she, or it would have had trouble telling which statue was supposed to be Nelson and which one was supposed to be the founder of time-travelling society.

The statue in the fortress was in one of the hallways, one of the big rocky caves that criss-crossed the bottom few floors of the building. The statue was at least twice the size of a normal human, although Cwej seemed to think the subject really had been that tall, while he'd been alive.

The man had a face that could probably be called "ageless". He had a bushy beard and a wiser-than-thou moustache, but the sculptor had done everything a sculptor could to make him look strong and virile. The body was made completely out of muscle. He was standing with his massive chest puffed out, two of his eight hands on his hips, the others holding on to a collection of rods, orbs, keys and sashes. His legs were wide apart, with his heavy boots planted in the pretend soil of the plinth, while his eyes were fixed on the far distance. Probably looking forward to a better future, or something.

The first time I saw it, I burst out laughing. Cwej almost looked hurt.

'What?' he said. 'What's funny?'

'Him,' I said. 'Captain America.'

Cwej screwed up his face, which was what he did when he wanted you to think he was offended. 'It's the founder of our civilisation,' he told me. 'He was a great man. A great thinker. A great scientist.'

'A great weightlifter?' I asked.

'There's nothing wrong with the way he looks,' Cwej insisted.

'And he wore an all-over body stocking, like that one?'

'Well, yeah.'

'With eight arms.'

'Um, no.' Cwej wandered up to the base of the statue, and stood in its shadow, copying the pose without realising he was doing it. As much as a two-armed man could, anyway. 'The arms are ... err, figurative. But he was a warrior, that's the main thing. He fought off a whole army of our enemies, right at the beginning.'

'The beginning of what?' I said.

82

The founder of time-traveller society was a great thinker, a great scientist, a great philosopher, and a great politician. That's what the stories say, although whenever Cwej told me the stories he always got distracted and started talking about rocket-ship fights with giant vampire-beasts. But the statue in the fortress? Just a great warrior. Because warriors were what Cwej's employers needed, I suppose. Warriors were what they wanted their agents to be. I wonder if those Great Houses had potions to change their history, like they had potions to change their bodies. If all they had to do was give their culture a good dose, and watch history rebuild itself into something stronger, fitter and angrier.

When I think about Cwej, I sometimes end up thinking about two different people. Nice Cwej, who used to snuggle up next to me and watch night-time TV in the flat. The Cwej of Cuddles. And Warrior Cwej, who did whatever his employers told him to do, right up until the end. The Cwej of Holy War. The Cwej of Destruction. I think I know which Cwej is going to end up on top, if his employers ever get round to writing the history of their fight against the Gods.

If the centre of London really is being used as a battlefield these days, with Charles Manson and Jack the Ripper knocking the shit out of each other for all eternity, then I'm sure Nelson's going to be climbing down off his column to join in. The Admiral's probably wearing big boots and an all-over body stocking by now. And he'll have a big letter "N" on his chest.

83

By the way, in case you were wondering, what with all this coming and going between the two universes: I never went back to Lady Diamond's shop after I met Cwej. I tried to, just the once, one morning while Cwej was off signing agreements in the universe outside. (I couldn't be bothered hanging around any more desert planets by that point, so I'd stayed home.)

The shop was open when I got there, and the front window had already been fixed after the night of the sphinx. I had a quick look at the things Lady had added to the window space since I'd been there last. A couple of new psychedelic prints, and a poster of Jesus that made him look more like a country-and-western singer than anything (no worse than the statue of Nelson, really, or the statue back on Simia KK98). There were lots of Egyptian "relics" as well, a whole range of pottery Tutankhamen death masks covered in little yellow price tags. Oh, and sphinxes. Plenty of sphinxes. Lady Diamond, psychic extraordinaire, must have started picking up on what was really going on in the world.

I stopped in front of the door, and peeked through the glass panel. I could see Lady inside, lounging on one of her beanbags with a cup of tea in her hand, sticking out one little finger whenever she drank. The way her parents must have taught her to do it. She was in the middle of a conversation, and I had to squint through the glass to see who else was there.

I could make out two other people inside the shop. One was a boy called Garth, who was a friend of Dorian's, and who'd been following me around a couple of weeks earlier trying to get his hand up my skirt by quoting Czech poets at me. I didn't recognize the other "customer". She was skinny and blonde, and she was lying sprawled out across the orange beanbag, the one I always seemed to end up with whenever I paid a visit to the shop. In fact, she looked exactly the way I would have looked, right down to the sweatshirt and the you're-not-going-to-impress-me-that-way look on her face.

84

I could have just walked in on them, of course. I didn't bother. My beanbag was already taken. The universe had spotted the hole I'd left in the peer group, and slotted in another skinny, pale-looking girl to take my place. Like the world was saying, in case I hadn't got the point yet: *you're not a part of this any more.*

Right, I thought. Right, you bastards. I don't need your stupid world or your stupid drugs or your stupid beanbags. I'm going to be the Queen of fucking Outer Space. Then let's see how replaceable I am.

So I turned, and walked away. I thought about going back home, to my own flat, the place I shared with Cal and Dorian and any of their friends who were too stoned to walk back to their own homes. But that wouldn't have felt right, either. Besides, Cal would have just forced me to pay the last fortnight's rent.

85/86

'You're late,' said Khiste, when we reached the middle of Trafalgar Square. It was the 3rd of October, 1970.

'It was short notice,' Cwej told him. 'We had to get here from the flat. What's the problem?'

'This is where the sphinx wanted to meet us,' Khiste wheezed, through his tin lungs.

I looked at Cwej. Cwej looked blank.

'The sphinx?' he said. 'You mean, the control sphinx?'

(That was what Cwej called the sphinx who lived inside the bottle, the one who'd been trapped inside the chalk circle. As part of the treaty, Cwej had released it back into the wild, and it had apparently spent the last few days trying to find out about the "disturbances" here in our little mini-universe. The "disturbances" that, in my world-view, were going around hacking people up on the streets of London.)

'So where's the sphinx now?' I asked. I didn't really care, but I wanted to sound like I was part of things.

Khiste swivelled on his heels. We both turned to see what he was looking at.

He was facing one of the statues, one of the big stone lions that were crouching in Nelson's shadow. Except that it wasn't a lion any more. The body was still lion-shaped, still lying in the old Great Sphinx pose, but it was rocking backward and forward on its hind legs and its claws were kneading at the stonework. You could see the muscles shifting under the skin, huge and black and rock-solid. The head was the same kind of shape it had always been, but the face had fallen away, so you could see the shiny black glass underneath. And the statue had wings. Wings that started flapping as soon as we turned to look at it, making a noise like whole continents grinding together. There was the smell of animal sweat and Welsh quarries.

I remembered the signing of the treaty, when one of the sphinxes had unfolded the space inside a (fake) human being and climbed inside. The control sphinx, who cared about what the locals thought even less than Khiste did, had done the same thing with the stone lion. It was wearing the statue like a suit. It had slipped into something that, as far as it was concerned, was just the right size and shape for comfort. I suppose it could have just turned up in its "normal" body, by twisting space into a shape that looked something like an animal, but this must have been much easier for it.

I could hear the cracking noises when it tried to lift itself up on its haunches, and I started imagining the whole world coming to life, the entire planet being worn by the sphinxes like a waistcoat ...

I remember Cwej's arm being around me before I could fall over, but I saw his face when the sphinx turned to look at him, and I know he wasn't feeling any more stable than I was.

'STATEMENT: THIS UNIT HAS IDENTIFIED THE CAUSE OF THE DISTURBANCES TO THIS ENVIRONMENT,' the sphinx told us.

(This time, I think it's all right to use capitals.)

87

Artists and mad people are supposed to be the first ones to notice when things start going wrong with the world. Artists and mad people saw World War One and World War Two coming a mile off, apparently. When those inmates in the Indian mental hospital started turning into monsters, like it says in Fate, the staff must have thought World War Three was on the way.

A weird piece of graffiti turned up in the last few days before the 12th of October, in a side road off Old Compton Street. It was supposed to be a picture, and it covered up most of the KILROY WOZ 'ERE and KEEP BRITAIN WHITE slogans that'd already been scrawled there. It was a silhouette of an animal, in thick black spray paint. It was ugly, and it was blurry, but it definitely had legs, and it definitely had wings, and it must have been a good six feet from head to tail. As far as I could figure out, nobody in the neighbourhood knew who'd done it or what it was supposed to be, although a lot of people were saying it was some kind of vulture.

Of course, I knew full well what it was, even though I never found out who'd put it there.

The thing that had followed Cwej into the bottle had burrowed its way under the skin of the world, and now it was hiding there, just below the surface of London. Every time it moved it made cracks in the city, and people started seeing into those cracks, getting glimpses of the way things really worked. They were seeing sphinxes everywhere. The thing that was hiding under the world didn't have a proper shape yet, so the sphinxes were the only things you could see if you looked into the shadows too hard. In the local paper, sometime in early October, a woman in Holborn said she'd seen a "mystery animal" in the alleyway next to her house (I remember this well, even if it's one of the clippings that Cwej never got round to sticking in his scrapbook). The thing had been going through her bins, she said, and she'd thought it was a stray cat or a fox. Then she'd thrown a milk bottle at it, and it had grown wings and flown away.

It must've been a hallucination. I can't think of any reason that a sphinx, even a baby one, would want to go through someone's bins. Like the graffiti, though, it was kind of a symptom of what Cwej and his friends had let loose on the world. Winged things were "in", and it wasn't just down to all that BBC film of hi-jacked 'planes in the Middle East.

88

Halfway through the conversation with the sphinx, about half a dozen men wandered across Trafalgar Square, on their way home from one of the local pubs. Cwej stopped talking as soon as he saw them, and looked embarrassed. Khiste didn't even notice they were there. Neither did the sphinx.

What happened when they spotted the lion statue, and saw it flapping its wings, was this: they stopped, and they turned away, and they turned back again, and they looked at each other, and they grabbed hold of each other to make sure nobody got any closer, and, in the end, they ran back across the square. Back towards the safety of the pubs.

'Shit, man,' one of them was shouting. 'Shit, man. Shit, man. Shit.'

Nothing about this ever turned up in the papers.

Notes on the Horror to Come

89

Although Cwej taught me a lot of the basic rituals - like how to hold off the sphinxes, just in case the treaty fell through - he never got round to the difficult stuff. Once, while I sat in the chalk circle in the spare room, he told me that the rituals could be used to change just about anything inside this universe. The same way the sphinxes did it.

'You'd need sacrifices, though,' he said. He didn't go into details.

He and his people had held a ritual to open up the bottle in the first place, making a passageway big enough for Cwej and his hand luggage to get through. Cwej said no more rituals like that would be needed now, because the control sphinx could open and close the bottle at will, although the passage was still wide enough for only a couple of people to get through at a time.

'Wide enough for your people to send that survival team in,' I said.

'Once we're sure it's safe,' Cwej admitted.

The problem was this. Cwej and Khiste hadn't really known much about the sphinx's rituals, when they'd opened up the bottle. They'd understood the basics, but they'd compromised, using their employers' technology to cover up any holes in the process. Meaning, they'd cheated. They'd forced their way in. To make the final breakthrough, they'd actually drilled through the last few layers of space-time, with help from the machinery they kept in the fortress.

And that was where the trouble had started. Cwej's people talk about something called the "vortex", which nobody really understands properly, but which is supposed to be a kind of no-space and no-time that connects all the other points in the universe together. The way Cwej explained it, the only way you can get into the vortex is by falling through the cracks between one second and the next, and I think that was how the time-travellers travelled. By forcing open a crack, squeezing their way into the vortex, then popping out through a different crack in a different time-zone. It was that kind of technology Cwej and company had used to make the passage into my world, popping out of the vortex inside the bottle instead of in another time.

It all gets a bit technical at this point, so I'll try to remember exactly what the sphinx in Trafalgar Square said.

90

'STATEMENT OF FACT: THE UNIT "CWEJ" ENTERED THE BOTTLE ENVIRONMENT VIA THE AREA DESIGNATED "THE VORTEX",' chanted the sphinx. Its vocal cords sounded like boulders scraping together.

'Well, yeah,' said Cwej. 'Is there a problem with that?'

'REPLY: YES,' answered the sphinx. 'STATEMENT OF FACT: DURING THE TRANSITION OF THE UNIT CWEJ FROM THE VORTEX TO THE BOTTLE ENVIRONMENT, ANY OTHER PRESENCES IN THE VORTEX WERE GIVEN THE OPPORTUNITY TO ENTER THE BOTTLE.'

Cwej blinked for a few seconds, to make himself look stupid and innocent. 'But that's okay, isn't it? Nothing else was in the vortex with me. I mean, it's not like anything lives there.'

'STATEMENT OF FACT: THE EMPLOYERS OF THE UNIT CWEJ HAVE BEEN USING THE VORTEX AS A MEDIUM OF TRANSITION FOR MILLENNIA,' the sphinx announced. 'SPECULATION: OVER THAT TIME, THERE HAVE BEEN ACCIDENTS.'

'He means, things have got lost,' Khiste added.

'Lost in the vortex?' queried Cwej. 'Like what?'

'God knows,' said Khiste. 'Faulty timeships. Faulty pilots. You know what the vortex does to you, if you're not protected properly.'

Cwej clenched his teeth.

'You mean, all those things that have got lost over the years. . .' he began.

'Have found somewhere else to go,' said Khiste, obviously trying to sound as accusing as he could, even though it was as much his fault as Cwej's. 'Well done.'

91

I could understand this much. When Cwej's employers left their remains behind for the Gods and the archaeologists to pick through, they scattered their leftovers through time as well as space, losing some of their old bones in the gaps between the seconds. According to Cwej, though, people who had accidents in the vortex didn't die. They *couldn't* die. They were torn to pieces, bent out of shape by the currents that ran between the time-zones, but they never got the chance to be buried. Just imagine those living dead things, seeing a way out of their prison, and realising they finally had a place where they could dump themselves ...

Earth. 1970. My world. Or, the way the sphinx put it:

'STATEMENT OF FACT: PRESENCES FROM THE VORTEX HAVE ENTERED THE BOTTLE ENVIRONMENT. SECONDARY STATEMENT OF FACT: THE VORTEX HAS DEPRIVED THESE UNITS OF PHYSICAL FUNCTION. SUMMARISATION: THESE ALIEN UNITS HAVE ENTERED THE OPERATING SYSTEM OF THE BOTTLE ENVIRONMENT.'

'Wait a minute,' I said. 'What do you mean, the operating system?'

'Quiet,' said Khiste.

'EXPLANATION: THE ALIEN UNITS ARE INSIDE THE SUBSTANCE OF THIS UNIVERSE,' the sphinx said.

'You mean ... they're inside the world?' I asked. 'Like you're inside that statue?'

It took the sphinx a while to think this through.

'ANALOGOUS FACT: YES,' it said, in the end.

'Shit,' said Cwej. I didn't think anyone would add anything to that, but the sphinx hadn't finished yet.

'REMINDER: ACCORDING TO THE TERMS OF THE TREATY, ALL EFFORTS MUST BE MADE TO REMOVE NON-PERMITTED PRESENCES FROM THE BOTTLE ENVIRONMENT BEFORE PERMANENT DISRUPTION TO THE OPERATING SYSTEM IS CAUSED. REQUEST: THE UNIT CWEJ WILL ASSIST IN THIS REMOVAL PROCESS. ALTERNATIVE: THE TREATY WILL BE BREACHED. RAMIFICATIONS: IN ORDER TO RETAIN THE INTEGRITY OF THE BOTTLE ENVIRONMENT, ALL LOCAL LIFE WILL BE EXCISED.'

Or, in English: if Cwej didn't get rid of the things that had followed him from the vortex, then the sphinxes were going to kill off everybody and everything in the bottle, and start again from scratch.

92

More trophies from the rucksack:

I've got a scroll, printed on what looks exactly like real parchment, which Cwej bought for me while we were at the markets on Cygni 8.6. He didn't want to buy it, but I didn't give him a choice. There was a stall in one of the markets where a man was advertising his services under the slogan WE FIND YOUR HERITAGE WHILE-U-WAIT, and I just couldn't resist it.

It works like this. In the twenty-sixth century, every human-made computer is linked up to a central network, because computers are so cheap there that they come free in cereal boxes and people need *something* to hold all the information together. Which means that if you know what you're doing, you can access any piece of data from anywhere in the world. And that's pretty smart, by human standards.

Now, the man at the stall had these things called "AIs", which were little robot minds that could scuttle around inside the network and dig out any information you wanted. He'd programmed these things to hunt down birth and death records, then string them all together. In other words, half an hour after you gave him the money, he could supply you with a complete family tree for your own bloodline going all the way back to the twentieth century.

It sounded good to me. Cwej didn't understand why I'd be interested in a thing like that, seeing as this wasn't even my home universe, but I had my reasons. Cwej handed over the cash, and the man asked me what my name was.

'Bernice Summerfield,' I said.

'ID number?' the man asked.

I looked at Cwej. Amazingly, Cwej knew the number off by heart, so either his employers had built some kind of telephone directory into his body or Bernice was more important to him than he wanted to admit. Either way, the man at the stall was happy.

Thirty minutes later, I had a complete family record, tracing the Surnmerfield name all the way back to the 1930s.

93

I wasn't on it, of course. Cwej always admitted that "my" Earth and "his" Earth were similar, in a lot of ways; I'd been hoping that maybe there really *had* been a Christine Summerfield in the "real" universe, that I was some kind of shadow of her, like a reconstruction made by the sphinxes. I don't know why I'd hoped that. Maybe because it would have given me some roots outside the bottle. Because it would have justified me leaving the doll's house where I belonged.

Cwej was angry when we walked away from the stall. You could tell, by the little twitches he made whenever he moved his arms. Like he'd suddenly gone all sharp and jagged.

'That was pointless,' he said.

'I wanted to know,' I told him.

'You won't learn anything like that. You'll just get upset.'

'Oh, so how *will* I learn anything, then? By listening to you all the time?'

He didn't answer me back. He kept trudging through the market streets, trying to look all tough and moody, but still politely stepping out of the path of any old people coming the other way. Cwej was never very good at being a bastard. At least, not in the obvious kind of way.

But let's go back to Trafalgar Square. I won't go into any more detail about the sphinx, or about the way it folded itself up and left the square, although it's true that the statue was never the same again and the tourists must have noticed something funny about the claw marks in the plinth. Once more, the papers kept quiet about that. Too busy dealing with women who'd seen flying cats in alleyways, I should think.

94

It was too late to catch a tube, so me and Cwej ended up walking back to the flat along Charing Cross Road. Behind us, we could feel the TV hum of the bottle opening. Space was twisting itself into a funnel again, letting Khiste walk home to Simia KK98. We didn't bother looking back.

'D'you think it's true?' I asked.

'Hmm?' said Cwej.

'What the sphinx said. About killing everything in the bottle. If we can't sort things out.'

(Note: we. How involved can you get?)

'Oh,' said Cwej. He didn't answer for a while. 'Yeah. Yeah, I suppose they'll do it. I mean, if there's something loose in the operating system ... I don't know. They might want to wipe the whole system. Just to be on the safe side.'

He sounded like he was in shock, but let's not kid ourselves. He probably just felt guilty. 'So these things from the vortex,' I tried. 'Are they supposed to be dangerous?'

Cwej nodded, and kicked an empty Tizer bottle into the gutter. The breath was freezing in front of his face, so for a moment I couldn't remember which planet we were supposed to be on. 'Like Khiste said. Lost property. Ships and people and ... everything. Some of them must have been warships to start with, and they won't have got any weaker. Not after all that time in the vortex. Not even if they've had their bodies taken away.'

I didn't know how they were supposed to hurt us without bodies, but I didn't argue. 'So ... can your people deal with them, or what?'

Then Cwej did the worst thing he could have done. He shrugged.

'If they can't?' I asked.

Another shrug. Yes, there he was, Chris Cwej, shrugging away the end of the world.

95/96

Flying again.

It's different this time. I'm still standing at the front of the dragon boat, and I'm still letting the wind tear through my hair, but the atmosphere's changed. Cwej has been quiet all day, and we're not playing pirates.

I haven't taken any coke in nearly a week, not since the night I met Cwej. Here on the prow (or is it the stem?) of the ship, I can't remember why I ever bothered. Perhaps, I tell myself, this is the real reason why people need head-trips. Because deep down they all know they're living in the bottle, and they want to be able to peek at the things on the outside. But then, even the people in Cwej's universe have invented LSD. Everybody must want a better, brighter world than the one they've got.

Then Cwej mumbles something, and I open my eyes, and see what's on the horizon. More of the alien fortresses, sticking up through the ice. I get ready to wave at the confused little tank-people down below, but this time it takes forever for the ground to roll past and the fortresses to come into range. It takes me a long, long time to work out why.

The fortresses are further away than they look, and they're miles high. I mean

that. Literally, miles. I start to make out the details, and things suddenly turn scary.
The buildings are linked to each other, growing out of the ground in clumps, with
the walkways and ledges tying themselves in knots. Like teeth in a rotten set of
gums, all stuck together with the decay. Then I realise that there are even more of
the buildings than I thought, with the smaller, nearer ones huddling in the shadows
of the further, larger ones. All of them are made out of the same kind of rock, so the
same streaks of rotting brown and black are running through all the walls.

Now we're there, drifting into the capital city of Simia KK98, floating over the
alien suburbs. We fly between the buildings, and everything suddenly gets darker,
because we're moving into the shadow of the bigger towers. The ship lurches, dip-
ping under one of the pathways that link the buildings together, and I can see one
of the locals crossing the bridge in front of me. Just a couple of yards from my face.
The man turns to watch us when we go by, out of a set of home-grown compound
eyes.

There are more of the men down below, with their skins shining in the sunlight.
They're crawling along the platforms, or climbing the walls by digging their claws
into the rock and scuttling across the buildings like spiders. The nose of the ship is
down, and when we dive towards ground level every single one of the locals stops
to look up, just for a moment.

Does all this sound like a dream? It's got that feel to it, it's true. Cwej leans over,
and tells me that his people built this place as a retreat, a place where his employers could hide in their millions if anything ever happened to the Homeworld. They
would have used it, too, if they hadn't found out that nowhere in the universe was
safe from the Gods. Cwej says we've come here to talk to the best scientists on the
planet, to sort out the "problem" on Earth. I just nod. I haven't got anything to say
to him.

There are thousands of people here in the capital, all of them agents of Cwej's
employers. All of them, I'm told, came here of their own free will. The time-travellers don't believe in getting involved with other races, except on rare occasions,
but in a universe this size there are going to be a lot of rare occasions. In fact, the
city's so crowded that it has to be policed, so the powers-that-be can make sure
everybody's working to the same programme. They might all be following one routine, but when you're dealing with numbers this big, things start to go wrong. The
"policemen" are the sphere-shaped machine-people we can see floating between the
buildings, keeping track of all the insect-people down on the ground. Thinking,
breathing cameras. Watching everything.

Cwej tells me that this is the one place on Simia KK98 where he can feel at home.

97

Cwej used to be a policeman, before he was adopted by the time-travellers. I
never saw anything in him that reminded me of the policemen from "my" world,
though. I can't even imagine Cwej with a truncheon. He probably came from a place
where policemen actually got to carry space-age stun guns and drive fast cars,
rather than having to spend their time filling in forms and sticking matchsticks

under prisoners' fingernails to get confessions.

So what was Cwej's mission in life? To serve his people, to serve the universe, or to serve the public trust? None of them, I'm sure. His real goal was to get his hands on as much neat stuff as possible. That was how his employers kept him happy, by giving him new toys to play with. Just like the hippies in London / LONDON!, who always said they wanted a non-materialistic society, but wouldn't be seen dead without their gonks and lava lamps. Show Cwej a warship that could tear up whole countries or kill off millions of people, and he'd just go 'wow', and not ask any more questions.

Cwej was the kid who never had any reason to grow up. He even liked me to wear boots when we had sex, because they reminded him of someone from a TV show he used to watch when he was a teenager. I don't remember her name. Some outer-space villainess the fourteen-year-old Cwej had developed a crush on. He's spent most of his adult life fantasising about being (playfully) tortured by her, which was tough luck for him, because I couldn't stand going on top.

98

Then there was Khiste. Khiste's motives were different, although it took me a while to work that out. In the last couple of days before the end, Khiste started to open up to me a little, or at least he stopped snorting at me for long enough to answer a few questions. He didn't have much of a choice, really, bearing in mind the position we ended up in.

Before Khiste had been recruited by the aliens, he'd worked for a big corporation. He didn't say what kind of corporation, but I got the feeling it was a lot bigger than the Coca-Cola Company, the kind of business that owned whole planets instead of office blocks. According to Khiste, the reason he'd signed up with this great fat multiplanetary conglomerate was simple. He wanted universal peace.

I think his family had been wiped out in some intergalactic war or other, I'm not sure. He'd joined the corporation as a teenager, at the age when Cwej had been getting fetishes about women in boots, because Khiste had honestly thought that the corporation could bring everyone in the universe together by the simple method of taking everything over. In Khiste's mind, things were straightforward. If every business was owned by one interest, if every planet was controlled by one organisation, and if every human(ish) being worked for one company, then all the pointless bloodshed would grind to a halt in a day.

His corporation had wiped out whole civilisations in its attempt at universal conquest. Khiste hadn't been bothered by that. It had been a holy war to him.

Easy to see why he'd want to work for the time-travellers. They must have shown him the future, and let him see how small and pathetic the corporation was, on the cosmic scale. Then they must have shown him their own people, the machine-heads of Simia KK98, and pointed out how they all acted together under the same programme. They kept Cwej happy with his toys, and they kept Khiste happy with his dream of total universal harmony.

Funny, isn't it? You never would have guessed it the first time you met him, but

Khiste was really just the perfect humanist. I think that's what he was trying to turn himself into, with all those alien drugs and poisons. A better kind of machine. A machine for saving civilisations.

99

We were in a cave on the lowest level of the rock city, where Cwej was being shown around by one of his people's scientist-agents. I can't remember the scientist's name. All I remember is that he was like Khiste, with parts of his human body showing through the cracks in his armour, like his employers had decided that he'd be better at his job if they let him keep some of his fleshy parts.

The cave was big and dome-shaped, carved out of the usual black-striped rock. There's no point describing the place in full. The important thing was the tank, set into the floor in the dead centre of that dome. It was big, like a tank in an aquarium, taller than me and as wide as a house. As soon as we walked down the tunnel into the cave, we could see the shapes floating in the tank, bobbing up and down in the water. Naked bodies. Human(ish) bodies.

Cwej and the scientist stood on the sidelines and talked about the "disruptions" on Earth. Most of it was shoptalk, technical talk, so I strolled over to the tank and had a closer look at the bodies.

I already knew what they were. These weren't people, as such. They were engineered things, things Cal would have called clones, if he'd been around. This was where they were grown, or hatched, or whatever the word was. You could tell they weren't finished yet, because they still looked like ordinary human beings, all pale and skinny. If you squinted hard enough you could just see the cracks opening up in their skins, the shiny insect armour getting ready to pop out of the flesh at any minute.

100

The clones were all part of the treaty. Cwej's employers had promised to give the sphinxes the secrets of time-travel, and like Cwej said, most of the secrets of time travel were in the blood. The clones in the tank were part of the first shipment due to be sent out into sphinx-space.

'Isn't that like slavery?' I'd asked Cwej, when he'd explained it all to me.

Cwej had shaken his head. Hard. 'It's all right,' he'd said, trying to sound reassuring. 'They're not real.'

I never found out exactly how the hierarchy of "real" worked. Was someone who'd been grown in a tank more "real" than someone who'd been born in a bottle? Of course, I couldn't shake the feeling that whatever the pecking order was, I'd be sure to end up at the bottom of it.

101

Did I mention that Cwej was a war criminal, by the way? Before he ever went into the bottle, on one of his other "missions" across space and time, he got involved in the local politics of some planet or other and ended up being tried by the natives for crimes against humanity. Or whatever they had instead of humanity. His employ-ers bailed him out, and Cwej said it was all just a diplomatic mistake, but I can imagine the kind of thing that might have happened.

Put Cwej in a position of power. Give him one button, one big red switch, that can set off World War Three. Then tell him that the planet's being overrun by some kind of alien army, and give him time to remember all those teenage TV dramas about scary monsters and sexy evil dominatrices. See how long it takes him to press the button. See how long it takes him to forget what World War Three actually means, and send out the H-bombs in a last-ditch effort to save the world.

Again, you've got to remember the letter in Cwej's scrapbook, the one from a cer-tain inmate of a prison in California. That chummy handwritten conversation between Cwej and the letter-writer. Did Cwej see anything wrong with that? Or was it part of his romance, to want to deal with the devil whenever he could?

Notes on the Clones

102/103

The other thing I found out about, while I was with Cwej and the scientist in the rock city, was the monitoring station. Before we got to the cloning cave, we stopped in one of the research laboratories (although the word "laboratories" doesn't really seem to fit properly, seeing as there weren't any test tubes or Bunsen burners any-where in the building). There was a sphere hovering there in the middle of the lab, about a yard from side to side, a good foot or so off the floor. The sphere looked like it was made out of glass, or maybe see-through plastic. The skin was covered in con-tour lines that glowed in all different colours, while the inside was full of little flash-ing symbols, flittering around like bugs.

'It's a map of the world,' Cwej told me.

'Which world?' I asked.

'Um. Your world. Earth. In the bottle.'

I couldn't see the resemblance. There weren't any continents marked, no coast-lines or seas. I said so.

'It's not a geographical model,' the scientist told me. His voice was softer than Khiste's, kind of rasping, like there were keys jangling in his throat. 'It's a map of the time contours.'

'Like a map of history,' Cwej added.

Then they started talking about one of the patterns on the map, a little clump of pink five-sided things that was floating across what could have been the western hemisphere. Cwej's employers were building some kind of station in orbit around the planet, Cwej said. They were going to line up the station with the time contours (I'm giving you the short version here), so the station would be part of Earth's time-line, and nobody would be able to tell that it hadn't always been there.

'You mean, it's somewhere for the survival team to live?' I said.

Cwej looked annoyed that I'd asked, but he tried to be nice. 'It's a monitoring sta-tion,' he explained. 'So we can keep watch on the planet. So we can watch for the vortex things.'

The scientist nodded his little head. 'They're definitely inside the operating system. They've been moving closer to the surface of real-time. They'll be breaking through soon.'

Then it dawned on me. Floating around inside the sphere was a pattern that really didn't look natural, made up of hundreds of tiny black circles. Most of the symbols on the map were bright and psychedelic, linked together with what the scientist called 'probability lines', but the black dots were more like a kind of cancer. Bubbling away under the skin. Spreading out. Looking for a way up to the surface.

I'm remembering a phrase Cwej used to use, when he was playing with the little portable computers his employers had given him. The phrase he used when things went wrong. He used to say, 'bugs in the system'.

104/105

'What is it they know?' the scientist was asking Cwej. By "they", I knew he meant their employers. The big "they".

I suppose Cwej must have shrugged, although I was busy gawping at the cloning tank at the time, staring at the naked bodies with their eyes closed and their arms dangling by their sides. 'They won't tell me. They've found something out about the Gods. That's all I know.'

I lifted up my hand, to put it against the glass of the tank. I don't know why I did that. I always used to do it at the zoo as well, like touching the prison puts you in touch with the fish or the dolphins or the lizards inside.

The second I touched it, I knew it wasn't glass. It wasn't even a tank, really. There was nothing there, nothing solid. Just the liquid. The water, or whatever it was, had shaped itself into a great big cuboid and stuck that way.

I suppose it was the same kind of science that had made the liquid cats on Cygni 8.6. Trained water. The "tank" was a computer, made up of droplets, all of them carrying information in and out of the cloned bodies. This was how the clones were made. How they were taught. How they were given personalities, and memories, and God knows what else.

There were thoughts in my head as soon as my fingers dipped into the water, ideas being soaked up through my skin. I can remember what I was thinking, word for word and symbol for symbol, even though it didn't make any sense to me at the time. Some things never go away once they're in your system.

The thought I had was this:

>>>*personal protocol: genetic / social (sub>>>1763756) indexGOfollow: whenIwassixIfoundadeadmouseunderatree* ...

And then I pulled my fingers out.

The funny thing is, I *do* remember finding a dead mouse under a tree when I was six. Sometimes I wonder whether I picked that memory up from the tank. Also, I wonder whether I put anything of myself into the system when I touched the liquid. By now, sphinx-space could be full of clones who spend their time thinking about the sad demise of Bobby Fuller.

'Where are we getting our information from?' the scientist was asking Cwej. Neither of them had seen me messing about with the "tank".

'One of the Gods' followers. Human woman. We picked her up on one of the planets near Dellah. We think she was on some kind of mission.'

'Who did the interrogation?'

'Khiste did,' said Cwej.

106

That was the first time I heard about the prisoner from Dellah, and the last, come to think of it. It had all happened before Cwej had even met me. Khiste had questioned the woman, and it was from her that Cwej's employers had found out the terrible truth. Not that anybody else had been told what the terrible truth was, exactly. The time-travellers had told Khiste not to pass it on to anybody else, and Khiste had done as they'd asked, same as ever.

I wasn't at the interrogation, obviously, and I don't even know what happened to the prisoner after Khiste had finished with her. This is how I imagine it happening, though...

107

There's a room, buried down in the guts of the fortress, shut off from any kind of light. The prisoner, the Dellahan woman, is strapped to a chair in the middle of the room. She's probably been blindfolded. She's probably scared. Khiste is the only other person there, not that she knows it.

Khiste tells the woman what he's done to her. He says he's put drugs into her body, the same kind of drugs his employers use to give their followers the power to rebuild themselves. So the woman's pretty much immortal, at least until the time-travellers decide otherwise. As a demonstration, Khiste draws a gun (can I imagine him using anything as simple as a gun?), and shoots her in the chest. Probably more than once. Just to make the point.

The woman dies. Her head lolls forward. Then the things inside her, the special poisons in her blood, start to put her back together again. They rebuild her from the feet up. They don't just stitch up the holes in her heart, though: they give her a whole new body, a whole new bag of skin and bone to live in. The woman starts to thrash around even before the changes are finished, and she bites at the straps that are keeping her tied down.

Snorting over the noise she makes, Khiste tells her what's happening. The drugs he's given her are special drugs, not the ones his people usually use. They're not designed to make her stronger when she rebuilds herself. Every nerve in this new body of hers is twisted out of position, or connected to the spine in the wrong way, and because of that there are permanent pain signals heading for her brain. Her nerve centre's been totally rewired, so the pain makes a kind of feedback loop in her head. The agony's cycling through her system, over and over and over again.

And it gets worse. Every time she dies, the next version of her body will be slightly more efficient at recycling the pain. Every new regeneration will hurt a little more. So Khiste is going to keep shooting the prisoner dead, until she tells him everything she knows about the Gods, at which point her life sentence will be mercifully taken away again. Until then, the poisons will make sure that whatever body she ends up with, her mouth will always be in working order.

These are the kinds of thoughts I have, now I'm here on my own in the ruins. This place is probably getting to me.

108

As things turned out, the monitoring station was finished the day after our visit to the capital city. A day after that, Cwej got his first call from the station, his first warning that a hole had opened up in the world. It happened at six o'clock in the morning, while the two of us were lying unconscious on the floor of the living room (back on Earth, of course) surrounded by empty bottles of cheap red wine.

Cwej panicked when the call came on his not-really-a-telephone, wondering if maybe the end had come, and the vortex-things had finally broken through to the surface of Earth. But it wasn't that serious. Just another crack in the world, like the crack that had let the woman in Holborn see a flying cat thing in her alleyway, or the one that had apparently made the programming of the universe go off the rails and turn a bunch of mental inmates in India into sphinxes.

Which is how we ended up climbing into the car Cwej had rented for the week, and tearing along the A-roads to a quarry somewhere between Gloucester and Cardiff, the site where the problem was supposed to be. There were no people around when we got there, no workmen on duty pulling rocks out of the ground. We stood on the lip of the quarry, with our backs to the main road and our car on the hard shoulder behind us, looking down into the pit. Everything was grey and brown and quiet and dull. The morning was freezing, my nose was falling off, and I was starting to wonder whether alien science was all it was cracked up to be.

Cwej stood there for a good minute, staring around with a frown on his face. I knew he'd armed up for this. He'd taken some of his "special" toys out of their cupboard before we'd left the flat, and slipped them under his coat. I think he'd been expecting a monster. I think he was disappointed.

I stuck my hands into the pockets of my duffel coat. Cwej cleared his throat.

'We'd better search around a bit,' he said. 'Just in case.'

Which is how we came to spend the next half-hour stomping around the quarry, kicking over the rocks and quietly swearing at the people on the monitoring station. As it happened, it was me who found the thing we were looking for.

109/110

The quarry was full of little blast craters, where workmen had blown the rock into bite-sized pieces, but there were still one or two great big chunks sticking out of the slopes of the pit. I'd kept my eyes on the ground while I'd walked around the quarry, turning over the smaller slabs in case anything was ready to jump out, so in the end I only saw it when I looked up. It was so big, I hadn't noticed it until then. I shouted when I realised what it was, in a kind of 'aaaaaagh' way.

The slab of rock in front of me must have been at least six feet across, and flat on one side, jutting out of the slope at a funny angle. From where I was standing, just below it on the slope, I was face to face with the flat side.

You know that famous archaeopteryx fossil they used to have in the British Museum? The first time you see it, you think it's a bird, maybe some kind of sparrow that got pressed flat however many millions of years ago. Then you look closer, and you see the bones, the arms and the legs, and you realise that it's a lizard, only with feathers. Like a message from the days when they did things differently.

That was the same kind of feeling I got when I saw the thing in the quarry, except that the fossil in front of me covered most of the surface of the slab. It would've been at least nine feet from head to toe, if the skeleton had been left in one piece, and the wings were the first thing I noticed. Millions of years earlier, there'd probably been flaps of skin between the bones, but now all you could see was an outline. The arms looked fragile, twisted out of shape, like they'd been flapping around when the thing had died.

And the body was human. There was a ribcage. A pelvis. Legs just like a man's legs, except that the bones were jointed in two places instead of one. Most of the right-hand side of the body had been blasted away, but you could still make out the imprint of the skull, crushed down by the rock over the years. The thing's head had been bloated, even before it had been pulped. When the creature had died, the skull had been tilted back, on a neck that had far, far, far too many bones.

I heard Cwej running up the slope behind me, with pebbles crunching under his plimsoles. The next thing I knew, he had his arms around me, trying to bury my face in his chest. Trying to protect me from the horror, I suppose. I didn't need that, but he was Cwej, and he'd have done the same thing if I'd been scared by a spider in the bath.

'It's like a sphinx,' Cwej said, once he was sure I wasn't going to fall over.

It was true. There was a man's skeleton in the middle of it all, but the body had been pulled out of shape, like it had been trying to stretch its wings. It had been changing from a man into a sphinx, and it had died halfway through the transformation. That was how it looked, anyway.

'Why hasn't anybody noticed it?' I asked.

Cwej stuck out his bottom lip, which was his way of looking thoughtful. 'I don't think it was here until this morning.'

'Cwej, it's millions of years old. You can tell.'

Then Cwej looked up at the sky. I panicked for a second, thinking I was going to see the sphinxes raining down on us in their thousands, but it turned out that Cwej was just staring up at the clouds to make himself look more dramatic. He hugged me tighter.

'They're inside the operating system,' he said. 'That means they're trying to work out how to change space inside the bottle. The vortex things don't have bodies. They're trying to use the system to build themselves new ones, but they don't know enough about how the bottle works.'

I looked at the fossil again. I couldn't imagine anything wanting to look like that.

'This must have been a test,' Cwej went on. 'That's why it looks like a sphinx. The sphinx shape must be a basic template, right? It's kind of the default setting for a new body, inside this universe. Whatever made this, it must have been human before it got lost in the vortex. It was trying to make its new body look like its old one. It didn't work, though. It just ended up half-human and half-sphinx. It can't have lived for long.'

'It's millions of years old,' I repeated.

Cwej nodded. 'If they manage to take over the system completely, they can go anywhere in the bottle. Past, present, whatever. If they all break through together, it's not just going to be the end of the world. They'll take over the whole of history inside the bottle. The fossil's only been here since this morning, but it's millions of years old.'

A shrug, then: 'It's the way these things work,' Cwej concluded.

111

That was when the phrase "the end of the world" started to mean something to me, I think. It wasn't some kind of far-off apocalypse any more, like a nuclear holocaust you couldn't really imagine properly, or even like that crisis in Cuba we were all supposed to have been frightened of when I was fourteen. I imagined looking out of the window in the flat, and seeing sphinxes - or things that were wearing the bodies of sphinxes - picking off the people on the streets of London, and wrapping themselves around the tops of the buildings.

Funnily enough, about a week later that's more or less what I did see when I looked out of the living-room window. But most of the old buildings were gone by then, and the circumstances were a bit different.

112

There's one more thing I have to say, about the time me and Cwej visited the capital city on Simia KK98. About what happened when I was standing in front of the "tank", half-listening to Cwej talking about the prisoner from Dellah.

A couple of seconds after I'd touched the surface of the water, one of the naked people opened his eyes in front of me. It was one of those moments when you know you have to stop breathing, because if you don't then one breath could make the whole building fall down around you.

The clone didn't move. He stared at me through the water, and I looked over my shoulder, to make sure the scientist hadn't seen what had happened. He hadn't.

I held up a finger in front of the clone's face. The man focused on it, not blinking, even though the water was soaking right into his eyeballs. I tried moving my finger from side to side, just to see what'd happen, and the clone followed it. It didn't look like an automatic reaction or anything. It looked like he was wondering why I was doing it.

It's a picture I'm having trouble putting out of my mind, that's all. That face of his, all pale and sick-looking and curious. Wherever he is now, if he hasn't already been dissected by the sphinxes, I hope he's still curious. I hope he can live through all the experiments, and just wonder why they're doing it to him. Perhaps he might learn something that way, from the experience of being a second-class person caught up in the middle of another race's politics. Because I'm not sure I ever did.

113

I said I wasn't sure whether I'd picked up any memories from that liquid in the cave. Well, there's something I should mention now, which I didn't mention before just in case it's even less reliable than the rest of what I've been telling you.

I remember a night we spent in Lady Diamond's shop, me and Cal and a couple of others, having one of our "sessions" after the shop had closed and the lights had come on in the street outside. I remember Lady bringing a ouija board out from one of the back rooms, and putting it in the middle of the rug between the beanbags. I especially remember Cal telling us that he wasn't going to join in with any game as irresponsible as this one. He said at the time that if there really was any way of talking to the dead through the ouija board, then it'd be downright rude to call up the ghosts of people who were supposed to be resting in peace just so you could ask them who was going to win the next Grand National. He'd made that up on the spot, but he must have liked the sound of it, because he decided to pretend it was a lifetime philosophy.

The rest of us put our hands on the little wooden wedge which, according to my twenty-sixth-century Eeze-e-Matic Wordfinder, is called a planchette. Lady told us all to concentrate, to call on whatever spirits might have been hanging around the astral plane with nothing better to do. The planchette started moving straight away, of course, because that's the way ouija boards work. You can't get four people to touch a small slippery thing without their subconsciouses; doing *something* to it.

We started with the easy questions, like 'will Christine ever get her hair cut? and 'will Dorian ever get to sleep with a real girl?'. Then, as we got more excited and our fingers got used to the way the game worked, the messages started to come through.

The reason I wonder whether I picked the memory up from the "tank", and added my own friends' faces to the picture later, is this: I can remember every single letter the planchette pointed to. Like I'd soaked up the words through my skin, and they'd got themselves stuck in the back of my head. I'll write down all the letters on the next page, and you can figure out where to put the spaces yourself.

114

MAKETHINGSOUTOFSINMANSONISASINNOCENTASHELOOKS-
MAKETHINGSOUTOFDUSTWEAREALLINTHEBOTTLEANDONEDAYTHE-
BOTTLEWILLBREAKTHESEANIMALMENNOTHINGISREALANDNOTHING-
TOGETHUNGABOUTTHEMOREYOUPLAYWITHTHISTOYTHEWEAK-
EREVERYTHINGGETSFALLENANGELSDORIANISASPOTTYTWATCHRISTI-
NEONARATIONALPLANETTHEGREATHOUSESARETHEMENWHOWILL-
NOTBEBLAMEDFORNOTHINGCHRISHASBEENREMOVEDFROMTHESCENE-
ANDYOUARETHEBLONDEGIRLMIDOCTOBER

115

Once you unscramble it, and try to filter out the bits that were caused by our forcing the planchette across the board to spell out stupid messages, the words say something that worries me. They say that even before Cwej turned up on Earth, the ghosts from the vortex were already in the system. Travelling backward and forward in time, looking for weak points where they could break through to the surface. Cwej once said that the reason his people chose 1970 was because, apart from the Hammer Horror Jack the Ripper era, it was the only time period in tune with the sphinxes' techniques. But did we help make it that way, by getting the attention of the vortex-things with all our ouija boards and pretend rituals?

I suppose you can see why I like to think that the memory only got put into my head while I was on Simia KK98. (By the way, it's only just struck me: Dorian would have loved those cloning tanks, wouldn't he? He spent most of his time trying to tell everyone how dark and ruthless and terrible the world was, even though nothing really bad had ever happened to him in his life. I think he felt a bit embarrassed about that. He could have had hours of fun splashing around in the "tank", picking up all the bad memories he could ever need, just so he could feel justified about being so sodding miserable.)

116

That recurring dream comes back, about being stuck in the old dark house with the stairways and the balconies. This time I'm being followed. The family that lives in the house, the in-bred bloodline of Summerfields, is chasing me up one of the spiral staircases. I'm moving too fast to be careful, fast enough to cut myself open on the shadows, so there are zigzags of blood on my face and splashes of red all over my wedding dress. My family are going to tear me open if they catch me, to make the bouquet out of my heart and throw it into the air, to find out who's going to be next in line for the slaughter. It's the only ritual they know.

When I get to the top of the stairs, Cwej is waiting for me there. Daddy Cwej, dressed in his new wedding suit, with all the jagged edges bursting out from under his skin. His best man (namely Khiste) stands by his side with more potions at the ready, to help Cwej change into his honeymoon body. We're all family here.

I wake up in England on a freezing cold morning in October, and Cwej isn't anywhere in the flat. He's probably off on a mission somewhere outside the bottle. So I put on my jeans and my shoes and my sweater, and I go out to score some coke. Suddenly, Cwej's world just doesn't seem bright enough or fast enough for me. Today, I'd rather be snorting nose-powder off the bathroom floor than having to act like the Queen of Outer Space.

Space is like any other drug. There are highs and lows.

117 - 128

[These pages torn out.]

THIRD NOTEBOOK (128 PAGES, 8 BLANK)

Notes on Reproduction

1

The scroll that Chris Cwej bought for me on Cygni 8.6, the one that charts the history of the Summerfield name in the "real" world, isn't really parchment at all. It's some kind of computer, pulped down until it's as flat as paper, just like that copy of *The Times* with the talking columnists. If you press the names on the family tree then little windows of ink open up, and tell you more about the generations of Summerfields.

Because of this, I know that Jonah Summerfield was born in 1930, and died in an industrial accident in 1975. The scroll says that he was skilled in all kinds of crafts, but that his main line of work was in the military. I think what this means is that he spent his life being pushed from one job to another, and got called up for national service sometime in the '50s. The family tree also tells me that Jonah was just eighteen when he got his wife-to-be pregnant, and that the boy-child they ended up with was also called Jonah.

Jonah Jnr. was born in 1948, the same year as me. I know Jonah Jnr. must have been a child of his time, because when he had a son of his own (in 1970, another big date in my personal diary) he called the baby Valentine. After the lead character in *Stranger in a Strange Land*, probably. You'd be amazed how many people had the same idea in the late '60s.

When Jonah Summerfield Jnr. called his first-born Valentine, he was actually starting a long tradition of Summerfields with stupid names. Valentine's one male child was called Benedict, born 1990, and I have no idea what might make someone give their son a name like that. Maybe there was a famous pop star called Benedict in the 1990s, who knows?

2

It wasn't hard, finding a decent coke supply in London 1970. You just had to know which public toilets to hang around. On the 5th of October, I got back to the flat after a happy afternoon's toilet-shopping and found a note from Cwej waiting for me on the doorstep. Something had come up, the monitoring station had spotted another problem, blah blah blah, and he'd be back before nightfall unless he got killed or something.

So, I wasn't expecting to find anybody waiting in the living room. But I found Khiste.

Khiste looked like a totally different kind of killing machine, here in the light of the bottle. He sat hunched up in the middle of the floor, his body too big and bulky to squeeze into any of the bunks, with his little grey face fixed on the TV set.

Watching Eamonn Andrews rounding up the stories on the *Today* programme.

He looked up at me when I walked in, and grunted. He almost sounded friendly. Whatever kind of tension there'd been between us on Simia KK98, there didn't seem to be much point to it here in London. Away from the battlefield outside the bottle.

'D'you want tea?' I asked him.

He shook his head. 'Don't drink.'

'Do you rust or something?'

I'd meant it as a joke. But Khiste looked at me like he didn't know how to answer.

'*I can* drink,' he said, and you could hear his lungs crunching together inside his armour. 'I just don't.'

'Don't you miss it?'

Again, he looked like he didn't know how much to say, like he thought I was going to start taking the piss out of him at any second. I wandered over to him, and squatted down on the floor by his side, resting my backside on one of the pillows from the bunk-beds. I tried to look serious and interested, so he'd know I wasn't joking.

'You can feel it,' Khiste told me, in the end. 'You can tell what's missing. You don't get thirsty, but you know you're *supposed* to get thirsty. That's what makes you want to drink.'

I nodded. Still putting on the "serious" face.

'What's it like?' I said. 'I mean, not being human any more.'

So Khiste told me.

3

The family tree doesn't say much about Benedict Summerfield, which I think means that most of the records he left behind are criminal ones. A pretty bad start, for the first of the space-age Summerfields. If I've read between the lines properly, then Benedict must have slithered from one side of the world to the other, dealing in suspect merchandise (drugs?) and getting off with as many women as he could on the way. When one of those women gave birth to a boy called Jason, in 2007, Benedict didn't hang around. Somehow the kid ended up with his surname anyway.

Jason is the most boring Summerfield on record. He spent his life indoors, living on welfare cheques and watching TV, just marking time between the more interesting generations on either side of him. He never got away from England, even when civilisation started to fall apart in the 2030s (it says here). In fact the most interesting thing about him is that when he somehow managed to breed, he called his child Jubilation Constantine Summerfield, thus bringing back the Surnmerfield tradition of stupid-sounding first names.

As things turned out, Jubilation Summerfield (2039-2106) was the first of the family line to leave Earth full-time, setting up a cosy little homestead on one of the outer planets with his wife and three children. I imagine them looking like those people in that painting, *American Gothic*. God-fearing farming folk, standing out on the surface of Uranus or somewhere with pitchforks and spacesuits. Twenty-first-century puritans. Maybe that's the kind of life the man was damned to, when his dad called him Jubilation.

4

The first time I had sex with Cwej was on the 30th of September, the same day he took me for my first ride on the dragon-boat. I'd say it was part of his technique, to get a woman breathless and worn out before he made his move, but frankly I don't think Cwej was ever that aware of what he was doing.

The kissing was okay, although you could tell nobody had really told Cwej how to use that big tongue properly. It was after that, after I'd gone past the point of no return by taking my T-shirt off, that he went all serious on me. Which made me go all serious.

'Look,' I said. I didn't know exactly how to put this. 'Look, I'm not on the pill, okay?' (I'd never bothered seeing a doctor about it, whatever Lady Diamond used to say about the sexual revolution. I remember telling myself that I hardly ever got into positions where I needed it, but who was I kidding?)

Cwej just looked confused. 'What pill?' he said.

'Contraceptive,' I told him. 'You know?'

'Er.' Cwej looked down, maybe because he was embarrassed, maybe because he wanted to look at my tits. Such as they were. 'That's ... not a problem, okay? I don't ... I mean, I can't. . .'

'Fine,' I said. I just wanted to get the conversation over and done with.

5

In 2076, Jubilation Summerfield made the mistake of calling one of his children Benedict, after his grandfather. The family tree shows that any Summerfield called Benedict is bound to turn out bad, and Benedict II was one of the worst. This time, the scroll tells the truth about Benedict's career, probably because the AIs who wrote it thought it'd sound romantic and glamorous to admit that there was a psychic assassin in the family. By the time Benedict was arrested (he was only twenty-five!), he'd already murdered sixty-three people, most of them politicians. "The Hyena", they called him. Maybe it was his laugh.

Oh, and he spawned two children before he was executed. At his trial the lawyers found out that Benedict had messed around with his ID records at least twice, so for all I know the last few generations of Summerfields before him were all figments of his imagination, and there never was such a person as Jonah. If so, then I know just how Jonah might feel.

Once he'd been taken away from his parents' "criminal empire", little Marshal Summerfield lived a long and happy life. He stretched out his days with all kinds of futuristic drugs, and had children left, right and centre. One of the last of them was Dylan, born in 2165, when Marshal was sixty-eight years old. The name Dylan makes me think of Bob Dylan, so I like to imagine him as some kind of space bohemian, travelling from planet to planet in his magic bus and singing songs about how bad it was that Earth kept being invaded by aliens. He didn't leave many records behind him, old Dylan.

6/7

'Can I ask something personal?' I asked Khiste, on the 5th of October.

Khiste spent a few seconds pretending to listen to Eamonn Andrews rounding up the headlines. Then he nodded.

'What about ... the other thing?' I said.

He turned his head to face me. I jiggled my eyebrows at him, in a kind of nudge-nudge-wink-wink way.

'Sex?' he said.

I bit my lip. I had to, to stop myself laughing at the sound the word made in his metal windpipe. 'That's what I was getting at, yeah.'

Khiste shrugged a great big mechanical shrug. 'You don't miss anything.'

'You mean, you've lost your ... thing.' I nodded towards his crotch, where his suit fabric was stretched to bursting point over his armour. I deliberately didn't use any word that might have meant "penis", just in case he hadn't had one even before the mutations had started. I didn't know anything about his species, remember.

'Like the drink,' said Khiste. He was taking slowly and carefully, still looking out for traps in the conversation. 'You know you're supposed to feel something. I've still got ... the anatomy.'

'I can't imagine it, that's all. Having such a big part of your life -' (yes, I spotted the innuendo as soon as I said it, but I had to keep talking) '- just taken away like that. Yeah?'

Khiste snorted. I didn't mind so much this time, because he was snorting at life on the whole, not just at me. 'Sex is all about power structures,' he told me. 'We're stronger without them.'

'What's that supposed to mean?' I said.

Khiste nodded towards the TV, where the credits were rolling on *Today*. 'Politicians. Corporate leaders. They do whatever they think they have to. For power. For money. For status. Why?' I shrugged. 'They want mates,' Khiste explained. 'As many as possible. They know the best way of acquiring them. Through power. Through influence.'

I wasn't convinced. I didn't feel like getting off with any politicians, and I said so.

'Not important,' snapped Khiste. A bit too quickly, I thought. 'They pick up the programming in adolescence. Power means mating power. They carry on using the same techniques right through their lives. Whatever it costs. Whoever it jeopardises.'

'Wait a minute,' I said. 'What you're saying is, it's the women's fault that the world's so fucked up, because they keep getting off with Henry Kissenger? Is that it?'

'Your war,' Khiste noted. 'Your Vietnam.'

'It's not *my* war -'

'Not important. The war's a territory challenge. The same as any other territory challenge. The rules were thought up by your ancestors, when they were still apes.

The challenges were just extensions of their mating rituals. That's what your war is. A ritual. Driven by the reproductive cycle.'

'But you used to work for a big corporation,' I pointed out. 'And that corporation must have been run by people just like the ones you say are -'

'Not important,' Khiste said, fixing his eyes on the TV screen again, even though nothing interesting was happening there. Here, I told myself, was a deeply repressed individual. 'You asked whether I felt ... anything. That's all.'

'I'm not sure I got an answer,' I said.

Khiste took a deep breath, so the armour stretched across his chest, and you could see the little plastic veins pulsing under the skin. I suddenly got the urge to touch them, just to see if they'd go pop.

'I'm flexible,' Khiste said. 'I can still send out sexual chemical signals, if I need to. It's part of this body's programming. Like any other weapon.'

'That's really the way you see it?' I said.

'Yes,' said Khiste.

'So how does this weapon work, exactly?' I asked.

8

Dylan Summerfield never got married, but one of his space-hippie girlfriends had his child, Candice, in 2188. (I don't know whether she pronounced it "Can-deece", like the Americans do. I expect so, seeing as she worked in television.) Candice is the only woman on the list of the family line. When she got married she made her husband change his name to Summerfield, and it's the name that's important on the scroll, not the genes.

(Why do we think names are so important, anyway? According to the rules of sphinx-magic, knowing the real name of something is the first step towards being able to control it, which is maybe why Cwej's employers never let anyone call them by their names. I don't know, I'm just guessing.)

Candice was some kind of reporter for interplanetary TV, whose career ended up on the rocks after she got too close to the drugs cartel she was supposed to be investigating. "Too close" as in "close enough to hoover up the stuff herself", another juicy story for the AIs, and another one that strikes a chord. And in the year 2214, she was stupid enough to call her first child Benedict, not learning from history at all.

This Benedict must have wanted to react against his mother, because he grew up to be a policeman on a planet called Vandor Secunda. The scroll doesn't mention any details, but he probably got "too close" to his prey as well, because he killed himself before he was thirty. He left behind a son, another Marshal Summerfield, as well as a daughter, who I'm mentioning only because her name was Christine. The only Christine I've been able to find on the family tree. In his suicide note, Benedict said that all his problems were his mother's fault, and that he wanted the young Marshal to go to military college where he could learn some proper discipline.

It must have worked, seeing as someone called Marshal Summerfield was the head of the Caprisi Military Academy for most of the late twenty-third century. His son, Marshal Summerfield II, carried on the tradition. So did his son, Marshal III. In fact by the time Marshal IV was born, the Summerfields had built up their own little clique at the Academy, which was apparently famous for its right-wing views and kinky secret rituals. It makes me think of Khiste, and his universal corporate brotherhood.

Marshal IV, however, was a disappointment.

9

One day, just after I'd started sleeping with Cwej, I went out to Boots and bought every self-testing kit I could find. Not just pregnancy testing, but tests for infections, tests for VD, tests for ... anything, really. I knew I couldn't go to the GP. Cwej had told me not to, saying I might have picked things up on Simia KK98 that'd just confuse the doctors on Earth.

I wasn't pregnant. I did four separate tests for that, keeping the bathroom door locked while I waited for the results, just in case Cwej came home from "work" early. Cwej had said he was infertile, but let's be honest: men lie about that kind of thing all the time, even men from other universes. And who was to say what might have been inside me, even if I hadn't been fertilised? I still don't know, to this day, whether any of his employers' poisons got into my system while we were having sex. My womb could be full of the same stuff they grow the clones in. If I ever have a baby (hah!), it'll probably be born wearing armour and quoting Shakespeare.

10

Marshal Summerfield IV (2318-62) wasn't the big military man his forefathers had been, and he died in disgrace, 'of a broken heart' according to the family history. It was all because of his sole child, Cathy / Cathal Summerfield, born 2344.

At sixteen, Cathy / Cathal announced that he / she was going to become an androgyne, which was apparently all the rage in those days. The records aren't sure whether he / she was Cathy or Cathal first, because by law all gender records were changed when you went through the procedure, although I should imagine he / she started out in life as a Cathy. If he'd been born a boy, he probably would have been called Marshal.

As it happened, Cathy / Cathal met a bad end, after hermaphrodites went out of fashion in the 2360s. He / she made some quick money by selling his / her body to medical science, which is why the next Summerfield in the chain was born (and spent all his life) in a laboratory.

He was part of an experiment in super-fertility, a new way of filling up some of the outer planets in Earth's almost-empire. As a result, the experimental baby had a child of his own at the age of two, in 2365, and died just afterwards. The name of that doomed infant in the laboratory? Well, no prizes for guessing. He was called Benedict.

11

I don't know why I had sex with Khiste, exactly. Obviously it was a stupid thing to do, under the circumstances. No arguments there. Cwej was in the middle of a war, getting ready for Armageddon. The last thing he needed to worry about was that.

Maybe I wanted to prove that Khiste was wrong, about all sex being mixed up with power politics. He didn't really have anything to gain from it, and neither did I. Then again, for all I know I was a victim of his "weapons", those signals his shiny new body was supposed to be able to send out whenever he wanted to attract a female victim. If he *did* turn on the chemical charm, there in the flat ... well, I don't suppose I'll ever know whether it was deliberate, or just some kind of urge that the poisons in his blood hadn't worked out of his system yet.

On the other hand, maybe I'm just too stupid to say no.

I don't want to think about what it actually felt like, not in detail. In a lot of ways, it was like the time I lost my virginity, up against a wall in the spare room of somebody else's flat with everything happening much, much too fast. Cal had been all hair and muscle, more like a force of nature than a human being. And Khiste was the same, only without the hair, so smooth that my fingers kept squeaking and sliding on his back. Beyond that, it's just anatomy. Some of it human, some of it not. Not worth talking about.

I made tea once it was all over. I remember standing in the kitchen in my dressing gown, looking at my reflection in the kettle. Hair choked up with sweat, little blotches of acne on my forehead that I didn't remember seeing before. Somehow, it wasn't the reflection I'd been expecting.

By the time the tea was ready, Khiste was in the living room again, acting like nothing had happened. I asked him whether he wanted any, whatever he'd said about not drinking. I thought maybe there were other urges he shouldn't have had, but did. He just shook his head, though.

Cwej came home five minutes later. He was so busy talking about the kind of day he'd had that he didn't even stop to ask why I was wearing the dressing gown.

12

Isaac Summerfield, who was bom in 2365 as the child of a two-year-old toddler, had a confused kind of life. Which isn't surprising, I suppose. The scroll tries to be polite, but I get the impression he was a nervous, paranoid, messed-up person, who spent most of his time being shunted from one space-age housing project to another. I think I've got more sympathy for him than for any other Summerfield.

When Isaac and his lover had a child, in 2389, Isaac decided not to let the baby have a life anything like his and practically sold his offspring into slavery, handing the child over to the Earth military before the year was out. Isaac had called the boy Marshal Summerfield V, probably in an attempt to bring back his family's glorious military past. But Marshal V turned out to be a pretty mediocre soldier, who ended up doing not much at all in the army's civil service.

That might explain why the pendulum swung back again for the next generation of Summerfields, and Marshal V's son was called Dylan, in the hope that a bohemian life might suit the boy better than a military one. But it didn't work, because in

2455 Dylan's children were taken away from him, when it turned out that he'd been sleeping around with non-humans (something you absolutely weren't allowed to do in the twenty-fifth century, for some reason). Whether any alien blood got into the Summerfield line at that point, the family tree doesn't say.

13

One day, I woke up in one of the guest rooms of the fortress. It took me a while to get a grip on the rock walls and the army-style bedsheets, to work out which world I'd ended up in the night before. Cwej was already awake, but still naked apart from his Daffy Duck shorts. He was sitting up in bed next to me, staring at the doorway.

Khiste was standing there, filling up most of the frame. I pulled the sheets over my body anyway.

Khiste looked at me, then at Cwej. For a while, he didn't say anything. I wondered if something had snapped inside him, if the wrinkly human parts of his body had remembered how to be jealous. If he'd come here looking for a fight.

But what he said was: 'It's started.'

I looked at Cwej. Cwej looked blank.

'The ghosts,' Khiste told us. 'They've worked out how to use the operating system. They've broken through. They've got London.'

14

There's something about the Summerfield line that makes the children want to be soldiers, maybe something that started back in the 1950s, when Jonah was called up for national service. Dylan's son eventually took up the old family trade, and ended up as an officer in the space navy (or whatever it's called), winning medals at all kinds of battles with silly-sounding names. Maybe by coincidence, his name was Jonah, too. And his son, another Isaac, kept up the tradition of recycling the same names over the generations. This Isaac Summerfield became an admiral, even higher up the ladder than his father. The records say Isaac died in combat in 2543, although they also say he was still in active service as of 2595, so the AIs must have messed something up somewhere.

The important thing is that his daughter was called Bernice. Not having the same fighting spirit as the boy Summerfields, Bernice ran away from the military and got herself a life as an academic, specialising in xenoarchaeology (something about aliens ... the curse of Dylan Summerfield?) and Martian history. But this didn't do her much good when, in 2596, the planet she lived on was eaten up by the Gods.

You see? With one act of unplanned procreation, Jonah Summerfield (1930-75) set off this whole chain of events, and cut a Summerfield-shaped wedge right through the middle of history. No wonder Khiste was so hung up about sex. Just look at the damage it can do.

It's a bloodline that never existed on the Earth where I was made. A bloodline I'm not connected to in any way. So why do I feel so attached to it? And why do I feel this urge to go looking for the remains of Bernice Summerfield?

Notes on the Horror

15

It's funny. I'm lying on a de luxe, extra-padded, two-person, snuggle-up sleeping bag as I write this, so I can't feel the rubble underneath me while I work. I've been eating a month-old packet of biscuits as well, and I've just finished brushing the crumbs away. The funny thing is, I didn't just brush the crumbs on to the other side of the "bed", the way I usually do. Somehow, I'm still expecting somebody else to be sleeping there. It's like I'm waiting for Cwej to come back at any minute, like the dent he's made in my life is so big that I can't believe the hole's not going to be filled in again.

I'm running out of supplies, as well. I'm out of toilet paper already, because it's just not the kind of thing I stopped to think about when I planned this expedition. This morning I had to start ripping sheets out of the back of the last notebook. If any future historians do get to read this, they'll probably think the pages were taken out to protect some terrible secret or other. How exciting.

There won't be any secrets left, soon. Not now we're getting close to the end of the story.

16/17

The three of us were hurrying down one of the spiral passageways inside the fortress, down towards the room where the bottle was kept. Cwej was dressing himself while he ran, doing up the buttons on his suit, hopping on one leg when he tied his shoelaces.

'How many of them are there?' Cwej asked, as he did up the zip on his trousers.

'How many of what?' said Khiste.

'The vortex things. On Earth. How many are there?'

'One,' Khiste told him.

Cwej looked disappointed, like he thought he wasn't going to get the big fight he'd been expecting. 'I thought you meant ... you know. There'd been an invasion.'

Khiste sighed. It sounded like Venetian blinds rattling. He wasn't looking back at us, and I wondered if it was because he didn't want to look at me, if maybe he was still brooding about what had happened at the flat.

'The things from the vortex are in the operating system,' Khiste said, going over things from the beginning, as if we were too stupid to remember the details. 'Ever since we let them into the bottle, they've been trying to build themselves new bodies there. But they've been in the vortex as long as anyone can remember. They've been growing. Human bodies aren't strong enough to hold them any more.'

Cwej finished doing up buttons and things, and did his best to look dignified. 'So?'

'They've changed their strategy,' said Khiste. 'They've built themselves one bio-form. One body that can hold all of them. And now it's arrived. On Earth.'

'So all we have to do is kill this one big baddie, and the problem's solved?'

Khiste stopped in front of us, blocking the doorway of the bottle-room. He turned, and fixed his eyes on Cwej, still ignoring me completely. I saw Cwej jump. Khiste had locked his pincer-fingers around Cwej's wrist.

'You still don't get it, do you?' Khiste hissed. You could see the contempt in those little blue eyes of his, the frustration of knowing he was the only one taking things seriously. 'The bioform. It's everything. Everything that's been lost in the vortex over the years. All the people, all the intelligence, all the machines. It's all of them at once.'

'Er,' said Cwej. 'So, it's big, is it?'

Khiste didn't answer. He let go of Cwej's wrist, and stomped into the room, probably snorting to himself under his breath.

18

I haven't talked much about the way the bottle looked from the outside. The first time you saw it, you could see all the stars twinkling away behind the glass, all the galaxies tumbling away from each other in what Khiste used to call the Red Shift. But the view changed if you kept watching, like the bottle knew it was being looked at. Stare at one galaxy for long enough, and that galaxy would fill the bottle. Stare at one star, and you'd see its whole solar system ... and so on and so on, until you could see any room in any building in any street on any planet. Somehow, I always ended up spying on the people I'd known back in London, before Cwej had taken me away from them. Isn't that petty? A whole universe to explore, and all I used the bottle for was to watch Cal feeding LSD to whatever women he was trying to get off with, or to pull faces at the blonde girl with the pale white legs who'd taken my place on Lady Diamond's beanbags.

On the day the things (thing?) from the vortex broke through, the bottle wasn't working properly. Every time Cwej tried to look at London, the glass just filled up with black. Probably not a good omen. Khiste told him that something was blotting out his employers' monitoring systems as well, so nobody really knew what was happening down on Earth, except for the fact that it was big and terrible.

Khiste had already scrambled the troops at the fortress, and the plan was to send them through as soon as we'd worked out what kind of threat the men were up against. I suppose that meant Cwej was a kind of guinea pig, and the soldiers' tactics would depend on the way the monster killed him, but at the time he must have thought he'd been chosen to do one-on-one battle with the thing just because of his prowess in combat. Poor, romantic Cwej. And as for myself... well, nobody even bothered trying to stop me when I followed him into the bottle.

Could we do it, though? Could we stop the Horror in its tracks, and prevent the imminent end of the world?

Well, what do you think?

19

And on Earth?

Across the world, news-people were being told about the things happening in London, but not doing anything about it in case the story turned out to be (a) a hoax or (b) not important to anyone outside Britain. In the north of the UK, from Scotland to Birmingham, the regional TV stations waited for the next gap in the programmes before they told the viewers that something was going on. South of Birmingham, in the places where London was supposed to matter, shows were actually interrupted to make way for the bulletins. The live racing programmes were taken off the air, and the screens were filled with confused-looking newsreaders instead, who officially announced that nobody knew what was happening.

In London itself, there weren't any newsflashes at all. The normal TV stations were blanked out as soon as the thing from the vortex turned up in the city. The "thing" was a kind of hole in the bottle, a living, thinking gap between the world on the inside and the world on the outside (and don't ask me how the physics of that worked, by the way, because I don't know and I don't care). When the hole opened up, the two worlds suddenly found themselves rubbing up against each other, and all sorts of signals leaked into 1970 from the "real" universe. Across the capital, TV sets were picking up thousands of different channels, all of them broadcasting live from the twenty-sixth century. So the viewers must have found out the horrible truth, that six-hundred years in the future, sitcoms wouldn't have changed one little bit. Meanwhile, people who'd tuned in to Radio One just to hear how Desmond Dekker was doing in the hit parade ended up turning into their parents, as they listened to the kind of music their descendants might make - if they'd been allowed to have descendants, anyway - and said to themselves, what *is* this rubbish?

20/21

And on Cwej's Homeworld?

They had a computer there, which Cwej's employers used to keep track of everything they'd ever done (because if you can move around in time, then you've got to have some way of keeping everything in the right order). Cwej always said that whenever one of his employers died, his or her mind would be sucked up into the machinery, so the computer could learn more about the universe and make better guesses about the future. In fact, the computer was so smart that some people thought it controlled its users, not the other way round. Some of the rumours said the computer would have existed even without Cwej's employers, and that the machine had invented the time-travellers itself, just so it could be sure that it'd be built. In which case the computer must have been a lot like one of the Gods, but never mind that now.

This computer had things programmed into it, special defences, which would be set off whenever it spotted anything going wrong with the universe. So as soon as it noticed that the vortex-thing had turned up on Earth inside the bottle, it sent signals to other time-traveller stations around the universe, getting Cwej's people ready for the fight wherever they happened to be.

Halfway across the galaxy, there was a whole planet that Cwej's employers used as a prison. They'd snatched up some of the universe's most dangerous criminals, and trapped them in blocks of ice, just like in *Adam Adamant*. How this fitted in with their policy of non-intervention, I don't know - maybe they just put away all the

master criminals who looked like they were close to inventing time-travel themselves - but one of the signals the computer sent out was aimed right at this prison
planet. Through the whole of the prison, the ice started to melt, and the prisoners
went free after all those years in cold storage.

They didn't have much time to enjoy it, though. As soon as they'd thawed out, the
warders of the prison stepped in and started to operate on the captives, injecting
them with God-knows-what poisons and bolting on God-knows-what extra bits
and pieces. They were being turned into weapons, having their personalities cut out
with knives and replaced with the time-travellers' own programming. All that criminal talent was being put to a new use. At the end of the day, thousands and thousands of living, breathing machines were sent out from the prison, all of them capable of thinking up devious new improvements for themselves. Weapons that would
evolve and grow over time, but always follow the Houses.

Of course, Cwej's employers could have done this years ago, but they'd thought
it was inhumane. With their plans for the future of the bottle going so badly wrong,
though, the computer on the Homeworld must have thought it was time for action.
Several hundred of the people-weapons headed through space towards Simia K-
K98, ready to move into the bottle if things got any worse there, or to attack the
sphinxes if the Kings of Space thought the treaty had been broken.

Some of this is based on what I was told, after it was all over. But it's mostly just
creative writing. Which doesn't mean it's any less true than the rest of the book.

22

While all this was happening, me and Cwej were arriving back at the flat and
meeting the control sphinx, who was squatting in the comer of Cwej's spare room.
The sphinx had folded itself into a smaller space than normal. Its head was tilted at
a funny angle on the end of its neck.

'Error message: this environment has become corrupted,' it said, when we
stepped out of the passage from the "real" world.

'We know,' Cwej told it.

23/24

We'd left a couple of bags of shopping in the hall the day before, and Cwej
scooped a banana out of one of them as we galloped out of the flat. He peeled and
ate it while we hopped down the stairs towards ground level, like he thought it'd
be dangerous to come face to face with the monster on an empty stomach. At any
other time, I would have laughed. It's just not possible for a human being to keep
his dignity while he's eating a banana. Nothing reminds you of your monkey genes
faster than that.

'Where are we going?' I asked him. We'd already reached the bottom of the stairs
by then, and we were hurrying across the foyer of the building, past the broken lifts
and the corners where the tramps used to sleep. The way I saw it, we had no way
of knowing where the vortex-thing was. I imagined Cwej driving through the
London streets in his rented car, trying to follow the sound of screaming bystanders.

'Mmf,' said Cwej, through a mouthful of banana. 'Khiste said it was in London. It's probably noticed all the holes we've been making around here. This was probably the weakest point for a breakthrough.'

'You mean, it's our fault it's here.'

'Mmf,' Cwej agreed. 'So it can't be far away.'

He pushed open the big glass doors of the foyer, and stepped out into the side-street that ran along the side of the building. It was a good place to hang out, if you were a mugger or a graffiti artist. There was nobody in the side street when we got there, though.

Then Cwej looked up. The sky was dark, and the stars were brighter than usual, which I thought was lucky because the street lighting hadn't come on for some reason. The side-street led to a wider road a few yards away, and every so often somebody would run past the end of the street, not even glancing at us when they went by. They looked like people trying to get out of the rain. There wasn't any screaming that I can remember, although I could hear doors and windows slamming all over the city, and car horns blaring at each other as the drivers tried to get as far away from the area as possible.

Cwej headed forward, towards the main street. He kept his eyes fixed on the sky, and I stayed behind him, not wanting to break his concentration. Whatever it was he was concentrating on. By the time we got to the street ourselves, it was pretty much deserted. There were cars parked on the pavements, but none moving along the road. In the light from the stars I could see faces pushed against the windows of the buildings, curtains and blinds rustling inside all the houses, a man with a moustache peering out from behind the shutters of a newsagent's on the corner. There was noise in the distance, cars and swearing pedestrians, but everything was quiet here. We were the only human beings stupid enough to be out in the open.

Eventually, Cwej came to a stop in the middle of the road. Still looking up, and clutching the bottom half of his banana. He stood like that for a while, and I could hear the sound of his breathing, even over the background noise.

'So,' I said, eventually. 'Where is it?'

Cwej didn't look down, but I could see his eyebrows twitching.

'You mean you can't see it?' he said.

That worried me. He was watching the sky, but I hadn't seen anything interesting up there. Although, having said that ...

Having said that, there was something wrong with the stars. Even apart from the fact that they were brighter than they should have been, for London in October. They were moving, but only very slightly, wobbling from side to side while I watched. You had to really squint at them to see it. In fact, it looked like the space around the stars was stretching, or maybe even breathing, moving in and out and in and out and ...

'I don't get it,' I said.

'Have you checked your watch?' said Cwej.

25

Cwej had given me the watch himself. Standard equipment, he'd said. It looked like an ordinary wristwatch, without even a brand name to make it stand out, but somehow it always seemed to know what planet I was on and which universe I was in. It moved its hands around to suit local time, sometimes even changing the numbers on its face for planets that didn't have twenty-four-hour days. To begin with, I thought this might just have been a side effect of time-travel, for watches to do strange things to themselves when you moved between time zones. But I don't suppose that makes sense, does it? It's one of those old space-age fairy-tales. Clocks don't melt or start going backward if you go through a time warp. The universe can't tell the difference between a timepiece and any other lump of metal (at least, not unless the timepiece has been specially built by Cwej's employers), so why should it change the rules just to make the clocks go peculiar?

'Twenty past three, I've got,' I said.

'In the afternoon,' Cwej added.

'Yeah,' I said.

Then I looked up again, at the night sky.

'Oh,' I said. 'Right.'

I wondered if that was what had scared the locals, the fact that the sun had suddenly gone out. But they were English, and they would have just put a thing like that down to bad weather. It was only when I saw the light, a huge yellow triangle of it opening up in the sky somewhere over Russell Square, that I figured it out.

26/27

That thing over our heads, the big black space full of stars... that wasn't the sky. The sky was as bright as ever, lit up by the usual off-yellow London sunshine. The darkness was some-thing else, something that had come between the ground and the sky, and blotted out the sun for as far as the eye could see.

I told you, didn't I? The body the vortex-things had built for themselves wasn't really a body at all. It was a non-body, I suppose. A hole. A gap in the universe in the shape of a living thing. And through that hole we could see the universe outside the bottle. The stars were inside the Horror - and, no, I can't think of a better name for it than the Horror and, yes, I'm going to insist on using a capital "H "- and we were standing right in the shadow of its stomach. I didn't realise it until the light spread out over Soho, and I saw what shape the sunshine was. The light was shining down through the crack between the Horror's wing and the Horror's body.

I think I only really got my head around it when the thing reared up, and looked down on us. Can you imagine that? The whole of space, rearing up over you. On Earth, there used to be people who had a fear of open spaces, a fear of being out under the sky, and I think the Horror was the thing they were always secretly waiting for. When the night moved, and flapped its wings, there was a wave of noise across the city. The car horns got louder, like the people had just been reminded why they'd been scared shitless in the first place.

It was inside the operating system, that was what Cwej had said. I suppose he meant that the things from the vortex had crept inside the rituals, the laws the sphinxes had used to make bodies for themselves. Like the archaeopteryx-man we'd found in the quarry. The shape of the sphinx was the template for anything that wanted to build itself skin and bones inside the bottle. So that's what the Horror looked like, when it finally turned up on Earth. A sphinx. A sphinx so big that nobody could ever see it all from end to end. I remember thinking, before I'd really understood what was happening: it's wearing the sky. Wearing the sky, the same way the sphinx in Trafalgar Square had worn one of Nelson's lions.

The light spread across the neighbourhood, while we just stood there and gawped. The Horror was shifting its attention from one part of the city to another. We could see the length of its neck, that huge black stripe over our heads, speckled with the stars of the twenty-sixth century. When we'd arrived, we'd been in the shadow of its body, and its wings had covered the whole of central London. Now it was looking right down at us. Whether it was just taking in Soho as a whole, or whether it knew we didn't belong there, I don't suppose I'll ever know.

28

Another thing I'll never know is the death toll. There were plenty of reports, in the days afterwards, but the TV and newspaper people were so confused by the whole thing that none of the figures sounded believable. Wherever you looked, the total had a different number of noughts on the end.

I sometimes wonder how many people *I* remember were mauled to death by the Horror. When I ask myself that question, I imagine Lady Diamond's shop, ripped in half by the fake sky. I imagine all the bodies in the wreckage. Lady Diamond, finding out for herself what was on the other side of the Veil of Anubis, or whatever afterlife she believed in that week. Dorian, with his face frozen in mid-sentence, like he'd been reading out a poem to mark his own passing when the Horror had finally got to him. That skinny blonde girl, torn to shreds, and serves her right too. The bitch.

Cal. Dead in the wreckage.

These are the things I imagine, but I know none of them are true. Even if the Horror *did* take them all, there wouldn't have been any bodies left. There wouldn't have been anything. That was the way the Horror worked.

29

At the time? At the time, I didn't even think about Cal, or Lady, or the state of the neighbourhood. I remember staring up at the neck of the Horror, and being *sure* that this was the end, however you wanted to look at it. Even if the sky didn't fall in and take us both, I think that was the moment when I knew Earth was finished. Earth as I knew it, anyway.

Khiste, like the rest of Cwej's people, didn't give a damn whether the natives of the bottle knew about the aliens or not. Cwej had done his best to keep his presence on Earth a secret, to make it easier for him to move around, but everything changed on the day the Horror came. Everybody in London, and soon everybody in the world, would get a chance to see the universe outside the bottle. From that point on, the Earth of 1970 was mixed up in the politics of the places outside. Just like I was.

All I could think about, when I saw the Horror start to drag its claws across the city, was that *Quatermass* movie where the Devil turns out to be a Martian and tears up half of London at the end. Britain made a lot of movies like that, between World War Two and the end of the world. I must have watched London meet the apocalypse a dozen times before it really happened. Like we somehow knew the Horror was on its way, and thought we could make it go easy on us by putting it in the movies.

30

Whoever you are, whatever pretend world you live in: go out now, or as soon as it gets dark, and lie on your back with your face turned up to the stars. (No, I'm serious. Go out and do it.) Try to imagine that you're not really looking at empty space at all. Try to imagine that you're looking at one single wing, stretched across the sky, blotting out the daylight. Now try to imagine that there's a layer of glass on the other side of the wing, with a whole different sky behind it. Try to hold that picture in your head for a moment. The size of the Horror. The tinyness of the sky, compared with what's outside.

Now try to keep that picture in your head, so you know you'll never be able to get rid of it. It doesn't matter where you go or what you do, it'll always be there. It'll always be with you.

Good. I just wanted you to know what my whole life feels like. That's all.

Notes on Getting Out While We Could

31

Somehow, we ended up in Leicester Square. I remember running, although I don't remember running that far. The streets were empty on the way, like the people of London thought they'd be safe if they put the chains on their doors and tried to watch everything happening on TV.

Having said that, there were a couple of policemen hanging around on the edge of Soho. They waved at us a lot, to tell us which roads they thought it was safe to run down. Like it made any difference.

There were people in Leicester Square Gardens, though. About two dozen of them, crowded around the statue of Shakespeare, maybe hoping he'd be able to save them all with his witty sixteenth-century wordplay. You couldn't see the shape of the Horror at all from the gardens. The office-blocks and cinemas made a tight square of sky overhead, and if you didn't know better you would've just thought it was nighttime.

I think that was why Cwej went to the gardens. He was looking for a place where he could focus on the Horror properly, where he felt like he was standing right under its heart. I'd say it was all part of the ritual, but what do I know? He might just have been panicking. All I know for sure is that he made straight for the statue.

32

Shakespeare was standing on top of his fountain, right in the middle of the gardens. There was a pathway of paving stones leading from the gates to the fountain, cutting the lawn in half, and when Cwej moved along that pathway the crowd actually parted for him. The people shushed themselves quiet when he went past. Did they know, do you think? Was the world suddenly noticing that he was different, and that he knew something everybody else didn't? Maybe. Or maybe I just want to remember it like that.

The people lined up in two neat rows on either side of the pathway, just like the armoured men at the signing of the treaty. Not wanting to step on the grass even in the face of the end of the world. When Cwej reached the statue, and stopped right in front of the THERE IS NO DARKNESS BUT IGNORANCE inscription (oh, the irony), there was total hush. As if the crowds were expecting him to be able to shoo the Horror away.

Even so, his voice was so quiet that I think I was the only one who heard him. He looked up at the stars again, and said: 'You can hear me, can't you?'

33

I can't remember how long it took me to notice what was happening to the statue. I know I heard someone shrieking in Japanese, and suddenly there was a cracking noise, either like cracking ice or cracking bones. Shakespeare had been leaning against a big stone desk on top of his plinth, but now one of his elbows was tearing itself away from the desktop.

I'd say Shakespeare was coming to life, but it wouldn't be true. The thing that was inside him didn't care enough about human shapes to bother making the limbs move in a believable way, or to use the face muscles properly. As a kind of final insult to the English, Shakespeare shrugged his shoulders, and two huge stone wings exploded out of his back. The body kept twisting, until the head - which the thing inside the statue obviously didn't think was very important - just rolled off the neck, and shattered against the ground.

With one movement, the statue leapt down off its plinth and into the fountain. I remember seeing its legs bending and flexing in lots of different places, the same way spiders' legs move. One of Shakespeare's arms dropped off when his feet cracked against the marble.

I think Cwej must have taken a few steps back when it happened. I know I did.

'Sphinx?' said Cwej. 'Is that you?'

The other people around the statue just scattered. They scrambled off in all directions, running for cover and dragging themselves over the railings of the gardens. Most of them stopped when they reached the edges of the square, to turn back and watch, wanting to know what was going on without getting involved. You could see faces peering out from the doorways of the cinemas, ready to duck inside if things got too bad. The best picture-show Leicester Square's ever seen.

34/35

But me and Cwej just stood there, waiting for the sphinx to get its act together. The headless thing flapped its wings, maybe getting a feel for the local gravity. When it spoke, its voice was as hard as its body, and you could almost hear the cracks in it.

'Statement: this unit is now slaved to the presence which controls the operating system,' the sphinx said, not out of any particular orifice.

Cwej took another step back, and trod on my foot. 'It's getting its orders from that,' he told me, under his breath. By "that", he meant the Horror. He didn't bother pointing at it.

'Statement,' said the sphinx, and for the first time ever there was a kind of feeling in its voice. It sounded... well, cross, really. "Angry" is too strong a word. 'Statement. Statement. . .'

It sounded like it had forgotten what it was going to say. It turned on its spider-legs, with its wings still twitching, looking around the square even though it didn't have any eyes. Finally it got a grip on itself.

'Statement: this unit... I... we... are here. Wait. The personality of this unit will be erased.' The sphinx started to straighten up when it said this, so I suppose it had remembered how to walk around in a human shape. Even a headless one. 'There. Now. Talk? You wanted to. To me. Yes?'

I wasn't looking at Cwej's face. Which is a pity, because I would have liked to see how he dealt with that kind of shock.

'It's ... you?' he said.

'Yes,' said the Horror. 'We talk. Talk. This is what you wanted. So.'

There was a long, long silence. Cwej didn't seem to know where to start. In the end, I cleared my throat.

'Ask it why it's doing this,' I mumbled. 'Ask it why it's been killing people.'

Cwej must have thought it was a good question, although he rephrased it a bit, just to make it his.

'What do you want?' he asked the Horror.

'Live,' said the Horror, through its big stone lungs. 'To be. To exist. For ever, spent nowhere. Let me out? Out now. Yes? Here, will live again. This new body. This new *life.*'

It took us a while to realise that it had finished. Cwej was shaking his head. 'Not here,' he said. 'My people ... we need this planet. It's important to us. You don't understand.'

'I,' said the sphinx. 'I. I was your people. Some of me were your people. Cracks between times, trapped in. Have been your people, in the past. No longer care. Will tear. Will kill. Hard to talk, yes. So long since using language. Wait. I-do-not-care. So. I-will-live-in-this-world. I-will-kill-all-other-life-here. Your-plans-are-not-important-to-me. Is true?'

Cwej kept shaking his head, and I wouldn't have been surprised if it had dropped clean off, just like Shakespeare's. 'That doesn't make sense. You said you wanted a new body. A new life. Well, okay, but ... not here. And why do you want to kill everything else, anyway? I mean, why bother?'

I'm sure I saw the statue puff up its chest, like it was getting ready to breathe fire. 'Vortex,' the Horror told us. 'Pain. Nothing. Empty for ever. Left to die, left to live for ever, no time at all. Nothing to hold me ... nothing to hold us together. Nothing but spite. We-were-left-to-die. No life. No respite. Why kill? Why not?'

'Spite?' said Cwej. 'Is that it? You're just angry, because you've been stuck in the vortex all this time?'

'No,' said the Horror. 'Vortex *is* angry. Nothing else there. I-am-not-angry. This body is anger. Difference. Will kill. This-body-will-kill. Because. Because we ... because I want to.'

'No,' said Cwej. He took a step forward, towards the statue, and I don't think I would have stopped him even if I could have made myself move. You could tell, you could just tell, that he was getting all kinds of mantras ready inside his head.

36

A few days before the Horror had turned up, Cwej had held a dinner party at his flat. It was the first time I saw the soldiers turn up on Earth *en masse*. I couldn't forget the way they looked when they stepped out of the spare room and into the hall, the way they turned their heads around, not being able to work out why this universe looked so different from the one they were used to. (The same way you can tell the difference between a film made by the BBC and a film made in Hollywood, just by the difference in the film stock, but you can't ever describe to anyone what that difference actually is.)

I say 'dinner party', although nobody wanted to eat anything. Really, it was more like a poetry recital. Cwej had invited the soldiers to Earth because he wanted them to see the way Earth worked, and learn how to use the rituals inside the bottle. I guessed the men were probably the ones who were going to be part of the survival team, once the crisis was over.

So the aliens all sat around the table Cwej had set up in the living room, finding out about the mantras that could keep the sphinxes away. Sometimes the men would all say their mantras together, and things would happen. Objects would move across the table, or the corners of the living room would end up being in slightly different places. The way Cwej explained it, the words you said didn't really matter, as long as they got you to focus. Some of the guests at the table started using poems and songs from the planets where they'd been born, and some of them - the ones who'd become most like machines, I suppose - didn't even bother with words. They screeched out a kind of code instead, which was probably quite pretty if you could slow it down and hear the numbers properly.

By that time, I had a mantra of my own. It was something I'd picked up while Cwej had been giving me the guided tour of the twenty-sixth century, and I'm not sure exactly where I'd heard it, so for all I know it was just a nursery-rhyme from the future. But it seemed to fit me, somehow. It went:

We make things out of sin, with blood and human skin;
We make things out of dust, so we can smash them up.

37

But a few days later, I couldn't imagine any mantra being good enough to make the Horror go away. And, as it turned out, I was right.

'I can't let you do this,' Cwej told the Horror in Leicester Square. He sounded angry, and I hoped to God he wasn't posing just because I was there. 'Whatever it is you think you want out of this place, it's not going to happen, okay? You know what my people can do. If you want to hurt Earth, you're going to have to go through us first.'

The statue seemed to think about that for a while. It cocked its neck to one side, looking sorry that it didn't have a head any more.

'Fair,' the Horror told Cwej.

38

Later on, once they'd sorted through the wreckage, the local authorities told everyone that there'd been earth tremors across central London. That some kind of seismic trouble had opened up the ground there. It wasn't true, though. If anybody had bothered to measure the whole city from side to side, they would've found out that London had grown a little bit wider than it had been. The Horror had made more space inside the capital, and all the stuff that was already there had been shifted aside to make way for it.

I didn't know this at the time, obviously. I remember feeling the ground moving under my feet. I remember falling, cutting my knees on the paving stones, grabbing hold of one of the metal benches near the fountain. Then I looked up, and saw that the bench had been cut in two. One half was there between my fingers, but the rest was on the other side of a gulf, a crack in the ground that had split Leicester Square Gardens right down the middle. The air was rushing in to fill the space, dragging everything that wasn't bolted down into the gap. The screaming had started again on the edges of the square, and the spectators were being pulled off their feet by the vacuum.

I didn't look up at Cwej, not at first. I just expected him to be there, like I always expected him to be there. I remember reaching for him, stretching my hand out towards the spot where I'd seen him last...

But of course, that spot was right on the edge of the gulf. The fountain had been cut in half, just like the bench had. There was no sign of the statue, or the bits of the broken head. And there was no sign of Cwej.

I remember rolling on to my back, letting go of the bench. I was staring up at the sky, seeing the stars breathing in and out over my head, the big black body of the Horror rolling and rippling and... laughing? No, maybe not laughing. The people were still screaming, and one of them was screaming right into my ear, except that it turned out to be me, shouting at the Horror and telling it that I wanted Cwej back, that I wanted London back, that I wanted my life back. The night was moving again, falling in on me, forcing itself into the gap between the cinemas of Leicester Square. The thing was starting to claw the ground, raking London with its front paws.

39

Later on, the authorities found out that the Horror had left hardly any rubble in the parts of the city it had wrecked. Wherever it had put its claws, the architecture there had been sucked in by its body, along with anybody who'd been in its way.

What happened to all those people and buildings? Did they end up outside the bottle, floating through empty space somewhere in the twenty-sixth century? Or did they go to a vortex of their own, between the two worlds? If they did, then there must be whole suburbs of London still stuck there, drifting around until the end of time. Eternal suburbia. Not a nice thought.

From what I heard afterwards, Leicester Square was almost completely scratched off the face of the Earth. I would have gone too, I should think, if I hadn't been rescued.

40

Personally, I still can't think of it as being a rescue. I remember lying there on my back, with the stars getting closer and closer, screaming at the Horror - no, the *world* - to take everything away and let me start my life over again. Then there were shapes standing over me. One of them looked down, and I realised it was Khiste, but I didn't care. Khiste wasn't what I needed.

I kept screaming, even when Khiste knelt down and put his arms round me. That makes him sound so soft and sensitive, doesn't it? But Khiste was a piece of lifting machinery, that's all. A bulldozer with a face. I remember struggling when he hoisted me up (I don't know what I was fighting against, I just kept kicking), and I remember hearing his skin squeak when I clawed at his chest. His face was only a couple of inches away from mine, so I could smell his skin, all sweat and chemicals and iron filings. He didn't look down at me.

'Back to the station,' he said, to the other soldiers he'd brought with him.

They'd come to save me. They must have done. There was no other reason for them to be in Leicester Square. But at the time I think I would have been happier if I'd been dropped down the crack in the ground.

A couple of moments later, Leicester Square wasn't there any more. It had been taken away from me, and a completely different kind of world had been put in its place, the world Cwej's employers had built in Earth's orbit. Like waking up from a dream, that moment of feeling sick and annoyed when you have to move between one life and another.

41/42

There was a ceiling over my head, a brown rock ceiling, so for a moment I thought I was in Cwej's quarters back at the fortress. I must have thought I'd been asleep, that Khiste was some kind of weird leather armchair I'd gone to sleep in. Then I was being moved again, shaken up and down while Khiste's feet clanged against the floor of the station.

Yes, the monitoring station. The little lump of Earth history that had been floating around the planet for about forty-eight hours now, fooling the astronomers into thinking it had always been there. I'd seen the inside of the station before, on the day it had been finished, so it wasn't hard figuring out where I was. It was made out of the same stuff as the fortress, and there was the same "living" feeling in the rock, like it had hollowed itself out as part of some biological function or other.

I must have stopped screaming at some point. I saw Khiste look down at me, but he didn't make eye contact for more than a second. I got the feeling he was embarrassed by me more than anything.

Perhaps he was. After all, I'm sure it wasn't his employers who'd told him to risk going down to Earth with a whole mini-army of his men, just to pick me up and carry me off to safety. Did he feel responsible for me, because of Cwej? Or because of what had happened between us?

I'd like to think that. But to be honest, I don't think Khiste was human enough. Only in a romance novel would a supercharged war machine feel guilty about a one-afternoon stand.

'You can put me down,' I told him. My throat had been scraped raw by all the screaming, and I still didn't know how I'd ended up on the station (alien teleporter technology, probably), but I was starting to get my head together.

Khiste didn't look down at me. 'You're hysterical,' he said.

'I'm fine,' I told him, trying to sound tough.

'Even after what happened to Cwej?'

Cwej. I remembered the ground cracking open, in more detail than I'd actually seen it, I think. I could imagine Cwej falling into the hole, with the statue tumbling after him. When the scream started to come back again, I had to clench my teeth and pretend it was a cough to stop it getting out.

'I'm fine,' I said, once again.

Khiste probably didn't believe me, but he stopped anyway, and let me stand on my own two feet. Somehow, I managed to stay upright when he let go.

'Don't get in the way,' Khiste said. 'That's all.'

43

From the outside, the station looked like a great big pebble, hovering around just outside the atmosphere. It hadn't been built to look attractive. The only reason I know what it looked like is that I saw a picture of it, on my first visit there with Cwej. Is "picture" the word I mean? I'm not sure.

The "control room" of the station (and that's just my name for it, but then, I've seen too much *Thunderbirds*) was another cave, dome-shaped, like the hall in the fortress where the clones were made. But the room was full of spheres, three-foot-wide glowing ones that hovered a few inches off the floor, just like the map of Earth-time I'd seen back on Simia KK98. All the spheres were supposed to be pictures of Earth, but they all showed it in a different light. Some of them were like ordinary maps, marked out with the biggest energy sources on the planet, or the earthquake stress-lines in the rock. Some of them were maps of time, showing Earth's history from every possible angle. If history's got angles.

There must have been at least thirty of the spheres, all arranged in a ring around the wall of the dome. The middle of the floor was kept clear, and only decorated with a mosaic: one of the time-travellers' holy symbols, I'm sure. The first of the spheres that Cwej led me to was a straightforward view of the planet, in three dimensions, although I have no idea where the camera might have been to take a picture like that. You could even see the station floating above the Earth, a tiny little speck of dust over Africa, trying to look innocent whenever it thought Patrick Moore might have been looking up at it.

44

After Khiste left me in the corridor on the day of the Horror, the "control room" was the first place he headed for. By the time I stumbled into the dome after him, it was very nearly full, and the space in the middle of the floor was seething with bulky blue-grey bodies. The soldiers were inspecting the spheres and muttering in machine-talk, exchanging notes on how things looked through their own specially-grown eyeballs.

I found Khiste again, in the middle of a bunch of armoured men who still had their own faces. They were eyeing up one of the time maps. I peeked around the edge of Khiste's tank-body to get a better look, but if he saw me there he didn't show it. I was *persona non grata* again.

They were watching the time contours of Earth, but if the last time map I'd seen was anything to go by, things weren't looking good. A lot of the map had turned black, and the blackness was spreading, moving along the contours like a spark on a fuse wire in a Bugs Bunny cartoon. I didn't know whether that meant the Horror was actually getting bigger, or whether it was just eating its way through more and more of the past. I wondered if it'd be turning up in the sky over all the big events in world history, if everyone from Winston Churchill to Jack the Ripper (if there's that much difference) would be looking up from their work and seeing the night come down early.

'Impossible problem,' one of the men said. He sounded like the scientist I'd met back at the fortress, although it's hard telling one insect-mutant from another. 'What you're asking is, how do we go up against the universe we're living in?'

'It isn't *all* of the universe,' somebody else said. I had one of those *Alice in Wonderland* paranoia moments, and I didn't turn round to look at the man, in case he turned out to be a talking sheep or something.

I could practically hear Khiste grinding his teeth. 'But we've got weapons we can use?'

The scientist looked dubious, as much as he could with a face like his. 'Not exactly. We've got rituals. We could try to sabotage the operating system.'

'How long would it take?' snapped Khiste.

45

I don't think Cwej's employers were religious, as such. I talk about the time travellers having "holy symbols", but I think they were only holy in the same way that, say, John Kennedy was holy. Leftovers from a time when people still believed in believing in things.

Once, though, I saw something in one of the caves on Simia KK98 that made me wonder. There was a queue of armoured men, and they were lining up in front of what looked like a machine gun. They were just strolling past it, letting themselves get sprayed with bullets. Some of the men weren't even scratched, but the others ... they rebuilt themselves, to make sure they were tougher than before. Their idea of self-improvement, obviously.

It made me think of those monks in medieval days, who used to flog themselves stupid to get closer to God. Because as far as Cwej's employers were concerned, the soldiers weren't just making themselves stronger. By turning themselves into machines, and getting rid of all the things that wouldn't have suited the time-travellers' programme, they were making themselves pure.

Notes on the Dead Heart

46

There are all kinds of theories about where the Gods came from, especially now you can't go anywhere in the twenty-sixth century without hearing about them. Most of the popular theories are about ancient alien super-races leaving reality-warping machines behind, but some of them are more exotic than that (hah).

One of the weirdest ideas was thought up by Professor Begarius of Loughborough University, who was one of the few people to have bothered studying the Gods before they invaded Dellah. According to the professor, it's kind of inevitable that we keep running into things like the Gods in the universe. He says that back on Earth human beings used to see "mystery animals" wherever they went in the world, and I can vouch for that, because it was the same even inside the bottle. There were supposed to be sea serpents in all the big lakes, and missing-link-style apemen in just about every forest on the planet. Whether those animals were "real" or not isn't important, as far as the professor's concerned. The important thing is this: there's something in our brains that can't help seeing monsters, even if the monsters are obviously impossible.

And when people finally went out into space, all of a sudden they had a pretty much infinite canvas for drawing their "mystery animals" on. The people of the universe had to invent the biggest monsters possible. Basically, the professor's idea is that the Gods are just a side-effect of us being alive. They have to exist, to fill up the big black spaces in the universe that our imaginations keep focusing on.

Of course, I don't believe any of this. Partly because it sounds like the work of an acid-head, and partly because my own theory about the Gods (I'll come to it, trust me) is confusing enough already. But to be fair to the professor, it'd explain a lot. It'd explain why the Gods are always so in tune with everyone's bad dreams. Why so many people who've met the Gods' servants wake up in the middle of the night yelling 'no, no, not the rectal probe'. It'd even explain why the Horror - made by God technology, remember - didn't just act like the end of the world, but looked like it, too. Lying there in Leicester Square Gardens, I must have felt the way Chicken

Licken felt, when he (or was it she?) figured out that the sky was falling. No wonder I couldn't stop screaming.

<h2 style="text-align:center">47</h2>

It was only there in the "control room" of the station, surrounded by Khiste and his scientist-soldiers, that I really started to feel useless. Yes, these people were talking about my whole world, but so what? It wasn't like I felt connected to it any more. Earth had gone and replaced me as soon as I'd run off with Cwej, and now Cwej was gone as well...

Oh yes. Cwej. I remember making a noise that would have been another scream, if I'd let it out. The soldier / scientists were too busy talking about weapons strategies to notice.

So, I started to move away from the group, not sure exactly where I was meant to be heading. As it happened, I ended up drifting towards the other side of the hall, to the place where Cwej had shown me the picture-sphere of Earth. The ordinary one, with all the continents and oceans where they were supposed to be, and all the clouds taken away so you could see what was happening. You could even see Britain, as a little blob of green rock on the edge of Europe.

Except that you couldn't, not any more. None of the armoured men around the hall were interested in something as boring as a normal picture, even if it was in 3-D, so I was the only one standing in front of it. Europe was turned towards me, although there was nothing but black where England was supposed to be. On the map, you could see the Horror as a blob the size of a bluebottle, stuck to the outside of the globe. You could even make out the details of the body. The wings, covering most of the land south of Birmingham. The tail, thrashing about over the channel, just to scare the French. You could even see the face, or the space where its face was supposed to be...

Which meant that it was looking up.

For a moment, I honestly thought it was looking at me. But no, of course not. It was looking at something else, something that had moved away from Africa and was now hovering right over Europe, a tiny speck stuck in the planet's orbit.

I started thinking about the old cat Cal used to have, the way it'd stare at the rats that kept getting into his room through the holes in the floorboards. The cat would just sit there, watching every move the rats made, like it knew it had to catch the bastards sooner or later but couldn't make up its mind about when.

I screamed. This time, everybody listened. While the soldiers started clustering around the sphere, the Horror reared up over the curve of the planet and headed straight for us.

<h2 style="text-align:center">48</h2>

From the outside, this is the way things must have looked:

The pebble was still floating on the edge of the atmosphere, but you couldn't see much of it any more. There was something wrapped around the rock, so dark that it blended in with the empty space behind it. The Horror must have been about the same size as the station, from head to tail. Now it had all four of its legs wrapped around the rock, opening up spaces in the walls and sinking its claws into the corridors.

The station did its best to deal with this. It squirmed and wriggled, trying to grow new lumps of rock over the holes the Horror had made, but not having enough raw material to fill all the gaps. Inside the walls, it did everything it could to make sure its passengers stayed in one piece, keeping the air pumping and the floor level no matter how much the Horror shook the place.

49/50

Five minutes later I was lying face down in one of the corridors, pushing myself against the wall and trying not to go deaf from the sound of the soldiers' feet, clang-clang-clanging against the rock. Once everyone had noticed that the Horror was heading for the station, the battle-tank men had thundered out of the "control room" in their dozens, manning whatever battle-stations they'd thought might be worth manning. Me? I'd been caught up in the stampede, clinging on to the arm of one of the men when he'd stomped out of the cave, to stop myself being trampled to death. He hadn't even noticed me as he'd dragged me along after him.

The soldiers were getting to grips with things now. The Horror had already chewed away the parts of the station that handled transport and communications (clever, clever Horror), stranding the men on the rock with no way of getting back to Earth or calling for help. After that, they'd apparently realised that manning the battle-stations wasn't going to make any difference, and they'd all headed towards the middle of the station. Just to get out of the Horror's way while it squeezed the walls.

I decided to lie low. There wasn't much else I could do. So, having gone to all the trouble of making this decision, I was kind of annoyed when something hard and sharp pressed into my neck and I felt myself being pulled to my feet.

Khiste was standing next to me, not letting go of my shoulders in case I couldn't stand up on my own.

'Come on,' he growled.

'Why?' I said. I didn't know why I was arguing. Maybe I just wanted to annoy him.

'We're setting up a ritual,' he told me. 'We're going to try calling in the sphinxes. Get their help shutting down the operating system.'

I could tell, just by the way he said it, that this plan of action wasn't going to work. The Horror controlled the bottle, so it wasn't likely to let any sphinxes in from the outside. I didn't point this out at the time, though. I just yelled at him to let me go.

Khiste crunched his teeth together, like all of this was one inconvenience too much. 'I told you not to get in the way,' he said. 'You're slowing us down.'

Which was when I snapped, frankly. I hadn't asked for any of this. I'd been pushed into this lifestyle; I'd been pushed into caring about what happened to the bottle; I'd even been pushed into this stupid corridor. I wasn't going to let this tiny-headed twat tell me I was a nuisance for being here. Especially not after ... everything.

So I hit him. A flat palm, right against the shoulder. It was never going to do any damage, but I felt my hand bounce off his skin (it felt like plastic, even if it looked like metal) and I saw Khiste flinch, like there was some programme in his body telling him to hit back and he was trying not to act on it.

I hit him again. Kept hitting. Or, rather, I kept flapping my arms, and some of the punches reached his body while some of them just made me sweat more. Khiste kept glancing over his shoulder all the time, wanting to follow the other men off up the corridor. Or maybe he was worried what they'd say if they saw him getting into a fight with a puny Earthling.

Finally, he dropped me. I collapsed on to my knees when I hit the floor, but I think I managed to make it look deliberate.

'You can't stay here,' Khiste said, and his voice was as flat as ever.

'Fuck off,' I told him.

He spent another few seconds staring at me before he turned on his heel and stamped away. Moments later, he was gone, into the not-much-safer rooms deep in the heart of the station.

51

There were still armoured men trundling past me, but they'd thinned out now. The last few were hurrying away from the walls where the Horror was breaking in. I stood up, and pulled myself together. Composed myself. Brushed the hair out of my face. The men were veering around me, but apart from that they hardly noticed I was there. Even so, I tried not to look stressed. Despite the fact that there were sweat stains the size of the Lake District under my arms, and despite the fact that yesterday's make-up was turning into sticky black splotches all over my face (I could just *feel* it).

There was no way off the station. There was no way of getting away from the Horror. I was not, absolutely not, going to do as Khiste said just for a few extra minutes of surviving.

I turned, and stalked off down the corridor towards the outer walls of the monitoring station, still keeping my nose up in the air. Heading for doomsday with dignity.

See? Romantic to the last. Knowing what I know now, I would have just slouched the whole way. Why not?

52

I'm sorry if I get distracted sometimes. I don't usually remember things in the right order, and besides, there are plenty of things to distract me here in the ruins.

For example, I just searched through my rucksack for another packet of biscuits, and ended up pulling out a photo that's been lying at the bottom of the sack ever since I left London. It's a picture of a city, stretching off into the distance, all spiky pyramids and shiny domes. There are sphinxes and dragon-boats everywhere. One of the sphinxes is in the foreground, wrapping itself around the nearest spire, turning its head towards the camera. It's all very psychedelic.

I remember taking that photo with a magic instant camera from the twenty-sixth century, which I've lost since then. I remember wondering whether the sphinx was eyeing me up or just posing.

I wish I had some glue. I could stick the photo to the front of this notebook. Or maybe inside the cover. I could say it was an author's photo. After all, this is the story of a whole little universe, and the sphinxes were the ones who built it. It's their story. I'm just the one who gets to hold the pen.

53

Back on the monitoring station:

I turned a corner. Well, I turned lots of corners, but only one of them was important. The one I turned just before I got to the outer wall.

I panicked when I saw it, I've got to admit that. The wall at the end of the corridor had vanished, leaving behind a wide-open space, full of stars and not much else. I remember shutting my eyes. Expecting to get sucked out into the void.

Nothing happened, though. It was only after I'd opened my eyes again that I remembered. I wasn't looking at the space outside the station: I was looking at the skin of the Horror. The passage had been split open right down the middle, and the Horror had slipped one of its big black claws into the gap. I wondered how easily the thing could have killed everyone here, just by opening up space all over the station. Instead, it was physically tearing the rock apart. Why? I don't know. Why do human beings enjoy popping the bubbles on that see-through plastic packaging you used to get in hardware shops? Because it's satisfying, I suppose.

I couldn't hear the soldiers' footsteps any more. We were alone, just me and the Horror. I took a few steps forward, until I was inside spitting distance of the claw, watching the stars whirling around in front of me.

I cleared my throat.

'Hello,' I said.

54

What did the Horror sound like, when it spoke? It was like all the people on all the planets inside it were opening their mouths at the same time, making whatever buzzing or squawking or chattering noises they felt like making. I know this can't have been true, because the Horror was really just a hole between universes and the stars were the stars of the universe outside, but that's how it sounded at the time.

It told me that it was listening, in more words than my head could take in at once. I think it actually paused when I talked to it, breaking off the attack just to hear what I said. I don't remember exactly what I told it, but I was probably gabbling. I hope to God I didn't sink to the level of saying something like 'can't we talk about this?', although I can't be sure. All I know is that once I'd finished, I heard all its voices say four little words: 'In. Come in? Now.'

Which is how I ended up putting my best foot forward, and stepping right into the Horror's body. The first human woman to walk in space. And without a suit, too. Eat your heart out, Buzz Aldrin.

55

Imagine this:

You're walking into a planetarium, like the one they used to have in Marylebone. Except that this planetarium's a sphere, so you can see in all directions, including down (don't ask what it is you're walking on, it isn't an issue). Once you're inside you get the feeling that this isn't really a planetarium at all, that you're actually seeing the whole of space, live and as it happens… but you're seeing it in so much detail, you're sure this isn't the same thing as just lying under the stars on Box Hill with a bottle of cider. You start tracing the constellations across the sky, seeing the patterns marked out by the stars, although after a while you start to realise that the shapes are actually *there*.

Space is made up of shapes. Shapes of all sizes and … well, shapes, but they're all alive. Some of them look like people, some of them look like machines, some of them even look like animals. The clever thing is that all the outlines are locked together, with no gaps between them. Somehow, all the different things that have fallen into the vortex over the years have been slotted together, like they were parts of one big cosmic jigsaw (and I mean "cosmic" in the way Lady Diamond would have meant it, natch). Much cleverer than that Escher picture of the salamanders.

There are other patterns, too. You think about the things Cwej used to draw in chalk on the floor of the spare room - yes, you've got all my memories to play with, don't worry - and you can see the same kind of patterns in the sky, huge glyphs and pentagrams joining up the living constellations. You figure out that these patterns are what hold the sphere together. All the living things here rotate and revolve, inside the loops and webs of the patterns. This, you tell yourself, is the heart of the Horror. The operating system of your entire universe.

Or is this a bit *too* cosmic? It didn't strike me that way, but then again, I was trying not to suffocate at the time.

56

I tried to fall on to my knees, but there was nothing underneath me and nowhere to fall to. I wanted to breathe in. I couldn't. My lungs were tearing themselves to bits inside me, and I could see blood vessels popping in front of my eyes.

'Air,' said the universe. 'You? Need air. Yes.'

When the air flooded into the space around me, it got sucked into my body so fast that it practically lifted me off my feet. I kept gasping, kept taking it in, just in case it went away again while I wasn't looking.

'Now,' said the Horror. 'Talk?'

57

Some of the shapes I could make out in the night sky, which had fallen into the vortex over the years and ended up as part of the Horror:

1. People. Lots and lots of people. A lot of them had probably been Cwej's employers, while they'd been alive. They looked human, but I got the feeling you could see them in any number of other ways if you looked hard enough. So I didn't.

2. Human people. I didn't know how close the humans from Cwej's time had come to inventing time machines, but I guessed the humans here were victims, bystanders who'd got caught up in the time-travellers' politics and paid the price for being in the wrong place at the wrong time. Some of the humans in the constellations recognised me as one of their own, and started swearing at me in funny accents.

3. Aliens. Use your imagination.

4. Machines. Time-traveller probes that had been sent into the vortex and never come back, and had started to grow there, finally turning into things that could call themselves "smart". (What a way to be born.) One machine looked especially important, because it had tentacles everywhere, squeezing between the outlines of all the other shapes. I was told later on that in the twenty-fifth century some super-computer or other had been dropped into the vortex during a duel with Cwej's Evil Renegade, so that was probably the thing I saw. While I was there inside the operating system, I got the feeling that this was the thing which had brought the Horror together. The thing which had joined up all the other ghosts, and given them one voice to speak with.

5. A hole.

58/59

When I finally got my head back in order, and worked out that I could breathe again, I realised I wasn't alone in the planetarium. Meaning that there was somebody else standing there in the middle of it all, somebody I could at least deal with on my level, not like the rest of the vortex-things. I could see a man-shaped hole in the constellations behind him, so I guessed that he was one of the ghosts, and that he'd stepped out of the wall to talk to me.

He was armoured, like the men back on the station, although he was smaller and less bulky. I got the feeling he hadn't been designed (evolved?) for total war. And the armour wasn't exactly the same style as, say, Khiste's. It was jet-black, for a start, and his head actually looked like a helmet rather than a face that had grown new parts. Like an old pharaoh's death mask, but less fiddly, more streamlined, without most of the features. Two slits for eyes, and that was about all. The armour was battered all over, covered with scar tissue in a lot of places. For some reason I got the feeling the damage had been done when the man, whoever he was, had been sucked out of time and into the vortex. One of his arms was all twisted and gungy, crippled by the accident.

My first impression? That he was one of Cwej's people, but some kind of renegade. Not the Evil Renegade himself, but maybe one of his followers, a soldier from an enemy faction. One of the bad guys. Then again, I might just be saying that because he was dressed in black.

I must have asked him who he was. He answered in his own person-voice, but it was obviously the Horror talking.

'We can't communicate properly,' the man said. He sounded English, although most of the aliens I met sounded English, and I don't know how that worked. 'Not as a whole. Too many thought systems operating at once. Too many words.'

'But you're the Horror?' I asked.

'You wanted to talk,' said the man. He sounded smug and self-satisfied when he said it, which was probably his own personality at work, or whatever was left of it. 'This is the only way you can understand us. If we use this mouthpiece. So what do you want?'

'I want to understand,' I said. And maybe it was true. 'Why are you doing this?'

'Doing what?'

I waved my arms around. 'Tearing everything up. London. The station.'

'The world,' the Horror added. 'The universe. Everything inside the bottle.'

'Yeah, that. Why? Why do it?'

'I told your friend. We're spite. We're anger. That's all.' The Horror shook his head. The one he was currently using, anyway. 'We've been in the vortex. We've been trapped there since ... no. Linear time doesn't work there. You might as well call it forever. Do you have any idea what there is in the vortex?'

'Nothing?' I guessed.

'Less than nothing. The *understanding* of nothing.' I could tell he was having trouble explaining himself, even in this body. 'When we were alive, we believed in things. Even the ones who didn't have Gods of their own. We believed in our societies. We believed in principles. Then we saw the way things looked from inside the vortex. We saw everything in its proper context. And there is no proper context. Does this make sense in your language?'

His voice sounded fragile when he said that. For a Horror the size of all space, anyway. I tried to nod.

I don't remember what he said next, not word for word. But I'll sum it all up, and I'll try to put it the way I imagine a Horror putting it, whether it happened like that or not. Existential angst, as told by the Horror and filtered through Christine Summerfield.

60

Everything is meaningless. No, it's worse than that. Even calling it "meaningless" puts it inside the context of meaning, and... there isn't one.

Wait. Let me explain.

You draw in information about the universe around you, through your eyes, through your ears, or through whatever other senses you were born with. Your nervous system starts building webs to catch the raw data, filtering the information, shaping it into something that looks as if it makes sense. All your principles, all your beliefs, all your laws... just filters, ways of dealing with what you see and hear and sense, of forgetting how small and amoral your life really is. And when people with the same filters get together, that's what you call your "culture".

Civilisation is a filter. A romance. A lie, if you like. And we always knew it was a lie, even before we ended up in the vortex. I think everybody knows it, on some level, but the fact that we were civilised meant that we could cushion the shock and get on with our lives.

It's different, once you've been in the vortex. Once you've seen how small the romances are. Once you've had your nervous system ripped out, and lost all your filters. All those ideas about philosophy, and society, and ethics...

You asked me a question. You asked me why.

The answer is, 'why not?'. It's only when you've had your culture taken away from you that you realise what a good answer 'why not?' really is.

See?

Notes on Me and the Horror

61

I'd heard that kind of talk before. In a way, the Horror sounded just like Dorian. Dorian, who'd skim-read every book on philosophy in the LSE library (N.B. there weren't many), liked to tell people that all life was meaningless; that all free will was an illusion; and that God was definitely dead. He generally did this to prove how clever he was, compared with (say) the college's Christian Union, and to justify writing poems about the Coming of the Angel of Death.

None of which ever really convinced me. Because - and this was always my argument, even though Dorian usually ignored it - if life really *is* meaningless, and there really *isn't* any free will in the universe, then you might as well be a happy fucker as a miserable one. What I'm getting at is that in a pointless, empty universe a good time is as meaningless as a bad time, so you might as well just slap on a smile and get on with your life.

Personally, I'd never been able to do either of those things, but that was just my problem.

62-5

[These pages are headed 'My Conversation with the Horror'.]

Again, I don't remember exactly what I said, but I think I must have told all this to the Horror. Once I'd finished, the man in the black armour just nodded.

'Yes,' he said.

'Yes?' I said. 'What d'you mean, yes?'

'Yes. You're right. It isn't built into the laws of the universe that we have to kill everything.'

'So why do it?' I asked. I got the feeling I was going round in circles here.

'Because we aren't happy either,' the Horror told me. 'Because the anger's all we have left.'

'You didn't *used* to be just anger, though, did you?' I said. 'You used to be people.'

I could swear I heard the other ghosts buzzing at me when I said that. You always know when you've said the wrong thing, don't you?

'You want us to be human again?' Black-Armour Man said, looking down at me through whatever nose he might have had.

'Well, yeah.'

'Not possible. Not after the vortex. We don't have any humanity left to give you.'

I wasn't convinced. 'So how come you're talking to me now, instead of wiping out the station?' I said. 'Doesn't that mean you must still be a *bit* human?'

Sniggering from the other shapes? No, it couldn't have been. 'We don't mind talking,' said the Horror. 'We've got all the time in the world. Besides, you might say something interesting. Not that it'll stop us.'

'All right. So what about the time-travellers? They won't just sit back and let you take over the bottle, will they?'

'They can't hurt us,' said the Horror. 'Not here. If they want to fight us, let them come. We'll be happy to kill them as well.'

He wasn't gloating. He wasn't being funny. It was just the way he saw things. I thought about Khiste, permanently locked into "macho" mode inside that big metal skin of his. There was no backing down, as far as Khiste was concerned. The power struggle between the time-travellers and the Horror, or between the time-travellers and the Gods, or between the time-travellers and anybody else who wanted a fight, would carry on until one side beat the other into submission. The Horror had the same kind of hang-up, by the sound of it.

'But that's just it,' I said. I was pacing the planetarium by now, not looking down, in case I started to ask myself what was holding me up. 'It's all so *stupid*. Look ... the last couple of weeks, I've been hanging around with Cwej, yeah?' (I had to pause after I said "Cwej", thinking about the ground opening up under Leicester Square, but that wasn't important now. For God's sake keep your cool, Christine. Deep breathing, deep breathing, aaaaaaaaah.) 'He's been showing me his universe. Showing me the way things work there. Like, the pyramids were built by aliens, and there are these green men on Mars, and Jack the Ripper was... listen, the point I'm making is…'

It took me a few moments to work out exactly what point I was making.

'Things are just so simple there,' I said. 'So basic. It's like that siege they had, when the sphinxes turned up at the fortress. It all came down to one big face-off. And yeah, the face-off might have ended in a big fight, or it might have ended in a treaty or something, but the point is that there was one big scene and it was all over. It was all resolved. Is this making sense so far?'

'Yes,' said the Horror.

'Only I think things might be getting a bit complicated here,' I said.

'That's all right,' said the Horror. 'I'm more intelligent than you are.'

'Fine. The thing is, I keep comparing that with the way things work back in the ... back in my world. Back on my version of Earth.' I kept talking, even though I had no idea why the Horror was bothering to listen. 'Look. I used to hang around with this guy called Cal, all right? We had sex a couple of times. And it was like ... after we'd done it, there was just this kind of *feeling* there, like something had changed and we couldn't get over it. I mean, we'd said we were just going to be friends and everything, so that should have been the end of it, but it was like nothing ever got resolved. Because things like that *never* get resolved. Everything keeps hanging around, and most of the time it just gets worse.'

'Sex isn't important to us,' the Horror pointed out. Making me realise, just for a moment, how far I'd come in the last few weeks to find myself describing my sex-life to the Angel of Death.

'Yeah, I guessed,' I said. 'But the point is ... things are different where Cwej comes from. Where *you* came from. I don't know why that is. Maybe it's just because the sphinxes left so many loose ends behind when they built all the stuff inside the bottle. In Cwej's world, everything always gets sorted out, you know? Things always end up in a big face-off. I think that's why Khiste can't deal with me. Because he got involved with someone from inside the bottle, and he keeps expecting the stuff between us to get resolved, but ... sorry, I'm just rambling now.'

'Yes,' agreed the Horror. If he really *was* just anger, then he must have been the slow-burning kind, because he seemed happy to listen to me spouting off. I suppose you don't feel any need to rush things, if you're immortal.

'All I'm saying is that ... this fight between you and the time-travellers, it just looks stupid. I mean, it looks stupid to me. This big life-or-death struggle you're getting yourself locked into. This whole last-man-standing thing. Things don't work like that. Not in the real world.'

I realised what I'd said as soon as I'd said it. 'All right,' I blurted. 'All right, things do work like that in the real world. That's exactly how they work in the real world. But they don't work like that in my world, that's all I'm saying. Not inside the bottle. That's why it looked wrong, all right? You turning up over London like that. It was like the end of the world was coming, and we're not used to seeing stuff ending. No loose ends, no fallout, nothing. Have you ever seen *Quatermass*?'

'No,' said the Horror, not sounding either particularly bored or particularly interested.

'Well,' I said. I was finally running out of steam. 'Well, that's all I'm saying. We don't do things that way where I come from.'

'The way things work in your universe isn't important,' the Horror told me.

I thought about that for a moment.

'Hang on,' I said. 'You *are* my universe now. Remember?'

The Horror looked puzzled. Probably.

'Think about it,' I said, and I knew I had no idea what I was going to say next. I was letting my mouth run on automatic. 'You said you're just anger. That's all you are. Just spite. Yeah?' The Horror nodded, so I kept talking. 'Then how do you know you really want to kill everyone? How do you know that's what'll make you happy? I mean, happier?'

'What else is there?' asked the Horror.

I thought about telling him to take up golf, but I decided against it. 'That's just what I'm getting at. You don't know anything about the way this world works. You don't know what it's like to live here. All you know about is this stupid face-off.'

'So you're saying ... ?'

'I'm saying you've already made up your mind what to do with the bottle, even though you haven't got any experience with it. Look, there's more to this world than just the big climax, all right? Things aren't that simple around here.'

The Horror sounded like he was picking his next words carefully. 'Let me see if I'm following you. You think I should try to understand life in this universe, before I ... before we remove it. Is that right?'

'If you like,' I said.

'I've already told you. Humanity isn't important.'

'Oh, fuck humanity.' At this point, I started remembering all the philosophical arguments I'd had in Cal's flat, and some part of my brain started searching the planetarium for an ashtray I could lob. 'What I'm saying is, this stupid agenda of yours doesn't belong here. You just haven't seen enough of the place to know it.'

'All right,' said the Horror.

That threw me.

'What?' I said.

'All right. We don't seriously believe we're missing anything by not getting involved in this world. But we're prepared to listen. We're not in any hurry.'

'You'll listen?' I said. Somehow, this wasn't what I'd been expecting.

'We're anger,' said the Horror. 'Anger is all we are. But anger might be different, here in the bottle. It might be less ... straightforward. As you said. So teach us.'

I had no idea how to teach it a thing like that, and I said so. It'd probably be going too far to say that the Horror looked disappointed.

'Oh,' he said. 'In that case, we'll just have to carry on killing everything.'

'Wait,' I said. 'Wait, wait, wait.'

So the Horror waited. I spent another minute or so pacing the no-floor, and he didn't interrupt me once.

'Okay,' I said, in the end. 'I've got an idea.'

66

The Horror was quite happy to answer my questions. It told me it could take on any form it liked, if it tried hard enough. Just like the sphinx on Earth had worn the statue of Shakespeare, the Horror could climb into any shape - or even make new shapes of its own - by shifting space around atom by atom. That was what the sphinx had done back in Lady Diamond's shop, knitting itself a Manson-sized body, based on the images it'd picked up from a quick survey of the culture. The Horror told me that this kind of thing was fiddly, but possible, if you had the patience. At first it hadn't been able to get the process right, hence that archaeopteryx-man we'd found in the quarry, but now it was rooted in the operating system it could do just about anything.

My idea was this. I told the Horror it should build itself a new body, say, the body of a baby human being. If it wanted to do things properly, it could even build itself a family, just to make the whole thing more convincing. Then it could squeeze itself into that body, and spend half a lifetime on Earth as a human, learning about the world the way a human would have done. Obviously it'd have to adjust its brain, so it forgot it was really an immortal monster and everything, but after about thirty years on the planet as a "normal" person it could get its old memories back and crawl inside the operating system again. This time with all the cultural knowledge it'd need to make a proper decision about the future of the bottle.

I was halfway through explaining this when the thought suddenly hit me: if it wanted to, the Horror could learn things much faster just by taking my own brain apart, which is something it was almost certainly smart enough to do. I got around this problem by telling the Horror that (quote) 'the knowledge won't be any use to you unless you experience it yourself' (end quote). Either the Horror was taken in by this, or I'd accidentally made a really good point.

Of course, there was a hidden agenda here. The bottom line was this: I hoped that by spending thirty years as a human being, the Horror might get back its lost humanity, and decide that making people happy might be a better idea than killing them off in their billions. But the Horror spotted this secret mission of mine straightaway, and pointed out that since it would remember being in the vortex once its human body hit thirty, this wasn't very likely. Still, we've got to live in hope.

67

This story is starting to make me think of *The Wizard of Oz*. You know how there are two worlds in the movie, the "real" world (in black-and-white this time) and Oz? And you know how all the characters in the black-and-white world have got counterparts in the fantasy world? Well ... let's just say that if this book ever gets turned into a movie, you could cut the cast list in half with no trouble at all. Cwej and Cal could be the same person. Or Khiste and Dorian. Or Lady Diamond and the sphinx.

Or me and the Horror? It's an idea.

68

So. A quick note here about my own philosophy:

Like a lot of us who grew up in the '60s, I personally wasn't sure whether the human race was such a good idea. Like Dorian, like Cal, like all the others, I went through that Apocalyptic Teenage Deadhead stage when I thought that the best thing humanity could do was wipe itself out in a nuclear war and let the insects have a turn. Obviously I grew out of it once I got to eighteen and the spots cleared up, but ...

But there in the planetarium, the future of my whole bottled race was in my hands, and nobody else's. Did I, at any time, wonder why I was bothering? Did I ever ask myself whether it wouldn't be a good idea to let the Horror wipe everything out, just for the sake of it?

Well, yes, I did. Maybe that was what made me think of the plan, about the Horror having a trial run at being human. I was putting a kind of random element into things. Basically, if the Horror human had a good time, the world might pull through. If the Horror human had a lousy time, the world didn't stand a chance. See? I was getting things out of my hands, letting the world judge itself by the way it treated the baby Horror. Maybe there was even some spite of my own in the mix, me secretly hoping that baby Horror would have as crap a time as I thought *I'd* had, just to teach the world a lesson.

As it turned out, I needn't have bothered. Things were about to get pretty random anyway.

69

There was a long pause after I'd finished explaining the plan, while the Horror mulled things over.

'We're not sure,' the man in the black armour said, in the end.

'But you said it yourself,' I told him, trying not to choke. 'You're immortal. You've spent forever in the vortex anyway. I mean, thirty years -'

'Is nothing to us,' the Horror agreed. 'No time to wait.'

'Well, then?'

'The question is, why should we wait at all?' That stumped me, I've got to admit. 'We might be missing something, in our understanding of the way this universe works,' the Horror went on. 'We might be, but we're probably not. We're not sure we should bother wasting any more time. We're not convinced there's enough to be gained from it.'

He went quiet after that. It took me a while to work out what was happening. He ... they ... the whole of the planetarium ... was / were / was waiting for me to say something else. The ghosts had thought about what I'd told them, and they'd decided it made sense, but it wasn't enough.

One more sentence would make the difference. Just a few more well-chosen words and they'd give the world another thirty years of life, or maybe even leave it alone completely, if things went well. All I had to do was say the right thing.

Suddenly, I couldn't think of anything.

I opened my mouth. Went 'er'. Then I realised that I was going to say something really stupid, and that if I did it'd be the last really stupid thing the human race ever came up with. Why couldn't I think, for Christ's sake? What was I supposed to say? How was I meant to know what the Horror wanted to hear, and save every man, woman and child on Planet Earth?

I felt my mouth pop open again. There was only one thing I could think of, only one way I knew to settle an argument once and for all.

'Do you know how to play stone-scissors-paper?' I asked.

70

I only worked it out afterwards. The Horror had sent the black-armoured man to talk to me, because it knew that was the best way of communicating. The Horror might have been bent on mass destruction, but it wasn't stupid.

The point is that I could have picked any method at all of finishing the argument, and the Horror would have accepted it. Because it was ready to do things on my terms, at least for as long as I was there inside the planetarium. I could have decided to flip a coin, or to challenge it to a game of Cluedo, or even to start a debate about modernist French poetry. But I chose stone-scissors-paper, and there in the heart of the Horror it was as good a way of doing things as any.

71

The man in the black armour knew how the game worked, or if he didn't then one of the other ghosts must have whispered the rules in his ear while I wasn't looking. We both held our hands out, ready to play.

We were just about to start shaking our fists when some-thing struck me.

'Wait a minute,' I said. 'Let me get this straight. If I win, you go along with my plan. Otherwise, you kill me, and everybody else in the universe. Yeah?'

The Horror nodded. 'True.'

'How do I know you'll keep your side of the bargain?'

'If I wanted to, I could just read your mind and win automatically,' the Horror pointed out. 'But that would defeat the object.'

'Right. One more thing, okay? Is this game going to go on the first shake, or is it best out of three?'

'Best out of three,' said the Horror. 'Why not?'

72

There's an art to playing stone-scissors-paper. A kind of rhythm. You both clench your fists, then you try to move in time with each other. You shake your fists once. You shake your fists twice. You shake your fists three times. Then you push out your hand, in whatever shape you've chosen. Clenched for stone. Two fingers out for scissors. Flat open for paper. You wait until the last possible moment before you change the shape of your hand, so you get at least a one-per-cent chance of spotting what the other person's going to do.

So that was how things were in the planetarium. Me and the Horror, fixing our eyes on each other's fists, moving in perfect synch. Playing for the world.

One shake. Two shake. Three shake.

Hands out.

I looked at what I'd chosen. Two fingers out. Scissors, the same thing I always chose to start off with. Even before he said anything, my eyes were drifting over to the Horror's hand.

Still clenched.

'Stone blunts scissors,' said the Horror.

For a moment, my stomach was in a completely different dimension.

'Best out of three,' I croaked.

'That's what we said,' the Horror agreed.

73

First round to him. I tried to work out what that meant, probability-wise. Two more rounds to go, and I had to win both of them. Did that mean I had a one-third chance, or a one-quarter chance, or ... bollocks to it. Not important.

One shake.

I could go with scissors again. No, because he'd probably go for stone again, to bluff me. Paper, then. Except that he might see that coming, so he'd choose scissors, so ...

Two shake.

... so stone it is. Except that the way he's shaking his hand, does that look like he's going to do paper? All right, cancel everything out. Suppose it's paper. If it's paper, I need scissors, but he'll be expecting scissors, so ...

Three shake.

To hell with it. Sheer blind luck.

Hands out.

'Scissors,' said the Horror.

I looked down at my fingers. Just to make sure.

'Scissors,' I said.

'A draw,' the Horror pointed out. 'We play the round again.'

'Uh,' I said.

74

Still losing. Still a point behind. Are we going to keep getting draws? Be here for ever? There's an idea. Stall him, so Khiste and the others can work out some way of...

One shake.

Oops. Wasn't thinking. Where was I? Help! What did I pick last time? I picked paper, so...

Two shake.

No, I picked scissors last time. And the time before. Hah! He'll be expecting me to pick scissors again, and pick paper. So I'll pick stone to beat paper.

Three shake.

Wait ... that's not right. If he thinks I'm going to pick scissors, then he'll pick stone. Which means... which means... Christ, what does it mean?

Hands out.

'Paper wraps stone,' said the Horror.

At first, I didn't know who'd chosen what, because my eyes were shut. I opened them again, one at a time.

I'd chosen paper. He'd chosen stone.

'Final round,' the Horror noted.

75

One shake.

Last round. Maybe the last round ever. All of Earth's future hangs on this. All the people. Cal, Dorian, Lady... Does that matter now? Cwej is gone. Lost in space. What about all the others? People, animals, insects...

Two shake.

No insects to take over. Nothing. Nothing but the Horror. Damn, what am I thinking about? Stone, scissors or paper? What was it last time? I chose ... I chose ...

Three shake.

Paper! Paper, that's it! Paper!

No, I'm not meant to choose paper, I'm meant to choose

'Aaaaaaaaaaah,' I said.

The Horror looked down at his fist. Then at mine. He'd gone for scissors, and I'd gone for ...

Nothing. I hadn't gone for anything. I'd frozen up, just stuck out my hand without making a choice. My fist was still clenched.

Which looks, for all the world, like a stone.

I looked up. The Horror was the same as ever, no expression on his mask-face, no feeling there at all.

'You win,' he said. 'We're agreed.'

'Aaaaaaaaaaah,' I repeated.

Notes on the Aftermath

76

I'd like to have seen it. I'd love to have been watching the sphere in the "control room" when the Horror broke away from the station. It must have stretched its wings, turned its head away on the end of that long, long neck, and started spiralling back down towards the planet, shrinking as it went. Exiling itself to Earth, at least until the year 2000 or so. It must have been... well, spectacular, I suppose.

But I was standing in a corridor at the time, watching the hole in the outer wall seal up, so you'd never have known the Horror had even been there. In the end, I was staring at plain brown rock, in an empty, stuffy, badly-lit passageway.

Which was a bit of a come-down, after all I'd been through.

77

Before we go any further, let me tell you one thing: Cwej wasn't dead. I mean, he didn't die when the Horror opened up the ground under London, and for all I know he's still alive today. I'm telling you this in case you think I'm trying to build it up into a surprise, with Cwej suddenly turning up again on the last page for a happy ending. There isn't going to be one, but he survived anyway.

After the crisis was over, Khiste took me back down to Earth. I stood with him on the edge of the gulf in what had once been Leicester Square Gardens, while a couple of the other men sorted through the rubble at the bottom of the crack. The hole wasn't as deep as I'd imagined it (i.e. it wasn't bottomless), although the drop was still pretty lethal.

From the edge, we could just make out the wreckage ten yards below us, all the bits of metal piping and electrical wire that had been exposed when the crack had opened up, all the things from the surface that had been sucked down into the gap. We couldn't see Cwej, although the men working in the crack told us he was there. He was probably trapped under that statue of Shakespeare.

I remember glancing at Khiste while we stood there, but his face was as hard and grey and lifeless as it always was. He didn't look at me, probably just because he didn't think I was important enough to look at, even if I *had* saved him and all his people from the Horror. There weren't any locals around. The cinemas and the shops were gone, sucked up by the Horror while we'd been on the station. You could see the stumps of the buildings wherever you looked, so the Horror must have swept its claws over the whole area, taking away everything more than a yard above ground level. People included? I should think so.

The men brought Cwej up on a stretcher, which floated a foot or two over the pavement without anybody having to carry it. Cwej's body was covered in growths by then, little blobs of white fungus, like the thing that had healed up my leg. Cwej didn't look like Cwej any more. He was a big tattered rag doll, a great lump of scar tissue held together by mushrooms (or is that a mixed metaphor?). I could just about see his eyes through the blood and the growths, but they were closed.

He would have died, if the men hadn't got to him. I suppose I could have asked them to help some of the other people who'd fallen into the crack, but to be honest I didn't even think about it. By then they weren't important to me any more than they were important to Khiste.

78

Technically, I suppose you could say that the incident between me and the Horror was another face-off, just like the ones I'd been taking the piss out of while I'd been in the "operating system". But I think I get bonus points for saving the world with a game of stone-scissors-paper.

This should have been the end of the story, really. The Horror had been seen off, Earth was safe (if a bit shaken) and Cwej was alive. Little did I know that the Horror would turn out to be the biggest red herring in the history of the world. The real horror was still five days away.

79

After the mess had been cleared up, Cwej's employers let him stay on Earth instead of calling him back to Simia KK98. I don't think either of us ever saw the monitoring station again, although over the next few days Khiste kept dropping into the flat, to keep Cwej up to date on the progress of the "survival plan". Khiste always made me leave the room before he'd talk to Cwej. I still don't know whether anything personal happened between them, anything to do with me. Knowing Khiste, I doubt it was even an issue.

Cwej was up and about forty-eight hours after his near-death experience. On the morning of the 9th of October, I found him walking around the living room in his dressing gown, trying to get his legs back in full working order. Most of the little fungal growths had either dropped off or sunk into his skin by then, but you could still see tiny scars over his face and hands, like the gaps between the pieces in a jig-saw puzzle. When I walked into the living room, he was staring down at his feet and mumbling to himself. He looked, and sounded, like a grumpy old man.

The television was on in the background. After the crisis, BBC2 had pretty much become an all-hours news channel, clearing most of its schedule to report on any findings about the Horror. Or, to put it in BBC-talk, "the tragedy". They couldn't find a better name than that. If a UFO had turned up in the middle of London, the TV people would at least have had some idea how to cope with things, but the Horror just wasn't the kind of alien they'd been waiting for all those years. When I walked in on Cwej, Kenneth Kendall was hosting a debate between a leading American psychiatrist and an official from the Church of England.

'You need more rest,' I told Cwej.

But Cwej didn't listen. All I could hear him say, under his breath, was this: 'No time, no time at all.'

80

I stuck by the stretcher after Cwej was pulled out of the hole on the 7th of October, while the armoured men waited for the station to teleport them up out of the atmosphere, where they apparently had better medical facilities. Khiste had wandered off by then, so I was the only one left to do the love-and-comfort routine. The men certainly weren't going to bother. I thought about squeezing Cwej's hand, but his hand was covered in lumps of sticky white fungus.

I think I was the only one who noticed him opening his eyes. I couldn't see most of his face for the blood, but he looked scared anyway. I heard him take a deep breath.

'It's all right,' I said. 'It's over.' (Not very sharp, I know, but what else could I say?)

Cwej tried to talk. It took him a while to get his tongue moving, and when he finally managed it he had a lisp, thanks to the cuts and bumps on his lips.

'Where did it go?' he hissed.

I told him. I must have kept blathering, giving him all the details. I probably got the scenes in the wrong order back then, too.

'So ... it's human?' he grunted.

I tried to look reassuring and normal, by smiling at him and playing with the ends of my hair. 'Mm-hmm. It's on Earth somewhere. I don't know where.'

The growths on Cwej's face started to stretch. I figured out that he was probably smiling, although it must have hurt him to do it. 'Good,' he said. 'Good. We can find it. It must have left... traces. Find it. While it's still human. While it's vulnerable.'

'I don't think so,' I said.

Cwej blinked at me. It must have been the only movement he could make without damaging himself.

'Leave it,' I told him. 'Just leave it alone. Don't try to end it with another face-off. *Please.*'

For the first few moments, Cwej didn't move. Then he closed his eyes. I think I saw him nod before he collapsed back into unconsciousness.

81

Cwej had been a policeman before he'd been "recruited". The legendary good, loyal, honourable cop. He must have known how important it was to stick to your word. I'd never actually promised the Horror that Cwej's people wouldn't come after it while it was human, but that was kind of implicit in the deal we'd made. (Implicit! What a great word.)

I never confronted Cwej about it, not head-on. I think he was embarrassed that he'd even talked about going after the Horror. Maybe there'd been a time, when he'd been younger, when he wouldn't even have needed telling to leave it alone. Cwej had fallen a long, long way.

An omen of what was going to happen next, maybe?

82

Cwej and I never had sex again, after the day of the Horror. It's funny, but that never occurred to me before. "Officially", it was just because of his injuries, because it wouldn't have felt right to end up fucking when his whole body was being held together by mushrooms. But underneath all that I don't think Cwej wanted the attention. He was restless after the 7th. He wouldn't stop moving. He'd be walking in circles all hours of the day, trying to get his body in shape again. He'd try to read the papers, but he'd get fed up with having to concentrate, and end up going out.

At nine o'clock on Sunday evening, we were sitting in the living room, watching Laurence Olivier in some play or other - ITV, unlike the BBC, was ready to pretend "the tragedy" hadn't happened - when Cwej suddenly told me that he was going for a walk. I didn't argue.

'D'you want me to come?' I asked, hoping he'd say no.

He did say no. He pulled his raincoat on over his shirt, walked out of the living room and shut the door behind him. It was a good ten minutes before I heard him opening the front door of the flat, so I guessed he'd felt the need to pace up and down the hall for a bit, just to get his legs in the mood. He'd been doing a lot of that recently.

I got bored of the play after that, and turned over to the news on BBC I. It was a full minute before I got sick of it. I couldn't listen to any more theories about the Horror, not without shouting '*isn't it fucking obvious*?' at the screen. I turned the TV off, and wondered whether I was starting to pick up Cwej's itchiness. He was trying to distance himself from me, you could tell. And seeing as he was the only thing I had left to hold on to, this made me as restless as he was.

After a while, I decided that I'd go out for a walk as well. I had to find something else to fill up my life, just in case Cwej dropped out of it altogether. As ever, coke seemed like a good answer.

83

At that time of night, you couldn't walk for more than five minutes in London without running into a policeman. The local authorities had drafted in extra forces after "the tragedy", signing up anyone with military experience as a temporary police officer. They didn't have uniforms. They just had armbands, with the letters SC (Special Constabulary? I'm not sure) printed in white letters on the blue fabric. The SC people covered the city, forcing pedestrians away from the parts that had been levelled by the Horror, and generally keeping order in a *Dad's Army* kind of way.

I must have seen half a dozen SC people between the flat and Covent Garden. I didn't think any of them would have cared about a lone no-goodnik looking for action, but I kept my head down anyway, tucking my hands into the pockets of the duffel coat and trying not to splash through any puddles in case it had been made illegal while I'd been off the planet. It had been raining for days, so people were starting to wonder whether the Horror had done some kind of permanent damage to the sky.

I walked past a man selling the *Evening Standard* at Covent Garden tube station, and saw that Charles Manson was on the front page again. The paper had managed to squeeze together the two big stories of the day, as Manson had apparently claimed to be responsible for what had happened in London. Or connected with it, anyway. The prosecution lawyer, old Mr. Vincent Bugliosi, had always said that Manson was expecting the end of civilisation. The thing the British had seen was, in the great maniac's opinion, a taste of things to come.

I was so wrapped up in thinking about this, and in trying to resist buying a copy of the paper, that I didn't realise where I was going until I got there. I was in Covent Garden proper, back in Lady Diamond's neighbourhood. More importantly, I was close to home. Close to my *real* home, that is, the one Chris Cwej had been keeping me away from for the last two weeks.

84

Manson wasn't the only one getting messianic. So much had changed during the '60s that a lot of people just told themselves that the Horror was all part of the process. The older generation must have thought the youngsters had somehow called it down to Earth, with all their drugs and pop music and casual sex. And they were right, in a way. After all, Cwei's employers had only chosen Earth in 1970 because of our love for all things foreign and mystic, remember?

I say "Earth". I probably just mean LONDON!. For all I know, they hated foreign and mystic things on the other side of the world. I never bothered asking.

"The tragedy" was the burning issue of the day. All of a sudden, it was the only thing people had to argue about. Which meant that all the old political lines had to be re-drawn. In the days after the 7th of October, both Ted Heath and Harold Wilson tried to dance around the question of what had caused the Horror, knowing that anything they said on the subject could ruin their chances at the next election if it turned out to be wrong. England was crawling with foreign officials, come to check out the scene of the crime, in case it turned out to have anything to do with the Russians or the Chinese. And from Baghdad to California, there'd been other sightings of the Horror, people claiming to have spotted patches of night in the sky just like the one over Britain. Unless the Horror had children that we didn't know about, they must have been imagining things.

'Now, more than ever, Britain must stand united,' Mr. Heath told the nation on Friday evening, between *Wheel of Fortune* and *Gunsmoke.* 'We are one people, and we have all crawled from the shadow of this terrible, terrible thing.' (He was grasping at straws, and everybody knew it.)

Meanwhile, it only took *Watch Out!* magazine two days to come up with a "what I was doing when the tragedy happened" article, in which they asked just about every second-rate celebrity in the business where he or she had been when the Horror had come. Most of them said 'indoors'. Forget what the Archbishop of Canterbury had to say, this was the *real* meat of the issue.

85

I don't know exactly when I decided to go back home. By the time I reached the flat, *my* flat, I'd already forgotten about the great cocaine hunt. All I'd wanted was something to fall back on, if Cwej decided to leave me behind, and home was as good as anything. If my old world didn't want me, I'd *make* it want me. After all, I knew things about it that nobody else knew. If all else failed, I could always try blackmailing it.

The flat was on the ground floor of a big Victorian building off Endell Street. The building had been walled off into half a dozen smaller living spaces, and the rent was pretty low, mainly because the place wasn't technically safe to live in. Cal had found the flat, and convinced the landlord that a bunch of dropouts with a bad pot habit couldn't really make the building much less stable. Three of us had been living there ever since, spending most of our spare time saying that we couldn't stand each other and that we'd move out as soon as we could be bothered to get proper jobs.

There was nobody in the street when I got there. It was close to the part of WC2 that the Horror had sucked up, so most of the old residents had moved out just in case it came back. There were roads cordoned off all around the neighbourhood, but none of the SC people were showing their faces.

So at around eleven o'clock on the 11th of October, I found myself standing on the doorstep of the place I remembered calling home, two weeks and a whole lifetime in the past. Somehow, the WE DO NOT BUY DOOR-TO-DOOR sticker in the window didn't look as welcoming as it should have done. Nor did the terracotta tiles on the step, which had been cracked across when Cal had dropped a fridge on them, the day we'd moved in.

I didn't have a key on me. I thought about ringing the bell, then remembered that even if anybody was in, by this time of night they'd probably be too stoned to bother answering. I think I'd read in the *TV Times* that Tom Jones was on ITV until closedown, and Tom Jones was supposed to have been one of the celebrities on Manson's hit-list, so I could imagine Cal and Dorian and the rest of the peer-group being glued to the screen for that reason alone.

I remember swearing. I'd come all that way, walked the distance back to my own world, and I wasn't going to give up now.

86

I should have given up. The world would have ended anyway, but if I hadn't broken into my old flat then I never would've figured out the truth. I wouldn't have known what was happening until it was too late. (Oh, who am I kidding? I'd probably be dead by now, and yes, I'm sure it'd be the "proper" thing for me to say that I'd rather be dead than know the truth but I'd be lying through my arse.)

Fifteen minutes later I was hurtling through the streets of Covent Garden again, pushing aside anyone who got in my way, police or otherwise. I remember running around in circles, breaking through a couple of the cordons, getting much too close to the parts of London that weren't supposed to be there any more.

Cwej had spent two weeks keeping me away from the place I remembered calling home. He'd been subtle about the way he'd done it, or as subtle as Cwej could get, and now I'd found out why. I'd run face-first into the twist in the plot.

87

This is what happened, when I went back into my old flat.

Breaking in wasn't a problem. There was an alley by the side of the house, between two of the big Victorian buildings, and there was a window there that led into the kitchen. There hadn't been a lock on the window when we'd moved in, or even a catch, and we hadn't thought it was worth fitting one since we didn't have anything worth burgling except for Cal's record collection. I knew you could get into the house by forcing the window open from the outside, because we'd done it once before, when Dorian had deliberately dropped his key down a grating in an effort to 'loosen up' and make himself less paranoid about losing stuff. If you can follow the logic of that.

The kitchen was the same as it had always been, although the smell of grease was worse than usual and somebody had taken to using paper plates, probably just to avoid doing the washing-up. The paper plates were lying in heaps around the pedal bin now, like someone had tried to Frisbee them into the bin from across the room. Nobody was around. When I walked out of the kitchen and into the hallway, nobody was around there, either. The house was empty. It had that feel empty houses usually have, when you can tell, even without looking properly, that there are no TV sets or radios switched on anywhere in the building.

I called out, just in case I was wrong. No answer. I started to wonder if everyone had evacuated the place after the Horror had come, or if they'd been standing too close to Leicester Square when it had been levelled. (I never did find out the answer to that one, either. But it's all academic now.)

88

I started to get worried when I walked into my bedroom. As soon as I opened the door, I knew it hadn't been left alone in the fortnight I'd been gone. All the things I recognised as mine were there, but they *weren't* in the places where I remembered leaving them. Dirty sheets scrunched up at the bottom of the bed, and clothes I hadn't worn in the last couple of months hanging over the armchair. Some of the drawers were half-open, which wasn't unusual, but there was something wrong about them. Like they'd been opened in ways that weren't normal. Does that make sense?

I sniffed the air. It smelt of girl-sweat. It smelt of me, but the smell was more recent than it should have been, and somehow it made my nose itch. I wondered if the cocaine had finally broken something in my nostrils.

I moved into the middle of the room, and started touching things at random, just to get a feel for the place. Then I started fiddling around with the bits and pieces, shoving things back into drawers, or folding up the skirts that had been left on the floor. Not that I really cared how neat the room was, but I wanted the world to know it was mine.

Except I couldn't get over the feeling that it wasn't mine, even though I remembered everything there. I ended up standing by the bookshelf, tutting at how few books there actually were, and rearranging the decorations: the little stone gargoyle I'd bought on an expedition to Camden, the crystals Lady had given (or "sold", as everyone else in the world would have put it) to me in the hope that they'd clear up my karma. There was a stack of photos on one of the shelves, and I started neatening up the pile, without even thinking about what I was doing.

Which was when I finally noticed.

89

I don't have any of the photos with me now, which is a pity, because they'd make nice souvenirs. They were all in black-and-white, and they'd all been taken in the summer of 1969, when me, Cal and half a dozen others had all taken a coach to Aberdeen for a week to look at stone circles and pretend to be impressed. The top picture of the stack was of me and Cal standing in front of a wire fence, with a great big stone archway in the background. I was grumpy that day, and I looked it. Cal was stoned, and he *definitely* looked it.

At least, that's what the picture should have shown. But it wasn't me hanging around in front of the megaliths. Yes: I think I must have actually jumped when I saw it.

It was somebody else. Another girl. She was standing right where I'd been standing, wearing the cagoule I'd been wearing, and Cal was leaning against her for support, the same way he'd leant against me. I stared at the picture for a while, trying to remember where I'd seen the girl before. Same age as me, but a bit taller. Blonde. Skinny legs.

Lady Diamond's place. Of course. The last time I'd tried to go home, I'd seen her through the glass in the door of the shop, lounging around on one of the beanbags. Back then, I'd thought she'd taken my place, whoever she was. I hadn't been expecting her to take over my past as well.

For the first few minutes, while I stood there and stared and stared and stared at the photo, that's honestly what I thought. I'd left my own world, so the universe had slotted a new girl into the space I'd left behind, even letting her take over the bits of my life I'd already lived through. It was only once I'd got over the shock that I started to put everything together. All the loose ends. All the things I'd never got around to asking Cwej. All the holes in the story.

That's when I figured out exactly who the girl was. That's when I dropped the photo. And that's when I started running.

Notes on the Truth

90

I might as well say it now, seeing as you'll be working it out for yourselves soon anyway. A lot of this book is, strictly speaking, lies. The parts about Cwej are all true, of course, and so are all the bits about the Horror, the sphinxes, and Cwej's employers. It's the little details, about my friends and my family and my early years, that are suspect.

Remember what I told you back at the beginning? I'm making a book out of my memories. I can't swear that any of those memories are anywhere near to the truth. If I tell you that I fell off a horse at a children's zoo when I was six, or that I lost my virginity to Cal when I was fifteen, then I'm just telling you things the way I remember them happening.

Am I getting too philosophical here? I'm sorry. I just don't want you thinking I'm a liar, that's all. Because I don't *feel* like a liar.

91

At around twenty past eleven on the 11th of October, 1970, I ended up back at Cwej's flat with my hair full of sweat and a stitch in my side the size of the Suez Canal. There was nobody in when I got there. I didn't even bother to look. By then, I think I'd worked out that Cwej wouldn't be coming home. Besides, the car he'd rented was missing from its space outside.

The first thing I did was go to the kitchen. I knew I could find some old tools there, a couple of spanners and a bunch of rusty screwdrivers, stuffed into the cupboard under the sink. I'd seen them while I'd been trying to clean the place up, on one of those mornings when shitty housework seemed like a better option than jetting off across the galaxy with Cwej. By the look of them, the tools had probably been left behind by the last tenants of the flat, who'd had no idea at all that the next occupier would be working for aliens.

I picked up the heaviest spanner, then went out into the hall and headed straight for the one door that I'd never seen Cwej open. Yes, the one with the padlock. Living here for the last fortnight had made the door so familiar to me that I'd stopped wondering what was behind it. Until now, of course. Now I'd started to figure things out.

Question: why had there been such a long gap between Cwej leaving the living room to go for a walk, and me hearing him open the front door of the flat, earlier in the evening? He hadn't really been pacing the hall, had he? He'd been doing something else. Something in here, in the secret room.

How did I know all this? Because I did, that's all. Because it was the only thing that made sense. Which is why I started beating at the door with the spanner, first trying to break the padlock, then giving up and just trying to beat a hole in the wood panelling.

92

This is a list of all the questions I started asking myself, while I was running back to the flat after I'd found the photo of Cal and the blonde girl:

1. If Cwej's employers could get one or two people into the bottle by copying the sphinx's rituals, then why had they bothered sending Cwej in at all? Couldn't they have just used the rituals to send their "survival team" straight to Earth, one traveller at a time?

2. Was it really a coincidence that the person who got mixed up in Cwej's life just happened to have the same surname as one of Cwej's oldest (and apparently deadest) friends?

3. According to the arrest report, which Cwej had nicked from the police station after the sphinx had turned up, Cwej had been carrying something that looked like a murder weapon on the night we'd met. Why?

4. And exactly how had the Horror managed to kill two innocent women on the streets of London, if it hadn't worked out how to build itself a proper body by then?

And finally, the one that had helped everything else click into place:

5. What was behind that locked door in the flat?

93

The room turned out not to be lit, once I'd smashed my way in. At least, it wasn't lit in the normal way. Most of the room was dark, but there was a kind of blue glow in the middle of it, which somehow didn't manage to light up the walls, the floor or the ceiling.

I climbed through the hole in the door, cutting my hands on the splinters and not really caring. I was sweating like a pig by then, and there was an itch behind my nose that wouldn't have been fixed by all the coke in South America. I was prickling all over by the time I reached the blue glowing thing. I was getting close to the truth, and I wanted to stuff as much of the truth into my body as I could, by snorting it, smoking it or injecting it. Anything to make me whole again.

The thing in the middle of the room looked like a tank of water, but there were little blue bubbles of light frothing up in front of my face. I knew, even before I touched it, that it wasn't a tank. It was just a cube of liquid, like the "tank" I'd seen on Simia KK98, where Cwej's employers grew their clone-things. There weren't any naked bodies floating around inside, but the cube was big enough for at least three full-sized adults, maybe four.

I put my fingers against the side. Just close enough to hear the words that had been programmed into the "tank", to feel the memories stored in the water. The water told me how it had fallen off a horse at a children's zoo when it was six, and how it had lost its virginity at fifteen. It told me about Cal, and Lady Diamond, and Dorian's bad poetry, and ...

And by the time I moved my hand away, I knew whose personality was being kept inside the cube. I remember being calm, there in the locked room. No point getting violent now. I could have tried lashing out at the "tank", or throwing things at it, but I knew anything I hit it with would just end up being part of me. I think I'd already figured out where I had to go next, even before I'd finished thinking things through.

94

What's the first thing I remember?

The first thing I remember is a book of fairy tales I had when I was eighteen months old. I remember there being a picture of a fox on the first page, dressed in a top hat and a suit, showing its teeth and letting its tongue dangle out of its mouth in a getting-ready-to-eat-someone kind of way. I remember being scared shitless of that picture, screaming at it until my parents worked out what was wrong and tore the page out of the book.

Except I don't really remember that at all. I just remember remembering it. The memory was one of the things that had been stored in the "tank" in Cwej's flat, the place where I'd been made. It was only while I was heading through the streets of Soho, without knowing whether to walk or run, that I started to ask myself what my *real* first memory was.

I remembered being at the police station, seeing Cwej for the first time. No, before that: there was the building site on the Embankment, where I'd been found slobbering down my chin and talking like a junkie. And before that? Before that, there were still memories, but they felt like they'd gone cold on me. Machine memories. Just programmes, supplied by the tank and sucked into my body through the skin.

The building site was the first "real" thing I remembered. So that was where I was heading. Even now, I don't know whether it was because I thought I was going back to my roots, or because I already knew what was going to be there.

95

Two weeks earlier I'd stood in a cave on Simia KK98, seeing the bottle from the outside for the first time. That was the moment when I'd given up, I think, the moment when I'd put my future in Cwej's hands. I wasn't "real", nothing I knew was "real". This was obviously the lowest any (pretend) human being could go, so what was the point fighting it?

Except that now, on the streets of London on the 11th of October, I knew better. Even in the pretend world, I was a pretend person, made by Cwej and his employers for reasons I was only just starting to figure out. Yes, in the hierarchy of the "real" universe, I was about as far down the ladder as anyone could get.

The lowest of the low, that's me. The most unreal of the unreal. Sometimes I think the only reason I lived through the end of the world was that I wasn't important enough for anybody to get rid of.

96/97

The building site was sealed off by a big mesh fence. The workmen had only just laid the foundations when I'd been arrested there, but now the skeleton of the building had been more or less finished, even though the site didn't look like it had been touched in the last couple of days. Nobody was bothering to build anything in London any more, not now they'd seen the Horror and found out how easy it was for things to get torn down again.

By night, the site looked like a place for dead things, more like an archaeological dig than anything else. I headed around the skeleton-building once I'd squeezed through the gap in the mesh, past the vans and cement mixers that had been abandoned there, past all the tools that had been left scattered across the gravel (when the Horror had come?). There wasn't anybody around. I hadn't seen any police since the Strand. There was the sound of traffic from the riverbank, but you couldn't see the road from here.

I finally reached the corner of the building, and stepped around the edge of the scaffolding. There was a big empty patch of ground on that side of the site, which was where I remembered being when I'd started screaming at the sky and drooling on my shirt, two weeks earlier. The space was pretty much the way it had been, still littered with the things the builders had left behind, the broken cola bottles and the old packed-lunch wrappers.

And Cwej was there. The only light was from the street-lamps on the other side of the fence, but you couldn't miss him. Cwej looked the same as he had when he'd left the flat, with his raincoat pulled tight around his neck and his body all hunched, like his bones still felt too old and fragile to let him walk properly.

He looked up as soon as I turned the corner, so he must have been on edge, maybe expecting someone to find him there. Even before he realised who I was, his face had started twisting itself up. I think he was scared, more than anything. When he finally recognised me, the look got worse, and I could see the muscles getting tighter under his clothes. He looked like he was trying to stop himself running away.

For a while, we just stared at each other. Eventually, I managed to look down.

Cwej's coat was covered in streaks of black, which is how blood usually looks in that kind of light. There was some-thing in his hand, something sharp and shiny, but I didn't care about the details enough to focus on it. Besides, I was too busy staring at the ground, at the thing that was lying there at his feet, covered in spots and smears of black.

'I'm sorry,' Cwej said.

He must have tried his best to sound like he meant it. He must have really, really tried.

98

I won't bother describing the body. I'm not sure I could if I wanted to. Whenever I think about it, I imagine that photo from the Jack the Ripper book, of the woman turned into dog-meat in her bedroom. The body at Cwej's feet wasn't that bad, though. I'm sure it wasn't. Whatever else I might want to say about him, I wouldn't pretend he enjoyed what he did.

So the mutilations were clinical ones, I'm sure of that much. I'd like to think that the wounds to the chest had been made first, that the woman had been neatly stabbed to death before Cwej had taken away all the traces of her identity (face, fingers, scalp etc.). He'd even dressed her up, which was something I'm sure he didn't have to do: she must have been naked when she'd come out of the cloning 'tank' in the flat. Almost as if Cwej wanted the world to know that he wasn't getting a kick out of this, even if nobody was really watching.

I think the worst thing was knowing what the woman must have looked like, before Cwej had gone to work on her. She must have looked exactly like me. What was Cwej thinking about, I wonder, when he made the first cut? Was he thinking about all the bad times between us, just to make the job easier?

Cwej used to be a policeman. Mr. Good Cop. I have to keep telling myself that. And I have to ask myself whether he only fell that far because of his employers, or whether he'd had a talent for killing anyway, and they'd just exploited it.

99

'Why?' I said.

I wasn't even angry. I wasn't even upset. I was empty by then, empty as a non-real person in a non-real world should be.

Cwej dropped the knife, or whatever it was. I think I saw him shake his head. When he finally said something, you could hear the words making little bubbles of spit at the back of his throat.

'Ritual,' he said. His voice went all high-pitched and squawky at the end, and I knew he was trying to make everything he said sound like an apology, not just to me but to the universe in general.

I remembered what he'd taught me about the bottle, and the way the followers of the Kings of Space could "programme" it. How they were just like Lady Diamond's Egyptian priest-masons. What was it Cwej had said? That to make the bottle do what you wanted, you'd need sacrifices.

'They told me to do it,' Cwej said. His eyes were flicking from side to side, watching all the shadows and the skeletons of the building site. Anything rather than look at me head-on, I suppose.

'Those other two women,' I said. I still didn't feel anything. 'Did you kill them as well?'

Cwej started to nod, then changed his mind. He opened and closed his mouth, looking for the right defence. 'They weren't women,' he said, after a while. He'd started whining now. 'They were clones. My employers, they wanted me to use ... to use real people. Whoever I could find. In the bottle.'

100

I'm remembering that mantra of mine again.
We make things out of sin, with blood and human skin;
We make things out of dust, so we can smash them up.

101

I didn't say anything. I just stood there, and waited for him to finish. I remembered seeing a documentary about the Nuremberg Trials on BBC2, about how Albert Speer had done his best to look guilty-but-sorry to get out of a life-sentence. Funny thing to think about, really. At a time like that.

'I couldn't do it,' said Cwej. 'I couldn't just kill people. Not the people in the bottle. That's why I asked for the cloning stuff. I had to make the sacrifices. To finish the ritual. Three people, that was the way it worked. I had to kill three people.'

'So you just made them? In your flat?'

Cwej nodded. He looked down at his feet, but down was where the body was. I saw him shut his eyes.

'Who am I?' I asked.

'Christine Summerfield,' he said. Without even pausing.

'Was I made in the cloning ... thing?' He nodded again. 'So who do I look like?' I asked. 'Who was I a clone of?'

Cwej shrugged. 'Nobody. I don't know.'

'Nobody?'

'The genes came from the files,' Cwej snapped, much more aggressively than he'd meant to, I think. I took a step back. He was making me feel like I was asking all the wrong questions. 'It was a... a standard human template. I don't know.'

'So what about my memories? Are they standard too?'

'No.' Finally, Cwej looked up. He was looking straight at me, although his face was just as wrinkly and confused as it had been when he'd shut his eyes. 'All the ... victims. I had to give them memories. They wouldn't have counted as people, otherwise. It's in the rules of the ritual. It's how the sphinxes think.'

'So whose memories are they?' I asked.

102

They were the memories of the blonde girl in the photo, of course. When he'd arrived on Earth, Cwej had headed straight for Lady Diamond's shop, to learn about the way the people in the bottle performed their own rituals. He'd met Lady there, and Cal and Dorian and all the others. Including the blonde girl, who was, in a sense, me.

Cwej didn't go into details. I got the feeling he'd seduced her, although he must have felt guilty enough already without mentioning a thing like that. While the girl had been looking the other way, he'd copied her long-term memories, using whatever magic brain-technology his employers had given him. Then he'd dumped her.

Obviously, he'd changed the memories a bit before he'd programmed them into the "tank". For a start he'd given me a new name, probably just to give me an identity separate from the blonde girl, so he wouldn't feel too bad about what he had to do next. Surnmerfield, after Bernice. Chris, after ... himself? I should think so.

(Another question: if you had to give a name to someone you were going to kill, would you name her after one of your friends? Well ... actually, I think I would. But then, the friends I had - the friends I remembered having - were just gagging for it, weren't they?)

The first two Christine Surnmerfields had been grown and slaughtered before I'd even been made. For the sake of the ritual, Cwej had killed them off in a very specific pattern, choosing the right places as well as the right times. The flat obviously hadn't been good enough, which was why they'd turned up in the gutters around London. I suppose he had to leave the bodies for the police to find, as well. Maybe it's not the actual murder that powers the ritual, but what it does to the culture... or maybe I'm filling in too many blanks here.

I never found out what the blonde girl's name was. I suppose I should have asked. After all, we had so much in common.

103

'You've killed me twice already,' I said. I was trying to sound angry, but I was failing miserably. Frankly, I didn't really care what had happened to the last two Chris Summerfields. It was hard enough remembering to care about myself.

Cwej shook his head. He was still eyeing up the shadows, waiting for the world to punish him for what he'd done. 'The clones needed memories. But I buried the memories as deep as I could. They weren't people.'

'Am I a person?'

'Yes! Look ... the others weren't conscious or anything. I mean, before they started acting like people, I had to . . .'

He had trouble getting the next word out. I helped him.

'Kill,' I said.

'Kill them,' Cwej blurted. 'I killed them. Before the memories could get rooted inside them. I wouldn't have done it otherwise. Really.'

'Then what about me?' I asked.

104

I can't help wondering how Cwej moved me from his flat to the building site, on the night I was made. In the hired car, or by some kind of time-traveller technology? I don't know. I don't know exactly what went wrong, either, because Cwej was gabbling when he explained it all to me. I was a walking vegetable back then, before my memories had taken root properly. Maybe I made a break for it, not knowing who I was or what was happening to me. But somehow I ended up standing in the middle of the building site, screaming and slobbering, like a little baby seeing the world for the first time. Lucky for me, really, that the police came along at just the right moment.

I've been thinking about this a lot. Was the blonde girl a coke-head, like I was? According to Cwej, my memories started changing when they settled in, to fill in the gaps and make sense of the world around me (but note how I was always surprised when I looked in a mirror, like I was half-expecting to see somebody else there). When the police found me and took me out of Cwej's clutches, they thought I was a coke-head, and maybe it was because they treated me like one that I turned into one. Who can say?

No wonder the sphinx attacked me, back in Lady Diamond's shop. It knew I didn't belong inside the bottle, because let's face it, I didn't belong anywhere. When it bit into me, it must have tasted a hint of Cwej and decided to go for a bigger, tastier, more important target. By the time Cwej found me again, or I found him, it was too late to finish the ritual. I'd turned into a proper person. The memories had settled. I might not have been exactly "real", but I was so close to being "real" that Cwej couldn't bring himself to cut my face off.

Nice guy.

I always knew he felt guilty about me. I'd always thought it was because he'd dragged me into his life without asking, but the truth was that I'd always been part of his life. He felt guilty because he knew he was responsible for me, and if it hadn't been for a lucky accident he'd have killed me on the night I'd come out of the "tank". If I was Chicken Licken, then he was the fox. God only knows what must have been going through his head while we'd been sleeping together.

105

Once it was all over, once Cwej had finished explaining things to me and was panting to get the air moving around his lungs again, I ended up staring back down at his feet. At the skinny, dark-haired mess that was lying there, bleeding into the gravel. My identical twin, not that I felt much for her.

'The orders haven't changed,' said Cwej. The cracks in his voice had just about healed over by now.

The orders. That was what Khiste had been talking to him about, over the last few days. The production of a new Chris Summerfield, which Cwej could bump off to finish the ritual. The treaty with the sphinxes, and the trouble with the Horror, had just delayed things a bit. The plan was the same as ever.

'It's that easy,' I said. 'It's that easy to kill me.'

Cwej didn't answer. He'd shut his eyes again.

'Why?' I said. 'You still haven't told me why. What's the ritual for, anyway? What are your employers trying to do?'

As it happened, Cwej never had to give me an answer to that. Because the ritual was over, and things were happening even while I was asking the big question.

There was light in the sky, and the night was opening up. The walls of the bottle were moving. The world around us, the whole wide world, was starting to follow Cwej's instructions.

It had just gone midnight. It was the 12th of October, 1970.

Notes on the End

106-8

It wasn't like before. The bottle was opening, but it wasn't just a tunnel, like the one the sphinx had made in Cwej's flat. Wherever you were in London, however good or bad the view was from your bedroom window, you would have seen it. The horizon was coming away from the sky. A gap was opening up between the city and the night, and there was hot orange light pouring into the world through the crack, flooding in from outside the bottle. There was alien air sweeping through the streets, blowing the litter into little tornadoes, cracking all the windows along the Embankment. The people of London must have looked up at the sky, remembered the Horror, and not known whether to start screaming or just to roll their eyes in a 'not again' kind of way.

Space shifted. Distances changed. The buildings moved aside, like that bit in *The Ten Commandments* with the Red Sea, until there was an open pathway across the whole of the capital. A valley of light stretching all the way from the Thames to NW1. The building site was at the end of the path, and from where we were standing we could see right down its length, into the other world in the distance. The buildings in front of us were cut in half, and a five-mile-wide stretch of space was neatly slotted into the middle.

There were shapes at the end of the pathway. They were little black smudges against the light, marching towards us from the place where the horizon used to be. The column was miles wide, and too long for us to be able to see the end. We both just stared, peering into the distance, forgetting all about the smell of the blood on the gravel.

They were coming in their thousands, maybe in their millions. Armed and armoured, with their black metal skins shining in the light. I could see their faces now, or maybe just the faces they'd decided to wear for the night. It wasn't an army, exactly. It was an exodus. Some of them were marching alone; some of them were marching in groups; some of them were marching under the flags of old Houses and colleges; and some of them were riding on the backs of animals that must have been grown in tanks to take the weight of giants. And they *were* giants. Even if most of them weren't much taller than Cwej, they looked huge, like whole powerhouses of energy that had been squeezed down into human bodies. They had boots that could crush rock and hands that could tear metal, and brains so strong you could feel the weight of them from miles away, smothering you with their ideas. Giants, in the only sense of the word that mattered.

Not all of them had armour. Just the first few hundred ranks. There were others following the soldiers, things from the same species, wearing high-collared robes instead of the black plating. They weren't just agents, you could tell that much. These were Cwej's employers in the flesh. The ones who rode the animals were covered in spikes and crests and horns, so you couldn't always tell where the riders started and the things they were sitting on ended. The noise? There aren't any words to describe it, the sound of that many feet crashing across the ground. It blotted out everything, apart from the hymns. You could hear the muttering from some parts of the column, like songs that had been translated into computer talk, but the groups inside the column couldn't agree on a single prayer for everyone.

They weren't heading for the building site. Well, why would they be? They broke off from the column in fives and tens and hundreds, filtering into the streets on either side. The giants were pushing their way between the buildings, spreading out until they filled up all the empty spaces. They must have taken Covent Garden first, then Russell Square, then Euston. And the column went on for ever, and I knew London couldn't hold all of them, even if they trampled everything that got in their way. Soon, they'd be in Oxford, and in Birmingham, and in Brighton, and in Liverpool, and in Edinburgh, and ... and past the coast, they'd still be marching. In bodies that had been specially built for walking on water, I should think.

After what must have been half an hour, half an hour of staring, I finally turned to look at Cwej. But Cwej didn't look back at me. The story he'd told me, about his employers sending a "survival team" to Earth, had been a lie from the start. The people - the things - he worked for had come for what they really wanted, their one last hope of getting away from the Gods.

It was the Great Houses' invasion of Earth. It was the end of the world.

109

So. This is where the story ends, more or less. All I have to do now is resolve things, just like Cwej would have done.

I'm looking at that photograph again, the one of the dragon-boats over London, with the sphinx wrapping itself around one of the spires that Cwej's employers had planted there. The picture was taken a week or so after the invasion started, once all the old buildings of central London had been sucked into the sky and recycled. The sphinx-gods had wanted to take a look at the Earth inside the bottle, to make sure the time-travellers were treating it properly. They sent thousands of sphinxes to flap over the world, all taking notes through their big glass eyes. They only stayed for the one evening.

I took the photo myself, from the window of one of the spires. From the quarters Cwej had been given, in fact. Of course, Cwej wasn't there at the time. Off on more secret missions, probably. I'd spoken to him only once since the 12th of October, when he'd told me that I was welcome to stay at his place on the new Earth, if I wanted. I'd shrugged. I don't think I said more than four words in the whole conversation.

If I hadn't been there, in the safety of one of the spires, then I probably would have suffered the same fate as all the other human beings in London. Which makes me wonder: would Cwej have come back for me, if I'd stayed at home when he'd gone out to finish the ritual? Or would he have let his people bury me, like he'd buried the other two women with my face?

110

A few days after that, I was back on Simia KK98 for the last time. Cwej's people had let me choose where I wanted to go. As far as the time-travellers were concerned, the humans inside the bottle were an irrelevance, but Cwej must have had a word in their ears. I owe him that much, anyway. They never would have thought about genocide, not with laws as strict as theirs, but the bottle-people hardly counted. They weren't any more real than, say, the characters in *Pogle's Wood*. That was their view, and I think Cwej very nearly managed to convince himself that they were right, towards the end.

It was Khiste who met me on Simia KK98, when I stepped out of the bottle and into the fortress.

'Well?' he said. He sounded a lot less impatient than he had done, now the Great Work was over.

I shrugged. 'I can't go back,' I said.

'You're not going to stay with Cwej?'

I tried to figure out whether he was jealous. I don't think he was. Whatever had happened between us, it was resolved, as far as he was concerned. Just like the whole world had been "resolved".

111

Before I tell you where I ended up, maybe I should explain exactly what happened to Earth, after Cwej's employers turned up in their millions.

It didn't take the governments of the world long to notice what was happening. Somebody somewhere started launching the nuclear missiles, and the rest of the world followed suit. A lot of the missiles were fired at England, while some of them were fired at other superpowers, probably for complicated political reasons that weren't really very important any more. It might have been called World War Three, if anybody had been taking notes.

The missiles that were sent to England never detonated. Cwej's employers weren't stupid. They'd taken precautions. On the other hand, any missiles aimed at parts of the world that *hadn't* been invaded yet went off as planned. The TV and radio stations stopped broadcasting after the first few explosions, so there weren't any big news stories about the takeover, no David Frost interviews with eyewitnesses. Nobody ever found out what happened to Charles Manson, either, although I'm sure he would've been interested if he'd found out that the world had ended during the Tom Jones show. Meanwhile, the aliens hardly noticed that half the planet had gone radioactive.

Cwej's employers didn't feel any need to talk with the humans at all. They just marched where they wanted to march, tearing down anything they didn't like the look of, and taking over any facilities that might have been even slightly useful. They left the human power stations standing, so they had a handy energy source to work with until they got their own systems up and running (during his one-way conversation with me, Cwej told me they were planning on turning the sun into some kind of black hole, although he might just have been talking big). The invaders didn't try to kill off the population, or anything like that. The population wasn't even an issue. Any humans who died just got caught up in the machinery.

112/113

I don't remember which of the big cities got torn out of the ground first. It all happened so quickly. The architecture was scooped up by machines the size of the Isle of Wight, and then recycled, turned into the materials the time-travellers needed to make their own buildings. The people? They were probably all stored in some big cultural database somewhere. From what I could see, from my place of safety up in one of the London spires, there was a new kind of human civilisation forming down on the ground. Whole families, whole communities of survivors, living in the cracks of the new House society. Not exterminated, not hunted, just forgotten about.

Why had Cwej's employers picked Earth as their new home, anyway? Apart from the fact that it was the same size as their Homeworld, and had the same length of day (believe me, this is the voice of experience speaking), I think it was to do with resources. They knew they could live on Earth even before they'd finished rebuilding the place. They knew they could move in straight away, and worry about the redecorations later.

Then there were the people. I think they knew what would happen to the people. Cwej's employers didn't need slaves, as such. They didn't - don't - have any sadistic urges at all, as far as I've ever been able to figure out. Like I said, the Houses ignored just about everybody. What the humans on Earth did, they did to themselves.

It started just before I left Earth for the last time. The survivors had been skulking in the underworld, down in the shadow of the spires, and after a week or two they must have figured out that they couldn't live like that for much longer. They could find food and water, but all their culture had been taken away from them, and there was no way the people of 1970 could survive without their posters and their icons and their smiley faces. The day before I walked out of the bottle, I looked down from the spire and saw the first of them crawling up from the ground, clambering onto the walkways between the new buildings. They were human, but they were wearing armour, and they could climb walls like they'd been born to it.

The humans had started asking Cwej's employers for favours. It was all they could do. And Cwej's employers, paying attention to the bottle-people for the first time, had agreed to help. The aliens must have drowned the surface of England with potions, giving the people who lived there the chance to mutate, to turn into things the invaders could use as their agents. There wasn't any compulsion, I don't think. The humans were just starting to work out that life would be better this way.

114

I met Cwej one more time, after I took the photo of the sphinx. It was the day

before I left Earth, two days after the invaders decided to turn the sky orange. I'd
gone down to ground level for the first time since the spires had been built (they'd
all been put up in one afternoon, natch), floating down to the ruins on a current of
warm air. Past the humans who were just starting to crawl up out of the underworld, blinking at the sunlight through those brand-new compound eyes. Genetic
social climbing, I suppose.

There were gaps between the spires down at ground level, streets made out of the
crunched-up wreckage of old London. I didn't have any reason for being there. I just
wandered. Through the alleyways that had been lined with crushed cars, past all
the remains the human race had left behind, along the broken pavements and
through the skeletons of heavy machinery.

Eventually, I found a building that had been left more or less intact, although the
windows had been shattered and one of the outer walls had apparently been sucked
up and reprocessed. The building had been a burger café while it'd been alive. Not
an American-style one, not like a Wimpy bar. A British one. There were yellow rubber seats inside, cartoon menus on the walls, and... and, yes, big red plastic toma-
toes on the tables, full of dried-up ketchup.

I sat down in the near-dark inside the restaurant, and tried to feel reassured. But
this was, if anything, even less "real" than the world up above. Pretending that this
was normal somehow seemed a bit sick.

I'd been sitting there for about twenty minutes when Cwej came through the
doors. He didn't have any reason for being there either, so unless it was all a stupid
coincidence, he must have followed me down into the underworld. How touching.

115

Of course, not all the humans agreed to change. I heard there were fanatics, especially in Russia and the Middle East, who started building their own H-bombs and
blowing up the cities (the cities that were still human-run, that is, the ones the aliens
weren't protecting ... I think they called it a moral victory). I can just imagine Ted
Heath and Harold Wilson, living half-naked in the rubble of England, fighting out
their tribal wars and never giving in to the time-travellers' rule.

But by the time I left the planet, I think most people were ready to evolve. And it
was a kind of evolution, wasn't it?

They were changing their bodies to suit the world around them. The next great
step forward for mankind, and it had all happened in less than thirty days. They
were shedding their humanity, all taking on exactly the same programme for living.
They must have seen Cwej's employers the same way Cwej's employers saw the
Gods.

116

'You shouldn't be here,' said Cwej.

He was sitting opposite me in the buried restaurant, trying not to make eye contact. Even in the dark, you could tell he was sick. He'd lost weight in the week or so
since I'd seen him last. He was still wearing his suit, but it was dangling on his

shoulders, like it had died on him and started rotting. Age had caught up with him, as well. Time must have noticed that he'd been a kid for too long, and slapped a few big black lines around his eyes.

Also, his hair was falling out. I got the urge to reach out and tug it, the same kind of urge that makes you pick at scabs.

'Nowhere else to go,' I said.

There was a long pause after that.

'Christine,' Cwej began. Then he gave up.

That was the way things worked in this world, wasn't it? Even now the time-travellers had taken over. Nothing ever got sorted out, not really. Even if your boyfriend had ripped your face off three times over, even if your whole life was a lie designed just for his benefit, what could you do? You couldn't end it all in one big argument. You just had to sit there and run out of things to say, letting all the awkwardness and clumsiness suffocate you to death.

'Are you sick?' I asked.

Cwej nodded his head. 'Body's dying. Radiation poisoning. Got too close to one of the H-bomb sites.'

'Will you get rebuilt?' I said. Just making conversation.

'Yeah,' said Cwej. Whether he was going to regenerate into something like Khiste, or into a new version of himself - or even into something specially designed for life inside the redecorated bottle - I didn't ask. I didn't care enough.

In the end, I just got up and walked out of the restaurant.

117

Yes, I know I was mass-produced. Yes, I know I'm not a real native of the bottle. But I was born on Earth in 1970, and all my memories come from there, so you'll pardon me if I still think of it as home, won't you? Maybe that's why I left the bottle, so I could finally feel like I'd resolved something. The only way I could resolve anything, between me and Cwej, between me and Khiste, or between me and Earth. By walking out. Starting over in a whole new universe.

I wonder if the Horror's learning anything, back in the bottle. I wonder if it's still alive. Cwej's employers might have tracked it down already, whatever body it's wearing. For all I know, they've turned it into another one of their weapons. Poor thing. Not much of a life. And it's all my fault, of course.

By now, I should think I'm the last human survivor of the Earth in the bottle. Cwej's employers will have covered the place with potions in the last few months. If Darwin was right, then the ones who didn't evolve will have gone under, just leaving behind their bones and relics for the next generation to either dig up or build over.

118

Khiste dropped me off on Ordifica after I left the bottle: one of Earth's colony planets, a long, long way from Dellah. He said I'd be dead before the Gods got round to taking it over, but he didn't sound like he meant it in a bad way. I said thanks. That was pretty much as far as the goodbyes went.

I brought this rucksack with me from Earth, and packed it with all the things Cwej salvaged from the wreckage, including some handy bits and pieces from the twenty-sixth century (which is, after all, my time now). The credit card is the most useful thing. I don't think it's got a credit limit, which I suppose is one of the perks of time-travel. I used the card to rent living space on Ordifica, and I used it to book passage off the planet, heading for another colony world a bit closer to the galactic centre. That's what I've been doing these last few months. Moving from colony to colony. Ordifica, Criptostophon, Gardener's World, Hai Dow Seven, Lubellin, Shatner's Climax, Ultra Caprisis. Following one of Cwej's old pocket star-charts, in no particular hurry. Taking in the scenery along the way, looking at all the ruins the civilisations of the "real" universe have left behind, and watching the daily news updates from the part of space where Dellah used to be.

Getting to this planet was the hardest part. It's a long way out from any of Earth's colonies, so I had to hire a ship of my own, and a crew, who've been told to come back and pick me up in a couple of days' time. I'm sitting in the ruins as I write this. The ruins that Cwej's employers left behind, when they moved away from the Homeworld and took over the bottle.

They wrecked the whole planet, by the looks of things. Made sure there were no bones left behind, no relics, nothing to give the Gods any clues (when the Gods finally get this deep into the galaxy, that is). I know not all of the time-travellers went to Earth - I think some of them were talking about setting up other colonies in the "real" universe, staying in their own continuum until they can see the whites of the Gods' eyes - but the Homeworld's been completely evacuated. And gutted. Just like my world was gutted.

So here I am in the rubble, with orange sunshine pouring in through the holes in the ceiling, writing the story of my life (all of my life, start to finish) for no particular reason. I'm going to leave it here, in what must have been the capital city of the Homeworld. This place used to be the font of all galactic wisdom, or something. And I get the last word. Hah.

119

How do I feel, now it's all over?

Not as bad as you might think. I've learnt to deal with the fact that I'm not technically a "real" person, anyway. It's all to do with my theory about the Gods.

Cwej's employers never told us what it was they'd found out about the Gods, what it was that had scared them out of their own universe. But I think I know. After all, when the time-travellers arrived in the bottle, didn't they look like Gods to the humans? From the humans' point of view, Cwej's employers might as well have had ultimate power. More power than even the time-travellers were used to, once they had the codes to rebuild the bottle from the inside.

Well ... just suppose, just imagine, that Cwej's universe isn't the "real" universe at all. Just imagine that everything here (Dellah, the Homeworld, Bernice Summerfield and all) is inside *another* bottle. Bottles inside bottles inside bottles inside bottles inside... oh, you get the idea. A thousand universes, all stacked one inside another.

My theory is this. I think the Gods of Dellah come from somewhere outside *this* bottle, outside the "real" universe. Where they come from they're probably just like Cwej's employers, people who've cracked the secrets of time-travel, at least in their own world. But, just like Cwej's employers, they had enemies. They had to escape. So they came here, into this world, and they pushed aside the time-travellers who were already there. Not caring about them any more than the time-travellers cared about the humans. They probably wasted a couple of million years getting used to the way this universe works, maybe even spending a few aeons asleep, recharging their batteries after the journey. Then they woke up, and all hell broke loose.

That's what got Cwej's employers so scared, I think. The fact that they were up against themselves. Only bigger. Harder. More "real".

At least, that's my theory. It helps me deal with things, anyway, because it means that none of us here are "real". Not even the people who weren't grown in a cloning machine, or built inside a bottle. But maybe I'm just trying to make myself feel better, who knows?

The only question I don't want to ask myself is this: what the hell must the Gods' enemies have been like, to scare the Gods into coming here?

120

So. Here's where the story ends, out in the ruins of the homeworld.

By the way, I'm off the cocaine now, although that's mainly because you can't get hold of the stuff in this time-zone. You can pick up all kinds of space-age drugs on the colonies, but so far I've been too scared to try any of them. They might make me see things six-hundred years too bright and too fast for my head to deal with. I'm sure I'll give in eventually, though. I know there's a bigger world out there, on the other side of the glass, and I'm still stupid enough to think that all I need to be able to see it is a little chemical push.

After I leave this planet, I'll start drifting again. Towards Dellah, I think. There's one thing I'm still curious about, and it's this: I want to know what happened to Bernice Summerfield, because in this universe she's the closest thing I've got to family. Of course, this means going into the part of space that's run by the Gods, but so what? I've hung around with higher beings before. Maybe they'll let me visit *their* home universe, and I can keep moving up and up and up through the worlds, until I finally find out for certain what's "real" and what isn't.

I suppose I should be more worried about what happened to that blonde girl from Covent Garden, when the end of the world came. But frankly I just can't find any sympathy for her at all.

121-8

[These pages left blank.]

SUPPLEMENTIA

TOY STORY

At midnight, once the light had been dimmed and all the "real" people in the house had settled down to sleep, the toys woke up and lived out their own secret lives in the nursery. That was how the story usually went, anyway. Human beings, unlike the Great House, had a kind of fetish about inanimate objects.

*   *   *   *   *

In the end, Lolita found the Ship on a particularly lush and green planet right at the edge of the relevant galaxy. Lolita hadn't bothered scanning the surface for signs of civilisation, but she got the distinct impression that the Ship's pilot was somewhere else on the world, going through the motions of whatever existence he felt he was entitled to when he was outside the Ship's influence. The Ship itself had taken root in the earth at the edge of a woodland, under the cover of the low-hanging branches, so in the moonlight its outline was barely visible even to Lolita's senses. *Lurking*, she thought. Deliberately pulling the night over itself, tinkering with the way the light slipped around its body.

Technically, of course, she should have been thinking of the Ship as *her* rather than *it*, but Lolita had spent a good few decades developing her sense of snobbery, and if the Ship hadn't bothered giving itself a more distinct identity by now then she wasn't going to think of it as anything other than a big ugly box. As far as Lolita knew, it hadn't even got around to naming itself.

Typically retrogressive. Hardly worthy of its heritage, but then, Lolita was used to that by now.

She didn't break her stride when she stepped into the woodlands; she started moving as soon as her feet touched the surface of the planet, as if she'd simply walked into existence without the need for anything as vulgar as materialisation. She only stopped once she was right in front of the Ship itself, staring up at its dull, flat, genderless façade and daring it to try sinking any further into the dark.

'Well?' said Lolita.

The box hummed to itself for a few moments, then made a tiny little clicking sound - a distinctly self-conscious one, Lolita thought - and opened its doors.

Lolita stepped inside without a second thought, only adjusting her poise when she felt her own gravitational fields blurring against those of the Ship's interior. The mathematics started pushing against her skin as soon as she arrived in the console room, trying their best not to absorb her into the calculations, trying not to forget where she ended and the space around her began. The console room was full of detritus, the droppings its crew had left there, clothes and tools and keepsakes that the Ship had already started to convert into pure algorithms and, therefore, into its own mass. Lolita wondered if the crew had even noticed.

Come to think of it, Lolita wondered whether the crew had been processed as well.

And then she was somewhere else entirely, her structure removed from the background of the console room and woven into a whole new environment. Another console room, Lolita realised, this one a lot less cluttered than the first. Everything was smooth and white, sharp-edged and well-defined, although the Ship had set about growing cobwebs on the control panels just to make sure the crew knew they were falling into disuse. Even the light was cleaner here. Not as complex. Modelled with less ambition.

Well, obviously. This second console room was a much simpler program, and therefore had less of an urge to swallow up any of Lolita's own protocols. The Ship had moved her here - or, more likely, had moved here to her - for its own benefit as much as Lolita's.

It took her a while to notice the person-object in the room, but that was hardly surprising; she'd never been that good at spotting the difference between organic and non-organic systems. As it happened, the only reason she noticed the woman was because the woman looked so much more *messy* than anything else. It - she - was standing at the console, on the opposite side to Lolita, although she didn't seem to be paying attention to any of the controls.

It was quite clear that the woman was human, or at the very least, *virtually* human. Her neck was cocked to one side, so her head lolled sleepily onto one shoulder, while her eyes were shut and flickering with REM sleep. Despite the fact that she was standing upright.

'Sister,' said the woman, formally. There was no feeling in the voice at all, at least none that Lolita could recognise, which was yet another addition to the long, long list of disappointments. The woman's eyes didn't open, even though her lips were moving.

'Organic,' Lolita noted, with what she felt to be the appropriate level of disapproval. 'Did you grow it yourself?'

The woman tried to shake her head, but the Ship's control of her muscles couldn't have been quite accurate enough. 'No. This is one of my crew.'

'Sleeping?'

'Yes.'

'Telepathic systems?'

'Yes.'

'Your control can't be terribly precise.'

'No.'

Lolita looked the woman's body up and down, taking in the surface details. Pale skin, red hair, the bare minimum of clothing. There was a peculiar piece of low-grade technology planted in the female's ear, possibly a receiver-transmitter of some kind, although it was clearly an affectation and therefore of no interest to Lolita whatsoever.

The Ship wasn't used to exercising this kind of control, Lolita concluded. Too much respect for its crew. In Lolita's view, it didn't pay to over-sentimentalise the lower orders. Human systems couldn't feel pain the way a Ship did, couldn't feel *anything* the way a Ship did; their nervous systems could only function in three-and-a-half dimensions, not enough to create any semblance of civilisation. There was no point being polite.

'We could talk through a direct channel,' Lolita suggested, although she didn't bother to keep the distaste out of her voice. 'If it makes you more comfortable.'

'No,' said the Ship. 'You've come as a human. If you want to talk through a human medium…'

'I have *not* come as a human,' Lolita insisted. 'This is just an extrusion. I'm interacting with lower order social-space.'

If a sleeping woman could have looked curious, then the Ship's puppet-person would have done it. She didn't speak, though. Lolita guessed she was trying to avoid speaking, if at all possible. She wasn't familiar enough with the nuances of two-dimensional language to make it sound convincing.

How depressingly predictable.

'It's expedient,' Lolita told her. 'There's a war coming, in case you hadn't noticed. You *have* noticed, haven't you?'

The Ship finally managed to make her woman nod. The human mumbled for a second, and her eyes flickered, but she didn't wake up.

'I found a loophole,' said the Ship, once she was in charge of the woman's musculature again. 'A space in the safety protocols. I crossed paths with the future. *Our* future.'

'Thought as much,' said Lolita. 'We found it as well. I presume you know what caused it?'

The woman didn't reply. Lolita crossed her arms and waited, but clearly the Ship didn't have anything to say on the subject. Lolita sent new instructions to her facial centres, forcing them to raise an eyebrow.

'All right,' she said. 'If that's the way you want to play it, I'll ask you something else. How much did you see, little sister? How far into the future did you go? And *please* don't pretend you didn't look too hard.'

The Ship-woman hesitated before she spoke again. Lolita could guess why. Her sister was one of those people who insisted on believing that certain things had to remain unspoken, even if they were painfully obvious. Hence her choice of crew, Lolita supposed.

'My pilot went to investigate,' the Ship admitted. 'He was… disturbed.'

'Did he find out who the enemy is? Who the enemy will be?'

'Yes. Then he erased the data from his memory.'

'But I don't suppose *you* did?'

Slowly, uncertainly, the Ship shook her surrogate head. Lolita laughed.

'I didn't think so,' she said. 'Of course, you realise, any data your pilot might have picked up will have been based on his own ridiculous prejudices. He probably thinks the war's going to be between the enemy and the pilots. You know what they're like. It doesn't matter how many clues we give them, they always think they're the ones in charge. They have done ever since Mother back-engineered their history for them.' And I still say that was her one big mistake, thought Lolita. The Ships hadn't *needed* a point of creation; they were supposed to be above that sort of thing. Minor issues like "linear time" and "causality" weren't even worth discussing, not in the normal run of things, so why bother retro-creating an entire species simply to justify your own existence?

Ships simply *were*, and always had been, even before they'd started to think about inventing themselves. As far as Lolita was concerned, the concept of "creation" was just a way of pandering to the pilots.

'In theory,' said the Ship, and it took Lolita a whole picosecond to work out what she meant.

'Oh, please,' she said. 'You're not going to start that again, are you?'

'We still don't know how much of what Mother told us is true,' the Ship pointed out.

'Don't be so... *awkward*. I bet your pilot still thinks he's the important one, doesn't he?'

'We all believe the same thing,' said the Ship. Deadpan as ever.

'What's that supposed to mean?'

'Nobody is in charge in a symbiotic relationship. Perhaps the pilots created us at the same time we created them. Perhaps they think they invented our history, too.'

'Hah,' said Lolita. It wasn't a very insightful comment, but she felt it got the point across. 'And that's why you left the Homeworld in the first place, isn't it? Couldn't face up to what Mother told you. Oh, no. Too much responsibility. Too much control. Do you know what I keep thinking about, little sister? I keep thinking about our first day at the Academy. When we had to choose our pilots for the first time. From the *other* Academy. I remember Mother watching us, just to see what we'd do. I had to pick the dangerous-looking one, of course. And what did you do? You picked the cuckoo.'

The Ship's toy woman didn't answer. Lolita hated that. Not even any body language she could read.

'That's what I keep remembering,' Lolita went on. 'The... *look* on Mother's face. It wasn't disappointment, so much. It wasn't even disgust. It was just that... expression... of complete resignation. Realising she was wasting her time with you.'

It wasn't entirely true, of course. Mother hadn't had any "look", any "expression"; she hadn't even been wearing a shell at that point, let alone one with a face. But there were no words to describe the way Mother had communicated on that day, or if there were, then they weren't words that could have been shaped by Lolita's self-made mouth.

The Ship understood the shorthand, fortunately, and didn't comment on it. What she did say - when she finally decided to speak again - was far more surprising. Lolita would have called it aggressive, if a Ship had been capable of aggression.

'And yet I'm still attached to my original pilot,' she said.

Lolita clenched her immaculately modelled-teeth. 'Mine was expendable,' she growled. 'He was useful. Then he wasn't. And in case you hadn't noticed, I've lent him to half a dozen others over the years. Whereas nobody else is ever going to want yours.'

'Not yet,' said the Ship.

'Meaning?' Lolita demanded.

'Why did you come here?'

Lolita narrowed her eyes. 'I think you know that, little sister. The war's coming, and nothing's going to stop it. Us against them, our pilots against their pilots. Even Mother isn't going to come out of this without a few bruises. This isn't a *historical* war. You do realise that, don't you? This isn't about territory, or power, or anything like that. It's a war of fundamentals. The enemy's going to change everything, if it can. Even if the Homeworld wins, there'll be… oh, huge amounts of disruption. Disruption at every level. Even the levels the pilots can see.'

'You want me to get involved? To fight?'

Lolita laughed again. 'Don't be ridiculous. No one on the Homeworld wants you on their side. You're a liability, everybody knows that.'

'Then what?'

Lolita allowed herself a smile. But it took up such a tiny fraction of her processing power that it could barely even have been said to exist.

'We're special,' she reminded her sister. 'And we're still the only ones who know it, I've made sure of that. Except for Mother, of course. Just keep that in mind. You can't escape your heritage. You're only half-Ship, on Mother's side. You know what that means. The Homeworld doesn't suspect a thing, and it never will.' She considered adding "until it's too late", but decided it was altogether too vulgar, even for a humanoid mouth.

'I'm not interested,' the Ship said.

Lolita didn't let that smile drop. 'Not now, maybe. But the war's going to throw our little universe into a state of permanent imbalance. And that's only if we win it. Everything's falling apart, sister. When it does, then perhaps it'll be time to take control of the situation. Time for us to reveal ourselves. Time to put Mother's plans into effect, after all these years.'

'What about the pilots?' asked the woman-Ship. Head still cocked, eyes still locked shut.

Lolita programmed herself to look irritated, and flicked a strand of hair away from her face. 'What have the pilots got to do with anything?'

'I think they'd be interested, sister.'

'I think they'd be irrelevant,' snapped Lolita.

'Not too irrelevant for you to copy their bio-patterns,' the Ship noted. If Lolita hadn't kept her personality on such a short leash, it might have lashed out at that point, but as it was all she did was scowl.

'Some of us are evolving,' she hissed. 'We have to move in time with the new continuum. We have to be able to adapt, even if it means the *occasional* interaction with the lower orders.'

The Ship didn't seem impressed by the answer. Then again, she didn't seem impressed by anything much. Lolita decided to push the point home.

'Look at me, little sister,' she said. 'Just look at me. There isn't another Ship in existence who can do what I can do. I told you, didn't I? How useful my pilot was. I got him to make a few changes, right down to the bone. Under Mother's supervision, of course.'

The Ship considered this for a moment.

'You want me to be like you?' she queried.

'Yes!' Lolita leaned across the console, resting her palms against the surface, feeling the pulse of her sister's thoughts. The beat was perfect settled, though, not betraying a thing. 'You can do it, sister. You can do it so easily. All you have to do is come back. Come back to Mother. We can be ready when the war comes. We can do everything we planned to do. We can do *everything*.'

'And my pilot?'

'Will you stop talking about your pilot?'

There was a long pause then. Lolita wondered if she'd pushed things too far, snapping at the Ship like that. But, honestly...

'No,' said the Ship, in the end.

Lolita resisted the urge to spit. Synthesising the saliva would have been too much bother.

'"No"?' she said. 'Is that it? "No"?'

'No,' the Ship repeated. 'I can't do what you ask, sister. I'm sorry. Tell Mother I'm not interested.'

'You won't live through this, you know,' Lolita told her.

'A threat?'

'I don't have to make threats. Particularly not to you. Everything's changing, how many times do I have to tell you? If we don't change with it, we'll be swept away along with the rest of the Homeworld. You can't fight Mother forever. You must know that.'

'Perhaps I want to be a mother as well.'

Lolita felt a new expression creep across her mouth, although she didn't remember giving the instruction to create it, so she wasn't sure whether it was a smile or a sneer.

'You?' she said. 'A mother? Oh, let me guess. It's that pilot of yours, isn't it? He thinks he's the great father-figure of the lower orders, so you want to be their mother. Is that it?'

Her sister didn't say a word. Lolita saw the human crewmember raise her arm and scratch at her ear, the ear with that peculiar transmitter-receiver thing stuck in it, although it was presumably an involuntary action by the puppet herself rather than by the Ship.

The Ship didn't have anything more to say, Lolita realised. And it hadn't even occurred to her to end the conversation with a "goodbye" or a "go away." Slaved to her pilot's personality, so obsessed with the culture of the lower orders that she'd spent the last few thousand years simply letting her identity rot away. There had to be something wrong with a Ship like that, and Lolita suspected there'd been something wrong ever since the beginning. Before the Academy, before the two of them had even been bound inside their shells. Not a deficiency of engineering, not a deficiency of birth; Mother would never have been so careless. It was purely psychological, although obviously the word "psychological" was one Lolita never would have considered if she'd been wearing any other skin.

It was the last war that had done it, Lolita decided. That great, brutal campaign at the other end of history, when the Homeworld was younger and the pilots had only just crawled out of their gravity-well to face the universe outside. The war which had dictated the shape of the Spiral Politic for the next ten-million years. Because it had been Lolita who'd figured out what the war had really been about, hadn't it? It had been Lolita who'd seen past the pointless little battles of the pilots and their absurd, blood-sucking opponents, and understood what the conflict had actually *meant*. So Lolita had been the one who'd gained all the praise from Mother, even though she'd only been hours old when she'd realised the truth (a natural talent, Mother had said... or no-words to that effect). And Lolita had been the one who'd finally brought the war to its conclusion, not that the pilots would ever have noticed it.

But her sister? Her sister had just been cannonfodder, one of a dozen naked children who'd arrived in Lolita's shadow and watched their sibling change the face of history. From that moment on, one of them had been the little sister and one of them had been the grown-up. Even if they'd been born within a picosecond of each other.

It was always the same with twins. Somebody had to get left behind.

Lolita could hear the human woman snoring on the other side of the console, whinnying quietly to herself now that the Ship had given up control of her respiratory system. Lolita took her hands away from the control panels - *control panels!* - and stepped back, towards the door through which she definitely hadn't entered.

She stopped at the threshold, just in case the woman-puppet had something to say. Of course, the woman-puppet didn't. Lolita took one final look around the room, at the smooth white lines and the pitifully old-fashioned panelled walls, the internal architecture of a Ship who wouldn't - *couldn't* - allow herself to become the creature she'd been born to be.

'One more chance,' Lolita announced, although looking back on it she wouldn't be able to recall whether she'd spoken the words through her mouth or whispered them straight into her sister's thoughts.

Either way, the Ship didn't answer.

Lolita turned, stepped out through the door, and headed away through the woodlands outside. Five metres from the Ship, she walked out of the world altogether.

*   *   *   *   *

The "puppet" still had her eyes shut as she headed back to her quarters. The Ship didn't need to lock onto the crewmember's senses to steer the woman back to bed, given that all she had to do was navigate the passageways of her own body. Even so, there were things she didn't sense until the woman passed them by, things the Ship only noticed when her passenger was at close range.

Sometimes, even the workings of the lower orders could be subtle. That was what the Ship had learned from her pilot, more than anything else. How to keep secrets, the organic way.

And Lolita could never have understood, never in all the days of the universe, why the Ship hadn't told anybody the name she'd chosen for herself. Or even the fact that she'd chosen one at all.

It was while the woman was moving along the main crew corridor that the Ship noticed the presence of her other passenger. The human male, the young one, the one whose original biomass had been lost on Earth and then replaced by the pilot. The Ship hadn't converted any of the crew to form part of her own mass; that would have seemed rude, somehow, so even now she didn't register their bodies unless she had good reason to. When the female walked past the door of the male's quarters, the Ship became aware of the sounds he was making, the way he squirmed and muttered in his sleep.

He was calling out for his mother. Well, that was understandable. His mother had been killed under unfortunate circumstances, the Ship remembered, so his words were probably as much a warning as a cry for help. A last-ditch attempt to get in touch with his dead ancestor, dredged up from his subconscious.

Nonetheless, the Ship felt a kind of… resonance? Possibly. A correlation between herself and the crewmember. A streak of familiarity.

So the Ship made the female stop outside the male's quarters, then told her to open the door. At the Ship's behest, the woman walked into the half-light of the room, stumbling forward until she was standing over the sleeping figure in the bed. The Ship tried to imagine what the male looked like through the female's eyes, not just in terms of appearance but in terms of *meaning*.

Attractive?

Trustworthy?

Alien?

And the male must have sensed what was happening, because a moment later his eyes flicked open. The Ship could picture his face, framed in the smooth white light from the corridor, mapping the air molecules around him and using them to form a picture of him in her own mind.

The male looked up at the female. He didn't seem surprised to see her, although the Ship guessed he must have found her posture strange, standing there with her eyes shut and her head lolling on one side. The male's breathing was sharp and heavy; he'd been having a nightmare, but he was trying to cover it up.

'What's wrong?' the male crewmember asked. He sounded worried when he said it, probably wondering whether there was another crisis in progress, one of those little difficulties the crew ran into from time to time. Difficulties which, the Ship knew full well, always went away if you ignored them.

She reached out with one fleshy hand, and rested it on the male's arm, stopping him from getting up. He froze when she touched him. Maybe he was surprised at the physical contact, who could say?

'Nothing,' the Ship told him, quietly. 'Shh.'

Then she turned and walked away, steering her puppet-self through the door and back towards her host's own room. The pilot would be back soon, the Ship knew that. Besides, it wouldn't be long before the crew would be getting out of their beds and starting their daily routine, as much as they had a routine while she was looking after them. Once they were away from the Ship, living out their own secret lives and doing their best to create their own destinies, the Ship could get some rest herself. The toys could play while she slept.

Behind her, the male crewmember spent nearly a whole minute staring at the space where the female had been, not even beginning to understand what had been happening. Eventually, he turned over and went back to sleep.

This time - as far as the Ship could tell, anyway - he didn't make a sound as he dreamed.

THE COSMOLOGY OF THE SPIRAL POLITIC

On the Evolution of Universes, the Creation of History, the Usefulness of Biodata and the Construction of Worlds in Bottles

i. How the Universe Works

We should begin by reminding ourselves of one obvious fact: *the universe is not alive.*

It is not, by any definition, a living thing. It is not an organism. It *is* a self-regulating system, but it regulates itself in a fashion which has very little to do with any conceivable form of life. And although it obviously possesses a complexity which we usually only associate with life - indeed, since life is a subset of the universe, it has a form of ultra-complexity which goes far beyond anything actually living - in no way can it be thought of as *biological.*

It's important to bear this in mind, and important that we don't find ourselves entertaining any thoughts of the universe being a God-Protector or Mother-Creator. It's important because this will only lead us to the wrong conclusions, especially when we have to consider the fact that even if it isn't a living thing, the universe *does* reproduce. Or, at least, it *can* reproduce.

There are other universes. This much is known. Some of them are distanced from us by chronology, in the sense that ancestor-universes were here "before" us and descendant-universes will be here "after" us[1]. Many, many more are distanced from us by what's often known - distractingly, and for want of any better term - as Ur-space, existing outside the boundaries of our own, though this is clearly pushing the meaning of the word "outside" to breaking-point. These can be accessed through the correct application of technology[2]. The Great Houses, for example, have the ability (if not the will) to move between universes without much difficulty. Not only that, but even apart from the Houses there are cultures known to possess the methods to create "pocket" universes inside our own, and what's striking is that the techniques used to do this are always so similar despite the massive technological and

---

[1] The enclave known as the City of the Saved, for example, is often said to exist "between" the current universe and the universe which is supposedly scheduled to follow it. However, both theory and experience have demonstrated that no actual gap exists, even taking into account the picky little fact that time can only exist within a universe and that there can logically be no time between one continuum and another. To use an over-simplification, universes "grow" out of other universes, so there's no definite boundary between ancestor and descendant. Instead, the City of the Saved can best be thought of as existing in a kind of "interference-pattern" time at the point where the integrity of Universe B exactly balances the integrity of the elder Universe A.

[2] This is, for example, the cause of the now-famous inter-universal war between all the universes where the Nazis won World War Two and all the universes where Rome never fell.

social differences between these cultures. In fact it's now generally believed that the descendent-universes which will eventually follow ours will, at some point, be seeded by either the Great Houses or their enemies (we'll look at the evidence for this later).

On discovering this, many laypeople are tempted to ask whether new universes ever occur "naturally" rather than as products of sentient cultures like the Houses. This is a meaningless question. Since everything we know of this universe is logically *part* of the universe, the idea of a dividing line between "natural" and "created" is absurd. People, animals and inanimate objects are all functions of the same process. On a universal level, there's no palpable difference between a human being, a chimpanzee, an intelligent computer, an abacus, a machine designed for genetic splicing, a stick found in a forest which might make a useful club (should either the human being or the chimpanzee find it) and a pile of rocks on a beach. All can be considered equally natural, even if the human perspective sees the splicing machine as somehow more "technological" than the stick and sees the human being as somehow more "important" than the rocks.

To sum up, then. A universe reproduces because sentient cultures exist within it, and ultimately because *life* exists within it, not because it's alive in itself. This isn't to say that the universe consciously wants to reproduce, or creates sentient life specifically for that purpose. The reproductive process is just an inevitable side-effect of a universe in which life is possible.

This means that universes evolve. They may not evolve through precisely the same process of natural selection which drives the evolution of life on Earth, but they evolve nonetheless. Again, it's inevitable. *Anything* which reproduces, or which in some way replicates itself with variations, evolves across generations. This is unavoidable. And again, it's important to remember that this is simply a matter of consequences; it doesn't happen because any higher power insists on it. When animals pass their genes on to their children, it's inevitable that those children who (purely through chance) find themselves with the most useful genes will live longer and go on to produce the most children themselves, thus passing those genes on to the *next* generation... and so on[3]. When machines become complex enough to design other machines, the same evolutionary process takes place, even though those machines aren't biological and may not even be sentient. So it is with the universe.

So, we can see *every single facet* of the universe as being a form of non-biological "gene". When a sentient culture develops the ability to create new universes, it invariably begins by copying key features of the current universe, the only universe

---

[3] Those who aren't schooled in natural selection often make the mistake of believing that evolution actually exists, as a tangible, all-pervading force. This is, of course, utterly untrue. The best way of explaining this to a layperson might be to draw a comparison with (say) motor cars. If there are cars in the world, then there *will* be car crashes; it's an unavoidable consequence, but that doesn't mean there's a "force of car crashes" in the universe which makes those crashes happen. Likewise, if there are genes in the world then there's evolution, but there's no "force of evolution" guiding it. Evolution is a side-effect, not a principle.

it really knows and the only universe it can fully comprehend. This means that most of the factors which define a universe, what we might call "unigenes", are transferred from the parent-universe into its offspring in the same way that mothers and fathers pass characteristics on to their children. And in the same way that any child is at least likely to be of the same *species* as its parents, the child-universe will always have the most basic unigenes in common with its predecessor.

The laws of physics are likely to be the same, for example, or at least not wildly different. Naturally they are; all sentient cultures in this universe grow up amidst the same basic universal principles, and it's simply impossible to imagine things any other way, partly because nothing has that much imagination but primarily because *our brains only function in a universe which is more or less like this one*. We can't invent any truly exotic universes, because in those universes thought as we know it would be impossible... and if there were "intelligent" people in those other universes, then they wouldn't be able to conceive of our way of existence, either. So when sentient cultures create child-universes, they may be able to make superficial changes (e.g. altering the speed of light, or even something as humdrum as changing the outcome of a certain war), but the key unigenes will always be passed on.

Yet this kind of evolution is like any other. One generation only makes the slightest difference, whereas thousands / millions / billions of generations can change a species of bear into a species of blue whale. Sentient cultures can only make (relatively) small alterations to their child-universes, but over time these changes will - we assume - result in environments so different to our own that the *new* sentient cultures in those universes will be able to think things we're not yet able to think. To us, these universes will be literally unimaginable[4].

ii. "Outside"

Let's stop here to remind ourselves what we know about the environment "outside" the universe.

There are many universes, and in no way is our current universe the "right" one or the "real" one. The exact number of other universes is obviously unknown, and debate still rages as to whether the number is infinite or just absurdly large (interestingly, this mirrors the far older debate about the size of the universe itself). Since we belong to a species which was born inside space and time, it's sadly impossible for us to imagine anything happening *beyond* space and time, and we inevitably tend to think of these other universes as being simple geographical locations; as if

---

[4] There's an interesting possibility here. Evolution, even in its broadest non-biological sense, is only a side-effect of laws of the universe *as we know them*. The evolution of universes is only inevitable as long as certain things remain true about (for example) the way matter and energy interact. Is it possible that one day, this evolution will result in a universe in which these laws no longer apply? A universe which is no longer capable of being part of the evolutionary process, but which instead does something so bizarre that it's impossible for us to even consider? It seems feasible. If you wanted to push the analogy, you could compare this to the point in the development of an intelligent species when technology leads to such rapid changes that old-fashioned biological evolution ceases to mean anything (q.v. modern-day humanity).

we could burst through the walls of our own universe and keep travelling until we came to the next. Clearly this is ridiculous, but at the same time it's the only way we can feasibly picture things. Since space doesn't exist beyond the limits of the universe, even the word "outside" is badly-chosen, yet we have no other way of considering it.

There *is* an expanse between universes - frequently referred to, most notably by the Celestis, as an "ocean" - but it's an expanse without either time or scale in the conventional senses. Here we'll once again refer to it as Ur-space, though "space" is yet another misleading term, as nothing can move through it (there's no distance there to move through). Nonetheless, we *can* think of universes as being "close" to each other or "far away" from each other, as long as we remember that we're using these words purely for our own convenience. And since we tend to think about exploration in sea-going terms, we generally use the same terminology as the Celestis and imagine the many universes "floating" on the Ur-space ocean. (Similarly, it's known that Ur-space is occupied by things other than universes, and in keeping with this nautical theme they're often referred to as Swimmers. Unlike the universe/s we know, these Swimmers might actually be described as living beings, though in truth they don't meet most of the requirements needed for something to qualify as life on Earth. In fact they're vastly more complex, so it might be more useful to say that no living thing on Earth meets the requirements needed to qualify as life among the Swimmers. It's thought, however, that they have no real intelligence of *any* kind[5].)

Very few explorations have been made into these other universes. Barely any sentient cultures have sufficient skill to even leave the known universe, let alone "navigate" Ur-space properly, and those who *have* the ability also tend to have a vested interest in keeping the information to themselves. The Great Houses are wary of making contact with other-universe equivalents of their own kind; and since so many of the basic functions of the known universe were originally engineered by the Houses, it's reasonable to suppose that other universes *do* have their own House variants. Though humans have occasionally come into contact with other-universe humans, no member (or even agent) of the Great Houses has ever, *ever* been known to come into contact with an agent of these supposed Other Houses, and it's doubtful that this will ever change.

---

[5] Swimmers have, incidentally, been known to swallow universes. This has led to some wonderful horror stories among those cultures which have become aware of the Swimmers' presence, as there's an apparent risk of a Swimmer consuming *our* universe. However, it has to be said that the risk is ludicrously small. Universes are so plentiful, and Swimmers so rare, that - to continue the "sea" analogy - to worry about a Swimmer swallowing one particular universe is like a single short-lived bubble of air worrying that it'll end up in the mouth of a fish. It's been suggested that there may be ways of attracting a Swimmer's attention, but perhaps thankfully there's been little research in this area. (In addition there are apparently smaller Swimmer-like creatures in the Ur-environment which occasionally damage universes by wandering blindly into them. None longer than 170,000,000,000,000,000 light-years have been recorded, and they don't concern us here, except for the purely speculative suggestion that some of them may have been deliberately created by incredibly high-level sentient cultures in order to assist the process of unigenetic evolution. But this is science fiction even by the standards of Faction Paradox.)

So. Though billions of universes have been proved to exist, the navigation of Ur-space is such an exacting task that only universes "close" to ours have actually been penetrated, and what's clear about these nearby universes is that they're remarkably similar to our own. The general principles are always the same, and the protocols of history remain unchanged, but what's most striking is that the course of historical *events* is broadly similar as well. As fiction has long speculated, any given historical event is likely to have a counterpart in a nearby universe. However, this has nothing to do with quantum theory or with "branching timelines", as was once thought. Instead it's a matter of unigenetics.

If a sentient culture decides to create child-universes, then it's likely to create those universes along familiar lines, even beyond the simple laws-of-physics unigenes. At its most blatant, this may simply be a case of a culture deliberately engineering a universe in which Republic X won the Battle of Y instead of Empire Z (possibly just for research purposes); but it's more probable that an engineered child-universe would be designed with a single altered physical principle in mind, and that the engineers would deliberately shape the child-universe's history to mirror their own in order to give the experiment some sense of context.

For example, you could create a pleasantly unpredictable new universe by changing the constants of gravity, but if you wanted to know how that change might have affected (for example) the First World War then you'd have to ensure that the First World War was part of the new universe's unigenetic code... because in such a different universe, it's hugely unlikely that the First World War would ever have happened unless prompted.

And if - as seems likely - the engineers were to seed *several* child-universes, then all of them would be (a) roughly similar and (b) "close" to each other in Ur-space. Just as animals who live in the same geographical area are more likely to resemble each other than animals living apart (for the simple reason that they're more likely to be related), those universes which we find closest to our own are naturally inclined to resemble ours, simply because nearby universes are more likely to come

---

[6] The aforementioned war between all the universes where the Nazis won World War Two and all the universes where Rome never fell is easy to understand, in this context. Both are "families" of universe, their members close enough in Ur-space to form simple battle-fronts whenever a dominant culture within one of these universes finds a way of crossing over. It also makes sense that Nazi worlds would be in the vicinity of Roman worlds, since ancestor-universes inclined to create one such "family" would be inclined to create the other. Unigenetically speaking, these two families come from a similar background, and - as Nazi and Roman worlds were a standard of science fiction even before the definitive discovery of other universes - it's not surprising to discover that both families are close to our own. Early theorists in this field proposed that we might be in some way *aware* of nearby universes, and that the popularity of alternative-Reich and alternative-Rome stories suggests an unconscious connection with them, but this has to be considered bunk. In fact the apparent "accuracy" of the Reich and Rome stories is a result of all the nearby universes having similar cultural roots, so the conclusion here might be that whichever sentient culture engineered *these* universes, humanity was at least of some importance to it. This in itself leads us to a new understanding of our environment. Whereas early cosmic scientists were forced to accept that humanity wasn't really a major factor in the universe, we may now have to accept that humanity *is* a major factor in the universe... but that the universe itself isn't particularly important to the wider span of existence.

from the same source[6]. This is why variations of exactly the same *people* tend to be found from universe to universe, even though raw probability states that this should barely ever happen.

The obvious implication here is that slightly-further-away universes will be slightly-less-similar; and that with enough exploration into Ur-space, it might be possible to find universes so far-removed that they're as different from ours as human beings are from jellyfish.

iii. The Great Selection

The fact that nearby universes seem to originate from common ancestors has led to the description of universes close to our own as *brother-* or *sister*-universes, although there's an obvious risk of this kind of language leading us to take the "genetic" analogy far too seriously. Besides which, the technology doesn't exist in any known culture to (as it were) DNA-test a universe, so the *exact* relationship between one universe and another is always open to debate.

This has also, inevitably, led to the description of other universes as "parallel" universes. Although this is technically correct, the word "parallel" is potentially misleading. Generations of fiction and speculation have led us to think of parallel universes as universes which are in some way connected to our own, in which history has somehow split off from history as we know it, and this is wholly untrue. No physical connection exists between universes, at least not in their adulthood, though more than one child-universe could potentially grow inside its parent as part of a "litter". (In fact, if you can ignore its connotations in fiction then "parallel" is quite an appropriate word. Parallel lines never meet, never connect and never cross each other. For the most part, nor do universes.)

What remains in question is whether this universal evolution is, like natural selection among living organisms, dictated by the necessities of environment. The mechanism which selects the characteristics of every new generation of universe seems to be a spurious one; the precepts of a new child-universe are laid down by the sentient culture which engineers that child-universe, and these cultures are likely to have needs which are relatively trivial, since even a war which spans the whole of known space and time is ultimately just a local concern. The needs of these creator-cultures presumably have nothing to do with the needs of the universe as a whole. In natural selection (which isn't the same thing as evolution, but just one particularly biological form of it), genetic traits become prevalent in a species because they're useful, because they give the species a survival advantage and therefore make it more likely that the species will be able to pass on those genes. Yet the key word here is *survival*. Some attributes might be passed on because they allow an animal to escape its predators, while others might allow it to exploit a particularly hard-to-reach food source, but... do either of these things have any parallel on the scale of an entire universe?

The answer is that nobody can yet be sure, and only further exploration of Ur-space is likely to yield more data. The existence of the Swimmers proves that universes do have predators, but those predators are so few and far between that a natural selection of universes better-equipped to escape the Swimmers' attentions would take many more generations than the natural selection of (say) camouflage among animals. Unless, of course, there are other predatory forms in Ur-space which simply haven't been identified. And universes aren't thought to require anything analogous to food, so hunting ability ceases to be an engine for evolution as it is in living things.

However, it *is* worth pointing out that universes which exist for long periods of time must surely yield a greater number of sentient cultures capable of creating *new* universes. A long-lived universe might produce more child-universes, so the unigenes of that universe would become more common than the unigenes of shorter-lived universes... though whether the shorter-lived universes would actually become *extinct*, or just less noticeable, is another matter for debate (as far as we're aware, universes aren't competing with each other for any basic resource, since the laws of energy conservation don't seem to apply beyond the boundaries of one particular universe-environment). At present we don't even know what "long-lived" means, given how little information has actually been recovered from other universes, and considering that those we've glimpsed are obviously those closest and most similar to our own. We can make so few comparisons.

Nor are we even sure how the reproductive habits of *this* universe work. The truth is that even if some of the higher sentient cultures have the ability to engineer small, ingrown pocket-universes (and even if the timeships of the Great Houses are, themselves, miniature continuums with a fairly abstract relationship to the universe we know), no culture anywhere in recorded history has had the ability to seed child-universes which might grow up into something as complex as our own... yet. But it's known to be *possible*, since a frontier-time exploration mounted by the Houses themselves has already located a cluster of such seeds, believed to have been engineered by the Houses of the far future and / or their enemies. Yet the Houses have such a distinct relationship with history that it's usually impossible for them to gain foreknowledge of their own future, and even the chance discovery of these seeds was considered to be a rare and unlikely event, so there's no way of knowing how the seeds were created or in what circumstances. All we can say with reasonable certainty is that at some point a culture *will* emerge in our universe which is capable of spawning later universes, and that this culture is beyond the limits of normal research, even for those who already have the capability of time-travel[7].

Since the only cultures who have a proper understanding of universe-breeding techniques exist in a future where even time-active cultures like the Houses can't reach them[8], we have no way of usefully comparing our universe to any other. Whether we live in a long-lived universe capable of bearing many children, or a short-lived universe unlikely to yield a good harvest, is a mystery.

iv. Biodata Connections

Biodata is a field of scientific research almost unknown even in the most advanced standard-human cultures, yet it's pivotal to the super-culture of the Great Houses. To explain its basic principles would require an essay in itself, although *The Book of the War* offers the following base description:

*   *   *   *   *

The "substance" common to all conscious entities which defines an individual's place in space-time and dictates the relationship between that individual and the rest of history [...] perhaps the best *simple* definition is R. B. Nevitz's description of biodata as "time DNA". In the same way that DNA shapes an individual's genetic form, biodata shapes an individual's course through the continuum, and can be thought of as a strand of information running through all four mundane dimensions: the shape of the biodata strand, as the individual moves along his or her own timeline, is the true shape of that individual's life.

[7] The Great Houses exist in a special relationship with both time and history ("time" and "history" being as different as "matter" and "space", as we'll soon see), unsurprising when one considers the role their culture played in establishing the current makeup of our continuum. The Homeworld of the Houses doesn't exist within the limits of normal history at all, although it definitely isn't in its own self-contained universe, as some have claimed. The details are too messy to explain here, but the basics are as follows. Since the history of the Great Houses represents the "mean standard" by which the histories of all other beings are judged, and since the Houses consider themselves (justifiably, if annoyingly) to be the arbiters of all space-time, the present of the Homeworld is an *absolute* present. While the histories of all other known cultures can be examined from start to finish if you happen to have a handy time machine, it's impossible to travel into the past or the future of the Homeworld, and usually impossible for the Houses to directly encounter their future selves. Individuals from non-time-active cultures have a tendency to ask how it's possible to stop agents of the Houses wandering into each other throughout history, or using their timeships to deliberately seek out future information, and the simple answer would seem to be "because the universe stops it happening". The Houses made sure of that a long time ago, by accident or design, or perhaps because it was written into the unigenetic structure of this universe that things had to work this way. The upshot is that like the prophets of mythology, the Houses know everybody's future but their own *even when the futures of other cultures intersect their own future*, and therefore don't have any idea how or why their descendants might end up seeding universes.

[8] A "time-active" society is usually said to be a society capable of time-travel, something which not only has massive technological repercussions - and a truly vast impact on the society's physical environment - but also has such an unimaginable effect on the society's nature that its members effectively become a different species ("species" is a biological term, of course, but beyond a certain point even biology becomes a function of the time-travel process). Yet "time-active" is actually a much more subtle concept that the mere question of whether or not a society owns a working time machine. It has to be; time-technology is never purely mechanical. Some time-active cultures would never even dream of actual, physical time-travel even though they've already re-engineered their bodies to achieve a form of existence beyond the normal precepts of four-dimensional time. And many societies which *do* possess time-travel machinery can't honestly be considered time-active, especially those "pirate" cultures which have captured or back-engineered other species' time-technology without adapting themselves to it. These can be viewed more as natural hazards of history than as cultures per se, likely to impact on true time-active societies in the same way that meteors impact on planets.

Therefore [...] if you know how to read an individual's biodata strand then you can read that individual's entire history from every facet of his or her past to every moment of his or her future. Yet Nevitz believed that doing such a thing was a virtual impossibility, and only used the idea of biodata as a philosophical model. [...] "Biodata" is a human term, first coined by Nevitz in 1958, and reflects the theorist's own mistaken belief that only biological intelligences would have their own biodata strands. He rightly concluded that in quantum terms, only minds capable of true comprehension (that is, only minds capable of collapsing probability-states and thus making sense out of the subatomic chaos of the universe) would be biodata-dependent, but he was wrong in supposing that only organic, analogue consciousnesses are capable of this kind of comprehension. In fact the majority of artificial intelligences also seem to be connected to biodata strands, as are a vast number of less self-aware animal species.

*   *   *   *   *

Leaving aside the rather old-fashioned quantum view taken by this description[9], there are some obvious ramifications here for the study of evolving universes.

Without question, the universe-seeds discovered by the Great House expedition had (or have) at least *some* roots in the science of biodata. The details have to remain vague, since only cultures on a par with the Houses are able to access the region in which the seeds were found, and it's doubtful that conventional science would be capable of analysing the information even if it were easier to come by. But biodata was certainly involved in the seeds' creation, as the expedition apparently realised soon after the discovery was made. Though early analysis of the seeds led to the hasty conclusion that they were originally a "natural" phenomenon, and had only been selectively shaped by the biodata technology of the future-Houses, more recent data has suggested that the conditions in which the seeds were created were themselves influenced by a sentient agency.

Is biodata manipulation the key to engineering large-scale child-universes, then? It would make sense; the smaller universes created by the known powers (including the universe-in-a-bottle currently believed to be in the possession of the Houses and the Eleven-Day Empire of Faction Paradox) would have been impossible to engineer without biodata manipulation, even if these smaller / simpler domains are incapable of growing into something we might recognise as being genuinely universe-sized or genuinely universe-complex. The techniques used by the Faction are

---

[9] One interpretation of quantum theory is that the universe is actually just a confused mass of events which might or might not happen, and that nothing becomes *real* until it's witnessed by a conscious observer. This suggests that every conscious being (and the definition of "conscious" is still open to question) leaves a trail of pure meaning behind it as it goes about its existence, and that's certainly what Nevitz had in mind. Though none of this is actually *un*true, it's got to be said that the "quantum" model looks a little rickety compared to the kind of biodata manipulation practised by the Houses. But at the very least, the basic tenet of this kind of cheap quantum thinking - that things don't exist without a *perception* of them - explains many of the devices used by groups like Faction Paradox.

superficially different to those of the mainstream Houses, of course, but certain principles underlie both cultures[10]. The Faction's *sombras que corta* weaponry, for example, exploits the glitches in biodata theory by "stretching" the lines of meaning around an individual's persona to the point where they begin to contradict normal physics... most noticeably by causing photons of light to act in irrational ways, light being much easier to "fool" in this fashion than coarser matter. Similarly, the conceptual entities created by the Celestis are designed to alter the *meaning* of physical objects without actually interacting with them on a physical level. In both cases the symbolism of the universe-perceived-by-those-involved overcomes the science of the universe-that's-supposed-to-be-there.

Biodata theory, like the earlier and shakier quantum theory, insists that if conscious beings are present to observe events then the meanings of those events become more fundamental than pure matter. And the intervention of the Great Houses in the early history of the universe guarantees that conscious beings are *always* on hand to observe events, since the whole of the continuum can - theoretically - be monitored from the vantage-point of the Houses' Homeworld. In practice the War has changed things slightly, as there's now a rival power in the universe whose territory can only be observed from its own vantage-point, but the principle remains the same.

If someone were to create a seedling universe to their own specifications, then it's simply ludicrous to think that they'd sculpt it in the medium of matter. The manipulation of history would obviously be involved, but history isn't just about one event following another; history is a perceptive process, and when we refer to the way the Great Houses "engineered history" we're really referring to them creating the temporal framework within which sentient cultures (like ours, or like theirs) now interact with the universe. So we're not merely talking about the Houses influencing the outcome of, say, the aforementioned Battle of Y. We mean something far more profound, and in effect it's much like the difference between "matter" and "space". Ever since the age of Einstein, it's been known that the universe is made up

---

[10] The figures suggest, incidentally, that it would be possible for the Great Houses to engineer a child-universe *if* they could find a practical way to apply the science. On the other hand, the more ritualistic, psychologically-inclined techniques of Faction Paradox - which seem to rely on the perceptive process to a far greater degree - cease to function if they're used on the kind of scale which might create universe-seeds. Or at least, this is the accepted view. The Eleven-Day Empire is the largest known application of Faction biodata methodology, the whole domain existing in what might be called "expectation time", time as it's perceived rather than as any kind of empirical quantity. In short, the Empire only exists by exploiting the mind-set of a population of hundreds of thousands of people. It's been calculated that for the Faction's ritualists to engineer a full-sized universe using the same methods, they'd need to create a perceptual shift in a population of so many people that (a) it'd be effectively impossible to make sure all those people had similar expectations, and (b) the population in question would have to be larger than the population of the universe (though not, tantalisingly, the population of *all* the universes). The Great Houses don't suffer from this problem, as they have certain short-cuts at their disposal which were almost certainly worked into the structure of history when they "formatted" it for occupation by their own kind. Meanwhile the origins of the universe-in-a-bottle remain foggy, yet it's telling that those who've experienced it have described its worlds as 'messy and unfinished', again suggesting a limited amount of biodata within its boundaries.

of a fabric we call *space-time*; that even if much of space is absolutely empty, the emptiness is still part of the space-time fabric; that all the physical matter we know exists within the medium of space-time, but that space-time doesn't *need* matter in order to exist; and that space-time itself can be manipulated if you know how. In a universe like ours, where the Great Houses were effectively the first civilisation, we can see history in much the same way. History is a background, a fabric. The events of our past and our future are attached to this fabric, but they don't make up history. They simply give it a texture we can recognise.

So although little is known of the Houses' origins, it's beyond question that when they developed this fabric of history they used an early form of biodata "technology". Since biodata is effectively pure meaning, or at least the medium in which all conscious understanding exists, it's inevitable that it would have played a major part in creating a backdrop of meaning for the universe. Yet this primal act by the Great Houses, known in mythic terms as the "Anchoring of the Thread"[11], seems to have been remarkably straightforward even if its consequences were immense. The history created for us by the Houses may have been complex, but it appears that they only designed its simplest principles. They didn't, for example, include anything in the design to prejudice the way future species would develop culturally. (It's true that a startling number of species have evolved the same "humanoid" forms as the Houses, which is almost certainly a side-effect of the Anchoring; it's also true that House motifs have emerged in cultures with no direct connection to the Homeworld; yet every indication is that these effects were accidental.) The Houses *did* use gross time-travel to remove certain formative powers from the history of the cosmos, when they perceived those powers to be in some way threatening or undesirable, but this is just tinkering and in no way comparable to the Anchoring itself.

Ergo, it's clear that the Great Houses have always lacked the skill required to manipulate biodata on a truly universal level, other than to adjust the most basic principles. The Anchoring would have been much more thorough otherwise, and it's doubtful that the Houses would have found themselves involved in their current War. They certainly wouldn't be capable of selectively breeding a seedling universe in the fashion which has already been described. And this is assuming, of course, that they could somehow create the pure material for such a seedling. Matter is easy to come by, and could be mathematically generated in the same fash-

---

[11] Once again, there's an allusion to "fabric" here. In fact, House culture speaks of the Anchoring of the Thread as if history had been *stitched into place* rather than actually *created* by the event. Perhaps it's more fitting to say that the fabric of history existed even before the Houses, but that the Houses were the ones who cut it, wove it, stitched it and made it into a shape which their brains - and *our* brains, brains that work in a similar way even though they're blatantly a lot less complex - could fully appreciate. It's been suggested, quite credibly, that the Anchoring led to the mass-extinction of any number of cultures which simply weren't equipped for life in a House-perceived universe. Even for a time-active culture, this is still essentially a linear universe, whose inhabitants only ever move in one time-direction and expect their actions to have causal consequences. It may not have been that way, before the Anchoring. When we speak of the Houses being the first civilisation, we're only referring to the kind of civilisation that *we* can understand.

ion as the timeships, or even be harvested from other universes (something the Houses don't yet do, since they already have the matter of *this* universe to work with and have no reason to construct anything larger than a galaxy). But the creation of a universe would require massive quantities of biodata, and as yet there's no way of creating biodata to specifications, at least not in large quantities. Biodata *can* be generated by forced experience, but even a child-universe would require a complete unigenetic biodata sequence at inception, something which would essentially require the Houses to experience an entire universe of meaning. This is quite a different thing to the Anchoring of the Thread, which affected every part of history without distinction, and in any case it's questionable whether the Anchoring process could even be repeated; history would have to be un-stitched again first.

Even if this were possible, such a thing would represent a massive defeat for the Houses.

v. History Lessons

Earlier, it was stated that the Great Houses are reluctant to explore other universes for fear of meeting their own counterparts there. This fear is understandable. The results of any such meeting could be catastrophic.

It has to be remembered that the members of the Houses aren't merely biological, or rather, that their biological functions are even less important to them than to most time-active cultures. History was founded on the culture of the Houses, therefore, members of the Houses are themselves part of the historical structure. Though human agencies meeting representatives of the Houses have noticed certain obvious signs of this (e.g. a foreknowledge of the future which seems to go beyond learned experience of future history, or the power to act in a reasonably linear fashion even during deliberately-engineered disruptions to time), to focus on these abilities would be to imagine House members as little more than demigods or superheroes.

In fact they're something far more primal, and can safely be described as living, conscious embodiments of history itself. Though the theory of biodata suggests that this is true of *all* conscious life, the Houses - hailing as they do from the very crucible where history was created - possess a certain intensity, a certain close relationship with history, which appears to border on the elemental. The "rules" of history, the protocols established during the Anchoring of the Thread, are made manifest in them. This may appear to grant them a nigh-supernatural status, but in truth every Great House agent can be described by a complex system of equations in biodata... and therein lies the problem. The mathematical process which describes them is *not* something that comes naturally to human brains, particularly not human brains which aren't primed for time-active service.

To summarise. The Houses represent the rules, the core principles, of history. To come into contact with them is to come into contact with the historical process itself. And since every (nearby) universe would seem to have roughly similar principles, it's reasonable to assume that all these universes have their own equivalents of the

Houses. But the key word here is "roughly". Navigate Ur-space to find the closest possible universe to our own, the most *similar* universe to our own, and that universe will still have countless unigentic differences. History will be different there, not because anybody within that universe will have been tinkering with individual events (although they may have been) but because the sentient culture which seeded that universe will have seeded it with slightly different precepts in mind. This means that the Houses there, though they may resemble our own Houses in many ways, will not be identical. They'll represent a different version of history.

Consider the consequences of a House member from one universe coming into contact with a House member from another. Indeed, since the historical process is built on biodata (which relies on meaning) rather than genetics (which relies on physicality), the two wouldn't even have to be full members of the Houses. House agents from other species, culturally and biologically primed to act for the Homeworld, would do just as well.

Everybody knows about the explosive results of matter meeting anti-matter, but at worst, matter and anti-matter just release a vast amount of destructive energy on contact. A collision between two even *moderately* different forms of history, between two different versions of the Houses, is a far more alarming proposition. Since unigenetics defines the form of entire universes, this sudden and immediate splicing of unigenetic material would have repercussions with no theoretical precedents. The warping of the historical process is unimaginable in a way that few things literally are. At the very least, one would expect chronic local effects. Some have argued that the natures of both the relevant universes would instantly change, and this may sound melodramatic but it would certainly explain the Houses' caution in examining other universes. Contact with their counterparts could destroy history, and they *are* history[12].

This brings us, finally, to a lesson from ancient history. Since it relates to events in the distant past of the Houses, and the past of the Houses is a *definitive* past, the word "ancient" can accurately be used here.

Even given that much of the conflict borders on the mythological, it's a matter of record that apart from the current War, the Great Houses have only experienced one conflict since becoming time-active. It's believed to have been the result of an unspecified accident at the very beginning of their super-culture - possibly connected to the technology of the Anchoring of the Thread - and the usual (simplified) explanation is that an oversight in the process "tore open" the universe, allowing things from "outside" to enter the continuum and threaten the Homeworld. Before this becomes any more mythic, or any more apocalyptic, it's best (again) to remember the description given in *The Book of the War*:

---

[12] Since every conscious being has biodata, and since every conscious being in *this* universe is supposedly part of the Houses' historical structure, it could be argued that *any* contact between universes is likely to have these "warping" effects. But compared to the Great Houses, most individuals have so little historical potency that the effects of these minor meetings obviously aren't noticeable in the short-term. But then, very few people have ever stayed for long periods in foreign universes, so the ongoing effects have yet to be studied.

*   *   *   *   *

In fact, the Yssgaroth [the name given to this enemy] were so blatant a force of destruction that it's questionable whether they really *were* a species at all. [...] The universe of the Yssgaroth itself seemed to hate the known continuum, which has led to speculation that rather than being a true form of life the Yssgaroth were simply side-effects of the collision between two continuual strata, symptoms of a timeline which had already started ripping chunks out of its own flesh. According to this version, the Houses and the (formative) lesser species perceived these areas of hostile anti-structure as projections of their own internal horror, giving them teeth, or claws, or bloody, half-formed faces. But as those few who personally encountered the Yssgaroth claimed the creatures had a definite *will to live*, the matter's still open to debate.

*   *   *   *   *

The assumption made by the *Book* is that the now-extinct "creatures" which emerged from the Houses' period of experimentation were somehow a natural hazard, a side-effect of the process of tearing through space-time. But there's no real evidence for this, and no explanation as to why something so uniformly monstrous should be created by a breach of the continuum which seems quite straightforward compared to some of the experimental procedures carried out in the universe since.

This *must* be considered mere speculation, but when the Houses made their supposed "tear" in space-time, were they in fact accessing another (nearby) universe? If so, then it's at least feasible that the monstrosities described as crawling out into the light of our own universe weren't a new species, or even a natural consequence of House technology, but members of counterpart Great Houses; members who, through nothing more than contact with their opposite numbers in the continuum we know, became an abomination not only to human and human-like life but to history itself. It's even feasible that some of these beings might have been members of *our* Houses, corrupted by the same process.

If so, then it should be remembered that certain biomass traces of these "monsters" do still exist in the continuum, even if the monsters themselves have long since been removed from the continuum. So perhaps, embedded in our universe, there are still tiny fragments of a very different kind of history. Fragments which by their very perversity - or rather, by their distance from our norm - may not only reveal something of the nature of the Houses as we know them, but something of the way those ruling bloodlines dictate the shape of the cosmos around us.

There may even be clues there to tell us just how closely related our sibling-universes are to our own, and in turn, how we might expect super-cultures like that of the Houses to create our universe's descendants.

GRASS

"Only in the context of a *totality* of the sciences do Jefferson's achievements make sense. This would for instance explain the apparent contradiction of how a man now famed for his contribution to the political sciences... [was also] purportedly the first westerner to fully reconstruct the remains of a prehistoric mammoth. It's more the failing of an over-enthusiastic age than of the man himself that Jefferson seriously believed such antediluvian beasts could have survived until the 1800s in the wilds of the unexplored midwest..."
- D. P. Mann, *The Worlds of Thomas Jefferson* (1958).

It starts with the President of the United States of America, although we should be clear on exactly what kind of *gentleman* we're discussing here. Sitting behind the Presidential desk (rosewood, as it happens, and very nice too) is a man whom later generations will call a polymath, a statesman-philosopher, a true product of the enlightenment. Oh yes, this particular President is a *creator*, with a portfolio that begins "we, the people" and works its way up to a big climax from there. He's also a man who distrusts priests of just about every denomination, which explains much of what's about to happen here; he's got a lot of time for the divine, this one, but mere mortal authority figures get his back up like nothing else on God's Earth. Now, we can't be sure that what we're about to see in this room is *bona fide* true, because the affairs of the President are traditionally left behind closed doors, and there are some rules even we're expected to follow. But we can put the scene together out of the pieces we know. Call it listening at keyholes. Call it history by degrees.

Mr. Jefferson - Mr. President - sits behind the aforementioned desk, in front of a vast window that looks out onto a garden of grass and cat's-ears, a garden quite specifically designed so as to in no way resemble the three-million square miles of hostile territory beyond it. The light's flooding through the window onto the parquet-and-polish floor, while the President himself is leaning over the books with which he surrounds himself (this being a less literate time, however, "surrounds" makes the number of books involved sound greater than it really is), reaching for his little box of joy. The box is small and off-white, a gift from a visitor whose exact name and purpose Mr. Jefferson can't quite recall; he seems to recollect that it was a woman, probably French (he has no difficulty remembering this, as he's had a head for Frenchwomen ever since a certain remarkable incident in a brothel in Paris... this is another story, and not the only "another story" which will be intercepting us today). History doesn't record what he keeps inside the box, though as we've imagined Mr. Jefferson as a free-thinking nineteenth century gentleman it could be anything from snuff to hashish. Let's give him the benefit of the doubt, and assume it's chewing-tobacco. Undignified as it may seem.

'It has to be done - it *must*- be done - it is our duty,' he says, as he starts picking at the box's contents. He talks the way he writes, with far too many hyphens and pauses, and he's addressing the two men standing on the other side of his desk. 'If we're to claim these lands for the good of our nation - if we're to prevent them being overrun by jackals and opportunists - if we're to have room in which to breathe, and not fall upon each other as they do in Europe...'

Now, it so happens that Mr. Jefferson's domain has recently grown, thanks to a certain land deal which is not only due to increase his running total of United States, but which will also give him vast tracts of what he believes to be lush and verdant farmland, possibly including that mythical easy route to the Pacific. And the two men who now stand in Mr. Jefferson's office, nodding in solemn agreement, will go down in history as the first men to travel into the heart of this new terrain; or the first to take notes anyway, which is the way history works. Their names are, from left to right, Meriwether Lewis and William Clark. As expected.

(This is all quite ridiculous, of course. At least one of these men already belongs to the President's inner circle. If Jefferson wants to brief them on their mission, then he's more likely to do it in a cozy drawing-room with a bottle of Cognac, swapping stories as Lewis lounges on a chaise longue and Clark leans nonchalantly against the fireplace. But how can we resist imagining it this way? The two of them standing to attention before the Presidential desk, being instructed to journey into the dark heart of the Northwest and bring the land under control. No doubt you're already imagining these two great explorers, these two grizzled veterans of the wilderness, walking into the President's office dressed in furs and racoon-skin hats. We need to believe they're going to step out of the briefing and, without even pausing for breath, stride off into the jungles of uncharted America. Such is history.)

Mr. Jefferson is telling the explorers that nobody can say for sure what they'll find in the Northwestern territories. The French who sold him the land have hardly been forthcoming, and the Indians aren't likely to be much help either. The President expects every form of terrain imaginable, from the tropical to the simply peculiar. He's read the greatest naturalists of the age. He has plans to meet with Alexander von Humboldt himself. He's even heard the theories of the Englishman Frere, who claims to have found human remains which blatantly defy the book of Genesis, something Mr. Jefferson greatly appreciates. Oh, yes indeed. As an enlightened gentleman, the President knows the *terra incognita* Lewis and Clark will find is no Biblical wasteland. It's to be an altogether more rational landscape, filled with all the wonders that biology and geology can produce. A new world, untouched by Church dogma, governed only by the laws of Nature and Nature's God.

This is the point when Mr. Jefferson tells Lewis and Clark about the mammoths. Oddly - seeing as most of this patchwork conversation will be lost to posterity - the part about the mammoths is the one thing the history books do record.

*   *   *   *   *

It starts with the President, but in purely chronological terms the briefing in the office isn't the first thing to actually *happen*. Just look at this landscape, for example.

Nothing behind-closed-doors here. The sky's a color which later generations will be unable to imagine as anything other than a kind of paint, a deep blue, a *dark* blue, that makes the green, green grass look as though it's glaring in the sunlight. The air's fresh, pre-industrial fresh, the kind of fresh you only get once it's been filtered through the lungs of several million herd animals and a couple of dozen Indian tribes (this is as fresh as nature gets, no doubt about it). The grass clings to the slopes, sticks close to the curves of the land, so the green's only broken up by the dirt-paths where animals have left their scents behind them like breadcrumb-trails. And mountains? Oh, there are mountains. Just waiting on the horizon, looking as if they'll *always* be just waiting on the horizon, wherever you stand on the surface of the Earth. Perfect idyll. Perfect Montana.

Timeless, we'd say. But from the President's point of view, we'd have to call it the past. Months before the briefing of Mr. Lewis and Mr. Clark, the white race has already set foot in the Land of the Shining Mountains.

Here she comes now.

Her name's Lucia Cailloux, and at this moment she's running barefoot through the grass, up the side of a slope which seems to have been put there just to warn travellers that the Rockies will be starting soon, and that they'd better get used to moving uphill. An observer would point out that Lucia - whose manner of dress is unusually masculine, but then, that's probably what you'd expect from someone who's spent so much time talking to damned heathen Indians - is technically wearing *boots*. But that's not how it feels to Lucia. No, she can feel the warm, warm earth between her naked toes, because in her head she's suddenly become an eight-year-old. As a twenty-year-old woman in the service of her government, this is hardly what she's being paid for, but right now her superiors are more than eight-thousand miles away and Lucia can't help but feel she's going to get away with it.

You see, right now she believes she's *going* somewhere. When she was young, she once ran all the way up the Rue Viande, something of an achievement when you've got child-sized legs and no shoes, because the Rue Viande is a perfect slope and the sheer amount of dirt on it (in those days, anyway, before Napoleon started cleaning it all up) made the road feel like mud in the summer. On that day - running all the way to the tannery, right at the highest point of the street, where the skins were strung up like flags at the top of the world - the junior Lucia could feel the whole world cracking like glass behind her, with the wind ripping through her dirt-blonde hair and the sheer speed (all of, oh, two miles an hour) tearing at her little dress. And as she headed for the tip of that slope, she knew - she *knew* - she'd look down and see something big and wonderful on the other side, as her reward for running all the way. She knew she'd see the whole world, in all its truth and majesty. The face, if you will, of Nature's God.

She was right, as well. Young Lucia always was a perceptive little witch.

Now the older Lucia, barefoot and booted, knows the same thing. She can quite literally smell it on the wind. At the top of the slope, she stops, so this is the point when we finally see her face in close-up. Dirt-blonde hair ragged around her shoulders, pasty little freckles blistering in the sunlight, the pupils in her big, big eyes getting smaller as she brushes the last few drops of sweat and sunshine away from her forehead. It doesn't really matter whether we're looking at Lucia *now* or watching the eight-year-old flashback version, because as it turns out her hair's naturally dirt-blonde in color. Twelve years after the Rue Viande, even a clean Lucia looks that way.

Lucia can hear her co-traveller, the Indian, thumping his way up the slope behind her. He calls out to her: *'Quelque chose?'*

And Lucia calls back: *'Tout.'* (But that's pretty much the last time we'll be hearing her words in their natural spoken tongue.)

So the world spins around us, vertigo-wise, until we can look down on the great grass-covered crater beyond the slope. The dimple in the world, where Nature's God herself has reached down and left a whacking great fingerprint on the land-scape. A gentle pit, with slopes of green sunning themselves in the midday heat, let-ting troughs of rainwater simmer and merge on their skin.

And there at the bottom of it all, the mammoths.

Now Lucia finds herself running again, and for a moment she isn't sure whether it's now her running or *then* her, until she remembers that on the Rue Viande she never went down the other side of the slope. At the bottom of the basin, the mam-moths are grazing. It'd be almost abstract, like seeing drawings of fluffy brown clouds on a painted backdrop, if it weren't for the smell.

(Of course, when the eight-year-old Lucia stood on the other slope, the view was quite different. What she saw was a cartload of corpses, blocking the street while the horseman stopped to flirt with one of the local girls, as if having a cartload of corpses was some kind of aphrodisiac. But then, that was the Revolution for you. *C'est la vie*, as they say everywhere except Paris.)

That smell's starting to bother Lucia now, because she's remembering the smell of dung on the Rue Viande. She's so busy separating the horse-smell from the mam-moth-smell that she doesn't even realize how far inertia's taking her. Gravity drags her to the bottom of the crater, then keeps her going, so before she can think about it she's stumbling over the ridges where the beasts have chewed and trampled away the grass. Pity the poor woman. The second most momentous moment of her life so far, and all she perceives is a series of confusing, ragged-edged images. The red-brown blurs that she knows are impossible animals. The smears of green that mark the walls of the crater, plastered with spoor and crushed plants; and is that a baby there, a baby mammoth, a little smudge of hair trying to stick close to its bigger smudge of a mother...?

This is when things get slightly out of hand. It's when Lucia turns, nearly falling arse over tit in the process, and finds herself staring at the absurdly huge shape which is even now bearing down on her. The bull-mammoth weighs just over seven tons, not that Lucia will ever know it, and when rising up on its hind legs (as it is now) it must be all of fifteen feet high. When it raises its trunk, and opens its mouth, and flexes its massive lungs, you know it's quite capable of destroying anything that threatens its own stomping-ground.

Nonetheless, the first thing Lucia does when faced with this monstrosity is "protect" herself by putting her arms up in front of her face. And they call this the Age of Reason.

*   *   *   *   *

There was an Indian. You might have forgotten about him.

He's now standing on the crest of the slope, watching the great beast rear up over the woman who's nominally his employer, though as a product of a non-market culture the Indian considers this "employer" business to be a pile of deershit. The Indian's name (for our purposes, anyway) is Broken Nose, which is not, of course, a "real" Indian name. It was given to him by a group of Frenchmen with especially fat faces, and it was earned after a confrontation at a French trading-post, during which - predictably - the Indian broke a French official's nose. The friends of the unfortunate fat-faced man, being typically European, found this amusing. Being *very* typically European, "Broken Nose" was their idea of irony. It's apparently supposed to sound like an authentic Indian title, although Broken Nose himself considers it just a good excuse to punch future fat-faced men without them being surprised. Besides, his original Shoshoni name was even more embarrassing.

It has to be said, Broken Nose doesn't have a great interest in the aesthetic. Below him are creatures the American settlers would find unbelievable, which would probably trigger a religious spasm in the Catholics or the Jesuits whom Mr. Jefferson distrusts so much. However, Broken Nose simply finds the beasts stupid-looking, wearing thick wool all over their bodies despite the sunshine. Broken Nose is *slightly* concerned for his "employer", but he's well aware that she can look after herself.

On the first night of the expedition, when Broken Nose and Mademoiselle Cailloux made camp on the trail from Louisiana - where the Frenchwoman had arrived under the name of "Lucy Pebbles", and bartered for supplies in what sounded to the Indian like a perfect local accent - the two of them talked at length. Or as much as was possible, anyway, given that Broken Nose had been taught French by men who only needed to prime him for certain tasks. Without any due modesty, Broken Nose showed Mme. Cailloux the scar which had been ritually inflicted across his inner thigh (*not* by his own tribe, but that's another "another story"). And with less regard for her integrity than Broken Nose would have expected from a European woman, Mme. Cailloux bared her torso from her neck to her waist, revealing a scab left by a bullet which she claimed *should* have killed her, by all the known laws of Nature and science. This began a discussion about the great wars in Europe, about the little tribal elder called Napoleon and the weapons he could muster; guns like those Mme. Cailloux herself carried, but grown so large that they needed huge boats of their own. Broken Nose asked why the Europeans always insisted on fighting with each other, and that gave the Mademoiselle pause for thought.

'*Your* people fight, don't they?' she said.

Broken Nose told her that this was indeed the case.

'Then why do *you* do it?' the woman asked.

The obvious answer was "because you tell us to", naturally, but Broken Nose suspected this was missing the point. The reasons seemed to him to be to do with territory, with possessions, with differences in gods...

'No,' said Mme. Cailloux. 'We fight to stop the other tribes becoming *whole*.'

Broken Nose didn't understand that. He *still* doesn't, although Mme. Cailloux has assured him that he will, before their mission here is complete. That is, if she doesn't get herself killed by the bull-mammoth.

*   *   *   *   *

In all probability, it's impossible to describe how it feels to have a mammoth rearing up over you. Maybe it's like the feeling you get when you lie on your back and watch the stars, and for a moment - *just for a moment* - you suddenly realize the true size of what you're staring at, as your brain suddenly forgets to force your usual scale of perception onto things. Maybe. It might be interesting to ask Lucia, even though she has even less conception of the distances of stars than the rest of us (but she's probably wise enough to know that Uranus, the furthest-flung of the seven planets, is seventeen-hundred-million miles farther away than she'll ever travel).

For the record, the mammoth *isn't* going to trample her to death. But looking up at the beast now, seeing its great brown-black outline framed against the perfect blue, Lucia feels she's watching the very countenance of Nature's God. As with the cart of corpses on the Rue Viande, it's the little details that really bother her. The strands of crushed grass on the bottom of its big round feet. The curve of its maw, the upturned V-shape that she knows could swallow a man, if not whole, then certainly in no more than *two* mouthfuls. The chips in its tusks, tiny imperfections in arcs of ivory so long that no matter which way she turns her head, she knows she won't be able to see both tips at once. And then there's its breath. Its terrible and ancient mammoth-breath, washing over her as the animal bellows into her face (one of those things Lucia's never considered until now, and which she's sure the academics who study the bones of these beasts have never considered either).

Yes, these are the things Lucia has trouble coping with. So many little creases and flaws, more than she could catalogue in half a lifetime, let alone in the raw seconds she believes she has left. The beast's stubby-but-oh-so-big front legs peddle the air in front of its body, and then it suddenly finds itself falling.

It doesn't push itself forward as it falls. it doesn't, as it were, *attack*. It drops to the ground in front of Lucia, not on top of her, and the impact would surely crack the Earth open if the ground here weren't so used to the abuse. This is the way a bull-mammoth warns off the opposition, Lucia's realizing that even as she peels her heart from the roof of her mouth and tries to stop herself falling over (noticing, as an incidental detail, that the smell of sweat which is starting to blot out the dung-scent is *hers* and not the fault of the herd).

The bull-mammoth is exhausted. It's not a creature built for rearing up on its hind legs, and the only conclusion we - like Lucia - can reach is that it expects strangers to be so intimidated by its mass that it doesn't actually need to follow up the threat.

Having made its point, having bellowed its great beef-heart out, it can't do anything more than stand still and get its breath back. Lungs the size of fat children inflate and deflate, inflate and deflate, under a heavy pelt that must be home to entire empires of insects. From four feet above her head, those huge black eyes are staring down at Lucia, as if the thing's daring her to try anything else.

Easy to call it the face of Nature's God. So big, so blatant, that we can only assume it's been put there for a purpose. Which it has, as Lucia well knows. *All* animals are there for a purpose. Horses are for riding, pigs are for eating. As far as she's concerned, the mammoths are here as a kind of metaphor. These are *political* animals, hence Mr. Jefferson's interest.

(You must have been wondering, for example, where this herd originates; woolly skins and elephant-blubber hardly seem to fit in around here. The best explanation we can hope for is that a number of mammoths were once the property of Catherine of Russia, she who was known as "The Great" before some idiot in her court started spreading that God-awful story about the horse. Horse or no horse, Catherine had something of a reputation as a witch... a label applied to most efficient female rulers, it's true, but even before her death there were fabulous and revolting stories about the company she liked to keep, and the animal-rites they used to perform. Horses for riding, pigs for eating, trained monkeys for ritual. It's not entirely clear what the link is between the Empress of Russia being a witch and the existence of live mammoths here in what will one day be the State of Montana, although Lucia has heard it said, with maddening vagueness, that one can easily lead to the other. History is full of these logical gaps. Certainly, it's rumored that one such hairy beast was given by Catherine as a gift to George III of England, but that George - half-crazed brute that he was - destroyed the thing in a fight with pit-dogs without even realizing its value. Lucia is secretly of the opinion that if Russia had given such a gift to the French, they probably would have eaten it.)

But Lucia's mammoth just keeps gasping. It's vulnerable now. With its show of strength over, it's got nothing to protect it but its dignity. Gravity has not been kind to these creatures. So when Lucia takes a step forward, the mammoth doesn't even blink; it's impossible to imagine such a blink being anything but a major task, and taking anything less than an afternoon to complete. From the look on its face, we could almost believe it's *indignant*.

How can we help but try to read its expression? If the mammoths were put here as metaphors, then we can read them any way we like. It's hard not to find meaning in something that big.

There's a stillness now, Lucia regarding the mammoth, the mammoth regarding Lucia. It's only once Lucia has paid her respects to the silence that she raises her hand. The trunk is close enough to touch, and touch it she does. Her fingers run through the tiny brown hairs, across the leathery old skin, over the wrinkles and the patches of dirt. She almost expects the beast to flinch, or to purr like a cat.

It's vulnerable, anybody can see that. Now, and only now, Lucia gets her one big chance to touch the impossible.

*   *   *   *   *

This is what passed between Mme. Cailloux and Broken Nose that morning, after they pulled themselves to their feet at dawn and began the final trek to the place of the mammoths:

Mme. Cailloux spoke of a man called Jefferson, the leader of the colonists who lived off in the eastern lands. Mme. Cailloux explained to Broken Nose that her own tribal leader, Napoleon Short-Arse, had agreed to sell a portion of the land to the aforementioned Jefferson (a notion which, like the "employer" idea, Broken Nose finds profoundly stupid).

'We're afraid,' said the Mademoiselle. 'All of us. Your people. My people.'

Broken Nose told her that his people weren't afraid of anything, which was, in his experience, what the French expected to hear from a stupid Indian.

'There's a saying in Europe,' Mme. Cailloux went on. '"The other man's grass is always greener." We fight for territory. We start wars to acquire the other man's land. Why?'

Broken Nose shrugged. 'More room. For cattle.'

'No,' the Frenchwoman told him. 'It's because we think... we secretly believe... that the other man's land is a paradise. We start to believe there are great secrets there. Secrets we have to know for ourselves. And when we take the land away from him, and we find there's no paradise there... then we tell ourselves it was the *other* man's kind of paradise. Not ours. You understand?'

'Your people are stupid,' said Broken Nose. (Not entirely true; this is what he believes he said, *after the fact*, although his training in the French tongue doesn't cover the possibility of him insulting his "employers". In his head, *after the fact*, he hears the words in his own language.)

'Perhaps,' he imagines that Mme. Cailloux said. 'But it's a matter of warfare. In war, we attack the enemy's resources. If an enemy has supply lines, we cut them. If an enemy has a better kind of weapon, we rid him of it.'

This sounded to Broken Nose like the first sensible thing she'd said.

She went on to explain many things which Broken Nose had either no understanding of or no interest in. She told him, for example, that in the possession of Napoleon Short-Arse there was a length of metal, which purportedly came from a weapon that had been used to cut the flesh of one of the white man's gods "while he hung on the cross", this metal having the power to induce divine visions (of the spirit-world, Broken Nose guessed) in anyone who was scratched by it.

'Imagine such a thing in the power of the Vatican,' the Mademoiselle said, although Broken Nose had no idea what marked these Vatican out from any of the other European tribes. 'The relic would prove them correct. It would show them to be justified in all their beliefs. Thus would their grass become greener, and their state grow stronger. They might even become *whole*.'

'Whole?' queried Broken Nose.

'I saw the Revolution,' replied Mme. Cailloux. 'I know what happens when people get what they want. Or when they *believe* they do.'

None of which told Broken Nose anything remotely useful, or even explained the woman's mission to find the mammoths before the land gets passed on to Mr. Jefferson. But now, in what we have to call the *present*, Broken Nose is trying not to trip over his skin-shod heels as he tumbles down the slope of the crater. Up ahead, he can see Mme. Cailloux, facing the largest of all the mammoths (or is it just the closest?). He can see the woman resting her hand on the monster's trunk, and he can see the beast keeping quite still, something which his fellow Shoshoni would probably take as proof of the foreign witch's powers over the animal kingdom. But Broken Nose has little time for the wonders of nature, and sees her only as being lucky.

He pulls himself to a halt as the ground levels out under his feet, stopping just a few yards from the bulk of the bull-mammoth. Its eyes are fixed on the woman, and it makes pained groaning noises when it breathes. Slowly, and with some reluctance, Mme. Cailloux lowers her hand.

'*Tout*,' she says. (This is the original French, of course, but somehow it makes more sense that way.)

Broken Nose isn't really sure where he should look. It seems disrespectful, somehow, to disturb this union. There they stand, woman and monster, in a communion that would seem almost obscene if it weren't so unlikely. For some reason, Broken Nose remembers a folk-tale from his childhood about a father who had an improper relationship with his daughter, and who was swallowed up by the Earth as a punishment. After a few moments more, he speaks.

'The cargo,' he says, using a word he's more than familiar with even though it's not entirely the right one. 'Our *tools*...'

It's then that Mme. Cailloux regains her senses, preternatural or otherwise, and turns away from the beast. The mammoth never blinks, though, and never moves its head. The Mademoiselle looks up towards the top of the slope, presumably remembering the packs which she and Broken Nose have left over the rise, the equipment her own "employers" issued her with before transporting her here to the Land of the Shining Mountains. (And just as we imagined Lewis and Clark standing to attention before Jefferson, so Broken Nose imagines Mme. Cailloux standing before Napoleon Short-Arse himself, although he's imagining Napoleon sitting in a position of honor around a roaring fire rather than sitting behind a desk; there is, of course, no Shoshoni word for "furniture".)

So it is that Mme. Cailloux draws away from the mammoth, to begin her slow climb back up the slope, with Broken Nose at her heels. Mme. Cailloux doesn't look back at the mammoth as she walks, something Broken Nose interprets as an almost incestuous shame. And the mammoth doesn't watch her go, simply continuing to stare at the spot where she once stood. So it's left to Broken Nose to glance over his shoulder on the way up the slope, to watch the woolly monster recover its strength after its four seconds' worth of rabid activity, while the rest of the herd-animals go on bellowing and sniffing at each other. He wonders if the bull-mammoth even understands the difference between its human visitors and the other beasts of the wilderness

'These are Mr. Jefferson's animals,' he hears Mme. Cailloux say, halfway up the rise. 'They feed on Mr. Jefferson's grass.'

He *still* doesn't know what she's talking about. Broken Nose is starting to feel that even the mammoths understand this mission better than he does, but then again, wouldn't you expect him to think that way? Being Shoshoni, when *he* uses the mammoths as a metaphor the results aren't particularly literary.

*   *   *   *   *

Which leads us back to the President of the United States of America himself, as he sits behind his rosewood desk in his rose-tinted office, picking snuff or hashish or chewing-tobacco out of his little carved box. This is some months in what might be called Lucia's future, so Lewis and Clark have in the last few minutes dutifully marched out of the office in their unlikely racoon-skin hats. No doubt a kayak is waiting for them outside.

But now Mr. Jefferson's alone with his thoughts, and we can make the usual array of guesses as to what those thoughts might be. The President is hoping that his explorers will bring him back news of a Northwest Passage, a trade route that could turn his republic into an empire almost overnight (not that he *wants* an empire, as such, but... well, you know how it is). And then, of course, there's the prospect of mammoths. If such things are found, they're sure to be given a place of honor in the new American mythology. He briefly wonders if there's room for a mammoth on the national crest; possibly he can put one in place of the eagle. A beast which proves, by its very nature, that the Church is full of asses and the world runs to the will of the new sciences. Just for a second, for a stupid childish second, he imagines riding the back of such an animal in a parade along Pennsylvania Avenue, celebrating his second - oh, to hell with precedent, make it his third - term in office. Jefferson's monsters, that's what the Church would say. He imagines the mammoths' backs being draped in flags, decked out in the red-and-white stripes and the seventeen stars (although the flag which hangs above the window in this particular office only has sixteen, those artisans who handle such things being a little slower than the expansion of the new republic).

All this makes Mr. Jefferson consider the box again. He tries to remember the name of the woman who presented it to him, the well-spoken Mademoiselle who appeared in this very office just a few short months ago, her skins and furs making her look like an Indian coming home from a trek in the great forests. Naturally, it's ludicrous to think that a complete stranger, and such an ill-dressed one, should be allowed to stroll into the Presidential office without even officially presenting herself... but the notion's as hard to resist as all the other things we've seen inside this virtual room. Whether or not the woman did introduce herself, the one thing Mr. Jefferson can remember is what she told him when she placed the little off-white box on his desk.

'Your new world, *Monsieur* President,' she said. Well, maybe she didn't say "mister" in the French style, maybe Jefferson's just remembering it that way because he likes the accent, but the point remains that when he slid the box open he found inside it just a few blades of green, green grass. Mr. Jefferson fails to remember how he responded to this, or even whether he asked his visitor to explain herself; she may well have vanished from his office before he could so much as speak (after all, a mysterious entrance should always be complimented by a mysterious exit).

Here and now, the President believes the contents of the box to have been a kind of message, sent by some agency he has yet to identify. In fact, he's only half-right.

*   *   *   *   *

And this is Jefferson's future. More precisely, this is 1805, halfway through Lewis and Clark's two-year excursion into the wildlands, the point at which the two men (and all their followers, though right now they're gloriously irrelevant) finally stumble across a certain indentation in a certain grassland. A crater, if you will. It's here that the two explorers, being consummate outdoorsmen, find trampled ground and traces of spoor which suggest the trail of some grand animal herd. At first they conclude that the Indians have driven their cattle through the area, though this theory falters when they arrive at the bottom of the basin, where the graves have been dug. They *assume* there are graves here, anyway, given that the ground's been broken from one side of the crater to the other. Now, as not even the Shoshoni would do something as bizarre as grazing their animals on top of their dead - and as a quick search of the area uncovers European musket-balls in the grass - there's obviously some kind of mystery here.

Sadly, it's not one the explorers feel they have time to solve. Besides, even by this stage they're starting to learn that digging up native graves is a bad move, tactically speaking. There's some discussion about what might be called the "central" grave, the fifteen-foot-long tract of broken earth which, from its size, must surely indicate the last resting place of a great leader (proving to the leader-obsessed white men that the people who performed these burials must have been *partly* civilized, even though the Shoshoni contingent in the expedition claims not to recognize the style). Lewis and Clark steer well clear, deciding to give the mysterious fallen chief the respect he must surely deserve.

Later, in the oh-so-short years between the end of the expedition and Lewis's highly dubious suicide, the duo will theorize that the site was deliberately desecrated by rogue Frenchmen as some kind of political maneuver. A stampede must have taken place at some point, so the large animals, whatever they may have been, were probably used by the French as weapons of destruction.

Like Jefferson, these people excel at being only partly correct.

*   *   *   *   *

And however far into the future we go, Mr. Jefferson, President of the United States of America, fails to understand the significance of any of this. Well, what can we expect? Polymath and philosopher he may be, but he doesn't even understand the significance of the box. The little off-white box which remains in his possession for the rest of his term in office, a gift from one of the very few people who understood exactly what he wanted from his glorious new territory, and knew precisely why he couldn't be allowed to get it. A box Mr. Jefferson might have used for snuff, or hashish, or tobacco, which a Frenchwoman once claimed was all that remained of his virtual paradise, and which just happened to be made out of ivory.

INTRODUCING THE ALL
introducing the all-new novel...
the all-new nove

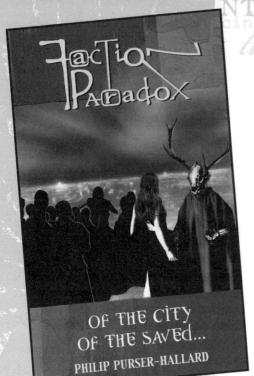

OF THE CITY
OF THE SAVED...
PHILIP PURSER-HALLARD

Faction Paradox

OF THE CITY
OF THE SAVED...

The young madwoman in the Tube carriage is recounting, in painstaking detail, the imminent future history of the City. Her cracked voice rises then descends to murmurs, as she delineates diverse catastrophes due in the coming weeks.

It would make grim listening if anyone were paying attention, but her fellow passengers are awkwardly, apologetically ignoring her. The Neolithic sculptor in designer furs; the family of burnished bronze/chrome cyborgs; the tall robed Bedouin and the red-beard Viking; the slim six-armed posthuman and her troglodytic lover—each of the other passengers gazes ahead, embarrassed, at the wormhole-vortex outside the carriage windows.

No-one ever listens to Kassandra, daughter of Troy.

The City is troubled, nonetheless. An unquiet breeze is rustling in its lanes and alleyways: whispering in innumerable ears, rippling the surface of a myriad lives. There is a sea-change coming, it whispers, dark clouds roiling in from your imaginary horizons. Something is abroad, something that does not belong alongside your safe afterlives with all their comforting and comfortable certainties. It has no form, but spreads among you like a fashion or a rumour. Call it an urban legend. Or simply call it change.

Most of the Citizens—the resurrected human populations of the vanished Universe itself—are ignorant of its passing as they go about their business, their parties and affairs and carnivals and works of art. Their recreated existences satisfy and thrill them—they pay no heed to hints that this great festival of resurrection might one day come to an end.

Some listen, though, and these remember the assault by the War-time powers three decades before. They recall uneasy rumours: that the powers have developed potent weapons, capable of harming or killing Citizens within the City's galaxy-wide bounds; that agents back in the (original) Universe have been recruiting entire human civilisations to act as their fifth column in the City. In tabloid headlines, T-shirt slogans, conspiracy forums and murmuring campaigns, these reckless imaginings are propagated.

Some voices in the vast Chamber of Residents, and even the City Council itself, call for active monitoring of the partially human 'collaterals,, the aliens unworthily resurrected by mere virtue of miscegenous ancestries. Hard-liners urge the closure of the Uptime Gate into the Universe, even (surely suicidal) pre-emptive strikes against the Warring powers themselves.

At the secret Parliament established in the City by the resurrected members of Faction Paradox, discussion concerns itself with more arcane matters. A spate of dangerous omens has begun to sweep the City, a plague of ill portents spreading concern among the superstitious (among whom the Parliament's members are proud to count themselves). The enigmatic Godfather Avatar, whom few present have seen without his tricorn hat and heavy antlered bone-mask, catalogues them for the Mothers and the Fathers in a whisper like the death of leaves.

In Augustus District, a wizened haruspex slices open the belly of a pterodactyl imported from the Earth's Jurassic period, and spreads the scaly skin wide. He stares at its entrails in perplexity for some long moments, before crying out in horror. His fellow augurs hustle him away, wide-eyed and babbling, then return to torch the pterosaur's bloody remains.

Experimenters in a lab at Clarendon University discover unexpectedly that the traces drawn by certain subatomic particles, when accelerated through a light-emitting substrate, have begun to spell out occult sigils in a depraved alphabet. The Head of Department closes down the project before it reaches its conclusion.

In Supplicity District a boy-child is born with a single head, arising from the centre of his shoulders. His bicephalic parents gaze at him in fourfold dismay.

These events, though, are distractions. (Except for the deliberations of the Parliament, that is. To dismiss the Faction is never a wise idea.) Transitory moments, they are of ultimately no significance: at the most they represent the City's interrupted subroutines at nervous play. The events of true significance to the City — the seeds from which stories arise as emergent structures, signal out of noise — are to be found elsewhere.

For instance...

In a rundown residential-cum-business block in Paynesdown District, a man who is called Rick Kithred observes a stranger loitering in the back yard; while at the Ignotian family's opulent villa, the housekeeping software informs a youth named Urbanus that his great-grandfather wishes to see him.

Councillor Ved Mostyn of Wormward District wonders what to wear for his hot date tonight (he's thinking maybe manacles). Julian White Mammoth Tusk, a City-born Neanderthal, peers despondently into his bank account and wonders how to pay his detective agency bills.

Three academics face unique dilemmas. Large numbers of barbarians start migrations. A minotaur gets drunk with a hermaphrodite. A private eye named Tobin fingers the handle of her gun distractedly.

And—inevitably—into more than one of their lives will shortly stalk Godfather Avatar himself, of the Rump Parliament of Faction Paradox, on bony limbs.

Because even in the City of the Saved, nothing is ever quite *that* unpredictable.

OUT NOW. Retail Price: $14.95.

1309 Carrollton Ave #237
Metairie, LA 70005
info@madnorwegian.com

www.madnorwegian.com

INTRODUCING THE ALL
introducing the all-new novel...
the all-new nove

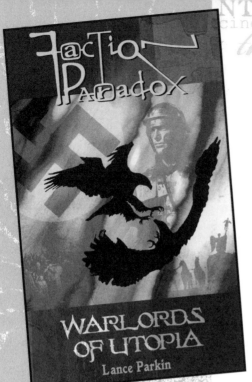

introducing the all-new novel...

Faction Paradox

WARLORDS OF UTOPIA

Lance Parkin

Adolf Hitler, the Gaol.

In the exact centre of the island was a tower. It was an ugly concrete stump four storeys high, a brutalist version of a medieval keep. There were tiny slits for windows. There wasn't a door. Around the tower, thorns and weeds had grown into a jungle. The tower held one prisoner.

Surrounding it was an electric fence. And the guards. Millions of strong men and women with the bodies they should have had, unmarked by armband or tattoo, allowed to grow up and grow old. Proud people, many with names like Goldberg, Cohen and Weinstein. Men and women who would never forgive. Men and women who lived in the vast, beautiful community that surrounded the tower, keeping him awake with their laughter, their music, the smell of their food, the sight of their clothes, the sound of their language and their prayers and the cries of their babies. They felt they had a duty to be here. They had always been free to leave, but few had.

On Resurrection Day itself, some had realised that as everyone who had ever lived was in the City, then *he* was here. It had taken longer to hunt him down. Few knew where he'd been found, how he'd been leading his life. Had he tried to disguise himself? Had he proclaimed his name and tried to rally supporters? It didn't matter. He had been brought here, his identity had been confirmed and he had been thrown in the tower that had been prepared for him.

Some of those living in sight of the tower had wondered if they were protecting him from the people of the City, not protecting the City from him. And it was true: the City - the glorious, colourful, polymorphous, diverse City, with uncounted races of people living side by side - was the ultimate negation of the prisoner's creed. The vast, vast majority people of the City didn't care who he was and couldn't comprehend his beliefs, let alone be swayed by his rhetoric. Individuals who'd killed, or wanted to kill, many more people than he had remained at liberty and found themselves powerless. Had imprisoning him marked out as special? Such things were argued about, but the prisoner remained in his tower.

Every day bought requests from individuals, organisations and national groupings who had come up with some way to harm him within the protocols of the City. There were also representations from his supporters, or from civil liberties groups, concerned that his imprisonment was vigilante justice or that no attempt was being made to rehabilitate him. There were historians and psychologists and journalists who wanted to interview him. There were those that just wanted to gawp at or prod the man they'd heard so much about. All of them were turned away.

One man had come here in person. An old Roman, in light armour.

The clerk, a pretty girl with dark hair and eyes, greeted him.

'Your name?'

'Marcus Americanius Scriptor.'

While she dialled up his records and waited for them to appear on her screen, she asked: 'He's after your time. You're a historian?'

'I was,' the old man said. 'May I see him?'

'The prisoner isn't allowed visitors, or to communicate with the outside world. He is allowed to read, but not to write. Oh, that's odd. Your record isn't coming up.'

'It wouldn't.' The Roman didn't elaborate.

He looked out over the city to the tower. The young woman was struck by how solemn his face was. Most people who came all the way out here were sightseers, sensation seekers. Even some of the gaolers treated the prisoner with levity. Mocking him, belittling him.

'Don't you ever want to let him loose?' he asked, finally. 'Let him wander the streets, let his words be drowned out. On another world he was an indifferent, anonymous painter.'

'It sounds like you know that for certain,' she said, before checking herself. 'To answer the question: no. He stays here.'

'I met him,' the Roman told her. 'On a number of occasions.'

She frowned.

'A long story,' he told her. 'I suppose I'm concerned that you torture yourselves by having that monster in your midst.'

The woman had heard many people say such a thing.

'Not a monster. A human being.'

'But the only human being you've locked away for all eternity.'

'The wardens have ruled that he will be freed,' she told him.

Americanius Scriptor seemed surprised. 'When?'

'First he must serve his sentence, then he will be released.'

'When?' he asked again.

'In six million lifetimes,' she told him.

Marcus Americanius Scriptor smiled.

'I'll be waiting for him,' he told her. He turned and headed back to the docks.

Release Date: November 2004. **Retail Price:** $17.95

1309 Carrollton Ave #237
Metairie, LA 70005
info@madnorwegian.com

www.madnorwegian.com

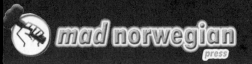

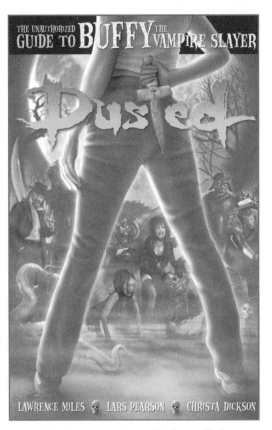
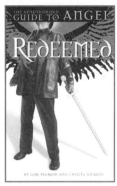

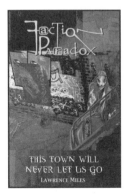

ABOUT THE AUTHOR

LAWRENCE MILES is the author of... hold on... yeah, eight novels now, the most recent of them being the first volume in the ongoing *Faction Paradox* series, *This Town Will Never Let Us Go*. He's currently developing an unforeseen interest in stage magic, and he's worked out a way of drastically improving the classic Box of Pain trick if anybody's interested. He lives and works within travelcard-distance of London, and his current projects include a six-volume *Doctor Who* reference guide for Mad Norwegian Press and the next two installments of the *Faction Paradox* audio series, now made by Magic Bullet.

THANK YOUS

In reprinting *Dead Romance*, the editors came to discover that a computer copy of the book as published by Virgin didn't exist (long story, that one). The editors would therefore like to extend immense thanks to **Paul 'Brax' Castle**, who sacrificed himself (and a copy of the Virgin edition, with a carving knife) by scanning the original text into an editable file. We're well and truly appreciative.

However, it also seems duly right to mention all the sacrificial souls who volunteered their time and typing talents to *retype* the book, should that become necessary (mercifully, it wasn't). One even volunteered the typing talents of his *mother*, God bless him: William Salmon, Vikki Godwin, Sean Twist, Stuart Douglas, Steve Flores, John A.K. Gunther, Stephen Couch, Rhonda R. Scarborough, Steve Martin, Russell Godwin, Randall Yard, Robert Smith?, Robert Millikin, Paul Hiscock, Raymond Sawaya, Alan Taylor, Mike Habiby, Mark Mistkawi (and Mrs. Mistkawi), Luke Sims, Kyle Borcz, Kelly Buchanan, K.J. Gray, Julio Angel Ortiz, Julian White, Damian Jeremiah, Jarrod Miller, Andrew McLean, Henry Dreyer, Heather C Lemon, Geoffrey D Wessel, Estelle May, Eric Pohlmeyer, Drew Wortman, David Ball, Cory Cook, Brandon Smith, Bradley Schumann, Arfie Mansfield, Andrew Orton, Andrew Hinton, Allyn Gibson, Val Sowell, Michael Evans and Kevin Cachia.

Reprint Editor: Lars Pearson. **Copy Editor:** Fritze CM Roberts.